JOY
LEWIS

A CROWN FOR THE CURSED

FAE CROWN BOOK TWO

CHAPTER ONE

Before the assassin's first arrow lodged deep inside her heart, Anova's eyes flew open. She shouldn't have been able to know that it was coming, but she did.

She leapt to her feet as the arrow's tip dug into the floorboards on which she'd been sleeping. The long-empty manor creaked with her movements. That was one reason why she'd chosen this place as shelter. Unlike well-maintained fae structures, this one made noises.

Well, there was another reason she'd chosen this manor.

Anova closed herself off to the memory. She had to keep her head.

The assassin swung to the floor from the rafters. The fae wore black clothing that hid them well in the shadows, concealing even their face. This one was better than many of the others that had come for her. The fact that this fae had even found her was enough proof.

But after three days of no sleep, Anova had slipped up.

Another arrow sailed above her head as she ducked out of its path, and her fingers dug into the fireplace poker that was her only weapon.

"Leave me alone or aim better," she said between clenched teeth.

Anova didn't allow herself to think on the possibility that the misses had been intentional. That this assassin's aim wasn't to kill her but to take her.

Like all fae, her assassin was inhumanly fast. They lodged themselves further in the shadows, and Anova lost the light to see by when they nocked their next arrow.

Her heart clanged in her chest like a bell in a tower. How could she hope to dodge arrows she couldn't even see? When they were faster and stronger from the start, how could she outmatch a fae on equal ground?

His voice filled the silence inside her.

"Fae, human, animal—it doesn't matter. All that matters is who has more to lose. Who can't *lose."*

But the problem was, she wasn't sure that she had much to lose anymore.

Use their position against them, sang another voice in her head. She had experience fighting against fae now, and their worst weaknesses were their ego and sense of superiority over humans.

They all thought humans weak just because they didn't have their reflexes or *moon magic.* Well, there was more to a fight than that.

Why not play into her attacker's misconceptions?

Anova darted to the side as if she were going to take cover behind the wide bed shoved against a wall.

Instead, she sprinted for the shadows where her fae assassin was. Two arrows had already stuck into the soft bed by the time her foe realized their mistake.

The only way she could hope to best this fae would be to fight close. Trying to flee the room would likely earn her an arrow in the spine.

Anova raised the metal poker above her head for a heavy strike. It left her open, but archers were generally useless at this distance.

The fae let out a hiss as they dropped and rolled on the floor. Anova followed like a shadow, her heart swelling with the desire for something that had been crafted for use as a weapon.

How much easier crossing the boundary forests would be if she had a bow and some arrows ...

Anova held the poker with both hands as she rushed forward. It was an all-or-nothing strike that would have been foolish to attempt under ordinary circumstances.

But that was what made the attack so brilliant.

To her satisfaction, the fae assassin's eyes visibly widened. They were already on their feet again, and it was too late to move out of the way enough to dodge her wide strike.

The assassin's hands clamped around the metal and steered it narrowly past where it should have pierced their insides.

But by doing so, they were brought closer than Anova would have liked. The dim light leaking through the room's curtained window fell on her assassin's face.

It was one she'd seen before.

"Did you already have a death wish?" the fae whispered into Anova's face.

Her eyes were beautiful and glittering like jewels. Like the last time she'd seen this fae, her hair had been styled and pinned tight to her head. Black clothes consumed her small frame.

It was the fae from the quarter moon fête. The same one who had nearly been executed by the king's guards for having so-called weapons—her mother's hairpins.

The same one who Anova had saved from that fate.

Except she hadn't anticipated that she truly was an assassin after the blood crown.

Anova's stomach turned, and she yanked the cold metal back. "I should have let you die."

Why had she been such a bleeding heart? She knew better when it came to the fae.

But not all fae are like this.

Something tangled in Anova's throat. She'd hardly allowed herself to think on him since the worst had happened. Since ...

A pain sparked at her temples. She was reminded against her will of the damned fae artifact that sat on top of her head. Anova ached to grab it and throw it at the assassin's feet.

But, as she'd discovered, she couldn't take it off.

Not without consequences.

"I should have killed more of you when I had the chance," Anova added. She didn't like the bite to her tone, but maybe if she killed this one for good, or at least scared her off, the others would learn not to pursue her anymore.

The fae assassin jerked out of striking distance, her hands already nocking another arrow.

"Your hate taints you," she said to Anova. "You think it makes you strong, but it makes you weak."

Anova's teeth gritted together. What did this fae know of hate? She would show her the meaning of it.

It was time to end this. The longer she entertained this fae, the more likely the others would find her, too. Anova brought herself low and swung wide with the metal for an immobilizing blow.

Pain streaked through her shoulder as an arrow tore past her, taking some of her skin with it. At once, the fae's legs were no longer in the path of her weapon.

Anova cursed under her breath as she realized something.

That hadn't been a killing hit. None of them had been. This fae assassin *was* trying to capture her alive—not kill her.

She lurched back, one palm tight against the wound. "Who hired you?" Anova spat. Pain danced along her nerves. She needed to get out of here.

The fae didn't respond except for a slight narrowing of her eyes. Anova's blood rushed through her faster. Anova needed to outwit her further.

Her opponent fired several arrows in succession at her feet, and each time, Anova managed to barely dodge each piercing blow.

"Careful. It wouldn't do to damage the fragile parcel you were paid by your master to retrieve," Anova said.

"I have no master," the assassin snarled back as she notched another one.

"Liar," Anova hissed. She could spot one of her own with ease. She angled the widest part of fireplace poker in front of her body to deflect her next arrow.

As she'd predicted, it had been aimed at somewhere non-lethal, and she blocked it easily. Anova breathed through her nose. What she needed to do now would break her heart, but it needed to be done.

With a clear swing to the fae's midsection, Anova heaved herself forward. The fae pivoted to protect herself from the poker, but Anova redirected her momentum at the same time. The other side of the poker slashed through the intricately carved wood of the bow, smashing it to pieces.

Anova resisted the temptation to drive the weapon through her heart for a fatal blow, and her fireplace poker hovered over the spot in a clear threat as Anova shoved her down.

"Now," Anova breathed, "you're going to tell me what I want to know."

The fae huffed, her eyes hard as she stared up at Anova. Her knee dug into the fae's chest where she'd gotten her on the ground.

"But first," she continued, "you're going to tell me who hired you."

Anova had done it. She was drunk on her success. She'd beaten one of them—not for the first time, but it was as sweet as if it was.

It was when her thoughts turned to *him* that it happened.

Sliver flashed in the dim light, and the fae assassin kicked away the poker as Anova recoiled from the hidden blade. She darted out of range of her strike, her chest heaving.

I should have expected that. I should have—

Anova's breath froze in her chest. "Where did you get that knife?"

"Surrender," the fae said, "and I won't hurt you."

Anova couldn't even laugh at the lie. Her eyes didn't leave the knife. It was one she'd seen many times before—as well as its sister.

It was one of Leander's.

She should have left by now. She should have run for the door now that her foe was fighting close. She should have run from the place and not looked back.

Instead, Anova dodged the edge of the knife while staying within arm's reach of her opponent. The wound along her arm throbbed with fresh blood flow.

"Where did you get it?" Anova repeated.

Her hand darted for the fae's wrist, but she was too fast for Anova. She cursed under her breath.

Her opponent didn't give an answer. Perhaps there was none.

And perhaps she'd already killed someone close to her. Her blood slogged through her veins.

What if she had hurt him?

It hit her all at once.

Anova didn't move fast enough to dodge the fae's strike. The pain seared into the skin of her cheek.

There was a reason this fae had found her here when others hadn't. There was a reason she was using his knife.

It can't be. No. He wouldn't.

But she had to know.

Anova shoved her palm against her new cut. Though it was shallow, more blood loss wouldn't help her. It was time for a gamble.

"Whatever Wolfsbane has promised you, he lied."

Anova saw in her eyes what she'd feared to see. Recognition.

"You babble like the moon-mad, Human," the assassin said through her teeth, but it was too late. Anova had seen the evidence.

The answer bubbled in her belly like vomit. It was no coincidence she'd been found here, in this manor where Leander had found her before. It had been on the night that he'd told her who he truly was.

It was no coincidence this fae was using one of Leander's weapons. He'd known to look for her here.

He was bent on destroying the fae artifact linked with her life.

And the only way to do that was to kill Anova.

CHAPTER TWO

A nova's heart raged in her chest like it could escape.

That couldn't be true, could it? He hadn't sent this fae after her. He couldn't have.

But his goal had always been to destroy the blood crown. At one point, Leander had planned to sacrifice his own life in order to ensure its destruction.

It was something she'd tried not to think about in the days since she'd woken up with the fae artifact attached to her head, but she couldn't avoid it any longer.

As long as she breathed, Leander couldn't get what he wanted. And he wanted that more than anything.

She'd been a fool to think otherwise.

But, a fragile part of her argued, *he wouldn't wish that. He would find another way.*

Anova bit into her tongue. She had to keep it together.

Her foe hadn't relented. In fact, her attacks had only quickened. The edge of Leander's knife flashed in the light, each one a deadly reminder of him.

As her breaths grew shallower, Anova kept moving. It was her only hope to prevent more attacks from landing, but her sleepless body could only cooperate with her wishes for so long. Pain flared at her temples again, nearly blinding her.

She had to get out of here *now*.

I can't out-maneuver my enemy. Nor can I outrun her.

But she had other talents.

Keeping out of reach of her foe's blade stole most of her breath, so Anova spoke in gasps. "Why are you working for him? If he promised you the crown, you must know by now that's a lie."

But the fae didn't flinch. She moved out of the way of Anova's kick to her shins and countered with a flurry of slashes.

"Either use your words for your surrender—or don't," the fae said. "If I must drag you from here unconscious, I don't mind."

Anova couldn't give up. Cheating was what she did best. Spears of pain drove into her head, eclipsing the pinpricks of pain along her cheek and arm.

"Do all your kind have such little honor?" she bit out. "A life debt must mean more to a mongrel."

This, the fae had no response for. Anova's heart pumped blood to her wounds faster.

While dodging, Anova lurched to the floor and grabbed the poker—only for her opponent to use her lapse in focus as a chance to stab her with Leander's knife.

It didn't hit. Narrowly, Anova had blocked the strike to her thigh with the metal rod. In the same instant, the edge of the long knife splintered from the blade and soared through the air until it stuck into the wall behind them.

Her assassin snarled at the sight, and Anova couldn't believe her luck. All that was left of it was a stump of the blade.

She'd won. She'd disarmed her assassin. Twice.

Time to go.

Anova turned to run, but a whistling sound chased her. Her heart was in her throat, but she knew if she didn't escape now, she wouldn't.

She gave in and looked. Seconds before it tore into her calf came the largest shard of the knife that had broken from it. Her assassin had flung it like a throwing knife at her legs.

Even though she dodged it, Anova hit the floor like a sack of potatoes to evade it. Her body bruised against the hard surface.

Quicker than a flame's tongue, her opponent had the rest of the knife's stump at her throat. Anova released the fire poker.

"It's over," the fae said.

Like hell it was. There had to be something she could do. All Anova needed was to create a break—an opening. It only had to be enough for her to flee.

What could be compelling enough for even one of the fae to ignore a life debt? There was little question that Anova had saved her life that day, and they both knew it.

Did the fae opposite her have so little sense of morality?

Though she was a poor judge of it herself, she didn't think that was entirely the case. Pain flickered through her brain like a hungry flame.

The words were out of her mouth before she could stop them.

"You don't care about the crown." Anova blinked. "It's *her* you care about."

She remembered the words she'd overheard this assassin speak in the hall during the fête.

"They're hair accessories."

"And you expect us to believe that?" the guards had said.

"They were my mother's—"

Her mother, Anova repeated in her mind. It was all she knew about this fae, other than that she was an assassin.

It was enough.

Her opponent's face froze for precious seconds. Anova didn't pause to reflect or even to take the fire poker with her. She slid from her grasp and ran.

Anova discovered from the fae's belongings and the horse which she'd hidden outside the abandoned manor that her name was Lyrin.

Lyrin's horse was a seasoned mare that was faster than she could have hoped. Anova dumped most of the rest of Lyrin's belongings. She narrowed her gaze on the forests looming before her. There hadn't been any weapons left behind in the fae's pack, which left her back to where she'd started.

No way to defend herself other than with her own nails and teeth.

As she raced under the ever-present canopy of the boundary forests, the shadows followed her. Now that she was properly alone again, she could lose the pretense of stability she'd donned in front of Lyrin.

Anova allowed a deranged laugh to escape her lips. The only one she'd ever come close to trusting in this warped land was trying to hunt her down. How had her life come to this?

She needed to remove the blood crown.

Too bad everything in Fae wanted to kill her for it first.

Anova pressed herself tighter against the mare as the forests rushed past them. She had exactly one true ally left. One who she could be sure wanted her alive more than he wanted anything to do with a fae artifact.

Juras.

The closer she edged to the boundary, the more her pulse throbbed. Getting anywhere near Irbess also meant coming dangerously close to Hinterfell.

And the only way she could stand Hinterfell was if she was on the important end of a sharp weapon. Something sparked in the base of her skull.

Don't worry. I'll be ready for you this time.

This time, she would free Juras and herself from the wretched woman permanently. She couldn't afford to ignore Hinterfell's threat to make both of them indentured to her and the brothel she ran.

Anova slowed her horse. They were closing on the border. The magic of Fae clung to her skin as if begging her to backtrack. She ignored it. After making certain no one had followed her this time, she dismounted.

The birds were quiet here, and the gnats that had dressed the air through most of the boundary forests were gone. Anova started to walk, her heart in her throat. A buzzing erupted in her head.

It grew louder with each step.

She held her breath. She'd barely dared to hope, but there could be no denying the possibility any longer.

The crown was reacting to the barrier. She felt drunk on the knowledge.

Humans were never meant to wear the blood crown. Once I leave the magic of Fae, it should dissolve all ties I have to it.

But as she took her next step to pass the invisible barrier, something held her in place. Anova jerked back, her heart racing. Her eyes darted everywhere, though there was nothing before her except the empty forest.

She extended one hand before her. Just as some force had repelled her body, something intangible stopped her palm.

A flurry of noises broke behind her, and she twisted so her back was to the barrier.

An army of fae emerged from all sides of the forest on the Fae side. She cursed out loud. In her inattentiveness, they'd surrounded her. She shouldn't have stopped to sleep at all.

And in the middle of them all was the fae she least wished to see.

As he stepped forward, a coat of gold and black enveloping him and shrouding him further in the gloom, the fae flooding the area started to lower themselves.

They were bowing to him.

His violet-black eyes glimmered in the darkness with a dangerous wickedness.

"Anova, my dear." Hellmyr paused as if savoring the sound of her name on the air. After a moment, a devilish grin spread across his face. "How I've been looking for you."

CHAPTER THREE

"I was hoping you'd come back to admire your work," Hellmyr continued, not bothering to gesture to the fae behind him that they could rise from their bows.

Anova watched, waiting for comprehension to arrive.

Fae had been without a ruler for only a few weeks. He'd seized power already.

Even without a blood crown, there could be no mistake. Hellmyr was the new Fae King. He hadn't even needed it.

Towards the trees, one fae remained standing. Anova's eyes adjusted to the gloom at the edges of the clearing, and she recognized another face. Letharia was draped in robes similar to her son's coat, and jewels tipped her ears which caught on the limited light. She watched the scene with what appeared to be an assumed indifference.

Anova's stomach tightened. Her own actions had made this possible, at least in part.

Hellmyr's words registered in Anova's brain, and she jerked her head back to where he stood, pacing the edge of his army. "My work?" she said.

She'd slipped up. She could see it in Hellmyr's face—the barely noticeable crease between his eyebrows. He'd figured something out.

He thinks I control the crown, and thus made the barrier, rather than the other way around, Anova realized. *Well, he assumed so until I proved otherwise.*

Anova's teeth grinded together. She needed to be better than this to get out of here. She was tired of running, but there was little choice before her. She was no match for an army of fae.

But first, she needed some information. And something told her that Hellmyr wouldn't hold back the truth.

"Where's Leander?" she asked.

Hellmyr stopped and let out an abrupt laugh. "No idea, I'm afraid. Although," he paused and stepped forward, his strange grackle-eyes drinking in the blackness around them, "I'm glad you got rid of him."

He took another step towards her as he continued talking. "There's something I need to discuss with you. And it's much easier without him."

"I'll kill you if you get any closer." Anova feared her heart thundered too loudly for the threat.

She didn't know how she'd make it happen, but she swore to herself then that she'd try.

"I hoped you'd say that." Hellmyr didn't break eye contact with her as he held out his hand behind him. One of his fae soldiers rose to his feet and gave him two swords. With his hands full of weapons, his eyes glimmered.

"I've heard you're quite the duelist," Hellmyr said. "Show me." He kicked one of the blades to her.

Her mind hadn't stopped buzzing. How was she going to get out of this? She couldn't fight them all.

Maybe I don't have to, she considered as she bent to pick up the fae-made silver. She didn't take her eyes off him, either.

If this fae boy wanted to play, then so be it.

She attached the sheath to a belt at her waist. No matter what she did here, she intended to keep his weapon. Anova suppressed the tremors in her hands when she gripped the hilt of the sword. It looked like it had been carved from ice, and a chunk of a white gemstone had been planted in the center of the hilt. The balance was better than she could have wanted.

She was out of practice, but it wouldn't do to let him know that. They circled each other like predatory birds. She kept her weapon low, aware of all the eyes on them.

"What do you want?" Anova said.

"You'll have to be more specific." Hellmyr revealed his teeth. "There's a lot."

Enough of this.

She rushed forward, aiming for the most carnage with a stab to his intestines. His response was lightning-fast, his blade grinding against hers as he leaned into the block.

"What do you want from me," she managed.

"I think you're aware." His face was too close, and his grackle-eyes devoured her.

She was. When they broke apart, Anova lurched several steps backward. Hellmyr was *not* out of practice.

Her blood thundered through her. This was just a demonstration for his fae army. A showing of his strength and power against the weak human who had gotten her hands on their most valued artifact.

Anova parried his flurry of attacks, and her breath came shorter with each second. Malice coated her words. "If you're going to kill me for the blood crown, why don't you just do it already?"

He was too good. *Let me at you, you coward.*

But he wasn't hurting her. Interesting.

Hellmyr's eyes glimmered behind his sword. "Because I'd rather have you as my queen."

Anova lost her footing and nearly fell on her face. That time when she'd been drugged by the High King and Hellmyr had told her that for the first time, she hadn't believed it.

But now, it was easy to see why he'd want that. He didn't want her—he wanted the crown.

"Or you'll kill me," Anova supplied. Her eyes narrowed. It was clearly the reason for the duel. "Isn't that right? Don't lie. You're not providing a choice."

Either way, he got the power of the crown.

Hellmyr gave a half-shrug though he didn't move his gaze. "My darling, you can refuse, but you're still coming with me." For barely a few seconds, his eyes flickered from her face someplace else. He was looking at her arm and cheek, she realized. Her wounds.

"I won't allow you to leave me only to be stabbed by the nearest goblin that lives under a tree trunk," he said. "Not as you are now, at least."

Her lower jaw felt like it came unhinged from the rest of her skull. Her cheeks burned. Why pretend to care?

She wouldn't be swindled into thinking that. Anova readied her next attack. It was time to end things.

But he didn't stop talking. He liked the sound of his voice too much.

"We'll rule, Anova. Together."

Anova stopped. She let herself envision it, if only for a moment. A world to rule over. All the power between them.

But she wanted nothing to do with Fae anymore—and that included the damned thing on her head. And the cruel beings that filled its borders.

Anova grinned a saccharine smile at him.

"No."

She moved, faster than she'd let on that she could do so, and aimed for his heart.

The strike was too close for him to defend against cleanly. Hellmyr moved like a demon, and metal cried against metal.

Her sword shattered to pieces. Fragments rained on the ground at their feet. Her arm holding the broken hilt went slack.

"As much as I've enjoyed this, the game is over, Anova."

He looked as he hadn't before—like a king over warriors. His expression was tight, and shadows had fallen over his face. Her stomach flipped.

He snapped his fingers, and his army rose to their feet and came forward several steps.

No. She wouldn't let this happen. She couldn't let them take her.

No matter what he said, they were going to use her or kill her. With such a powerful artifact connected to her blood, those were the only options.

A new idea sparked in Anova's brain—a dangerous, foolhardy one. But it had to work.

She would use her assassin's tactics. All she needed was something sharp enough to cut through a throat.

Night would soon come. She needed to do it now before they had access to their magic.

Anova raised her arm that held the hilt of the broken sword. In its center was the jaggedly sharp remainder of its blade. It was as clean as the edge of broken glass.

Perfect.

Anova held the shard at her throat.

"Keep them away. Or else I'll destroy it."

The eyes of all the fae moved to her. They were attracted to it despite themselves. He was right. Every stump goblin would kill for the power of the crown.

They couldn't let it be destroyed before their eyes, or so she hoped.

None of them moved except for Hellmyr.

His lips were tight, and his eyes were hard. "Don't."

This was her ticket out. Their king.

She stared back at him. "Come here and turn around. And drop your weapons."

He did as she commanded, pausing only a moment to stare back at her before turning. She felt cold.

"Don't move, or else," she threatened.

Who was faster didn't matter now.

Anova pressed her front against Hellmyr's back. His raven hair engulfed her vision. She buried the thoughts of how his body felt against hers.

All fae were like this, she reminded herself. Too pretty for their own good.

Across the wide gulf of bodies between them, she locked eyes with Letharia. The mask had slipped.

It was like staring into the eyes of a wolf.

Anova almost lost her nerve then.

No. She had to get out of here. She had to find a way to destroy the crown. Anova started to walk some steps backward, aware that her heart must have been louder than a drum to the new fae king.

"Do I make you nervous?" he whispered.

She should have ignored that. It was a daft question.

But there was something about him that made her lose control of her mouth. "Hostages don't normally talk unless to plead."

The trees consumed them, and the shadows started to bathe them in their shroud. Before they were out of sight of his army, he commanded to them, "Don't move. Don't come after me."

And then, a few steps later, they were alone.

Her pulse raced even faster. This was the end of her plan.

He shifted in front of her, moving his head so he could glance at her halfway. His lids were low. "Is this how you would keep your fae husband? At knifepoint? On a leash?"

Her face was on fire. She suppressed the thoughts of it as well as she could. "I'm not marrying you." The fire spread to her blood. He'd once wanted to hunt her down for sport. "Ever."

His expression sobered. "A human queen and her fae king. We would be unstoppable."

Anova moved so her mouth hovered over his ear. "You will never catch me alive."

"I won't have to," he murmured. "You'll come to me at Eastwoe palace."

Anova pulled back from him and ran, clinging to the broken piece of sword.

CHAPTER FOUR

When Anova woke up, she was stiff as a board. Brief surprise flickered through her. She hadn't been attacked in the night.

Even more surprising was that she'd gotten away from Hellmyr.

She rolled from under the brush and leaves she'd used as cover while sleeping. A glance skywards revealed a sun bright and high.

Has it been hours or days?

She supposed it didn't matter. After escaping Hellmyr's army, she hadn't stopped to sleep for a day and a half.

Anova's eyes narrowed when she glimpsed her nose. Something dark had dripped along the side of it. When she touched it, her fingers came away red.

She was bleeding.

Anova jumped to her feet and shoved her broken sword in her belt. Her fingers felt for the wound when she realized. It wasn't just a little blood.

Her hands trembled and she found the pond a few paces away that she'd drunk from before her slumber.

In her reflection, she saw rivers of blood falling from around the crown. Her fingers could find no ridges digging into her skin, yet several cuts had formed along her head. Her pulse pounded in her ears.

She dunked her head into the water, tinting it pink. She needed to stop the bleeding.

Anova tore the sleeve of her shirt off and wrapped it around the wounds she found. She slumped against a tree as she pressed tight to the spot where her blood leaked the most.

There were too many reasons to number why she needed to rid herself of the fae crown. She didn't need another one. Her vision doubled, and she took several deep breaths. The sun crept overhead.

After several minutes, Anova stood slowly. She needed to remove it. Destroy it, preferably. Now.

But how?

The first method was most obvious, and she'd tried it before without success.

I'll do it this time. No matter what.

She gritted her teeth. It was her or the crown. And she'd been through worse.

Anova walked some distance to a wide clearing in the woods she'd slept in. For several minutes, she ensured sure no one was hiding in the bushes watching her.

There'd been too much of that recently.

Anova stood in the clearing's center and removed the crown from her head. She placed the gleaming black object on the grass. Here, it looked innocuous.

How could such a thing cause so much bloodshed? It didn't look like the bearer of a curse.

As soon as it left her head, the pain at her temples lessened. She breathed. She entertained the thought that she could even leave it and come back to destroy it.

But at least this part was done.

I imagined it last time, then. All the power and evil contained in one object is enough to drive one mad.

Anova took one step away when she heard it.

Don't. Don't. Don't.

Screeching pierced the wilderness. Screams of animals she'd never heard filled her ears.

Don't. DON'T. DON'T.

Anova sprinted another few steps before the screams reached a pitch unimaginable. She heaved at the ground and threw up, her body shaking.

The crown. She needed it.

She just needed to hold it. Then she would be fine.

But to put it on her head—

NO. It was evil. Cursed.

It was better to be cursed than not. Better to keep it. Safe on her head.

She needed it. She would give anything for it. She would trade the rest of the blood in her body for it. Her fingers touched the cold metal already. How right the world would be.

NO.

Anova jerked another step and started sobbing. "I don't want it. Don't. Don't make me take it."

Her fingers shook. She would bleed for it. Kill for it.

"Please." She didn't know who she pleaded with until she sank to her knees.

She was pleading with herself.

"Please."

Pain burst through her like a star against the sky. It burned like the sun. The part of her that didn't want it left her and stared. Ashamed. Disgusted.

Anova lurched to her feet and ran to it.

It hadn't moved. It was still cold despite the stream of sunlight falling on it.

Her hands didn't move to put it on her head, yet it was there already.

Anova sank to her knees again, her palms spread on the ground. Something was wrong with her.

She would just have to remove it through other means. She swallowed. Nothing could ever be easy, could it?

A laugh pierced the air, though she didn't look up. She didn't have time for more of the crown's illusions.

But the laughing didn't stop.

She looked up. In the boughs of the tree on the far edge of the clearing was a creature with coal black eyes. Its ears came to sharp points among snow-white hair.

It was a goblin.

When the goblin spoke, she guessed from its voice that it was male. "Don't stop for my sake. I do love it when humans go mad."

Anova stared and found that she could say only one thing. "And does that happen often around you?"

His expression was flat. "Not often enough."

Anova suppressed a shiver. She shouldn't linger in these woods.

"I won't allow you to leave me only to be stabbed by the nearest goblin that lives under a tree trunk."

Especially with the blood crown. She turned back to where her scant supplies where stashed, shouldered her bag, and started in the other direction when he spoke again.

"Aren't you trying to go somewhere?"

Anova gritted her teeth together. "As a matter of fact, yes."

As she took another few steps, he called again. "You have no idea where you are."

Anova turned around and glared at the goblin. Of course, she knew where she was. But as she was about to say the words, she noticed the sun overhead. It had moved.

In the other direction from where she'd thought west was. Her mouth hung open for a moment before she started in a new direction.

No matter. This way is north, then.

The goblin started laughing again. He was only a few feet away from her, and the hairs on the back of her neck rose. Her fingers hovered over the hilt of her broken sword.

"Where am I, then?" she said between her teeth.

His eyes were like shiny beetles as he wiped his face of tears. "The Lost Forest. Where else?" He cocked his head at her. "Did you not think it strange that nothing followed you within these woods? Not even your shadow?"

Anova's eyebrows pushed together. This goblin had already gone mad, and he was trying to take her with him. It didn't matter which way was east or west—only that she walked in the opposite direction of this creature.

Despite herself, her gaze went to her feet. The sun was only a few degrees off its zenith, so she threw no shadow. Even so, her skin crawled.

She shook her head. She'd already wasted too much time. As soon as she left this forest, she would find her way to the fae settlement she was trying to get to.

I shouldn't have stopped at all, Anova considered. The faster she got to civilization, the sooner she could find the knowledge she needed. She didn't linger on the fact that she might not find any information on what she sought at all—how to destroy fae artifacts.

She couldn't go back to his estate, despite the wealth of books there. And the archives in Eastwoe were too close to Hellmyr. She would have to find some other source of information.

While not getting caught.

"It's because she wishes to speak to you. It's why you can't leave yet."

Anova stopped under the swaying canopy of branches crisscrossed above her. Without turning around, she said with a flat voice, "And who would that be?"

"I know not her name," the goblin replied. "She is one of those from the other side that inhabit this space. One of the unliving. I'm sure it's you she wants."

Anova turned around, words tight in her throat. "What do you mean *unliving*?"

But when she looked behind her, the goblin was gone. The skin on her arms rose in pimples.

From the other side ...

Could it be?

Anova's head pounded. She felt as if she'd gone as mad as the goblin had thought her to be. But a new thought burned through her brain.

Is it her?

Or did the goblin make it all up?

How would he have known?

With a stuttering heartbeat, she continued through the Lost Forest. She looked to the skies again, but it was as if no time had passed from when she'd woken. It hung above her like an eye.

The longer she walked, the more she realized that the goblin was at least partially truthful. She was getting nowhere, but she couldn't allow herself to believe all of what he'd said.

Is she really here?

Anova shook her head again. It was too much to hope.

Her mother was dead.

But what if he wasn't lying?

Anova stared above her. The branches were empty of the laughing goblin, but she asked it anyway. "Where am I supposed to go?"

A great wind nearly knocked her to her feet. It whistled through the trees, disturbing the strange midday quiet. Anova shuddered. It was blowing in the direction the sun was angled overhead, so she followed it.

She'd lost her mind. There was little other explanation for it.

The blood crown had finally driven her mad.

Anova's steps were too quiet, and she came to the edge of the pond where she'd washed her face before. The wind settled to a whisper in the trees. Her pulse galloped ahead of her.

There was nothing here but the placid surface of the water.

It was that moment that shadows engulfed the area. Her head shot up, and she saw a thick, bloated cloud eclipse the sun. Chills ran down her spine as she gripped her broken weapon tight.

Mother?

She couldn't allow herself to think it, but it had been so long since she'd seen her face. She'd been the only family she'd ever known. The only truly safe place in the world.

Anova closed her eyes. The twin pains of longing and loss in her chest were too much to stand.

Someone was watching her. It was an unignorable feeling.

When Anova opened her eyes, the figure standing on top of the water stared back at her.

CHAPTER FIVE

It wasn't her mother.

She was fae, and she was unearthly beautiful.

Her pointed ears parted her corn silk hair that came to her waist. Eyes the color of a blue moon watched Anova. Sapphires and garnets draped her body from her ears to the bottom of her skirts where they were sewn into the fabric.

Anova had never seen this fae before, but she knew who she was at once.

Above her regal brow was an exact copy of the crown she now wore. This was the fae princess from the fae tale whose human lover had been murdered. And the fae who had taken her own father's life for doing so.

When she spoke, her voice was lilting, delicate, and dangerous.

"You know who I am, human."

It wasn't a question, though Anova treated it was one. She couldn't seem to move her body or say anything else. "Yes."

"Then you know what I did."

"Yes." The word hardly came out of her throat. "This crown," Anova said in a hushed voice, "really is the same one, isn't it?"

As she said it, a cloud of mist rose up from the water underneath her feet and blurred the fae princess's outline.

When the fae spoke again, her voice came from behind Anova. She jerked around to see the princess hovering barely off the ground, her dress rippling from a nonexistent breeze.

"The same. It carries the curse born from blood and tears."

Anova's heart soared. This was who she needed to speak to. "I need to know everything you can tell me about destroying it. I want to break the curse."

The phantom of the fae princess stared back at her. "Such a thing is impossible."

The words were out of her mouth before she could stop them. "Just tell me what you know. About the spell that caused it. About anything—any little detail could help—"

"It was not the spell's doing," the princess interrupted. "Not by itself. My treacherous father and the witch Gwenore started it, but I carried out her murderous intention." She stopped herself. "But this is not the reason I have summoned you here."

For the first time since the fae princess had appeared, Anova's hand gripped the handle of her broken weapon tighter. Something in her stomach soured.

"Why, then?" she asked. Her muscles tensed.

The princess took a step towards her. "The crown was not meant for your kind."

Anova's legs were stiff, but she forced them backwards a step. It mirrored the one the fae had taken. "It is not something I would have chosen to accept, had I known it would be like this."

As if you could call what I had to do a choice, Anova thought, but she kept this to herself.

The fae princess's blue eyes glimmered. "Power always has a cost, Anova."

Her teeth clamped together. "I never wanted its power. Don't you understand?"

The princess's eyes dulled. "It matters not. But surely you realize what it is I must tell you? I can see that you know it in your heart."

Anova took another step back. Her boot sank into wet earth. Much farther, and her ankles would be submerged. "I don't know what you're talking about."

"You do," the princess said. The shadow of a bloated cloud fell on her, obscuring her further except for her piercing eyes. "You have already heard it. Felt it."

Anova's eyebrows came together. This was just a spirit before her. She was the one made of flesh and bone. What did beings of dust and air and mist know?

Riddles and dreams.

But something deeper inside Anova did know.

Perhaps it was that she hadn't wanted to understand what it meant—the crown's effect on her. Perhaps it was because she already had figured it out from the first time that she'd tried to pry it off her head. Or the first time it had drawn blood from her. Or caused her pain.

"The blood crown will kill you."

Anova heard the fae princess's words, but they sounded far-off. It was if she were underwater already, drowning among the river stones and fleeting minnows.

It had started killing her already. Anova could barely remember a day that had passed since she'd woken with it that she hadn't had splitting pain at her temples.

When Nerium had told her that the blood crown would kill any human who attempted to use it, she had assumed that death would come immediately—if it were to come at all.

A swallow scraped along her throat.

Does Leander know?

"No." Anova's voice trembled despite her best efforts. "There must be something I can do." She would do anything, trade anything, to live. She was, from the moment of her birth, a survivor.

She would claw out bits of life from around her until it was enough to save her. It was what she'd always done.

The fae princess's lips were tight. She allowed a handful of words past them, however.

"You have one moon left."

CHAPTER SIX

Anova felt when she took her last step in the Lost Forest. The goblin had been right. Her shadow returned as soon as she was free of the area.

Time passed in a blur for her. Her feet plodded forward, and her senses were too numb to notice where she was. But her mind didn't stop.

One moon.

She had a month left. Anova couldn't afford to doubt what the fae princess had said. She was right—Anova had already known that it was hurting her.

That it hadn't been meant for the likes of her.

But to kill her?

One more moon.

Her temples throbbed as if in reminder. She had a month to destroy it. A month to save herself.

As she walked, two things became clear to her.

First, she needed power. Or rather, protection. She needed enough of it to stop the constant attacks on her life.

She couldn't break the curse on the crown if she was always defending her life.

Second, she needed knowledge. The spirit of the fae princess hadn't believed there was a way to break the curse.

Anova couldn't let herself believe that. She couldn't give up like she had.

But first, she needed to stop wasting time. It took her only a few hours to find a fae estate with a stable. As Anova crouched in the bushes and observed, her stomach twisted. Unlike the abandoned manor she'd taken shelter in on her way to the border forest, this manor was clearly inhabited. Flowers spilled from window boxes. The hedges had been immaculately formed into swans that looked to be on the verge of flight. It was perhaps the most beautiful home she'd seen in Fae.

A figure emerged from the house and walked to the stables. Anova chewed on her lip.

It was likely just the stable boy, but she couldn't let anyone see her. It was then she heard a soft chuckle on the wind.

Anova's gaze shot up. Her heart pounded with suspicion. Above her, the goblin with white hair lounged in a tree branch.

I should have taken care of him in the forest.

But it had been hard to convince herself that he hadn't been a spirit, too.

"Stop following me," she bit out. "You're not getting the crown."

She didn't have time for another assassin. Things were getting out of hand.

"Oh, I don't care about that." His black eyes shined in the shadows. "But I can't resist a bargain with a human."

"What are you talking about?" Anova said. "I'm not bargaining with you for anything."

"Are you so sure about that?" His coal eyes flickered to the fae manor on the hill ahead of them. "You are in want of something they have. It's in your eyes."

Before she could say anything in response, he was on the ground before her. Although he was shorter than she was by several heads, she knew to not underestimate him. Her hand itched to draw her sword fragment.

Anova was careful. If the goblin thought he had the upper hand, he would abuse it. With a masked expression, she said, "And what is it you think you can give me?"

He cocked his head to one side, and his lips revealed teeth as pointed as a sea monster's. "A distraction. I am singularly gifted in them."

Anova crossed her arms. She believed it, but that wasn't the problem. She needed to be specific about the wording when dealing with fae bargains. "And exactly what would such a bargain require of me?"

The white-haired goblin's smile widened. "Only a drop or two of blood."

Her blood ran cold, and her voice was flat when she spoke. "No."

There was power in blood. The crown on her head wouldn't let her forget that.

The goblin shrugged. "Fine. One act of service to me, the nature of which will be determined at a later date."

Anova's mouth hung open. This was worse. Much worse. But a drop of her blood?

She didn't know enough about the kind of magic that goblin fae could do, and she was sorely aware of that fact now. Other fae drew their power from the moon. The crowned fae had their own magic which came from the earth.

But goblin fae were something else entirely.

A loophole occurred to her, then. The dead couldn't pay their debts.

And if she lived—well, even better. She would be more equipped to deal with a mad goblin's request once she ridded herself of the blood crown.

"I'll agree on a few conditions," Anova said. "First, this act of service will be repaid in more than one month from now. Second, it will not endanger my life. Third, I would know who you are before entering into a deal with you."

The goblin appeared to consider these conditions for a few seconds before saying, "Yes. Yes." He paused and added, "Rietvar is what they call me."

Anova blinked. Somehow, she hadn't thought he would agree. When she looked back to the fae estate before them, the keeper of the horses was brushing the hide of one of them.

I would be in Eastwoe in a day by horseback.

One month.

The words were out of her mouth before she'd realized. "I agree."

Rietvar smiled his pointy grin again. "The bargain is set, then."

Anova kept to the bushes surrounding the estate. The sun would set soon, and she needed to get a horse before nightfall. As she passed among the shadows, she caught sight of the fae she'd assumed to be their stable boy.

Up close, he looked far from it. The fae was tall and muscled, and something hit his back at regular intervals.

A swordstaff.

This was one of the king's guard. Anova's stomach sank. He'd likely tried to kill her at one point.

It doesn't matter if it's the dead fae king himself. I need a horse.

Even in the day, there were shadows to hide in. She edged around the structure, awaiting the goblin's distraction.

As the minutes started to crawl by and her shadow grew longer, she realized something.

The fae was starting to walk towards her hiding place—exactly where the horse feed was. She cursed her judgement.

And Rietvar had tricked her. He'd never intended to help her.

Sweat coated her back. *That bastard.*

She grabbed her broken sword with ferocity. It would be little match against his swordstaff, but it would have to do.

Anova shifted in preparation for her attack, and it was enough to catch the fae's attention. His gaze shot to where she waited in shadows. It was time to create her own distraction, then.

Before she could emerge, a shadow flickered through the area like a moon blotting out the sun.

The fae pulled out his swordstaff and swiveled away from her hiding spot. For, suddenly, opposite him was a monster.

She might have called it a wolf if it weren't three times the size of one. She might have called it a bear if it weren't faster than she'd ever seen one move.

Oversized claws dug up the earth as it darted around the fae. Its coal black eyes gleamed underneath white fur.

Anova held back a gasp.

Somehow, it was Rietvar.

Stop standing about slack-jawed. This is your chance.

But, looking at the beast that had been the goblin, she could hardly move. Fear burrowed into the marrow of her bones. This was a predator of predators.

Anova pushed her feet forward, making far too much noise despite herself. But a roar covered up the noise, and she ran towards the bay mare that had skittered off at the sight of the clawed creature in their midst.

As she fixed her with the saddle she'd stolen near the stables, Anova tried to calm her horse. Her own breath still drew too short, and she knew the mare could sense her fear.

As they kicked up a storm of dirt at the edge of the forest where she'd made the deal with Rietvar, she spared one last look behind her.

The thing that had been Rietvar had opened its wide maw, and each tooth was as thick as her forearm. Spittle flew from its mouth.

She'd made a deal with a monster.

And she had a feeling it wouldn't be the last one she would make before this place killed her.

CHAPTER SEVEN

S he hoped there weren't fae here.

Night had fallen, and she felt as jumpy as a field mouse in a snake den. Anova couldn't shake the feeling that the folk were nearby.

Anova and her horse had made considerable progress, and she was certain she was already in Eastwoe. The air felt cooler, and the ground was soaked with mud in places. Moss draped from lazy trees that leaned to one side. She missed the vibrancy of the Sorrelands.

Is this the right decision? Or am I heading into the maws of another monster?

Anova's hands shook. The possibility that this was all a trick to get the blood crown was too likely for her comfort. The possibility that her blood would be splattered on the palace floor as soon as she stepped foot inside it was also too likely.

If there was one thing that she knew about Hellmyr, it was that he was hungry for power. What more powerful object existed in this world?

But there was no other option before her. No other path. No other assistance except—

Anova squeezed the mare to encourage her to stop her light gallop. Someone had already come through these trees. Branches had been cleared, and although they had nearly been hidden, she saw evidence of tracks when they stopped.

Anova breathed in the silence for several minutes, debating. She could turn around and go the other way. She should.

It was then she heard something through the trees.

It can't be.

It sounded like a voice that she'd once known. Shallow breath filled her and left her for several seconds.

The blood crown was going to drive her to madness before it could kill her. Anova raised the mare's reins, preparing to speed them into a fresh direction, when she heard it again.

His voice.

Her heart jumped into her throat. Leander was nearby. But the problem was, she didn't know if they were on the same side any longer.

Anova slid off the mare and removed her saddle and reins, stuffing what she could into the pack she'd stolen from Lyrin. She patted the horse's hide and hoped that she wouldn't wander too far.

Next, Anova removed the pack from her shoulder and gathered a bundle of fallen leaves to pour over her. The smells of earth and rotting vegetation clung to her. Fae could smell better than humans, and if she were going to sneak up on him, she needed to disguise her scent.

And she needed to prove to herself she could still best him in this way. That she could still outwit any fae. She gritted her teeth.

Anova stuffed her stolen belongings in the hollow of a twisted juniper tree. She brushed against the branches for good measure before she turned in the direction which she'd heard his voice.

Anticipation flooded her veins. She hadn't seen him since she'd killed the fae king. Surely, he'd wish to work with her to destroy the blood crown.

And yet, he had been willing to kill himself to destroy it before. Why would it be hard for him to kill a human to destroy it now?

Her heart throbbed. Despite the charade they had played together, Anova knew there had been something between the two of them.

Her brain had taunted her for believing it, but her heart remembered. It remembered the gentleness with which he'd moved her hair out of her face. How he'd broken past her carefully constructed walls. How he'd given himself to their enemy to keep her safe.

No, she hadn't imagined that.

Leander's voice was loud enough to be on the other side of the cluster of trees ahead of her. As noiselessly as she could, Anova slipped into a bramble of jewel-like berries.

Silence fell upon the air. She bit into the edge of her tongue. So much for disguising her presence.

Stop this. Enough of this hiding. If he really did—if he sent that assassin after me, then I'll know soon enough.

And she would show him exactly what she did with her enemies.

Before she could emerge from her hiding place with her broken sword in hand, she heard a voice from the other side of the bramble bush, though it wasn't Leander's this time.

It was Lycasta.

When her voice broke the silence, Anova kept deathly still to hear it.

"I can check it if you'd like."

"No, I don't think that's necessary. There's nothing else here. I made sure of it myself." The sound of Leander's voice made her freeze.

What were they doing together? He despised her. She'd been the one to shred his mother's dress, framing Anova for it in the process.

And yet, Leander continued to speak to her. "Ly, I can't believe it. All of it."

Her heart thudded too loudly. *Ly?* Who was Ly?

"I know," Lycasta responded. "When I thought I'd lost you—"

"It's okay. You can say it." Leander's voice went too soft.

"Are you really here, Leander?" Lycasta asked. The sound of his name made Anova cringe with a strange sort of pain. "I mean, you won't vanish on thin air, will you? You won't ... leave?"

The fae fell silent. Anova couldn't help herself. With the utmost care, she shifted herself within the shield of brambles around her until she could see a small space between the leaves and berries.

Her worst fears were confirmed. It was Leander—there could be no doubt about it. He was as strikingly handsome as she'd remembered, his raven hair falling to one side and his arrogant mouth twitched half-way up in a smirk. His second dagger was sheathed at his waist.

He was even wearing the coat he'd worn as the fae king's second in command. It framed his body as he leaned over Lycasta to kiss her fully on the mouth.

"Not for her," he said between kisses. "Not for anyone."

Anova stared, unmoving. She could no longer hear their voices—or anything, for that matter. She pulled herself deeper into the brambles, hardly aware of the thorns digging into her skin.

She couldn't hear them anymore. She didn't want to.

At some point, Anova pulled herself out of the berry bush. Like a worried mother, her shadow followed her.

How could she have been so dense?

What was she compared to another fae? She was human.

Not just a human, she reminded herself. Her hands shook. *A lying thief. Street trash.*

All fae used humans like they were disposable. Why had she thought him any different?

No, there was only one path before her. One way to get the power she needed.

No one else would care to save a human's life here. It was daft and dangerous to assume otherwise.

She left the two fae behind and headed for Eastwoe palace.

Even if she had to lie and cheat to do it, she would destroy the blood crown. Anova released a breath that had been tightly held in her chest.

At least she was good at lying.

CHAPTER EIGHT

The palace rose before her like a dark sun. Dawn broke behind it, draping it more in shadow.

She'd never seen it in the light. The memory of that night tugged low in her belly.

No. Anova was leaving that behind. She would get stronger.

But she wasn't going to blindly trust Hellmyr, either. She would observe him before accepting what he'd proposed. She'd already released the mare just outside of Eastwoe's streets. Her pack was light on her back.

The building was grand even by Fae's standards. Columns supported the black roof, and black metal twisted into roses formed walls around it. The soft glow of lanterns hanging from poles illuminated the area. Near the center of the palace, she knew there to be the hall where the fae king had hosted the quarter moon fête.

There's a window there. But knowing fae design, there will be more than one moon-facing window.

It took her less than five minutes to find a window that was accessible by the ground. A twisted tree leaned too close to the palace, points of lantern light filling its branches. It was almost begging her to scale it and use it to enter the palace.

Anova pulled herself up, branch over branch, until she reached the farthest that she could drag herself. She shimmied down the length of the most horizontal branch, the one scraping next to the window.

Goblins had been carved into the palace's exterior, and they glared at her as she climbed closer to the window. They were strikingly lifelike, and a part of her worried that they'd been alive at one point.

Stop distracting yourself.

If she fell from this distance, it would probably not be fatal, though she would surely be discovered. And possibly injured.

And if she were going to enter this situation with an advantage, that wouldn't do. Hellmyr could have been lying to get her to surrender more easily.

I could be climbing into a trap right now, she reminded herself.

She silenced the voice within her as she eyed the distance between the windowsill and the branch. Anova breathed in slowly. She could do this. She'd jumped as far before from her and Juras's attic window.

She didn't care to think on how many times she'd bruised herself from doing that, though.

A moment passed, and she leaped. Anova's hands and body found the ledge she'd aimed for, and she hadn't even made a noise.

After waiting a moment for her heart to calm, she pried open the glass of the window. It helped that this wasn't the first window she'd used to enter a fae dwelling; she knew better now how the locking mechanism worked.

The problem with fae architecture is that it's more concerned with aesthetics than functionality. Or rather, security.

Much like the fae themselves.

Anova was inside one of the corridors that snaked through the palace. After finding no guards nearby, she lowered herself to the floor carefully. Somewhere within were the great hall and the archives, but beyond those, there was a king's bedroom.

She might have been walking into the jaws of the monster, but she would do it on her terms. Anova flitted from bust to bust carved out of marble.

She froze. The sound of their voices and footsteps bounced around the polished surfaces surrounding her. Holding herself close, she crouched near to the floor and held her breath, listening.

Not Hellmyr. Good.

Dawn was breaking, which meant most fae would be sleeping or retired by now.

They passed, and she sprinted to her next cover. She fit perfectly behind a podium with a pot of orchids on it.

As soon as she got into cover, pain split into her head. It assaulted her body, spreading from her cranium to her ends. Her body slammed against the ground, and her senses betrayed her.

She hoped none of them found her like this.

Anova was being dragged. The pain in her skull had retreated somewhere in her body like a coward, hiding in wait.

In a flurry of limbs, bites, and scratches, she tried to get out of the rough grasp of the guards forcing her forward. But too soon, the edge of a blade had found her back.

The fae whispered to her, "Blood crown or not, if you don't comply, we will make you. You don't wish to experience that, human."

Anova didn't respond, though she allowed her limbs to slacken. Her mind raced.

Was she being taken to her execution?

Or to the dungeons?

She shouldn't have come here.

The guards flung her inside a room with only a chair and a lantern hanging from the wall. Her blood raged inside her. She never let a male touch her without touching him back just as hard.

They flooded the room, and her irritation overflowed. Why did they think they needed no less than five fully armed fae to apprehend an unarmed human?

"Sit," the guard who had whispered to her ordered.

Anova did not. "What do you want with me?"

"Spies are always questioned," he said.

She ground out, "I'm not a spy."

He moved so that his face consumed her vision. A vein in his jaw flicked. "Why are you acting like one, then?"

"I'm here to speak to him," Anova said. "Or didn't you hear him at the border forests?"

A suspicion dawned on her. He wasn't here at all. She'd broken in for no reason.

"You'll speak to us," he said. "Then we'll see what we'll do with you."

This wasn't cutting it. She would need to take them out. Breath flowed in and out of her. She needed to take his sword.

It was then that a commotion rose outside the room. It was her chance. If she could rush them, even without a weapon, she could get out of this room.

But when the door burst open, slamming on the wall next to it, the very fae she had been looking for walked in.

A stream of foul curses flooded from his mouth, some of which even she hadn't heard before. A sword of gleaming silver hung at his waist, and blood had flecked it.

His face was fixed into an expression of pure fury. It looked like it belonged on one of the busts lining the halls outside the room.

He didn't look at her. His sword came loose from where it had been at his waist, and he held it at the back of the guard's head that stood between them.

Hellmyr's voice was tight. Controlled. "Before I take off your head, I'll allow you to decide if you prefer to beg for mercy or apologize to her first."

The guard said through his teeth, "She broke in."

"I wouldn't care if she lit the archives on fire with you in it." Hellmyr moved in a blur, and something hit the ground with a smack. The guard's body followed a second later.

To the remaining guards, Hellmyr promised, "If you touch her again, I will do something much worse to you."

Anova refused to look at the floor in case the sight made her falter and instead leveled her gaze on the new fae king. "I'm here to speak with you." She was proud of how even her voice came out.

Hellmyr's grackle eyes held her there, his lashes brushing against his skin. "I knew you'd come."

She swallowed, hoping that the fae king couldn't hear how her heartbeat had sped up at his words.

What had she gotten herself into?

CHAPTER NINE

It was bigger than Anova even imagined it could be. The first room she stepped into was cathedral-like.

It was almost as big as Hellmyr's ego.

As soon as she stepped into the suite that she'd been told was hers alone and not for some army of a hundred men, she was pushed and prodded and poked until she'd surrendered all her clothes down to her underthings.

Fae servants flitted around like buzzing insects, taking measurements and holding fabric against her skin like seafoam or lavender could bring out the rosiness of her skin. She knew the truth, though, even without having to look in the floor-length mirrors angled at her from different directions.

She looked like she'd been sleeping in a dumpster for at least a week.

A frown twitched across her face. It wasn't as if she had to imagine how that felt.

"Does it hurt, my lady?" asked one of the fae attending to her. Before Anova could answer, however, the fae had already turned her head to one of the others and hissed out, "Don't jab her, Sera."

With horror, she realized that the one the other servant had yelled at was a girl. A human girl.

Her hair had been pinned into a tight bun, revealing the soft curve of her distinctly human ears. Her face still had the roundness of childhood, and her eyes had darted to the floor from the admonishment. At most, she must have been a year or so past her first decade.

She's at the age I lost Mother.

"I'm fine." Anova looked at the fae servant. "Don't yell at her."

The fae servant had the decency to avert her eyes. "Yes, my lady."

Anova stared. She wasn't used to such a response so much that it unnerved her. She decided then.

The servants had moved on from taking her measurements to applying ointment and gauze to her scrapes and bruises. In truth, she could already feel the stinging pain mingled with relief that came with healing a wound. But she had to speak to the girl alone.

She straightened. Despite the hatred of her that burned her veins like a poison, Anova channeled the only person she could think of who always got her way.

Madam Hinterfell.

"That's enough," Anova snapped. "You have what you need. Leave the medicines. The girl will apply the rest."

At once, her retinue retreated from the room like she'd told them that the slowest one would be executed. Anova suppressed a shiver.

Perhaps that's because Hellmyr already has.

As they left, some of them snuck glances at the blood crown. Something itched at the back of her throat. She couldn't forget the target she was now.

It could be the last one I make.

The human girl stood to her side, her eyes still to the floor as she awaited further instruction. Anova wasn't quite sure where to start, but something had to be done.

She flew to the drawers at the edges of the room, but she found that most of those contained only things like necklaces and earrings.

On second thought, these may be useful. She'll need money to survive out there. Anova grabbed a bundle of dangle earrings like they were the neck of a chicken.

Anova turned around. Sera had snuck up on her. "Pardon, my lady, but I could put those on for you. And your medicine, as well."

"Do you remember how you were transported here?" Anova said. "I can't go back to the human lands with you, so we'll have to wait until there's an opportunity to get you closer to the border forests."

Except the barrier to the human lands is impenetrable right now, Anova remembered. She silently cursed.

Sera blinked. She had a tin of ointment in her hands. "I'm not sure I understand. My lady."

She was getting ahead of herself. Anova breathed through her nose. If she had to, she would wait until the perfect moment to sneak out the girl.

Better to be careful than to be caught.

But if she were caught, as long as she had successfully snuck the girl out of Fae, what could Hellmyr do? Punish her? She'd like to see him try. And relieving her of servants would be a blessing.

Anova put down the earrings. When she eyed the doorway for shadows and found none lingering under its eaves, she turned towards Sera.

"I promise, I'll get you out of this place. Out of Fae," she clarified.

Sera took a step back from Anova, seemed to realize her misstep in doing so, and froze. "I don't want to leave." She bit on her lip. "My lady."

She stared at the human servant. "You don't have to pretend with me. I know they trick humans and steal children from our lands."

Against her will, she remembered the cage of human children that the previous fae king had procured to start his war against their kind. Her stomach twisted like a wet rag. She hoped that, when Leander had freed them, they'd gotten to the other side of the barrier.

Remembering *him* made her stomach cramp even more.

But the girl was shaking her head. "That's not how I came to be here. I made a bargain." Her chin raised to look Anova in the eye. "I don't want to leave."

Anova frowned. "Their bargains always benefit them more than us." But she sat down, abandoning her search for supplies. "What were the terms?"

Sera looked away. "Three years of service here, and my grandfather's life is saved."

Anova swallowed. She could understand her reluctance to leave now. What was more, this bargain was unusually fair—by fae standards. But there were always loopholes. "And he ... he yet lives?"

"I receive letters from him. My benefactor has already healed him, though he is still recovering from his illness."

Anova nodded to herself. Unusually fair.

She looked over at her. Apparently satisfied that Anova wasn't going to try to force her back to Irbess early, Sera had picked up the tin of medicine and approached her once more.

Anova remained as still as a statue for Sera while she applied the cream to her cuts. "How much time do you have left here?"

"Most of it," Sera admitted. "I came here only recently. My lady," she added.

There was a knock at the door leading outside her rooms. Anova called for the fae on the other side of it to come inside, her thoughts on her broken piece of sword that they'd confiscated from her. Her hands itched for it.

A fae servant emerged, his eyes flying to the floor. She'd forgotten to throw something on besides her underthings, but it was done now. Enough of them had already seen and poked at her earlier for her to lose most of her shame, she figured.

"His Majesty requests your presence when you are ready, my lady," he said.

She nodded her head, forgot that he wasn't looking at her, and said, "Wait outside the door. I'll be ready in a second."

"As you wish," he said, still looking at the floor. "Will your maidservant be coming with you, my lady?"

"Yes. Please." Anova shut her mouth. People used to getting what they wanted didn't say *please*.

A secret smile pulled at her lips, though she suppressed it. She could get used to ordering about fae. And, now that she'd stolen the girl for herself, she would make sure Sera had the easiest job in the palace.

The nascent smile dissolved on her mouth. *You won't be in this place for long.*

Remember why you're doing this.

No matter if she reached her goal or not, she wouldn't be staying here.

When she and Sera emerged from her suite, the fae servant led them through Eastwoe palace. Anova's eyes scoured her surroundings, mapping within her brain where they were and where they headed. If she were going to find out anything here, she'd need to be able to move about undetected.

The archives will be the obvious place to start, she considered. Her fingers twitched.

One month. I have to find something here.

The fae servant suddenly stopped before them. They'd scaled many more stairs than she'd guessed there could fit inside the palace. He opened the door and stepped to the side to allow them in.

Only it wasn't *in* at all. The coolness of fresh air filled her lungs, and she stepped outside on a wide balcony.

The first thing she noticed was the sunrise, shafts of golden light piercing the gray and blue sky. The second thing she noticed was the flood of flowers.

Black and red roses were everywhere she could see. It was as lush as a garden—except for directly ahead of her.

It was where he was seated in a black metal chair. Next to him was an empty one.

The servant who had led her to the balcony excused himself and closed the door. Except for Sera, they were alone. And the human girl had taken to gazing out over the edge of the balcony a few paces from her as if to give them space.

Anova wasn't sure if that was going to be a good thing or not. She swallowed. At least the day had properly dawned, which meant his magic had gone with the night. But he still wore his blood-stained sword.

"I knew you'd be back for me." He leaned back in his chair, and Anova suddenly noticed that the dress the servants had procured for her to wear on such short notice *coincidentally* matched his clothes.

He seemed to have observed the same thing. His eyes lingered on the shape her dress made.

She gritted her teeth. She'd forgotten how insufferable this one was.

Lie. Fake your way through it. This is a charade. He is a means to an end.

And yet, what came out of her mouth was much closer to the truth than she would have liked.

"You think I came for you? And not your power?" she said through her teeth.

She should have started constructing the mask she was to wear here. If he found out that she only wanted this power in order to crumple it under her foot, he would likely have her chained up.

Hellmyr shrugged. "Soon, you will."

Anova narrowed her eyes at him. Before she could respond to *that*, he stood. Something about her face made him stop. He closed the distance between them, and with hardly a touch at all, traced the cut on her face.

"Didn't they do their job?" he said.

At once, she knew what he was talking about. "They did," Anova said. Although she hadn't agreed with the fae servant yelling at Sera, they didn't deserve to be punished for simply following her orders and leaving her alone.

Hellmyr's eyes went to her expression. "I heard you dismissed them. Well, most of them."

"I don't ... trust them," she said. It was honest enough, and she felt it was something that a human would say regardless.

For what she needed to do here, she couldn't have a crowd following her around.

His gaze narrowed. "Smart." He pulled away from her after a quick glance at the blood crown still on her head.

She shifted. She hadn't missed that. "You can't fool me, you know. You're just after the blood crown."

"And if I was, what would you do?" Hellmyr was before her in a blur. His finger found the base of her throat, and her heartbeat bumped into it too quickly. "Kill me first?"

Anova didn't respond. She felt in her bones she should've. After a moment, he laughed.

"Leander trained you well. Or have you been like this from the start?" he said.

She flinched at the mention of *him*. She needed to say something so they could stop talking about Leander. Or herself.

"You never answered my question," she said. "What's to stop you from doing the same?"

"You haven't tried to kill me yet, which means you're already convinced I'm not." His eyes gleamed dangerously, and he pulled his hand away from her. "But you still don't realize it, do you?"

He took several steps until he was before the balcony railing. His back was still to her as he said, "It's not only the blood crown. You're the key. I meant what I said that day."

Something scratched at the back of her throat. She remembered.

"Because, when I'm High King, I want you to be my queen."

"A human queen. A fae king. Together, we will rule uncontested." Hellmyr turned around. "And not just over Fae." He stepped forward. "Over *all* lands. Everything."

Hellmyr was before her too quickly. His finger found the underside of her chin.

"Which brings me to the reason you're here. Do you accept these terms, Anova?" He lifted her face with a slight pull. "Would you wed yourself to a wicked fae?" A smirk appeared on his lips. "Think hard on it. I can't promise such a thing wouldn't make you even worse than me."

She was using him for protection and the access to the knowledge she needed. That's all this was.

So why was her heart pounding this much?

This was what she did. Pretend.

She had one moon left, and she would need all the power he offered her. Too bad it wasn't going to be for what he thought it was—an ultimate reign over both fae and humans.

She was going to destroy his tyranny from the inside out, beginning with the blood crown. When the time came, she would wipe the smirk from his face.

Or she would die trying.

"I will," she answered.

CHAPTER TEN

They expected her to sleep. Which was exactly why she shouldn't.

Anova had picked clean the plate of food they'd delivered to her rooms, a light breakfast of glazed pears, cheese, and bread. Fae didn't normally eat at this hour—in fact, most of the fae in the palace would have retired at dawn had she not broken in.

This fact made this the perfect time for her to do her work.

She guessed that all but his day guards had likely gone to bed by now. The pull of the moon and night on them was strong, and she'd seen it with her own eyes on many occasions. Wakefulness during the day meant that more time under the moon was stolen from them.

Judging from the angle of the sun outside her windows, it was still early morning. The landscape of Fae beyond the palace was bathed in morning light, though plenty of shadows still lurked from the night. *Perfect.*

Anova changed out of the striking blue dress that she'd worn to meet Hellmyr in. When she'd arrived back to her rooms from their conversation, she'd found the closets full to the brim already.

It was day now, so it couldn't have been made by magic. All items influenced by fae magic returned to their original state upon daybreak. She frowned. *Of course, there are more than enough servants to work to the bone here to have produced these.*

Anova silenced herself and pulled out a pair of what looked to be riding breeches and a simple cotton shirt that puffed at the arms. They were the most practical-looking pieces she could find, and among the few garments that weren't dresses.

As much as she itched to try all the dresses on and steal her favorites, there would be nowhere to go with them. What would she do—go back to Irbess and fence them for money? That didn't matter now.

Anova shook her head. She needed to think clearly.

After dressing, she left the part of the suite that she'd claimed as her bedroom and walked through the other rooms until she came to the door to the halls outside. She crouched near the ground to see a shadow fall from the other side.

Of course, there was no chance they'd ever leave her alone. But that wasn't about to stop her.

Anova opened the door, and her armed fae guard pivoted to her. Anova suppressed a curse. He didn't even look sleepy.

"What's wrong?" he said. "My lady," he added at the end.

The words sounded especially wrong coming from a fae guard. Anova tried to remember if he had been one of the guards who had apprehended her when she'd broken in. She supposed it didn't matter.

"Nothing. I'll be going out of my rooms for a bit," Anova said and side-stepped him.

He stepped so he was once again before her. "Perhaps you'd like to wait until this afternoon."

It wasn't a question but a command. Anova's teeth dug into her tongue, but despite her brewing agitation, she returned to her rooms, mumbling her acquiescence as she did so.

At least she knew she was right; there weren't enough guards awake now to keep an eye on her.

It was a good thing, really.

But this could also mean she was much more of a prisoner than even she'd feared.

Both, most likely.

Good thing she had help this time.

"What's wrong, my lady?" Sera's eyes went to the closed door that separated them from their fae guard. The similarity between their reactions was unnerving.

Anova shook her head. "Nothing."

When Sera had emerged from her room within Anova's suite, she'd worried that she'd woken her. However, Sera seemed just as awake as Anova and the guard.

She added, "I need some help if you're able."

"Of course," Sera said. "Anything you wish."

Anova frowned at her response, though she wasn't sure why. It was time for a different approach.

She pressed herself close to Sera's ear and lowered her voice. "Are you up for tricking some fae?"

When she didn't respond, Anova pulled away from her. Sera's eyes were on the door. She must have realized they had a guard, too.

Anova bit at her lip. She shouldn't involve her. What if she was punished for Anova's actions?

Just as she was about to tell her to forget the matter, Sera turned to face her again. But this time, her eyes gleamed in the light.

"I am, my lady."

Anova mirrored her small smile with a bigger one. "Good."

After they went over Anova's plan, she got into place. The reception room of her suite was filled with fae-made furniture, and she fitted herself in the narrow gap between the back of a dresser and the wall.

The door to the halls nearly came off its hinges when it slammed open. Anova kept still.

The guard's voice filled the space. "Where is it? Is it here?"

"Through here, sir." Sera's voice sounded as if she'd been crying.

Anova's heart soared. The girl was proving to be a natural at this. She might have to use her help for other things …

As soon as she heard Sera's door open and close, Anova ducked out from behind her cover and sprinted for the door. She was out of her suite and into the halls, though not before she heard the fae guard swear in the closed room behind her.

She grinned. He must have found the spider that Sera was pretending to cry over.

Most males were happiest playing the hero and savior. It seemed this one was no exception. By the time he killed the spider they'd found dangling from the ceiling, she would be long gone from this part of the palace.

While it might have been more cathartic to knock the fae unconscious for a few hours while she left her rooms, that would have been far messier. It was hard to explain away the loss of several hours without the fae raising important questions.

Once she reached the bottom floor of the palace, the archives were easy to find. As she'd hoped, there were few guards patrolling the palace, and their presence thinned the farther she went from the suite.

Her memory of that night was burnt into her mind, and she used it as a guide.

How things change.

She'd wanted to escape Hellmyr and find Leander.

No, even then, Leander had found Lycasta to enjoy his night with.

She bit into her cheek. She needed to stop thinking like she'd had some sort of hold on him. Like they'd been something to each other.

Maybe that's because it only meant something to you.

A noise tried to escape her throat, but she swallowed it down. They'd gone their separate ways, hadn't they?

No, actually. Leander likely wants you dead.

Her heart throbbed like the pain at her temples.

Well, maybe he'll get his wish after all.

The math in her head screamed at her, yelling that she'd wasted so much time already.

If you die, it's your fault. You didn't do enough.

Anova was inside the archives. She didn't remember slipping inside the doors, but the smell of old pages was enough to break the spell that had fallen on her. It was time to do some work.

She started in the section of the archives where she'd found the book of fae tales. It wasn't still here, of course, but maybe she'd find ones like it.

Or so she hoped.

After shelving the third copy of the same book on war strategy, her fingers shook too much to hold another one. She flexed her stiff fingers and massaged blood into them. She'd searched perhaps eight entire bookshelves.

She needed to try something else.

Curses. Fae artifacts. Where else would this information be?

Through the windows into the archives, the angle of the sun sharpened. Her nails dug into her palms. Her unsupervised time was coming to an end too quickly.

She closed her eyes. *Leave now and they won't discover that I ever left.*

Or stay and risk being caught.

And never leave my room again.

Anova sank to the floor, stirring up a cloud of dust. Her head fell into her hands. There was only one person for this job, and she was pretty sure he wanted her dead right now.

Actually, Leander was only pretending to be the scholar. That was his brother.

She was beginning to realize she'd never really known him at all.

They were going to find her here and drag her back to her rooms. She needed to get up, but she couldn't move.

Anova lurched to her feet. There had to be something here. A clue. A word or two. Something to prove that the blood crown could be destroyed.

That she could *live.*

As she walked past the sections of shelves, scanning their spines, something occurred to her. She stopped. There was no mention of the crown at all in these books.

Someone had removed them all.

And she was fairly certain she knew *who.*

Moving twice as fast as she had before, Anova arrived at the correct section of the archives out of breath. But she didn't pause to catch her breath as she pulled every folder and book free that she could reach.

This was the section she'd wanted to find upon her first arrival here. These were the personal folios of the fae king, specifically the High King that she had killed.

When Hellmyr seized power, the fae guards must have moved the previous fae king's notes and records here.

The reason she'd originally wanted to search these documents stung in her mouth. She had never discovered which of the fae had killed her mother.

Anova blinked back a tear. She needed to focus. The stack of parchment in her hand had a title written over the front, and it made her want to throw the entire thing through the window.

The Human War.

They'd narrowly kept his fae army from invading Irbess. Anova didn't wish to read what he'd planned to do to her people after getting out of the boundary forests. And yet, she started reading his war notes.

Her stomach clenched. *It would have been merciless.*

He'd planned to make the survivors their slaves. No bargains. No illusion of trade between them.

When she read what was on the last page, Anova's heart froze.

She read it again. It didn't make sense.

A third time.

The war that never was …

Was a front.

It had intended to be a cover for what the High King had wanted much, much more than human slaves.

A voice pierced the dimness of the archives.

"A good sneak covers her tracks. One would think you'd have learned that by now."

It was far too much like the first time she'd been here when the High King had caught her and Leander in the archives.

But this time, she couldn't hide.

Dressed in a gray silk dress that likened her to a shadow, Letharia stepped into a shaft of lantern light seeping between two bookshelves. Her golden eyes were sly like a predatory bird's, and the tips of her ears were laden with gold jewelry that caught the light against her dark hair.

The information she'd learned seconds ago rattled around in her head like coins dropped on a busy street. Anova couldn't let her know that she knew this.

Does Hellmyr know?

He can't. Or they would have continued the invasion at once.

And the only way to cover her tracks now was to destroy the papers.

It was less a decision and more an instinct. Anova ran.

Because Letharia wasn't expecting it, she had a healthy head start. But if there was one thing Anova had had proven to her—over and over—it was that the fae were faster than her.

Already, her lead was vanishing. She ducked between stacks, changing directions. Ultimately, it didn't matter if she were caught. It mattered if they discovered why she'd come here in the first place and what she'd learned in the archives.

Her gaze darted from one end of the archives to the other. There was nothing here but pages older than her great-grandmother.

It was then that she remembered something Hellmyr had said to her when she'd broken inside his palace. She smiled.

Letharia's voice floated above the stacks. "This is fruitless. You are doing nothing but incriminating yourself."

"You knew what I was when you helped me that night in the High King's castle," she called back. "You knew when you helped me in the boundary forests. But then," Anova said, barely pausing as she silently plucked a lantern from a table, "like recognizes like, doesn't it?"

The key was to get as far away as possible from the place her pursuer thought she was at any given moment. Anova picked up a book and threw it over her head where it sailed clear over two shelves. It produced a solid *thunk* where it smacked the floor, and she ran in the other direction.

"You stumbled into a plan orchestrated by others and claim yourself the mastermind, do you?" Letharia asked.

I still kept the blood crown out of your son's hands.

She bit down on her response. This was where the magic needed to happen.

Judging from Letharia's voice, they were as far apart as she could hope. Anova shoved herself against the end of a bookshelf and carefully removed the top of the lantern. The heat from the flame brushed against her face, and she fed the parchment inside. It licked each paper until it turned to ash.

She couldn't let this information out—not if she wanted to live. Her heart galloped in her chest fast enough for make her dizzy. She couldn't let them know she'd destroyed anything, either.

Anova rushed to hang the lantern on a wall hook, but when she started to run for the exit, a shadow stepped out from behind a shelf, blocking her path.

In Letharia's hand was a long blade well within reach of Anova's neck. She froze before the sight of the weapon. Sweat coated her back.

Anova cocked her head. "What is it you want, Letharia?"

"A reason not to have one of my guards kill you in your sleep," she said. Her golden eyes held her there, and Anova was suddenly quite sure she wasn't exaggerating.

Anova felt as if a spider walked on her spine. When she spoke, her voice was tight. "We're on the same side. That should be reason enough."

"Are we? It didn't seem so when you took my son hostage." Her expression was flat. She narrowed her eyes and took a step forward. The tip of the sword was nearly at her throat. "And it doesn't seem so now. What are you doing here, Anova?"

She swallowed. Things were almost going the worst possible way.

At least I destroyed the war notes.

Her pulse climbed higher. She had to convince her. She had to get out of this. She'd found the key—the one that might've been enough to end the crown permanently—but it would do her no good if the secret died with her.

But there was no lie convincing enough.

It doesn't matter if I can get away. A poisoned sip of water, a knife in the night. That's all it would take.

Anova cursed to herself. Where was the power she'd supposedly stolen now?

She said the only thing she could. The truth.

"I wanted to know more about the blood crown. How it works. Where it came from."

Instead of stepping closer to use her blade on Anova, Letharia stood there. She wasn't sure what the fae was searching for in her face, but she seemed to have found it when she lowered her weapon.

"You'll not find that here. He had all physical records destroyed," Letharia said. A look flickered in her eyes, and it was like watching the center of a fire writhe and dance. She was remembering something.

Anova stared back at the fae. Something clicked into place.

She knew these things. Or, at least, she knew more than Anova did about the blood crown.

"You want to know," Letharia said when Anova hadn't responded. She stepped forward. Though she'd lowered the sword, Anova didn't relish any fae this close to her.

"Prove to me you're more than a sneak thief, Anova." Letharia turned in one motion and strode for the exit of the archives. She stopped, and without looking back, she said, "Convince me you're here to do what you say. Set a date. And make it soon."

CHAPTER ELEVEN

Anova's eyes bolted open. The pain was like a light in her brain: bright, merciless, and exacting.

A scream tore through her lips before she could clamp down on it. Her body trembled with the burden of it, and she pulled her limbs close like she could hold the pain inside.

It felt like someone was trying to pry apart her skull. Anova pulled the crown from her head, but the pain didn't stop. It grew, monstrous and ravenous. She shoved it back on, and her body shuddered.

Sera's voice was at the door. It was high and strained. She'd heard it all. "My lady, is something wrong?"

She must have fallen asleep. Sometime between sneaking back inside her suite and planning for her next steps, her body had taken what it had needed from her. The sunlight was too angled. It was nearly dusk.

The memory of what she'd learned in the archives—along with Letharia's threat—lingered in her mind. She needed to do something about it all. Now.

Anova lurched from the too-big bed, wiped her face with the back of her hand and opened the door to prove that she wasn't getting murdered in her sheets.

But instead of showing relief, Sera's eyes widened at what she saw on Anova's face. "Bad dreams." Anova's voice sounded hollow to herself.

Sera's lips pressed together. She still didn't look entirely convinced that Anova wasn't attacked. A thought occurred to Anova then, and she didn't like it.

She's no fighter. So that means they intend her to double as a body shield should an assassin make it inside. They would expect her to lay down her life before mine.

Sera spoke again, disrupting Anova's morbid thoughts.

"The feast will be in an hour, my lady. Please allow me to prepare you for it."

Anova narrowed her eyes at nothing in particular. "Feast?"

"To celebrate the announcement of your engagement," Sera said. "Most of Fae will be there, I imagine."

Anova felt like she was going to throw up. How had the bastard organized all this within less than twenty-four hours?

Anova sat and allowed Sera to do what she wanted with her, though only after Sera had insisted that she should do something. As she brushed and pinned parts of her hair to her head around the blood crown, Anova allowed the details of what she'd learned to coalesce within her.

She needed to get back to the human lands as soon as possible. There was no way around it. And she needed a reason that wouldn't arouse Hellmyr's suspicions or tip him off as to what was so important there.

Because the real reason that the High King had wanted to invade the human lands was to ensure the blood crown could never be destroyed. That was where the last hope of destroying it was.

The descendant of the witch who had created the blood crown.

The last human with magic. The last witch.

During his conquest, he'd planned to root out this person and kill them.

The proof of it all had been written plainly among his war notes. Anova sagged in her chair. At least she'd been able to destroy the papers.

Her next steps were plain before her: convince Hellmyr that she needed to go back to Irbess and set a date for their wedding.

Anova shivered at the thought of being tied to him in such a way.

It's only a front. I'll set it for a month from now.

She seemed to be pushing a lot of obligations out lately—but her first priority over most anything else was living. And if she didn't, well, that was one less thing to worry about.

And she'd done this before, even if under different circumstances. Her stomach twisted at the thought of *him*.

Sera helped her into her dress, a low-cut gauzy black one with a slit along the leg. It would have been stunning if she weren't wearing it solely to tie her life with that of a fae monster.

A knock sounded at the door to her suite. It was time.

When she entered the hall, Sera beside her in a beautiful fae-made dress of her own, she couldn't help but draw the parallels between this night and the last one that she'd been here.

The tables spread across the hall were filled with steaming food. Above them, night had fallen already, and the soft light of the stars brightened the room through the sky window. Moonrise would happen soon if it hadn't yet.

As the train of servants guided her to her seat, Hellmyr and his guards entered at the same time. She scowled. Of course, Hellmyr was in a black coat and suit that matched her dress. It was trimmed in gleaming silver, and on his head was a crown of the same color that must have been made to mirror hers.

They were a matching pair, or so he certainly wanted them all to believe.

Anova felt their eyes on her as she took her seat. The smell of the roasted chicken near her made her mouth water.

She tried to ignore their stares, but it was becoming difficult.

Most of them weren't at the battle in the boundary forests. Perhaps they didn't know what happened there. Or they thought it was a rumor.

And there was the fact that never before had a human worn the blood crown.

She felt when Hellmyr sat beside her at the head of the long feast table. He was within arm's reach, though she didn't look at him. It was tiring being his doll and figurehead all in one.

I'll need to convince him soon that I need to go to Irbess.

Now wasn't the time, but she didn't have time to begin with.

Suddenly, a commotion erupted at one end of the feast table. A fae stood with a feral look in his eyes.

"Right there! Somebody kill it. It's not meant to have it."

Hellmyr stood so quickly that his chair fell against the floor. "Kill him," he growled.

A flurry of guards carried out his will. They held the fae against the ground, but she could still see him. His eyes were on her.

Silver starlight glinted off a blade, and the fae was freed of his head. Anova could feel the bloodlust rise in the room. Eyes flickered between her and the dead fae.

"Anyone else care to be relieved of a head?" Hellmyr said with a dangerous look in his eyes.

Silence fell upon the room. He stood before his seat. "An attack on my bride is an attack on me. Misinterpret that to your folly."

Murmurs broke out among the feast tables as they realized what his words meant.

Hellmyr took his seat. Moonlight fell around him, highlighting his almost violet-toned black hair. He looked every part an angry fae king.

"Anova is to be your queen. For the first time in ages, you will have a High King and High Queen. Together, we will be stronger than any fae ruler our history has known. Fae will be stronger." He waited until the furor dissolved.

After a moment, he added, "We will combine our houses in two weeks under the full moon."

The words echoed within Anova's skull.

Two weeks. Two weeks.

Her gaze shot to Letharia, her lip curling already. *You couldn't wait for me to prove myself, is that so? You set the date yourself.*

Anova cursed the fae lady for interfering, but then again, that's what the fae did best.

But she noticed a strange thing then. Letharia didn't look the part of a self-satisfied cat who ate the mouse.

Instead, she looked approving. Her mouth moved quickly, almost too quick for Anova to read her lips. But it was clear enough to her.

You've done well.

Anova could feel her brow wrinkling. Letharia didn't do this, and she thought that Anova had selected the date. Her gaze shot to the fae king next to her.

He had said more words to his gathered court and allowed them to start eating. Sera was testing Anova's food, as was Hellmyr's servant doing for him. He waited, almost bored, for his taster to finish chewing a glistening piece of meat seasoned with lemon pepper.

She whispered to him, "Had enough of waiting, have you?"

Hellmyr's eyes swept to hers as he smirked, his sharp teeth showing. "My dear, you'll find human moralities have little influence here. Whatever waiting you're suggesting doing—there's no need. You may come to my chambers whenever you wish."

Anova's face reddened. "You know of what I speak," she grinded out.

"I'm afraid I don't," he said, turning his head to bite into a plum that resembled the shade of her face.

She stared at him. "The full moon is two weeks away?"

The fae king's eyes flicked back to hers. "Your servant spoke like you knew that."

My servant?

"Sera?" she said in a whisper. Her throat closed around the name. *Why would she ...?*

He shook his head, ever so slightly. "One of the others." He narrowed his eyes at her. "What are you saying?"

"Nothing. I just—" She chewed her lip. What did it mean? "I'll have one of them find me a more current moon calendar."

She started to eat the food placed in front of her, but she couldn't taste it despite knowing how mouthwatering fae food was. The muscles in her jaws moved without her directing them to.

What was going on?

Hellmyr hadn't decided it. Someone else had set their wedding date so close. But who?

More importantly, why?

She had more enemies than she'd known. There were other players in this game, and she hadn't even realized it.

The hand holding her fork had started to shake. She clamped down on her bottom lip and speared the meat on her plate. She couldn't expose her vulnerabilities. Someone else was out there, watching. Pulling strings that she hadn't realized were attached to her limbs.

Someone needed them to be wed on the full moon. Did someone else know she was to die so soon?

Anova breathed. Hellmyr was staring at her. Watching.

Perhaps he'd already pieced it together. Someone was among them, pulling them along like puppets. She couldn't let him know her true intentions.

She needed to act already.

The words passed between her lips, soft and fast. "Is that offer good for tonight?"

His response was a smile that showed his teeth again.

"For you, it is."

CHAPTER TWELVE

Anova's heart thundered inside her chest so much that she felt dizzy. She stopped when her guards came to a set of wide doors illuminated on either side by wall sconces.

Reminding herself why she was here and what she needed to accomplish helped move her feet through them, but it did nothing for her heart.

But when she walked inside his chambers, they were empty. After the guard closed the doors, Anova walked around the first room. The fact that she was alone couldn't placate her heart—not when she considered this would be the perfect time for an assassination.

She swallowed. What she was trying to do here now seemed the epitome of foolish. Trying to seduce a disturbed fae king into letting her return to the human lands without tipping him off to the real reason—well, she'd done more difficult things.

Hadn't she?

One month left. One month left.

It kept her feet moving.

You've done this plenty of times with Juras's help. She closed her eyes and envisioned that Hellmyr was no more than her drunk mark in a tavern. She even saw the gold jewelry and coins that she would steal from him.

When she opened her eyes, she realized that on the other side of the room was a balcony. The glass and metal door was ajar, and a warm breeze leaked into the room from it. She held her breath and passed through it.

"I knew it was only a matter of time," he said.

He was propped against a lounge chair, letting the moonlight fall on his skin and highlight the planes of his bare chest. Thankfully, he was wearing pants, because Anova wasn't sure what she would have done otherwise.

Beside him on a low table was a glass of what looked like human-made wine. Her mouth popped open.

The smell of grapes and earth hit her. It was human-made.

"Do you want some?" Hellmyr's grackle eyes took her in. She hadn't changed from the gauzy dress she'd worn to the dinner.

Her tongue danced inside her mouth for the thought of something from her home, but she thought better of it and refused him. She needed a clear head for this.

Her eyes darted to his waist. There was nothing there. No weapon. But then again, she could always try to throw him off the balcony if she needed to.

"Fond of balconies, aren't you?" she asked.

And of showing off. And generally being full of yourself.

He shrugged. "One of the improvements here I made upon becoming king."

She tapped her foot. "I need to speak with you. Alone." Anova looked pointedly out across the land. While the landscape of Eastwoe was undeniably beautiful with its autumnal forests and lanterns glowing like will-o-wisps in the night, this was surely less private than speaking inside. Even if they were high in the air.

Hellmyr's palm faced the moon, and a small light flashed in his hand before disappearing. A shimmer danced on the air before he faced her again. "It was already spelled for wayward arrows in case you were wondering."

She suppressed a shudder. Attacks on her life had become mundane to her now, which oddly bothered her more than the idea of being attacked.

His eyes were still on her. "If you're tired of standing, you can sit."

Anova crossed her arms, glaring at his reclining form. "You're taking up the only—"

She shut her mouth just as quickly. *That's his point.*

She should be doing better at this, she felt. But this fae had a way of bringing out the worst in her.

"Fine," she said between her teeth.

Before she could convince herself not to, she sat down on his lap, bringing her legs across his so she was perched sideways on him. She crossed her legs together as the breeze ruffled her dress.

I'm the one using him, she reminded herself. *Then I can be quit of him as I like.*

Hellmyr watched her, saying nothing—blessedly. He didn't even shift his weight under her.

The plan she'd worked so hard to concoct during dinner sat in her mind, but her lips were pressed tight together. As she mulled over what the words to convince him of what she wanted, she started tracing the divots and hills of his hard chest.

As quickly as a bolt of lightning, one of his hands grabbed hers, stopping her where she'd coaxed out a line of goosebumps.

He brought his mouth to her ear. "You're here to seduce me, aren't you?" He breathed against her neck. "Then do it already."

Anova swallowed. "What are you talking about—"

"I can tell when you want something. It gets in your eyes," he murmured. His sudden, barking laugh surprised her. "It must be important for you to stoop to this. Perhaps it's the real reason you came here."

But something rose in Anova like a wave. She didn't realize what it was until she started speaking.

"You should care that I'm using you," she said with a bite to her voice. She pulled herself up from him. This was the densest thing she could say to him, but something inside her wouldn't keep it bottled up when he acted like this.

She felt as if her heart were being throttled. She could barely breathe for the anger that consumed her. He was the fae king. He was the only thing holding these feral creatures back from bedlam.

And he'd let her in knowing she had intents other than what he wanted. Murderous, traitorous intents.

"You should care," she repeated, her frantic heartbeat barely allowing her to speak, "but you don't."

His mouth was on hers before she could understand what had happened. Her fingers found the back of his neck to pull him closer to her. Sometime, her legs had moved so she'd started to straddle him.

Kissing Hellmyr was like falling into darkness. Adrenaline rushed her body, but she let herself fall deeper.

One of his hands found her back where her dress surrendered to bare skin, and he traced shapes into her skin that made her shiver. Heat rose inside her like the plume of a wildfire and spread through her veins.

Hellmyr pressed his mouth against her throat. The fire continued through her, and she arched herself against him.

Against her throat, his voice rumbled through her. "Why is it that you came back to me?"

Because I'm dying. Because I need help and there was no one else.

But instead of those things, those horrid, ugly, truthful things, she murmured into the cool night, "Don't. Don't ask."

If she were going to die anyway, what did it matter who knew?

She didn't want his pity. But she wanted *this.*

"You will tell me," he said against her skin.

The haze lifted from her mind as she breathed in fresh air. No, she needed to do something here. She was going to live, and she'd better start acting like it. She needed to remember that.

His mouth had moved to other places, and she tried to keep her voice even as she spoke. "I need to go back to the human lands."

Hellmyr stopped and looked up at her. "Darling, I don't know if you've noticed, but you tend to stick out as you are. I don't think they'll allow the one crowned with that to walk around. Not after recent events." His lips formed a startling smile at a new thought. "Unless, of course, you wish to invade and start your reign over those lands, as well."

Something bubbled up her throat at the thought. "No," she blurted. "We are not invading Irbess."

Hellmyr shrugged. "As you wish. I personally agree. We need only target the humans' corrupt, old king in order to take control of those lands."

Her teeth grinded against one another, and she pulled away from him. "We are not taking control of the humans' lands." Something flashed in Hellmyr's eyes at those words, and she amended them with, "Not right now. No, I just need to take care of some business there."

Hellmyr's gaze narrowed on her. "Business?"

"I have some ... associates who are in debt to their employer." She chewed at her lip as she decided whether or not to tell him more. "Juras. And the women who were my mother's friends. I want to pay off their debts so they can leave."

It was the truth. She'd wanted to help them get out of the Rosebud since she'd escaped it. Now that she had the power to do so, she would seize the opportunity.

And Juras ... she hadn't seen him since she'd murdered the High King. She needed to make sure he was free of Hinterfell.

It also happened to be the perfect cover for her to find the last human witch.

As Hellmyr opened his mouth to surely say *no*, he said something else instead. "I'll get you past the boundary and even into the city under cover, but only if you do something for me, as well. I'll make a deal with you."

She didn't like the sound of this, but she figured she should have expected no less.

"What is it?" she asked.

But Hellmyr wasn't looking at her. He was examining one of her hands. She felt something cold, and she slid her hand out of his before something could happen to it.

When she saw what was on it, her stomach dropped.

Ah, there's my new problem.

"Wear this," he said.

It was a silver ring that wrapped perfectly around her finger. On it was a heavy onyx gem, cut so its facets collected the light around it.

There was no other word for it. It was beautiful.

And it was a reminder of what was quickly becoming one of her biggest problems, second only to her death coming in less than a month.

Her engagement to this fae.

There's always a catch to fae bargains.

CHAPTER THIRTEEN

The last light of the day streaked through the trees of the boundary forests. Anova leaned towards her horse. She couldn't quite believe how painless it had proven to convince Hellmyr of this whole operation.

She snuck a glance down at her hands holding the horse's reins.

That's because I paid a price for it.

She steadied herself. It would be worth it to see the blood crown destroyed.

Anova concealed her smile. It was a demented smile, but something in her took joy from the thought. *No matter if I can save myself or not, it will be destroyed for good.*

Ahead of her, Hellmyr signaled for their party to stop. Anova could feel the tension in the air. The magic of Fae fought against the neutrality on the other side of the boundary.

They descended their mounts, and she walked to where she knew the invisible barrier to be. Just like last time, she felt the intangible block before them.

This needed to work. Or else she would be stuck in Fae until she died.

Hellmyr's violet-black eyes beheld her. A smile quirked to his lips as she approached.

"Ordinarily, feats of magic performed by the wearer of the blood crown are difficult to reverse." Anova narrowed her eyes at him. She hadn't done this, but she didn't interrupt. All that mattered was that they could pass through it.

Hellmyr continued, "But in this case, a little assistance will suffice to lift the spell."

He held his hand out towards her. Anova frowned but came forward to clasp his in her hand. She felt his thumb run over the onyx of her ring before they proceeded.

She bit the inside of her cheek. Fae were obsessed with ownership and possessing.

Anova felt a rush of warmth spread through her, going all the way to her ends. She breathed slowly, trying not to panic at the feeling of magic invading her limbs.

With his other hand, he drew magic from the moon in his palm. It was as light as water as it collected in the creases of his skin.

A ripple in the air formed, and it reminded Anova of how light bent in water. With her breath held, they walked through the ripple together.

The air clung to her oddly as she stepped through to what she knew was the human realm. She tried to breathe normally, but a pressure held tight to her chest. She swallowed.

You'll be fine here. This is your home.

But why did it feel so different now?

As soon as the last of his guards were through, Hellmyr dropped his hand, and she pulled hers back to herself. The ripple was gone.

Hellmyr stepped to where it had been, his hand before him. He made a noise and turned back to her.

"It's closed again." Before her heart could jump out of her throat, he added, "I should be able to open it to go back, but it'll need to happen while the moon is out. I'll be waiting here. Don't be late." Hellmyr sniffed in the general direction of Irbess like he could smell the stink of the city.

He probably can, she reminded herself.

"Fine by me," she said, her arms crossing. "I'll be back before the night is over."

She turned to lead her horse out of this side of the boundary forests, but Hellmyr stopped her, blocking her path with his body.

"I may be staying here, but your guards are coming with you. Besides, I need to glamor all of you before you go."

She looked back at the retinue of guards he'd dragged here. There must have been a dozen or so of them. She'd assumed they'd been for him.

She gawked at them. No less than twelve fully armed fae, most of which were pure sculpted muscle. She turned to look back at Hellmyr. "There's no way we can sneak through the human lands like this. Even with fae glamor, they're too noticeable."

Some of them had started to glare back at her. She didn't care.

Hellmyr took a step closer to her. "You're taking them or you're not going at all."

Anova felt a vein pop against her temple. "The constables will stop us as soon as we pass into the city. There's too many. I work best by myself."

For her plan, one fae guard was too many, but he didn't know that.

Hellmyr closed his eyes and breathed. His voice lowered. "I'm coming. Or they are."

Her heart raced. She couldn't have that *at all.* Short of killing him, there would be no fooling him as to her true motivations once she got farther in.

His eyes opened again. He surely could hear her frantic heart, and she needed to say something to distract him from it.

"One. I'll take one of them."

"You'll take two."

Hellmyr looked back at them and pulled two from the group, a male and female guard.

They went to work glamoring themselves. Out of her peripherals, she watched their ears round from points. Even their brutal beauty softened.

They became human-like, though she thought she'd have been able to tell if she looked hard enough.

Her mind raced ahead of her as she allowed Hellmyr to disguise the crown on her head with fae magic.

How am I going to lose them?

They didn't look particularly thrilled that he'd chosen them out of the rest. In fact, she'd have said they looked bored.

I'll just have to find a way out of their supervision.

She'd bet her life that Hellmyr had intended just that for these fae—not just as her guards but as watchful eyes on her.

"Before dawn. Don't be late," he reminded her as they mounted their horses once more.

She rolled her eyes. It helped with the tension tangled in her gut. "I wouldn't dare."

With one fae guard on either side of her, they rode through the rest of the boundary forests. From the help of the steeds bred in Fae, they were on the outside of Irbess well before she'd perfected a plan.

They left their horses at the edge of the forest and slipped into the city's shadows like wraiths. She should have felt at home here, but all she felt was unease.

I need to start driving us to the other side of Irbess where the hills are.

In her mind, she envisioned a map of the city. Where she needed to go was on the opposite side, where the city surrendered to foothills that eventually gave way to more coast. That was where the last witch was said to reside.

She hoped this person still lived.

Anova crouched by a crate pushed against a warehouse. She'd come as close to the Rosebud as possible without veering off path from her first destination. How she would do all this in one night would be a miracle, but she only had tonight.

She felt them behind her in the shadows. It was now or never.

Anova whispered behind her, "I'm going to the south side of Irbess first. There's something I have to take care of there."

No plan. No tricks. Just a command.

But her fae guards weren't looking at her. They'd glanced at each other, and Anova tried to interpret the strange, fleeting look before it was gone.

It was then they attacked.

Silver flames filled their palms, writhing and alive. Anova slammed herself against the other corner of the crate as she dodged their fireballs.

Her nails dug into her hands. What were they doing?

All fae are bastards, remember.

Anova dodged another of their assaults before pulling free the weapon she'd taken with her upon leaving Eastwoe. But a blade was little defense against fae magic. She swore out loud.

"You'll give us all away with your ill-thought-out treason," she said through her teeth. She pushed herself against another crate.

The female guard leaped in front of her, her eyes gleaming. "If it means we kill you and gain the crown, so be it."

The heat of her flames grazed Anova's skin, and she rolled under her to dodge the worst of it. She ran.

They were being far worse than reckless. This was deranged.

Flames blasted the street ahead of her. Anova turned around, her weapon raised.

The male had his hands behind his back. A smile as sharp as a dagger bolted to his face, highlighting his cheekbones. "It should go to a fae. One who can use its power." Even human, he was much too beautiful. His eyebrows raised in question. "Don't you agree?"

Anova bit her tongue. No one deserved the unrestrained power that came with such an artifact.

The female joined him. Her eyes were much more cunning than his, and in her palm already was a dagger. If Anova had to bet, this fae was planning on killing the other once she killed Anova.

I don't have time for any of this.

She was on the streets she'd been raised on. It was time to fight dirty.

Suddenly, Anova raised her hands to the sky and looked at a point just past their shoulders. Her eyes widened, and her voice was tight with pleading when she spoke.

"They're fae," she gasped. "They tried kidnapping me. Please—arrest them!"

As soon as their backs twisted to look behind them, Anova ran, jumping over the dying flames in the street.

There were no constables.

It was one of the oldest tricks known to the street rats here. She smiled to herself, and she started for the route that would hide her best in this city.

CHAPTER FOURTEEN

Anova's feet were sore and blistered in her boots, but she couldn't stop. She'd already passed the area in which the High King's war notes had claimed the last witch lived.

Trees shifted, and she glimpsed the sliver of moon overhead. She prayed the night would be long enough.

Through the last of the trees that bordered Irbess on its south and west sides, Anova came to rolling fields scattered here and there with more tree clusters. It was undeniably the most beautiful part of the land this side of the boundary.

It looked empty, but a quiet tug that started in her stomach told her otherwise.

The witch was here.

Anova started forward, listening to how the grass bending against themselves was like a chorus. The sky above her was clear except for puffs of clouds that raced under the moon crescent like children.

How far does this deception go? Now that she was far from their flames and the streets she'd been cornered on, she considered which was worse.

If her guards had acted independently or if they had something to do with the servant who had told Hellmyr that their wedding date was to be in two weeks.

Either way, it wasn't good.

At once, the ground fell away from her, and her stomach twisted itself into a tight knot. The world was a blur of motion and color as she fell.

It wasn't until she stopped moving that Anova realized that she hadn't fallen. Or rather, she hadn't fallen *down*.

The breeze stirring the grass made her sway. She was hanging from a loop of rope around her ankles that was tied to a tree branch. As she tried to bend herself up to reach her ankles, she discovered that her arms wouldn't budge.

Anova cursed. When she'd been flipped over, her hands had caught a loop of rope that had tightened as a part of the trap.

The rope stretched her too tightly for her to be able to move. How had she not seen it before?

Rocks and leaves had hidden the trap. She'd let her guard down, and she'd paid for it.

I don't have time for this. Her teeth grinded against each other. All her things were on the ground below her, including the blood crown that had been on top her of her head.

Anova's nails dug into the rope at her wrists. Her circulation already suffered for it, but it was the surest way out.

It was then she heard the ticking noise. It reminded her of a wooden clock, which was why she'd ignored it at first. The first sign of blood crown madness was always auditory and visual hallucinations.

But it's usually far more insistent, she thought.

Anova looked ahead at the upside-down land around her and stopped moving. It was well-hidden inside a bramble bush, but there was no mistaking it now that the clicking was all that she could hear.

It most resembled a bow gun, though she'd never seen one quite like this. Attached to one end of it was a wooden dial that clicked on its own at regular intervals.

Like a clock, she realized. Her next thought came a second later.

It's counting down.

And aimed straight at her heart was an arrow with a deadly metal tip.

This was the point of the trap—not only to capture but to kill, as well.

It's an illusion. Nothing more. It's the crown.

But the blood thundering through her veins told her otherwise.

It's real. It's real. It's real. You can't afford to find out if it's real or not.

Her vision danced before her eyes, swirling to the beat of the timer. The blood had gathered in her head and hands. She couldn't move.

Don't give up.

Her extremities had numbed by now, but Anova couldn't stop. Her nails barely pierced the thick rope, and she swayed with the movement of her frenzied attempts.

It wasn't working. There wasn't anything she could do.

Her heart stuttered, pumping more blood like it knew the sharp metal would soon be inside of it.

I can't do anything.

It hit her like a punch to the gut.

That was the point. Rather than automatically release the arrow when the trap's prey was still unaware of it, a timer had been affixed to the trigger.

But why?

To allow the hunter to come and investigate his kill.

She blinked. *For the prey to beg for its life.*

This was either the work of a sadist or …

When she spoke, her voice was unnaturally high. "I'm not here to hurt you. Please. I need your help."

The calm breeze mocked her, pulling at her binds. Between the ticking noise, silence was heavy on the plains.

"I can't die yet. I'm trying to destroy it." She didn't like the sound of her own voice, but she was sure no one was listening anyway.

"If I knew that dying would destroy it, I would gladly die. But I don't." Her memories showed her the first time she'd decided that her life was worth trading to destroy the crown.

It hadn't worked then.

"Not anymore," she said through her teeth. The ticking was louder than ever. "But no matter what it takes, I vow to do it."

Her heartbeat was so loud for several seconds that she didn't realize the ticking sound had stopped. Anova blinked through her distorted vision.

There was a hooded figure standing in the brambles.

It was one last illusion from the crown before she died. Except, this illusion stepped forward, pulled her hood back, and revealed a face she shouldn't have recognized.

She'd never seen her before.

But it was like she'd seen her in a dream years ago.

Her hair was pulled away from her face in a loose braid. She was young, perhaps just a year shy of adulthood or even a year into it. Anova felt her dark brown eyes missed nothing.

"You're the witch," Anova said. "The last one."

The witch's eyes tightened at the edges. "And you have glamor on you."

She closed the distance between them. As quick as a snake, her hand slipped into her pocket and out again. Loosened from between her fingers, she spread something over Anova in a wide spray.

She spat out the pieces that had landed on her mouth. Anova looked at the witch with incredulousness. "*Salt?*"

The young witch thumbed at her closed mouth. "You're still human." Her eyes raked over Anova's hanging form. "But what were you hiding?"

Her gaze caught at something among Anova's possessions, and she lurched backward, her hand in her knapsack like she was about to spill a load of salt on the ground.

Anova could guess what she'd seen. The blood crown.

It seemed to trigger Anova's pain of removing the blood crown. She winced as it begged to be fixed atop her head again.

Soon, she said to herself, soothing the cursed thing below her that was also inside her head.

The witch's teeth were gritted together, and her eyes flicked from the cursed crown to Anova hanging in her trap. Her hand remained in her bag.

Each word the witch spoke was like stone scraping against stone. "Why. Do. You. Have. *That*?"

Anova endeavored to make her voice as even as possible despite the fact that she was hanging upside down and covered in salt. "By rights, I am its owner."

The witch's deep brown eyes stared at Anova. Her voice was a hoarse whisper. "You killed their king. And yet—" Her gaze narrowed by the smallest degree. "Why are you here?"

"As I said, I want to destroy it. For good."

For several seconds, the witch's gaze was fixed on her. The breeze stirred the grasses again and lifted a strand of the witch's brown hair.

As she stepped close to Anova again, she braced herself for more salt. Instead, the binds at her hands loosened. The witch stretched to untie the rope at Anova's feet, and her palms smacked against the ground as she was lowered to the earth with the help of the one who had set the trap.

At once, Anova shoved the crown against her head, and she nearly sagged as the pain sapped away from her body. She took several moments to breathe and massage the skin at her wrists and ankles.

The stranger watched her in silence, waiting for her to collect her things. Clearly, there was no apology forthcoming for nearly killing her moments ago, and Anova didn't expect one. This girl's existence had been the sole reason for the High King's war on humans.

She had to be aware of the threat she posed to fae, even if she wasn't aware of what had nearly befallen the human lands. In a similar situation, Anova would have taken the same precautions.

Anova stepped towards her when she was done gathering her things. "I came here to find you." She swallowed. It was time to face something she'd buried for a long while. "And to find out if it can be destroyed. If the curse can be broken."

The witch girl looked from the glistening fae crown on her head back to her face before turning away from Anova. "Come. We'll go to my cabin." Her eyes went to the treeline of the forest at the edge of the plains.

"On nights when the moon is out, even the trees have ears."

CHAPTER FIFTEEN

Th	he witch's cabin was only a short distance away from her fatal trap,
but it was well hidden.

The air smelled wet, and Anova guessed they were near the coast. Moss soaked every surface in sight, especially a great oak that had a thick trunk. Its branches spread to the sky like fingers.

She didn't realize until the witch stopped that this was her cabin. Or rather, the witch's cabin was almost indistinguishable from the tree's wide girth.

Moss covered it as well, except for glass windows that seemed to have been tinted green from the breath of the plants around it. It was pushed against the tree so that the oak's roots looked to be part of the cabin's foundation. Birds had nested on the roof, and they picked at their feathers at the sight of Anova.

She squinted back at them, just as suspicious.

The witch stretched to reach above her door frame. A rope fell away, freely hanging from a close branch until she looped it around it once more. Anova reminded herself not to touch anything of the witch's. She hadn't seen that one, either.

After Anova walked inside, the witch turned and sprinkled salt at the threshold. She wanted to ask for some—Hellmyr's face sprang to her mind—but they had more serious matters to speak of.

And there's only so much of the night left.

But before she could say anything about the blood crown, Anova couldn't help noticing something. Her gaze drifted across the interior of her cabin. In one corner was a single, wide bed. Quilts with frayed edges were piled on top of it.

The table in her kitchen was loaded with dried leaves, bottled liquids, more salt, flowers, and books. Even more books lined the shelf near her bed, some with covers that were falling away from their pages.

While the witch removed her shoes, Anova noticed another pair of worn boots sitting near the door. The soles were nearly detached, and they had been scuffed to the point that Anova was unsure of their original color.

Anova held the witch girl's gaze. "How long have you been alone here?"

The witch froze, her lips tight against each other. "You don't—"

Letharia's words came to Anova then, and she quoted the fae lady. "Like recognizes like."

The witch looked away from her. "Ten years. Or so."

Anova steadied herself against the back of the single chair propped against the kitchen table. The calculations were simple.

She'd been just a child when she'd been left alone.

Anova didn't know anything about her other than the fact that she was the descendant of the original witch in the fae tale and the last living human with magic.

But this, she recognized.

When the witch spoke again, her voice was quiet. "What about you? How long has it been?"

Anova counted the years back in her head. *Too long,* she wanted to say, but her mouth said, "Five years."

Five years since she'd lost her mother.

Anova added after a moment, "They killed her. They came here and killed her themselves."

The witch was looking at the crown again. "So, that's why. That's why you risked death to kill the High King and destroy their crown."

In truth, it was one of many reasons, but how could she admit that she'd done it mostly to save the life of a fae who thought of her as nothing but a useful tool? The words soured on her tongue.

The witch met her gaze once more. "My name is Alys. You're right. I am the last of the witches and descendant of Gwenore, the human who helped make that."

"Anova," she said in offering. She wasn't sure where else to start.

Alys shed the last of her boots and coat as she said in response to Anova's unspoken question, "Ten years ago, they found my mother and killed her. They thought that our line was ended then. And with her death, they thought to preserve their cursed power."

Anova's heart raced faster than her words. "But they found out about you, didn't they? A glimpse. A rumor was leaked." She swallowed. "You were in the High King's war notes."

Alys's head snapped up from where she'd been going through her knapsack. "War notes. War," she repeated dully.

Anova gritted her teeth. There was much ground to cover here, but she didn't have the time. Irbess didn't have the time.

Hellmyr would unleash hell on the human city if she wasn't safely back before dawn. She had little doubt of it.

Anova stepped forward, avoiding the creeping vine that dominated the space under a green-tinted window. "What do you know about the blood crown?" Her voice was tight. "I need your help to end this."

I need to know if it can *be ended.*

The witch's hands hovered around the crown, and her gaze turned empty. At once, she stepped back several paces.

"My mother told me stories. But its evil is so plainly felt." Alys's words came out like a hiss. "As is its power."

Alys's chest rose up and down frantically, and Anova noticed that her hands were blistered around the pads. The crown had *burned* her.

Anova stepped forward. "Your hands—"

"Yet despite all its pure fae power, what made it so was the curse and blessing of *witch* magic." Her eyes were bright on it. "What was made can be unmade. Even if such a thing can only be destroyed by what brought it into existence." Alys's smile was exultant. "With this, we will destroy the line of their kings and queens."

Anova couldn't believe it. She wanted to, but she couldn't allow herself to be so easily lured by the relief. She closed her eyes.

"How? What will it require?"

When Alys didn't respond, she opened her eyes.

The witch was staring fixedly at her books, occasionally looking back to the crown. Anova frowned. She knew that look.

"Before it became the blood crown, it was just a crown, a token of the reigning fae monarch's power," Alys explained. "The problem, of course, is the witch magic within it. While the wearer is cursed to be hunted by rivals and assassins, the witch magic imbued in it also gives them power unlike what most fae can harness by moonlight. It's a power warped by the hate, grief, and blood loss that crafted the curse in the first place. It's what makes their position of power so covetable."

Her lips pursed together. Alys added, "I can't be sure yet, but what should destroy it would be another ritual by a witch, one to nullify the one that created it."

Anova exhaled. It made too much sense not to be true. Only a witch should have been capable of destroying what had been created by one. And the High King had been desperate to kill the last witch—desperate enough to start a war between their kind.

This was the answer. She felt it in her bones.

"How much time will you need to find the right ritual?" Anova's pulse raced.

Alys tilted her head to one side. "A few days at least." Her eyes went to her bed, her lips tight. "I'll make room for you ... should you decide to stay here rather than trek back every day."

Anova's stomach twisted into knots. She didn't have days to come back. She had one night in the human lands.

"I have to go back tonight. Back to Fae." Anova took a step towards her. "Come with me. I'll help you find the answer. We'll destroy it together."

Alys's brown eyes were fixed on her. She hadn't moved. "You're going back *there*? After what they've done?" Her voice was coated in slick bitterness.

"I have to." Anova clenched her teeth. How much could she reveal to this witch? "There's a fae who will raze Irbess to the ground if I don't return before dawn." And the first place where he'd look for her?

The Rosebud. Anova's stomach lurched.

Anova added, breaking the silence, "And there are people who I need to return to. Depending on me."

Alys didn't respond. She only stared at her and the crown atop her head that shouldn't have been there.

She didn't have time for this.

Her life depended on Alys's help. But others were in danger now because of her lies.

Maybe she could fail herself, but she couldn't fail them.

Anova left.

CHAPTER SIXTEEN

H er body and mind were numb as she ran. Anova tried not to think of what she'd left behind in that cabin.

She would have to do this by herself. As she always had.

Not when I was with Juras, though.

The reminder of him drove her forward. At least this crown would be good for something.

It was a long time coming, but she could finally pay off their debt to that vile woman for both her and Juras. And even if she was doomed to die, she could at least free her closest friend from their past.

She chewed on her lip as she ran. Would he still be at the home they'd once shared? Anova didn't have time to look anywhere else.

He had to be there.

Against her will, she recalled those harrowing moments in the border forests. She'd coerced Juras into helping her poison the High King, thereby poisoning herself. After she remained conscious long enough to see the fae king afflicted with it, Anova had fallen ill from the wolfsbane to the point of death.

That was the last we saw of each other.

He likely thinks he helped kill me.

As she flew through the streets, she knew she had no time. The night's shadows were already dissipating from their corners and nooks. Dawn was less than an hour away.

She smelled the bakery before she saw it. The aroma of rising bread filled her like it was solid food.

Mara's already up. I'll have to be quiet.

Her footsteps were noiseless, an impressive feat when she scaled the barely-attached metal staircase that led to their attic home above the bakery. The door was locked, but it was hardly a challenge as she jimmied the familiar mechanism.

As it opened, Anova pressed into the shadows of their shared single room, his name in her throat.

It was empty.

Or rather, it was empty of *him*. Their belongings remained, left behind like ghosts in the corners. Clothes, trinkets, blankets, and knives were all where she'd remembered them.

Would he have left this here if he relocated?

The question hung in her mind, alone like she was. It was a possibility—if he were being hunted by the constables or worse.

She noticed it then.

The note was neatly folded and placed on Juras's trunk. She read it once, twice, and a third time before crumpling it in her fist.

If you're reading this, you know he's mine now.

But I'm open to trades.

H.

Anova didn't think. There wasn't room for it within the storm that had started inside of her. There was no way for her to know how long the note had been here.

She left what had once been their home as noiselessly as she's broken inside it.

Anova crouched low. She was within sight of the Rosebud. She licked her teeth. This night hadn't come soon enough.

For a handful of seconds, Anova seriously debated killing her before conceding to the fact that it would have been far too much hassle tonight.

Without having to scout it out, she knew the fastest and quietest way to sneak inside. She'd been doing it until she was twelve or so.

Anova shimmied up the gutter, hanging halfway off the side of the building for support. Even though she knew where to step to avoid creaks, they were inevitable. Anova hoped that whoever was inside attributed it to the wind.

As she came to the part of the sloping roof where she knew the window was, she crouched, hung on to the side of the establishment, and shoved it open as quickly as possible. Anova lowered herself to the window ledge, balanced on it for less than a second, and climbed inside.

Her stomach lurched to acknowledge it, but she knew that the building had been designed so that the windows were too high to reach from the ground. Anova clung to the inside of the window ledge for a moment before carefully lowering herself to the ground of the empty room.

It wasn't empty.

Anova turned fast enough to make herself dizzy. One of the figures on the bed rose from the shadows and approached.

When the candle light hit her face, Anova held back a gasp. She was in the woman's arms a moment later.

"Anova, is that really you?" Della whispered in her ear.

"Yes," she whispered back. "Yes, it's me."

When they pulled apart, Anova's eyes went to the bed. "Is he ...?"

Della smothered her laugh with a hand. "Paid for the whole night. Fell asleep within an hour."

Anova smiled back at her. Della and Maris had been her mother's closest friends. She'd missed them.

"You've grown so much," Della was saying. She frowned as she saw Anova better. "Are you eating enough? What is—"

Anova stepped back. She'd forgotten to pull her hood up around her crown. Her stomach dropped at the expression on Della's face.

"Anova, where did you get that?" Her wide eyes focused on her face. "What's going on?"

She had a job to do here. She had to start moving or she would be late.

"Della, where is Juras?" She took Della by the shoulders. "I need to find his room."

"Anova—I—What—" Della seemed to settle on answering her question rather than getting out the dozens of questions she must've had. "He's not here. I haven't seen him since the two of you stopped paying her off."

Anova stared back at her. A sour feeling rose in her stomach. She had to leave.

Now.

Somewhere, Della continued to speak. "Anova, what's going on? Are you in trouble?"

At that, Anova's fingers dug through her bag for the coins.

"I can't stay to explain. I'm not in any trouble, but I can't stay." She found them and fished them out. "I'm buying you and Maris out. Here." She shoved the golden coins into Della's arms. Crown pieces gleamed in the candlelight.

Della's jaw looked like it had unhinged from the rest of her skull. It was more than enough to pay for Della and Maris's debts and for them both to start a new life somewhere. Courtesy of the new fae king's treasury.

Her mother's friend looked at her. "Anova—"

"I have to go. There's no time left," Anova said as she backed up towards the window.

"Won't you stay, Anova?"

Della hadn't spoken. In the doorway of Della's rooms was the person she'd dreamt of killing more than any other, including the High King.

Madam Hinterfell.

Beside her materialized her favorite hired muscle, Strego and Bron. Hinterfell's gaze went to what was on her head. "That's a pretty thing. It'll go toward what you owe me."

Several things happened at once. The man who had paid for Della's time ran out of the room with nothing more than a loose shirt on. Della shrieked as Bron tackled her. And Anova pulled free her sword for the second time that night as Strego tried to do the same to her.

Strego stopped before the sight of her steel. *Good.*

She needed to repay him for taking her dagger. She watched as he took it out of a holster at his waist.

Her eyes flickered back to his face. She held out her hand. "I'd like that back."

Instead, he sneered down at her. "It stays here now. As you will too, soon."

Anova gritted her teeth at his words and dodged his quick flurry of stabs. *It should be easy to best him with my longer range.* She swiped him once along his shoulder.

His eyes narrowed at her. She smiled, though it was joyless. "I've gotten better from last time," she said.

Strego responded with a strike aimed down. Anova deflected it and retaliated with a swing for his other side. Adrenaline soaked her veins. For too long, she'd wanted to do this against the men who had intimidated her mother and her friends. She wanted to scare the men who had hunted her and Juras for the last five years.

Her tongue ran across her lips. Hurt them, even.

A commotion on the other side of the room caught her attention for a second. As she dodged Strego's next blow, three others were tangled in a mass of limbs and screams.

"Get off her, you cretin!" Maris was trying to pull Bron off Della.

She must have come when she heard Della scream.

Over it all, Madam Hinterfell swore and twitched with anger.

Something rose in Anova's chest like a bird soaring through the air. She was winning against Strego. But what was even better was witnessing Strego realize it.

His lips pulled back in a toothy snarl, his breath coming in huffs. Despite his realization, he didn't give up.

Well, that was fine with her. She was used to opponents much faster and cleverer than this one.

She hadn't even broken a sweat yet.

Anova's strike cut him again when she heard Madam Hinterfell's voice change among the stream of curses.

Her voice was breathy. "Wait. I know what that is." She paused and leered at her. "You naughty girl."

Anova back up against the wall. Her heart dropped into her stomach. She saw it for what it was.

The blood crown, the single most powerful object of the fae people.

"What monster did you steal that from?" she said with narrowed eyes.

"Call off your men," Anova said. "Or else." She bit the inside of her cheek. This time, she wasn't the thief Hinterfell thought she was.

"No matter," Hinterfell said. "It's worth more than all the lives in this whorehouse anyway." Her fingers snapped. "Bron, kill the two girls."

Anova screamed for them.

Maris's face was bruised and bleeding. She'd fought hard against Bron, but it hadn't been enough. He'd pinned both them against the ground, and it was clear they couldn't move against his weight.

But, somehow, her hand had found Della's. Della had been sobbing from the moment Bron had tried to attack her, but her eyes were clear as they looked to Anova.

Anova stared back.

She saw a face that she hadn't seen in five years except in the nightmares where she died in front of her. Where Anova could do nothing but hold her hand as the blood left her body.

Anova dropped both objects at once. Together, her sword and the blood crown made an awful clatter against the floor. And then silence flooded the room where there had been nothing but.

The pain from separating herself from the crown was instant. A cry came to her lips, but she swallowed it. This was multitudes easier to tolerate than watching her mother's friends die.

"Strego," Hinterfell said.

It was all the command he needed. He picked up the objects, adding her sword to the growing collection of her weapons at his waist.

Anova ignored the screams in the back of her head that was the crown's delirium. She didn't have time for hallucinations when her reality was worse. Sweat dribbled along her back, and she resisted the pain that carved into her body.

"Where is Juras?" Anova croaked over the noises inside her head.

"Anova, my girl." She hated the familiarity with which Hinterfell said her name. "I've known you your entire life. It's not a hard thing to get you to come back to where you belong."

It was a lie.

She knew anger was the only rational response to Hinterfell's manipulations. But she couldn't help but feel a twinge of relief flood through her at the realization that Juras hadn't been caught in this net, too.

Even if she was the fool in the snare.

Hinterfell walked forward. Bron had pulled Della and Maris upright. At their feet were the coins she'd intended to use to buy out their debt here. Hinterfell didn't even look at them as she kicked the crown coins with the tips of her boots.

The screams became a rhythm in her brain like a hammer against the head of a nail.

Put it back on. Put it back on. Put it back on.
NOW.

"You should have stayed out of this. This didn't concern you," she said to Maris.

All too fast, Madam Hinterfell's hand dove into her cloak and retrieved a blade that curved open.

"No!" The scream ripped from Anova's throat.

Anova lost track of what happened then as all the world burst into a blinding white. A high-pitched whine lingered in her ears, and a wave of heat pushed against her skin. The smell of burning fat forced into her nostrils, and she coughed it out.

As the whiteness thinned into a smog, she blinked against it to see a wide hole in the wall made from the blast. Warm hands found hers and whispered into her ear.

"Anova, are you okay?"

It was Della. She could barely see her.

Her voice was a croak. "Is Maris with you?"

"Yes, she is. She's fine, as well. Anova, are you okay?"

She realized then the reason for Della's question. On the floor near what had been the wall was a mass of what looked to be strange coal.

Anova's stomach pushed its contents up into her throat. It was a body. Or, it once had been. It was charred beyond recognition now.

"Grab Maris," she said with Della's hand tight in hers.

Whoever that had been, there was no turning back, now.

A scream pierced the white-gray miasma that hung in the air. It sounded too human to have been an illusion from the blood crown.

When Della returned and squeezed her hand again, Anova pulled the three of them forward. The smog was thinning, and they needed to get out before it was gone altogether.

Anova stepped over the charred corpse, keeping her gaze as far away from it as possible. They were nearly out, and her lungs begged for clean air.

A whistle cried in one of her ears, and a whoosh of air rushed past her.

After the three of them contorted themselves through the cracked wood, they ran.

Hinterfell's curved blade had landed deep inside the wall next to them.

CHAPTER SEVENTEEN

I t was too late already.

The new day had broken. Streaks of light painted the ground and buildings around them.

Anova, Della, and Maris ran through Irbess, their breaths coming in fits of gusty exhales and inhales. The bakers, smithies, and dockworkers were already on the streets, staring at the three of them.

It was also too late to worry about Hellmyr.

"Where *did* you get that, Anova?"

Maris's dark eyes were on her. Well, not on her face, exactly …

Anova's hand flew to the top of her head. It was back. The blood crown was back on her head. Her mouth hung open.

She hadn't picked it up. She hadn't even touched it after Strego had picked it up from the floor.

"I … there's a lot to explain." Her mouth tasted of ash as she remembered. Her voice was dull. "That was Strego, wasn't it?"

The crown did that.

"He deserved it, my sweet." Della's hand grazed her upper arm, squeezing it for a second as they ran.

Anova nodded. She could feel them looking at her, waiting for an explanation for any of the things that had happened moments ago.

Where was she going to take them? They couldn't remain in the city. Hinterfell would make bloodsport out of finding them.

And what of Juras? If not in Hinterfell's clutches, where was he?

She knew in her heart where she had to take them, even if she hated herself for putting them in more danger.

"We'll head to the boundary forests. I have horses there. Enough for each of us." Her stomach lurched at their expressions. Perhaps they were piecing it together now. The fae crown. The forests. She was sure she smelled of danger.

She swallowed. She owed them an explanation. And a choice.

Through gasps, Anova said, "I have some ... allies waiting for me inside the forests. I'll leave it to you to decide if you wish to follow me there. I should be able to get you to safety after that. Away from Hinterfell."

They hadn't said anything yet. She added, "I'm truly sorry I brought this upon you both. I never meant for any of this. I just wanted to buy out your debts."

"We know. It's alright, Anova." Maris's face was bruised and scraped, but a quick smile flickered across her face. "If I didn't want to get involved, I wouldn't have."

Della laughed next to her. "Besides, it was worth it to see her so scared. And to be quit of her." She paused. "Away from Hinterfell ..." Della arched her eyebrow. "I don't know how you managed it, but I haven't seen you at the Rosebud to pay off your debts in a while."

Maris glanced at Anova sideways. She completed Della's thought. "Long enough to barely recognize her, as a matter of fact."

The boundary forests were before them, now. They'd made it through Irbess safely.

Anova bit at her lower lip as she debated how to say it. There was no good way to admit to it. As they made it under the cover of the leaves, she said in a rush, "Some weeks ago, I killed the High King of Fae. It's why I need to go back there."

Actually, my only hope of living was in this land. And I failed at that.

Anova ignored the voice in her head. She had no other options right now. Hinterfell would hunt them as soon as they got inside Irbess, and Hellmyr might, too.

The other two didn't say anything to that. Anova considered that there was no response fitting for it all.

Her heart felt pinched in her chest. She'd failed at something else tonight, too.

"Juras wasn't ever there. The note she left for me was false. It was all a trap," Anova muttered. "And I fell for it."

"It's also a sign that she can't find him, either." Anova's gaze darted to Maris's face as she processed her words. Maris continued, "If that's the only way the hag can hope to trick one of you, she's getting desperate."

Anova swallowed. She hoped that was the case and that Juras was well and away from her. She continued forward, even if all she wanted to do was run through the streets they used to stalk and call his name.

But she couldn't, not if she wanted him to live free from their enemies.

I've become a walking target for no less than four parties.

Hinterfell's men, the constables, the fae who had turned on her, or even Hellmyr. By now, she had to assume they all knew she was in the city and likely were hunting her tracks even then.

She stopped. They'd reached the point where she and her fae guards had tethered their horses. Except, there was only one left now.

He chomped grass under the dim light of the dawn. There was no sign of the other two horses.

They've been here already.

Anova's palms became clammy.

Maris was looking at her. "What's wrong?"

"There should be three here." She swallowed, though her mouth was dry. "We should leave this area."

It stank of a trap.

"We can't go back inside the city," Maris said. "She'll have alerted the constables by now."

Della stepped towards the horse. "I'm not going back there."

Anova got to work releasing the horse's tether. "We won't," she assured them.

Her heart thrummed out an erratic beat. She shouldn't load the horse with all three of them, but they had no other choice. She wasn't leaving one of them behind. Anova got on after Della, and Maris drove them forward in the front.

"Towards the boundary line," Anova called to her, and they started off at a lively gallop.

The forest rushed past them, and Anova leaned into Della. She had no plan for her confrontation with Hellmyr.

If he's even still there.

Morning light streaked through the branches. Anova worked on keeping her breaths even. It hadn't all been a waste if she could just get these two out of Madam Hinterfell's clutches.

Anova's head jerked up.

Maris's voice rang through the trees. "Who's there?"

So, it wasn't just me.

Shapes, things more shadow than anything else, moved among the trees near them.

Her pulse galloped in time with their steed. Anova called out, "Leave us!"

She'd traveled these forests more times than she'd cared to by now. She'd never seen something like this here.

The shadows were getting closer to either side of them. Something in the back of Anova's skull buzzed.

She whipped her gaze behind them. "Someone's gaining on us," she said through the wind.

Maris urged the horse faster, but Anova feared that it was too late. They were straining the horse too much already.

The gallops of another horse reached her ears. They were almost caught up to them.

Anova put one hand on the blood crown. Her teeth gritted together as a flicker of pain traveled down her nerve endings.

Had the crown truly done that to Strego? Or had she?

Does it matter?

She closed her eyes. A voice shouted through the trees at her.

"Anova!"

Her eyes opened, and she saw someone she knew tailing them on horseback.

I can't believe it.

Alys's braided hair hit her back in regular *thumps* as she spurred her horse towards theirs. Her knapsack was strapped tight to her, which was fortunate because the two of them were nearly flying.

Anova's voice was almost stolen by the wind. "What are you doing here?"

When she caught up to them, she shouted to Anova, "I'm coming with you." Her gaze burned into hers. "We'll do it. Together."

Anova felt like she was soaring, too. *With Alys, this might be possible.*

Alys threw another look at the three of them. "But something chases you."

"We can go no faster," Maris said between her teeth up front.

She had a horrible feeling in her stomach that this was related to the fae guards who had turned on her in Irbess. They would all be hunted down because of her.

"Can you do anything?" Anova asked the witch.

She didn't spare time for an answer. Her horse veered away from theirs some distance ahead.

A moment later, the sound of shattering glass filled the trees, and smoke snaked through the branches around them. Anova smiled despite the situation.

This witch was proving to be infinitely useful.

Anova held tight to Della, and the trees around them thinned to a sunlit break in the foliage. Anova's heart hammered in her chest.

Hellmyr stopped his pacing. His guards were several steps away, or as far away as they could be without leaving.

Their horse came to a dead stop in front of them. A moment later, Alys and her horse broke through the trees. She looked from her to the gathered fae around them and froze.

Hellmyr was beside her in a second, barely sparing the other humans around her a glance.

"Will you mind telling me *what in the hells was that*?"

Anova breathed. She had to handle this well if she was to convince him to bring along the others.

"Those two wanted the crown," she said with a flat voice. "Your kingsguard attacked me for it in Irbess."

His expression changed at once. He put himself between her and the rest of the forest, his eyes scanning the trees around them.

He'd noticed it, too, then.

"They came here with magic reserves so they could attack after moonfall." His eyes lost their focus for a moment. His voice lowered to barely a murmur. "They knew. They were planning it."

Her stomach dropped. This wasn't good by any measure. Anova resisted turning to look at the rest of his guard.

How many more of them are traitors?

He turned back to her again. "This doesn't change the fact that we can't get back to Fae now. We'll have to wait until the next moonrise."

She found she couldn't speak. *No. Hinterfell is after me now, too. We can't stay here.*

Hellmyr seemed to finally notice the other humans with her. One of his eyebrows arched.

"Pets, my love? I thought you were beyond such things yourself." His eyes brightened despite his seemingly sour mood. "Unless you mean them for me."

At once, Alys turned to him. "If this is to be how it is, you can kill me now, Fae."

Hellmyr smiled his hair-raising grin. "Humans like you are the easiest to drive mad."

He can't find out what she is ... Or what we're trying to do.

Anova shoved herself between them before they started hurting each other with more than words.

"As your bride-to-be, I have chosen these three as my attendants and witnesses to our ceremony. They will be coming with us to Fae."

He narrowed his eyes. "More humans." He said it like a curse. But, just for a second, he glanced out of his peripherals as if towards his guards. Perhaps he was thinking what she was thinking.

How many more fae will try to kill her? How many of them were in his guard right now?

Hellmyr turned from them. "Just keep them out of the way."

She could feel the three humans staring at her for what she'd just said.

Bride. Yes, I am to be the monster's bride.

Alys approached her first. With a quick look to see that the fae king was busy doling out orders, Anova mouthed to her, *"They can't know."*

Alys gave the smallest nod. They couldn't know they were sneaking in a witch to destroy the crown.

Della's eyes were on the fae, as well, but Anova sensed her thoughts were bent in a different direction. "Are we to stay here, then? Until the night?"

Maris joined them. "She recognized it, Anova. She'll know to come here."

As always, Maris was right. She wasn't just losing a day by staying here. Surrounding her were potentially traitorous fae, Hellmyr, the last living witch, and Hinterfell's stolen property. There were too many things after them in the forest and city to stay in the same place for an entire day.

She wasn't sure if a day was a short enough measure of time to start the human-fae war, but she didn't wish to find out.

And besides, something told her that a day would be more than enough time when the blood crown was involved.

Anova stifled a gasp before the others could look at her. *That* was the answer. Her stomach twisted into parts at the thought. But there was no other way.

She approached the area where she could feel it in the air. It was nearly physical. The more she walked, the more pressure gathered in her chest until it was a choice of breathing or walking forward. Her hand reached towards it.

That's where it is.

Anova closed her eyes. None of the fae were paying much attention to her or the other humans, which was exactly how she preferred it.

How did it happen last time?

Anova remembered the fear and anger of almost losing Maris and Della. She remembered the gleam shining off Hinterfell's hidden knife. Losing the crown was a bearable thing compared to that.

She couldn't fail them. Not like how she failed *her*.

I love you, little Nove.

The feeling started in her aching skull and spiked from her palm before she could stop it. A burst of harsh light exploded from her touch just as soon as the pain burst from her, too.

The thought came an instant later.

Last time, I killed Strego. What if—

It was the last thought she held onto before falling into the white abyss around her.

CHAPTER EIGHTEEN

The white haze lingered around her brain for longer than she sensed that the explosion happened. Time passed, and she drifted.

She felt her body being carried in the arms of another. He whispered in her ear, but the words were lost to her. She felt the rhythm of a horse underneath her. She felt when they left the lands that she'd been born in.

When Anova opened her eyes, she was inside a tent. Her bed was too soft, but she dared not question it in case it reverted to stone. Her head ached dully.

Alys was in the same room with her, sitting on a stool and scanning a book she must have brought with her.

The witch's head jerked up. "You're awake."

Anova's head felt too heavy to speak, but she needed to know. "How long?" she said. "How many days?"

She hated not knowing, though she hated the witch's answer more.

"Two days," said Alys.

Anova leaned back. They were well into Fae, then. But to lose that much time when her days were so few was unforgiveable. She clenched her fists. To save a day, she'd given up two.

Was it better that she'd gotten them inside Fae immediately or would it have been better to keep her days as her own?

What a fool you are.

Her eyes stung, but she didn't want to cry. Not like this.

She forced other words from her mouth because they had concerns besides that. "Della and Maris? Are they safe?"

Not only had she gambled away her time, but she'd left them alone with these creatures.

Alys nodded, and Anova's head sank to her hands in relief. "They are in the next tent." Alys paused before continuing. "You're in luck. This is the first he's let you out of his sight."

Anova looked up at the mention of Hellmyr. Had that been him carrying her? Or had that been a dream—an echo of that night she'd been poisoned by his father?

Out loud, she asked, "Where is he now?"

"Sleeping. It's the first time since we've crossed into this place." Alys shook her head. "I knew it would be at least this long before you woke, but of course I couldn't tell them that. Not that they would have believed me, anyway."

"They still don't know, then?" Anova asked.

Her heartbeat quickened. Keeping Alys's identity and skills a secret was the only way they would let her freely go. As long as the fae thought of Alys as just a human girl, they were safe to investigate ways to destroy the blood crown, the object of every fae's power-hungry dreams.

Alys looked to the corners of the tent before answering, "They don't suspect it. Not yet." Her eyes flashed back to her face. "Though I've been slipping you some tonic of my own making when they haven't been looking. Which is practically never." She muttered, "Damned fae."

Anova closed her eyes. "I did it, then? I got us through the barrier? Safely?"

The paused stretched on too long. She opened her eyes.

At the witch's expression, Anova came to her feet. The world swirled around her, but she ignored it. Either it would stabilize or it wouldn't.

"What's wrong?" Anova said. "What happened?"

Alys seemed to choose her words carefully. "You've done something like that before, haven't you?"

Anova swallowed. "Once. Perhaps an hour or so before that."

Alys looked away from her. "It's killing you. Faster."

Anova nearly fell on her face. She couldn't speak.

"Yes, I've known. Since we met." Alys was still looking at the floor when she spoke. "Doing things like that is shortening your time."

Her thoughts were like a wind storm in her mind, furious and consuming. But one thought broke through the rest.

It must have been what changed her mind that night, Anova realized.

Or a part of it.

There was only one question she could force from her lips.

"How much?" Anova said. "How much shorter?"

"Hours, seconds, days," Alys said and shook her head. "I know not." She finally met her eyes. "But using the magic inside it is not helping you, Anova."

Of course it's not. Anova slipped a hand to her temple. She'd gambled more than she'd thought.

She'd been using a cursed fae artifact for its magic. What had she expected?

She bit into her tongue, and her eyelids pinched shut. She couldn't unravel. Not now. Not for any reason. She had too far to go still.

Her eyes snapped open. *Two days into Fae from the border. Going straight from the boundary line towards Eastwoe.*

That would place this camp…

She needed to get out of this fae encampment. Now.

There was someone she had to talk to again. And the forest where she resided should have been close to where they were now.

Anova moved to where her bag and a new sword awaited her on top of a table. *At least Hellmyr likes his women armed,* she considered.

Whether that was smart of him was another matter entirely.

"Can you keep them from discovering that I've woken? Just for a while longer—perhaps another hour?" Anova asked.

Alys had been watching her. She nodded.

With some scant supplies and a sword, Anova slipped through the back of the tent and into the sunlight outside. Despite the brightness, she wasn't overly concerned of fae eyes catching her.

This was when humans rose, not their kind.

The Lost Forest should have been here.

It was as if Anova had dreamt it up. She worried her lower lip. She wouldn't have been able to dream up Rietvar. Besides, he'd appeared outside the forest, hadn't he?

But then, if only I've seen him, that's grounds for a hallucination, isn't it?

Sunlight streamed through the trees. Every so often, Anova checked to see that her shadow still followed her. It was persistent, attached to her feet like shackles.

The farther she went, the clearer it became.

The forest didn't want to find *her*.

She heard something behind her like the rustling of leaves when there should have been silence. Someone—or thing—was following her.

Anova kept walking as if she hadn't noticed it yet.

Better to get as much information and time to think as possible.

From their steps, she judged them to be several paces behind her. Close enough to track her. Far away enough that most human ears wouldn't have detected it.

However, she wasn't merely any human.

Casually enough that it might have been called a reflex to an outside observer, Anova ran her thumb down the guard of her sheathed sword. On her other side, a sheathed knife hit softly against her hipbone.

It didn't matter who it was—only that they were willing to kill her to get what sat on her head.

A second after she heard their breath again, Anova pivoted on her heels. At the same time, she released from their sheaths her sword and the knife. As she spun, she threw the knife in a deadly arc towards her assailant.

Just before it pierced his heart, he deflected it with his own blade.

It was Leander.

The breath was driven out of her.

A pain spider-webbed from within Anova that had nothing to do with the blood crown.

She lurched forward with her sword before her at a dangerous angle. Her blood pumped through her too quickly as it ran hot.

She should have been fleeing before he killed her for the blood crown. But she needed to know a few things first.

Leander raised his weapon in response, twisting to block her attack. Through gritted teeth, he said, "What are you doing?"

"Attacking you first." Anova rushed forward to land a blunt blow to his head. He dodged it by a few hairs.

His dark eyes narrowed from behind his weapon. "I don't wish to fight you, Anova. I want to talk."

They could do both.

Anova didn't relent. A distracted opponent gave up more answers than he bargained for. Always.

And she'd learned too well by now—either the fae manipulated you or you them.

"How long have you been following me?" Her question was accompanied by another lunge to his heart.

There.

It was a flicker of something in his eyes. He wanted to lie to her about this.

Her heart throbbed faster. He'd been tailing her for much longer than she'd been out here looking for the Lost Forest. It was obvious that he hadn't just happened across her out in the fae wild.

Sweat trailed her spine. He'd been following Hellmyr's camp. For days, likely.

Finally, he said, "I had to see for myself."

Anova watched him from the other side of her blade. She paced around him, looking for the moment he'd give up his guard. "See what?"

Even in the unbecoming sunlight, his eyes gleamed with a promise of darkness. "Whether you were his captive … or his conspirator."

The pain in her skull flared. What did he care what she did?

It was time. She'd had enough of these answers. Any more of this, and her anger would make her the fool here.

She'd feint to his side and then run. She couldn't outrun a fae, but her camp wasn't so far away for a sprint.

Or so she hoped.

"It seems you have your answer, don't you?" she said, aiming her sword for a swift and brutal strike. She needed him to believe that she would take the shot, and her body moved like she needed him dead.

Before she could complete the motion, a cold tip hovered near the skin at her throat. The edge of her sword grazed his arm, and it drew a small flicker of blood which ran down the steel.

She jerked into stillness before she cut herself on the point he held at her. Leander had seen through her feint. He pointed his blade straight at her jugular.

But his eyes were elsewhere.

They were cold. Dark. Calculating. He was looking at the ring on her hand.

"What is that?"

"What that is is my own business." Anova forced the words out from some cold, pitiful place. "Why should it matter to you?"

While carefully keeping the point of his blade at the same spot, Leander came closer to her. His eyes were an abyss that she didn't recognize. "It becomes my business when you just hand him the crown on a gilded platter."

She wanted to punch him.

It had never been about her. It had been about the crown.

Always.

Anova hated the low creature that was her heart. She wanted to rip it out of her.

"Leave me alone," Anova said through her teeth.

"Are you so eager to hand the most power-hungry fae that?" Leander pointed his chin towards the crown.

"I'm not handing him anything," she snarled.

He articulated each word with a sharp breath. "You're *marrying* him."

As if she didn't understand what it meant. As if she didn't understand the risks.

This was what she did.

But instead of pointing any of that out, she laughed, and it was a sudden, harsh thing. "Are you *jealous*?" She cut off the sound abruptly. Anova craned her neck to meet his stare. "It's too late to pretend to care about that anymore, fae."

Leander pulled back his blade slowly. "Don't be ridiculous." He snorted, though bitterness coated his voice when he spoke again. "I shouldn't have traded a thing to find you. I should have guessed that you weren't his prisoner—that this is all by your own volition."

Her heart felt as if it were being squeezed. She gnawed at the inside of her lip to keep moisture from gathering along her eyelids.

Not in front of him, something inside her bade. *You can unravel later.*

"I don't need your help," Anova said.

"That's been clear from the start." His eyes narrowed on her.

"Then what are you doing here?" At the same time, Anova ducked out of his reach.

He didn't say anything. He didn't try to stop her, either.

Anova took another step away from him and towards her camp. "I can do this myself."

Before she could take another step, a noise in the tree branches above them made her freeze. Standing among a cloud of moths on a thick branch, her hair in ringlets around her face, was Lycasta.

"Leave the crown." Her head tilted, and the sun hit the strands of her hair and turned them gold. "You don't intend to use it, do you? Then we'll be the ones to destroy it."

Anova felt her lips curl back to reveal her teeth. "I'll be the one to do that."

"You haven't yet." Lycasta stared down at her with a flat expression. "And yet it's been weeks, hasn't it?"

Unwillingly, Anova remembered the night she'd discovered that Lycasta and Leander were working together. It was the same night she'd seen them kiss.

She held back the emotions warring to escape her throat. They would do her no good here. But the words slipped out of her anyway.

Anova looked to Leander across from her. "This is what you want?" she asked. He stared back at her. "What you really want?"

Of course, this was what he wanted. It had been his goal to destroy the blood crown from the day the High King had slaughtered his family.

But is that what you meant? she asked herself.

Her heart tightened in her chest. He stood there, a thing of both her nightmares and daydreams. The skin that she'd once traced and kissed bathed in the filtered sunlight. The bare throat that she'd once buried herself against flickered with his heartbeat.

The silence filled the air between them, heavy and resolute. Suddenly, she didn't want an answer anymore.

Anova ran.

CHAPTER NINETEEN

"I've found a ritual. It's an old one, mind you, but ..."

Alys stopped herself and locked eyes with Anova. "It could work."

Anova leaned back against the desk. It was too good to be true. But Alys had been researching how to destroy the blood crown since they'd left the human lands.

They'd made it back to the Eastwoe palace shortly after her encounter in the forest. Anova hadn't been able to relax until she'd been assured that the humans accompanying her would be protected from harm here and given their own rooms.

Della had taken to Fae surprisingly well so far. Maris, too, despite her refusal to eat anything but the smallest amount of fae foods.

She couldn't blame her. She'd been the same way in Leander's manor. The breath in her lungs staled when she thought of him.

He's not coming back. He knows I'm not his prisoner. He can't pretend to be the knight anymore.

She wondered if that was supposed to make her feel relieved. She wondered if she was or not.

Anova cleared her head. She straightened from where she'd propped herself on Hellmyr's furniture in her suite. They were alone for the first time in days. "What do you need? How can I help you?"

Alys thumbed at her chin where she sat in a chair opposite her. "You mentioned there were archives housed here?"

"It's how I found out about you," she admitted.

A strange look crossed Alys's face for just a moment before it was gone.

Anova remembered then. She'd already told her about that—and the High King's war notes.

"Right," Alys said, and she wondered if she had remembered the same thing. The witch's lips pressed together.

"What is it?" Anova asked.

"There's ... information there I need to check," she said.

Anova frowned. She'd been caught when she'd broken in, and she considered herself a good sneak.

"They've assigned me more guards since then," Anova said. "It will be hard to pull off, even in the daytime hours."

"Is there any time when they'd be most distracted? It would be a matter of minutes, up to an hour." Alys leaned forward. "I need you to think, Anova. I'm close to piecing together what's required. But if I don't have the information, I may as well not be here."

Anova considered it. Hellmyr had barely let her out of his sight since they'd crossed back into Fae. And the guards went where he went, for better or worse. After leaving the human lands, they had hardly allowed her to walk down a hall without a cast of guards.

But that's the point, isn't it?

The answer came to her at once.

"I can distract him. I'll lead him out of the palace for the night. It's the only way to ensure enough of his guard will go with us."

The light from a lantern on the table next to her caught in the witch's eye. "You know, for someone who isn't a witch, you think like one."

Anova smiled back. It faded a moment later. "Just ... be careful. Not that I need to tell you, but this isn't safe here. For human or others."

"What is it?" The witch's eyes narrowed on her. "What's happened?"

Nothing escapes her, Anova thought.

Out loud, she said, "Someone is trying to kill me for the blood crown. Perhaps several fae."

"What?" Alys straightened. "Tell me everything."

Anova started with her encounters with assassins in the fae wilds. She wasn't sure which incidents were related and which were simply a result of the target she wore, so she told her all of it. Alys didn't move throughout it as she explained how someone had moved up their wedding date through to when she told her about his guards attacking her in Irbess.

"What do you think?" Anova said when she finished.

Alys got to her feet and started pacing. She stopped in front of her after a few minutes. "There are no coincidences in this world. Or rather, we must assume the events are related. Whoever has masterminded it likely intends to act at your wedding."

Her stomach dropped. It was all so close. They were days away from it, now. Anova started to breathe too shallowly.

She had to stop. She had to focus on something else. "How?" she gasped. "We can't know for certain."

Alys looked at her. "Why else move up the date?" She looked away and added, "Besides, you will be considered their queen after that. You'll hold more power, and also be less able to be poisoned, likely."

Anova suppressed the shudder that wanted to rise out of her at the thought. They needed to end this as soon as possible.

Or someone else would take it from her.

The double doors burst apart as Anova stalked through them. For once, she'd outran her guards.

But after they'd let slip he was here, there had been no stopping her.

"Then find them. None of my guard rests until they're caught." Hellmyr's eyes blazed where he leaned across a long table. On it were scattered documents, maps, and letters with torn seals.

All the gazes in the room jumped to her. Hellmyr straightened where he was at the far end of the table and locked eyes with her.

She raised her chin to meet his gaze. This wouldn't work if she wasn't confident enough. "I need to speak with you," Anova said.

She could feel her guards on either side of her, filling up the doorframe. She could sense their desire to take her out of the room by force, but she refused to look at them.

Without taking his eyes from her, he said, "Everyone else. Out."

Her guards departed after his fae advisors and his kingsguard. Their gazes were the last to leave.

Anova came to the table, her arms crossed at her chest. His eyes hadn't left her. For her own sake, this had to work.

She swallowed. "I wish to ride somewhere with you. Somewhere away from here. Today."

He turned from her so she couldn't judge his expression anymore. When he spoke, she could gather no clue from his tone of voice.

"Why?"

"Do I need a motive?" she asked.

Suddenly, too suddenly for her comfort, he was behind her.

"You always have a motive." His fingers moved a strand of hair behind her ear. "My human bride."

She couldn't help the shiver that she gave at his touch. Even so, she kept her eyes forward and her arms crossed. "Is that a *no*?"

His fingers left her skin, and he moved to one of the wide windows in the room. As he leaned over it, he said, "Meet me at the gate in half an hour. I'll send servants to saddle your horse." He glanced back at her, too quickly for her to catch what he was thinking. "Wear something a queen would wear."

Anova's brow furrowed. During that half hour, she hadn't stopped picking apart what he could have meant by his parting comment.

She hadn't thought the clothes she'd been wearing had been all that bad, but she'd given up and changed into something else anyway. She wore a silver dress that clung to her skin and glimmered with tiny gems sewn into the skirts like a shower of stars.

She'd never seen a queen with her own eyes, but she imagined that one might wear something like this. It was one of the dozens of dresses that filled her suite. She probably wouldn't be able to touch all of them before she was done here.

But when she saw him, she felt sorely overdressed.

He wore simple riding pants and a white shirt that was unbuttoned to the middle of his chest. She resisted rolling her eyes. *Vain creatures.*

He looked like a scout, not a king.

When the fae guards led her to the front of the palace near the gate, her lips parted. His entire court was before them.

He'd waited for her on his steed. Next to him, hers waited, adorned with shimmering gold reigns.

What's going on?

Red crawled up her throat. She itched to pull out her sword. When he caught her eye, he mouthed to her, *Follow my lead.*

He moved before them. "The full moon is days away." Her stomach lurched at the reminder.

Too soon.

He continued, "But you will not gain a queen that night." Hellmyr paused, and the murmurs stopped almost as fast as they'd started. She stared at him. "She is your queen now. Every creature, low and high, shall bow to her."

Like a wave upon a vast sea, they did as he said. She wanted to fidget. She wanted to look away.

But a horde of people bowing to you isn't something to look away from. Hellmyr dismounted from his horse and lowered his head towards the ground.

Something caught in her throat. This was insanity.

Likely, never before had fae bowed to a human. She felt as if she were about to slide to the ground with them.

Anova realized with a jolt that no one was moving because she hadn't yet told them they could.

When she spoke, her voice was hoarse at first. "I release you. All of you."

They rose, their eyes still on her. Suddenly, Hellmyr was beside her.

"Are you ready, my bride?"

"I thought this was my idea," Anova said. She still felt a little dizzy from what had happened. *This was why he said that.*

"I took the liberty of choosing a destination for us." Hellmyr put his mouth against her ear and spoke softly. "If I've overstepped your authority, my queen, there can be punishments later."

Her neck grew hot. His court was still staring at them, most likely awaiting a more formal command about what to do next. He ignored them completely.

"No, it's fine," she said in a voice that barely came out. *Damned fae.*

They were all masters of this, apparently.

When they rode out, a company of guards flanked them on either side. Undoubtedly, it was an excessive show, but the more that she could get away from the palace, the better.

Her horse was a well-cared for steed who seemed as at ease among the forests of Eastwoe as he had before Hellmyr's court. Anova followed closely behind Hellmyr, though there was little chance of losing him. Strapped to his horse were several lanterns filled with glowing beetles.

She furrowed her brow at the sight. Where were they going? Not knowing didn't sit well with her.

You're doing this for Alys. To allow her time to investigate the archives for the answers you need.

As the forests blurred past them, Anova thought she saw the will-o-wisps flicker in and out of existence that supposedly haunted this part of Fae. She pulled herself closer to her horse.

The moonlight was too strong here to be careless.

Soon, Hellmyr signaled for them to slow, but she couldn't see what was so special about this part of the woods.

That was, until she moved past the last of the moss-soaked trees and saw the enclosure ahead of them. The breath in her lungs stilled.

Before her was perhaps the clearest water she'd ever seen. In its center was the nearly full moon, an orb of white in the center of the crystalline lake. Honeysuckle laced the air, making it heavy as she breathed it in.

"It's beautiful," she said. There was no other word for it.

Hellmyr turned to the entourage of guards surrounding them. "Line the perimeter." He looked at their steeds for a moment before adding, "And take these two for now."

They scattered to obey his orders, and Anova saw no more of them as they took to their stations beyond the trees around them.

Anova walked to the edge of the water and bent to examine it. "This isn't something ... magical, is it?" She frowned down at her reflection.

Hellmyr laughed among the branches.

Anova's gaze shot up. "What are you doing?" she said as she lurched to her feet. "This is a trap," she hissed.

She looked around her, but there was nothing coming for her. Hellmyr examined her from his position in a nearby tree. How he'd gotten up there so fast eluded her.

"No to the first one. And ... maybe to the second," he replied, looking at the cuff of his shirt as if there was a smudge of dirt there.

"You fae bastard," she said between her teeth. She went for her sword, but there was something already approaching from the other side of the lake.

Something not fae or human or goblin, even.

CHAPTER TWENTY

When she saw what it was, she still didn't understand.

Her sword hung at her side in a loose grip. She hadn't thought they were real. No one had told her that they were.

Anova couldn't help but put away her sword. It felt sacrilegious to have it out in front of a unicorn.

She watched Anova carefully on the other side of the lake. Her hide was cream-white, all the way to the horn at her head. Her eyes were a soft shade of lavender.

"Hellmyr," she said in a whisper. "I need to understand. This is a ..."

"Unicorn," he finished for her from his perch. "Very rare things. Easily spooked."

She had bent her head to sip at the edge of the lake, though her eyes didn't leave Anova.

"Almost as moon-mad as we are," he added. He shifted where he sat on the branch. "I only found this one after discovering the lake here."

Anova couldn't move. Something was happening. The unicorn was walking towards her.

"I still don't understand why you're up there," Anova said. It was making her nervous that he didn't dare come down.

Hellmyr was silent as she approached Anova. Up close, she was even more breathtaking than she'd thought. Her mane was like threads of silver and white.

She held her hand out, expecting the creature to turn and run for the forest around them. Instead, she nuzzled Anova's hand.

"They like maidens more than us," he said. As he watched her, a gleam sparked in his eye. "And ones pure-hearted most of all."

Her head snapped over to where he lurked in his tree. "What are you talking about?" Heat rose in her cheeks.

Pure-hearted. There couldn't be a thing I'm further from.

Hellmyr jumped from his perch in the tree. At the same time, the unicorn's lavender eyes narrowed on his form.

He smiled at the creature, revealing the sharp points of his teeth. It only took a few seconds for the unicorn to gallop to the treeline in response.

He shrugged at Anova. "I'm not sorry."

"Have you ever been?"

He appeared to give it some thought and said, "Not yet."

Anova walked to the edge of the lake and looked down into the sky's reflection. Neither of them broke the silence.

Finally, she asked, "Why did you betray him? You were friends, weren't you?"

When he didn't respond, Anova looked back at him. He had shed his shirt and jacket and walked towards her.

The moonlight found the violet in his grackle eyes. It was a stark contrast to the unicorn's soft lavender eyes. "Has it occurred to you that I'm simply not a good person?"

He stopped before her and tilted her head towards his, his thumb resting under her mouth. Her lips parted, and the words she'd been about to say struggled to remain in her head.

Unbidden, she remembered what it felt like to kiss him. How it felt like falling. She blinked and focused on what she was trying to find out.

"I want to hear the reason," she said.

Hellmyr's face was thoughtful. His hand left her face as he considered something. "I'll tell you the reason. But only if you win against me."

Anova's eyes narrowed. "Win?"

Hellmyr shrugged. "Only a modest wager. It's quite simple, really. You win if you do nothing."

She crossed her arms. "You're not telling me what's important, Fae."

More fae tricks.

Hellmyr started to pace behind her. She itched to twist herself and keep him in her sight at all times. "I win if you move at all. If I can ... persuade you to move. If you don't," he said, "I'll tell you the reason I betrayed him."

Anova bit at the inside of her lip but didn't allow her face to show any expression. It was too easy.

"For how long?"

"Let's say ten minutes," he replied from behind her. "Or until the clouds obscure the moon again."

Her hand hovered over the hilt of her sword. Her muscles tightened for the moment she would pull it out of its sheath upon his attack. She didn't think he was armed—there was nowhere to hide anything since he'd shed his shirt and jacket—but the fae had other weapons than ones made out of metal.

"Starting now," he said.

She braced herself, but all she felt was a hand lifting her hair to one side. His lips pressed against her neck a moment later, soft and searching.

Anova gasped but didn't budge. She should have known the fae wouldn't play fair. A slow breath left her.

His arrogance will be his undoing.

His mouth moved to her back where the silver dress plunged low. Heat raced across her skin, smudging red along her neck and cheeks. He laughed to see it, though it sounded low and forced from his chest.

She gritted her teeth, but she comforted herself with the thought that she didn't need to last long without punching him.

Just a handful of minutes more.

His mouth traveled up again, and this time, his hands pulled her head to the side where his thumb brushed against her bottom lip.

"Why are you here, Anova?" His voice was low as he said her name. "What do you want?"

His question didn't sit well with her. She didn't know why until she realized it was the same one that Leander had asked her.

She barely moved as she spoke. "This isn't about me."

Hellmyr's thumb found the edge of her mouth. His lashes brushed against his cheeks as he looked down at her. "What if I want it to be? What if I think I can make you tell me what I want to know?"

His other hand went to her throat, and her pulse tapped against his touch. He added, "What if I can make you tell me the truth?"

He's going to tell when I'm lying by using my heartbeat.

Anova's mouth popped open. "You *cheat*."

"This is why your unicorn friend doesn't like me," he whispered in her ear. "I don't play fair." He adjusted his thumb where it pressed against her pulse. "Now, are you here to unseat me? To bathe in my blood?"

"No." Her eyes swept away. "Though the night is early yet."

Perhaps this will be easier than I thought.

"Hm. Perhaps you're a pathological liar," he mused. His mouth found her ear again, and his other hand traced her hips. "Do you like this?"

Heat spread through her at the proximity of his touch. She remembered at the last second not to move. There were too many pieces to the game they were playing.

"No," she ground out.

She could feel how her heartbeat had sped up, so there was little chance he hadn't felt and heard it.

"Liar," he whispered into her ear. He sounded like he was smiling.

"You're wasting your minutes," she reminded him.

"This is not a waste of either of our time," he said, though he pulled his hand away from her lower half. "Though it's a shame. I do love a murderess."

"Sorry to disappoint." She hoped she didn't sound sorry at all.

One of Hellmyr's eyebrows arched. "Are you trying to steal something from me? Or from the palace?"

"No," she said. *Not this time,* she considered. Out loud, she added, "This won't work how you hope it will."

"We'll see about that, Darling," he murmured against her skin. He was kissing her neck again.

Hellmyr waited for her heartbeat to calm down again before he asked another question.

With his other hand, he examined a lock of her hair. "Are you ... afraid to tell me why?"

Dammit.

Her teeth were locked together. It didn't matter if she tried to deny it. He'd felt it clearly enough.

Something in his voice changed. She ached to crane her neck to look at his expression, but she resisted the urge. "Are you afraid?"

"You need to specify—" She bit into her own tongue.

Calm. Calm down. It's not like you're going to die tonight. Or tomorrow.

But her heart rate had raced ahead of her to betray her.

"That's not fair," she said. "This isn't going to tell you anything."

She bit into her tongue again. Anova knew how much she was contradicting herself, but she needed to speak of something else *now.*

"It's about the crown," he guessed.

She felt dizzy. There was no time to stop and think about it. It was easy to do—too easy. Anova twisted herself in his grasp and kissed him.

Once more, she felt like she was falling into darkness. The heat that had been building in her belly spread through her like fire.

It was only a moment later that he kissed her back. His hands curled around her, one around her neck and the other at her waist.

"Anova," he said between kisses.

Hearing him say her name did strange, embarrassing things to her heart. She knew he was trying to say something more, perhaps something about the cursed thing on her head, but she didn't want that.

"No," she said. "I've won."

She knew it was childish, but she needed this not to be a surrender.

He laughed against her mouth, and it was a rough sound. "The only way to play this game, Darling, is make sure you are the victor in every outcome."

His eyes gleamed with wickedness as he moved his mouth from hers to the front of her neck where her pulse raged. He moved down until he was kissing her bare chest where her dress exposed much of her skin.

Between kissing her skin, he said, "Tell me *why*."

"No," she said.

He paused. "No ... to what?"

"There's no why," she said. Her breaths came in uneven gasps. "There's nothing to tell. So, no."

His ear pressed against her heart. "But there is," he said before his mouth was somewhere else.

Anova swallowed the gasp that her lungs had tried to force out. "This isn't going to tell you anything, you know," she said.

"We'll see about that," he said.

Heat spread across her skin like a fever, and desire weighed deep in her belly when some of his bare chest brushed against her. She swallowed.

One of his hands locked against her hip as he continued to kiss her skin, and the pad of his thumb brushed against her dress in circles.

"Tell me why you came to me. Tell me what you're after," he murmured.

There was little use lying anymore. But that didn't mean she had to tell him. Unless he wanted to torture her for it.

"Isn't it good enough that I'm not trying to kill you?" she said.

Her heart raged. It should have been enough, but she knew it wasn't. Not with a fae like Hellmyr.

A sound broke the stillness around them. A fae's voice carried across to them. "Your Highness."

Anova clenched her teeth. It was one of Hellmyr's kingsguard. Her skin flushed with redness at being found like this.

But Hellmyr didn't stop kissing her chest between her plunging dress. "I'm sure you can see I'm busy, Unferth."

She looked to Unferth. He looked to be about as happy to be here as Hellmyr sounded.

"We found something nearby, Your Highness. Evidence of the enemy. We must leave immediately."

Hellmyr stopped what he'd been doing. At once, he twisted and planted himself between Anova and the trees surrounding them.

In his palm gathered a pool of moonlight, and the air shimmered. Anova unsheathed her sword.

She looked from Unferth to Hellmyr. "Enemy?"

"Those trying to kill you," he explained.

Sweat ran into her eyes. "Where?"

Unferth's jaw was tight. "We don't know."

"Get her horse," Hellmyr said. "He's faster than mine."

What happened next was a blur. His guards brought her horse forth, and they mounted him. Their fae guards clustered around them in a tight formation as they flew through the woods, Unferth and a few other fae leading the charge.

One of Hellmyr's arms was around her waist, holding her close against him. Magic glimmered on the air around them like a visible distortion.

The fae in front came to a circle around something on the ground. As their horse approached, her stomach dropped.

On the trail before them were two mangled bodies. From what she could tell, they were fae. Relief raced through her that it wasn't someone she knew and cared for.

But then, something about one of their faces sparked recognition within her. She stiffened.

"The guards," she whispered.

Hellmyr swore behind her.

She could see the face of only one of them, but it was clear who they were. On the ground were the two fae guards who had attacked Anova in Irbess for the blood crown.

Someone had slit their throats and dumped their bodies on their path home.

CHAPTER TWENTY-ONE

"They're moving against you," Alys said as she and Sera helped Anova out of her dress.

Anova had to admit, there was little room in which to interpret the act otherwise.

Someone is pulling the strings above these assassins, Anova considered. *Someone who can sacrifice their pawns with ease.*

Someone with several pawns, she added silently.

Anova hadn't been sure where to start when she'd told Alys what had happened that night. None of it had felt real.

Although, she had omitted much of her conversation with Hellmyr.

If that's what that was.

She pushed those thoughts aside. She had more pressing matters to deal with than an arrogant fae princeling who always got his way.

Like how she was two days away from wedding him. Anova's knees nearly buckled at the thought.

"Did you find what you needed ... in your books?" Anova finished the thought with a quick glance at Sera. She was busy combing out the rat's nest that had taken hold of her hair on the journey back to the palace.

Anova hoped that she'd at least bought the witch enough time to get the answers she'd needed in the archives.

Alys was watching her carefully. "About that—"

A series of knocks interrupted her. Anova grabbed her sheathed sword from a nearby table, and Alys's hands went to her pockets. She could only guess what weapons she'd hidden in them. Even Sera had tensed at the sound.

With a nod to Anova, Sera opened the door to reveal the fae guard, Unferth. He closed the door after him, and after seeming to assure himself that there were no hidden assassins in the rafters, he spoke.

"His Majesty would like to inform you he will be leaving shortly, my lady."

Anova came to her feet. "Leaving where?"

Unferth's lips pressed tight together. He looked pointedly at the humans beside her. Anova gnashed her teeth together.

"Oh, come on. Do you really think them assassins?" she said. She took a step towards the guard. "I trust them more than anyone else here."

He narrowed his eyes on her when he spoke. "A training grounds in Westvalde for his guards. He's launching a hunt on the fae behind your attack."

Anova exhaled. It was almost unnerving to see a fae so concerned about someone besides himself.

Then again, an attack on his bride must be an affront to his massive pride. She resisted rolling her eyes.

Anova realized how far away that was. "How long will he be gone?"

"Until the night of the full moon."

Our wedding.

Anova sank into the nearest chair. She realized that Unferth must have been commanded to do as she'd said because he was still standing in the corner of her suite. "You may leave," she mumbled, and he did.

I'm out of time. I'm out of time already.

Afterwards, Sera excused herself to her room. Anova was still staring into nothingness when Alys grabbed her hands. She hadn't realized they'd been shaking.

The witch pulled a small vial of clear liquid out of a pocket on the inside of her shirt. She passed it to Anova who shoved the glass against her thigh to keep it from shaking with the rest of her.

"Drink it. You'll feel better."

Anova did as she was told. She expected the tonic to burn her throat as most medicine did, but it didn't. In fact, it reminded her of the earthiness of the human lands.

"It's good." She blinked and focused on her breathing.

"I found the rest of the ritual."

She nearly broke the thin glass in her hands to shards. Hope was greedy and unforgiving. She couldn't let it take too much of her.

"Is it something we can prepare in two days?" she said in a tight voice.

"I think so." Alys stared at the door that Unferth had taken back to the halls of the palace. After a moment of silence, she added, "But we're probably going to need *him*."

In her bones, she knew there could have been no other fae that she was referring to besides the arrogant fae princeling.

"Likely?" Anova repeated. "Is there another way? Any other one?"

Alys looked away from her.

"What is it?" Even without her consent, hope had started to root inside her. Anova swallowed it down.

Alys shook her head. "It's not that. It's ..." She looked at her straight. "I have almost everything the ritual to undo the crown will require. But you'll need to contribute something specifically." She paused before adding, "The blood of a fae you love. And the blood of a fae who loves you."

Anova didn't speak. She couldn't seem to form the words.

Love? It was a ludicrous word to begin with. That her fate should be tied to such a thing was unthinkable.

After a moment, she managed to say it. "Why?"

"The crown was made from the merging of fae and human magic, and from a magic entirely something else—hate. It will need something like its opposite to break it."

"Your weapons."

Anova couldn't believe it. Her teeth clenched together.

She stood outside the fae king's chambers facing one of his guards. Her eyes were a pure blue that dazzled her if she looked into them too long. She avoided doing so—her anger might dissolve if she fell under the fae's spell of beauty.

"My weapons are here to protect me," she said. "Hellmyr would agree."

Her eyes narrowed on Anova. "They're his orders, my lady. Anyone entering his chambers during day hours must forfeit weaponry."

"I'm not the danger here," she said through her teeth. But she did as the guard said and clicked her sheathed sword from her belt.

The guard was still staring at her. She didn't have to say anything more.

Anova swore under her breath and removed her hidden dagger from where she'd shoved it inside her dress's bodice.

"That's it," she said. "Or did he order you to check?"

Her heart hammered inside her ribs. She'd held onto the hope that she could bleed him before he left for Westvalde. She swallowed drily. There was only one path left to her, now.

As the fae guard moved aside for her, Anova's head still buzzed with what Alys had said.

"The blood of a fae you love. And the blood of a fae who loves you."

Did she love him? Did he love her? Her stomach felt sick.

She was going to die because she hated him. And not just him. Quite possibly, all of them.

Inside his suite, dawn light filtered through the glass of his balcony doors. When she saw him, her eyes flew to the ceiling at once.

Anova itched to bleed him now. Without looking at him directly, she searched the room for a needle, a knife—anything with a sharp edge. Or even things without a sharp edge.

Just a drop of his blood, and she could be quit of all this.

"Could you put something on?" Her cheeks heated.

He had nothing on but a towel that clung precariously to his hips.

"You're the one who so valiantly barged in." Hellmyr paused, and she could hear the wicked smile in his voice. "Besides, my human bride, one would think you'd want to know what you're getting out of this entire affair. I could see why you'd be curious."

She bit into the edge of her tongue to suppress the memories of what had happened over the night. "Modest, aren't you?"

"Kings are neither modest nor meek. Nor are queens," he added after a moment.

"I'm coming with you," she said.

Finally, she dared to look at him again. His back was to her. He'd put on some pants at last. The muscles in his back bunched up as he pulled out a cuffed shirt from his wardrobe.

His voice was low. "You will stay here."

"I'm not. Or was that an order, Your Majesty?"

Her heart was too loud, and she knew it. She needed this to work. Too much hung in the balance than was fair. Her life and death. The destruction of the blood crown. The rule of Fae and the human lands.

Hellmyr had stopped buttoning his shirt. His back was still to her. Silence was his only answer.

She was failing. How had she thought she could do this?

Maybe, once I die, the blood crown will at least die with me.

But she didn't know that, either.

At one point, she had thought sacrificing her own life would end it. She'd been wrong, then.

Was she wrong now?

Anova opened her mouth and closed it again. Her heartrate pulverized her insides.

"I'm …" Anova stopped herself. It was just a lie, wasn't it? When had she been bothered by her lies? "I'm afraid of what will happen."

It wasn't a lie, she realized with a jolt. She was afraid of what the blood crown was doing to her. She was afraid of the fae trying to kill her.

She was afraid of what was going to happen in two days.

Hellmyr stared at her. She wondered then what he'd heard from her chest.

At once, he was before her.

"Don't leave my side when we get there. Or even before," he added. His expression was tight, and when he spoke, she saw the sharp edges of his teeth. "The camp where we're going will be dangerous."

"About that," she said. "Unferth mentioned a training grounds. What kind of danger are you talking about?"

"It's not that it's ordinarily this dangerous there, though certainly for a human who wears the blood crown, it would be," he said with an arched eyebrow. "It's essentially a camp for what had been the High King's army. It's where our guards train."

He turned from her again to look out the glass doors to his balcony. "This has gone too far. I'll be calling a hunt using the only evidence we have."

The tone of her voice crept up. "Evidence?"

"Any lingering scent left on the guards' bodies … and in your room."

Anova stepped back. "What?"

"When we returned from the human lands, my guards informed me that someone had broken inside the palace." He turned to look at her. "Specifically, your rooms."

Someone was in there. Someone looking for me.

To kill me.

Anova couldn't process all the implications of what Hellmyr had said, so her brain chose one for her.

"Sera," she gasped.

Hellmyr shook his head. "She was untouched. I don't think the girl even knows something happened. Whoever it was wanted the blood crown only. They were very careful."

Anova felt dizzy. She swallowed it down. This was no time for fainting spells or even the throbbing sensation at her temples reminding her of the deadly thing on her head.

Something else occurred to her. Hellmyr's words repeated inside her head.

"Whoever it was wanted the blood crown only."

Lycasta's voice joined his.

"Leave the crown. You don't intend to use it, do you? Then let us find a way to destroy it."

He was following me from the moment we reentered Fae, she recalled.

She faced the very real possibility that it had been Leander who had broken inside her rooms.

And that Hellmyr was about to set his entire army on him.

CHAPTER TWENTY-TWO

Anova rose as she saw the sun's rays peek underneath the sides of the tent. This evening, they were to arrive at the camp and start the hunt.

This was the first time Hellmyr had slept during their trip to Westvalde. She was nearly out of time. Before she could pass into Hellmyr's part of their tent to check that he'd truly started sleeping, she heard raised voices.

Her heart lodged in her throat. Any noise too loud could wake him.

And there might not be another chance after today.

Anova shoved through to the entrance of the tent where two guards were blocking someone's entry inside.

"Don't *touch* me, fae," Alys's voice hissed.

The fae she was talking to sneered back at her. "All who enter his Majesty's quarters will be searched for weapons and accompanied at all times. That includes you."

Anova pushed herself between them. A fight wasn't what they needed now. "She's with me," she said to the guards. "I will be responsible for her."

The fae's jaw ticked with repressed words, but he stepped aside for Alys. Anova didn't breathe again until they were both inside the tents that she shared with the fae king.

Anova barely made a sound when she spoke. The fae had better hearing than humans did, and they couldn't forget that.

"Did you bring it?" she whispered to the witch.

Instead of verbally responding, Alys pulled two glass vials out of her pockets. One was empty, and the other was filled with a cream-like liquid.

Anova led them through Hellmyr's tents until they entered the room where he slept. Upon seeing him, she froze.

He seemed too still to be asleep. His lips that normally smirked were parted slightly, and a slow breath filled and left him. Anova moved again.

As she crouched near his sleeping form, Alys joined her. First, she handed her the vial with the liquid in it. When she unstoppered the numbing agent for where they would prick his skin, Anova hesitated.

Does he love me?

Do I love him?

This had to work. There would be no second chance for her.

Her heart hammered in her chest too loudly as she considered the matter before her. In little over a day, she would be wed to this beautiful monster.

Unbidden, she remembered his lips against her skin, and the words he'd spoken there.

"Why is it that you came back to me?"

Anova swallowed and, with as light a touch as possible, spread the salve across the pad of his thumb. Hellmyr didn't seem to notice as breath filled his chest in a slow rise.

He was spread out, one arm over the edge of his bed and the other stretched out in the other direction. In this state, he looked almost vulnerable.

Anova didn't linger on the thought. Fae were hardly vulnerable, especially one who had seized power as the new fae king and who wanted to bolster his position of power by marrying the wearer of the blood crown.

It would have been smart of her, then, to accept his proposal—had she truly wanted the power and authority that he offered her.

And yet, he saw through me too easily.

What else has he seen?

Anova frowned, but she pricked his skin with the needle nevertheless. Ruby drops of blood beaded at the site, and she pressed the neck of the glass against his skin to collect them. She quickly corked it and handed it to the witch.

Alys didn't hesitate as she shoved it into her pockets among other objects certainly as arcane as the blood of a fae king.

As Anova moved to the front of the tent to allow her out, Alys didn't move. She stared at her.

"What's wrong?"

"We need to talk," Alys whispered. "There's something else. Something urgent I need your assistance with."

Anova pursed her lips but led her into her room, farther inside their tents. After they were out of earshot of even a sleeping Hellmyr, she finally spoke.

"What's going on?" Anova asked. She looked for an immediate threat but saw none.

Alys looked at the edges of the tent like she expected fae to be listening in on their every word. Her gaze went to Anova's at last. "There's something else here other than guards in training. Something the fae are hiding."

Anova's heart plummeted. "What is it?"

"A weapon." She turned to look at Anova again. "A weapon they plan to use against us. Humans."

"What—he's not—" She stopped herself. What did she know about the fae king, exactly? That he coveted power like a rare gem?

Maybe he doesn't know about it.

Maybe he doesn't plan to use it.

She swallowed. *And maybe swine will fly.*

"What are you saying?" Anova said in a voice that was too loud to be a whisper. "How do you know this?"

"I ... saw it in the archives, Anova." Alys stepped forward. "They won't stop. Not until they're masters of all humans."

Not Hellmyr. He can't know about it. He can't condone this.

And then the question she couldn't ask came out of her mouth. "Does he know?"

At her words, Alys looked away. "I don't know." She was still looking away from her when she said, "But there's something I'll need you to do when he calls the hunt."

Her brown eyes were depthless when she looked over at Anova. "I need you to keep him distracted. No matter what."

"You're going to destroy it? This weapon?" Anova asked.

Alys nodded, once.

Her stomach bubbled with nausea. She couldn't believe the fae were keeping such a thing here.

She couldn't afford *not* to believe it.

Anova remembered Hellmyr's words from many nights ago.

"Unless, of course, you wish to invade and start your reign over those lands, as well."

"What does it look like?" Anova lunged forward to catch Alys's gaze. "What does it do?" She needed as much information as possible about this new threat.

"I don't know what it looks like besides that it's another fae artifact," Alys said simply. "They must have made it in secret in an attempt to match the power of the blood crown."

Her stomach dropped. Another all-powerful fae artifact.

"Is it?" she ground out. "Is it as bad?"

Alys pressed her lips together. "It will target humans specifically. In that sense, perhaps it is more dangerous than the artifact you wear."

Anova felt ill. She sat into a plush chair that some poor servant must have dragged there. "We have to destroy it," she said in barely a breath.

Does he know?

It doesn't matter if he knows or not, another part of her argued. *It exists.*

Another thought occurred to her. She jerked to her feet. "It will be dangerous for you to leave the protection of his guards. Every one of his trained fae soldiers will be hunting for someone who smells even slightly of me. Alys—"

"No." She stepped away from her. "I will do this myself." Her facial expression calmed after a second. She gave Anova a small, sheepish smile. "Have you no faith in me? Fooling them is my best talent."

Anova returned her smile even if she felt like doing the opposite—that was, running from the fae king's tent until she found somewhere entirely absent of guards, magic artifacts, moonlight, and anything with pointed ears.

Anova breathed. "Forgive me," she said with a smirk. "I promised myself many nights ago never to underestimate you again."

Alys's eyes gleamed. She saw the witch whose trap she'd unwittingly walked into that night. "And you'd be wise to live by it."

Dusk had draped the land of the Westvalde in hues of blue and purple. All atop horses, Anova, Hellmyr, Letharia, and a small army of guards around them stood at the hill overlooking the camp below.

From this eagle's eye view, she was starting to understand Alys's conviction of there being something hidden here.

She'd expected more tents strung together by poles and canvas clothes like the ones they'd traveled here with. A smithy, perhaps. A grounds for training with blades.

What faced them below was an expanse of buildings. Several training fields. More than one smithy, from the looks of it.

This wasn't a training camp. It was more like a compound.

It was the kind of sight that she was sure the former High King would have feared, if it hadn't been used to train his personal guard.

What remained of the fae king's armies had gathered below. Anova tried to estimate how many hundreds there were and soon gave up.

It was more than any forces the humans had. Her thoughts went to Alys, and her eyes flickered to the edges of the compound, but she saw no sign of her yet.

Good. Just let her not be hurt in the hunt.

It wouldn't be long, now. The moonrise was about to come.

Atop his steed, Hellmyr came forward. His grackle eyes were like dark pits, and shadows fell across his face in the dusk gloom. A cloak of bird feathers fell across his shoulders. He looked every part like a moon-mad fae king. Anova suppressed a shiver.

Hellmyr nodded to one of his generals near the base of the hill. The fae stepped forward and started to distribute something among their audience. She realized a moment later what it was.

It was clothing that the dead fae guards had been wearing. And pieces of her clothing that she'd left in her room after they'd departed for the human lands.

"Soldiers. Generals. Fae in training. And all those who serve me." His voice rang out over the space. It was tightly controlled, yet she could hear the fury he held back. "You will find the commonality between these scents. The party responsible for these attacks will be put to death immediately. Tonight, your moon madness will be sated with one of our most revered traditions."

The edges of Hellmyr's mouth rose and his teeth were exposed, but it was anything but a smile.

"Tonight, I call a blood hunt."

Anova's hairs stood on end, and she looked to the east. Just beyond the tops of the trees, a band of white light had pierced the dusk gloom. The moon had risen.

The hunt was on.

CHAPTER TWENTY-THREE

Just as Hellmyr snapped his fingers and the air around them shimmered silver-gray, the fae in the valley below them began their frenzy.

Some pulled weapons out of their sheaths or straps, but many relied on claws or teeth. They started for their barrier at once, clawing at an invisible barricade that kept them from touching her, Hellmyr, Letharia, and their guards.

Anova's hand twitched over her own sheathed sword. She would do well not to forget how quickly the fae could turn from beautiful and civilized to these monsters hungry for blood.

Hellmyr dismounted his horse and joined her where she watched them. When he spoke, his voice was low.

"Had you called them to the hunt, they likely would have found a way to break our defenses. It would have been too much for them."

Anova stared at him. "What do you mean?"

"Their rationality is enough to keep them from tearing it apart, but only just so. The lust for the approaching full moon and the promise of blood drives them insane enough, however." He arched one of his eyebrows as he looked at her. "The combination of the moon and the commands of the blood crown would have been likely a bit much for them."

Anova stared forward, processing the information. It wasn't as if she were planning to wear the blood crown for much longer, but what he'd said didn't sit well with her. She didn't want dominion over these creatures. She wanted them to leave her and her kind alone.

She wanted them to stop trying to kill her.

As if summoned by the thought, Anova saw a figure move in the peripheries of the trees lining the area. Among the chaos of the blood-frenzied fae, she thought she recognized this figure.

It wasn't moving like the others—like dogs with the taste for meat on their tongues. She hoped it was Alys and that she was safely avoiding the hunt.

Keep him distracted.

As she stared out over the scattering fae, she started to realize something.

"At the quarter moon fête under the last High King, Leander said that these events were necessary for the flow of magic. That ... the High King had a part to play in returning the magic to the earth from the moon." She squinted at the lands below them. It had gone something like that, hadn't it? "The wedding ..."

When Hellmyr was silent, she looked to him.

His hand found its way under her chin. He brushed his thumb along her jaw until he found her bottom lip.

Anova tried to breathe, but she already felt like she was falling.

"Perceptive, my human bride," he murmured. He traced the outline of her lip. After a moment, he stopped and moved his eyes away from hers. "That's right. The wearer of the blood crown typically does hold these celebrations at least once per month. It is said to restore the balance between what our kind take from the moon and what we give back."

Anova raised her eyebrows. "It's truly not an excuse to have a celebration, then? A reason to give in to moon-madness?"

But the king of fae didn't smile, laugh, or even sneer at her comments.

"What's wrong?" she asked.

Hellmyr shook his head. "It doesn't matter."

"You want me to do this," she guessed. "You wish me to try to … do that at the next full moon. To facilitate such a thing."

Her throat felt tight. She was trying to destroy the blood crown.

What would it mean to destroy it?

His voice was flat. "There are those who don't think a human can."

She turned towards him. "Is this why?" She searched his face. Surely, he knew what she was asking.

Is this part of why they've been trying to assassinate me? Because they think I could break their link to their magic?

Something in her chest tightened. She almost didn't blame them for it.

"With any luck, we'll have answers by the end of the night," he murmured.

Her stomach flopped. He was supporting her at risk of alienating his people.

He can't know about the weapon, she decided.

Hellmyr had been watching her face. "What is it?" he asked with narrowed eyes.

Where Anova stared out over the land stretching before them, she saw a plume of smoke rise and twist into the dark sky.

Alys, what's going on?

Distract him, a voice in her bade.

Tell him, something else said.

There was little other explanation. He …

Somehow, this fae seemed to care deeply for her.

This power-hungry, manipulative fae.

A fae who loves you.

Around her, her world was collapsing. Hellmyr had followed her gaze to see that one of the forges for his training headquarters had caught fire. His guard had clustered around him as he barked orders.

They were to douse the fire. They were to find who started it and drag them to him.

Anova came to his ear. He stilled. His guards scattered to carry out their lord's will.

"I've heard them speaking of a weapon." She breathed. "One that can destroy humans. One designed only to do that."

Her heart throbbed in her chest. If it was a half-truth, could he tell that?

He pulled away to look at her. "There is no such thing."

"What if they were hiding it from you?" She swallowed. "Because they knew you'd side with me?" Anova stepped closer to him. They were almost touching. "There is a cell of resistance already, isn't there?" she guessed. "Or rumors of one?"

For a protracted moment, he stared at her. "There is no such weapon in Fae."

He turned then, and he sent more guards to extinguish the flames that were spreading. Beyond the barrier, the blood-crazed fae had been unleashed on the surrounding lands. Flashes of light pierced the darkness.

They were looking for the one who had orchestrated the attacks on her life. But what if there was more to it than merely seizing the power of the crown?

What if they're hunting Leander?

"There is no such weapon in Fae."

The seconds were slipping out of her fist. What was really going on? Who was telling the truth?

What could she not afford to believe?

Distract him.

When all eyes were on the valley below them, Anova slipped to the edge where Hellmyr's barrier protected them all from the fae participating in the blood hunt.

If she couldn't convince him, she would have to force him to believe her.

Sweat beaded at her forehead, and a painful flicker started in the back of her head in anticipation.

What if I pass out? What if ... I hurt myself?

Her eyes went to the fae watching the bedlam below. *What if I hurt others?*

Anova closed her eyes. She just needed a sliver of magic to do this. She knew so. All she needed was to slip past his barrier for a second—to create a hole only big enough to let her through and only for a few seconds.

Somewhere in the recesses of her mind came a primal scream. She opened her eyes, and her chest heaved to see a glimmer of angry white light appear in the barrier before her.

Anova couldn't look back now. She needed to do something.

As she ran through the white shimmer, her body felt like it was vibrating. Her lungs filled with joy. She was flying. Somehow, she was *flying*.

The world was blurring past her. The exaltation that filled her left her just as quickly. With an impact that was hard enough to break bones, she slammed into earth.

Anova opened her eyes and tried to lift her head.

Before she could, overwhelming pain bolted through her cranium. Her hands pressed against her forehead, and her teeth grinded into each other. It felt as if her head were coming apart.

Heat brushed against her cheek. Anova opened her eyes again, and shoved her body to the side. A streak of searing light struck the ground where she'd been seconds before.

A fae with fangs extending past his lips emerged from the shadows cast by the trees around her. His hair was wild, and his eyes were wilder as he beheld her. White magic grew in his palms.

"You …" He sniffed the air. "You smell like prey. You'll be in my clutches before night's end, little human."

"I don't think so," she said between her teeth. The pain was making it hard to get words out. She came to her feet and found a blade still strapped to her waist. But a new pain erupted through her. It felt as if she'd broken something in her arm.

His tongue ran over his teeth. "Give up. Or run and give sport like the game you are."

She drew a ragged breath. Even with a weapon, she could barely dodge the magic that he drew from his palms. That left one option.

Anova ran faster than she could remember running before. Her head swam, but she pushed the feeling deep down inside her. All she had to know was which way was farthest away from that fae.

A burst of fae magic fell the tree in the path before her, creaking before its full weight dropped against the ground. Anova darted to the side to avoid it, scraping her skin as she flew between brambles. But the longer she ran, the more she started to notice something.

An acrid smell began to stuff her nostrils. Her breath came shorter as she breathed in the heavy air.

Smoke. I'm going towards smoke. It must have spread.

He's herding me towards the fire.

Her hand went to the sheath that had been hitting her thigh at regular intervals. *I could stand and fight. I could last … for several minutes, at least.*

Her chest tightened. She was in no state to fight. But she was running out of options.

Another thought occurred to her. She had a purpose here.

Distract him.

Lead him to you.

Starting with the tree trunk before her, Anova shoved herself against the vegetation. Her teeth dug into her lip as her shoulder hit the wood. She brushed against bushes as she leapt through them.

This will either lead the king of fae to me ... or the rest of his army.

As Anova scraped her arm against a low branch, the pain demanded its price at last. She swallowed down the howl that wanted to escape her lips and fell against the ground in a heap.

She felt him loom before her.

The fae made a sound against his teeth. Above his open palm, an arrow made of pure light hovered. "Too easy." The black in his eyes grew like a cat's pupils, and he crouched to an angle. "But the moon demands a blood price tonight."

He's moon-mad, she realized. *He can't be reasoned with.*

Her blood pulverized her veins. She wasn't ready to die at the hands of a fae just yet. But as her hand went to her sword, agony seized it instead.

There was only one thing left to try.

"By the authority of your queen, you will stop this," she shouted. Her breaths heaved in and out of her. Her broken arm hung at her side.

The fae's eyes gleamed in the dimness. "I know no queen. Only the broken prey before me."

He took a step forward, and the magicked arrow above his palm fixed at her heart. When it hit her, would it feel like one made of stone and wood?

The words rushed out of her. With her good arm, her fingers dug into the thorned crown on her head.

"By the only power your kin cower at, I bid you to stop!"

All else was silent besides her uneven breathing. Smoke snaked through the branches nearby.

His pitch-black eyes were frozen on her. The arrow didn't budge. So slowly that she thought she'd imagined it, his eyes returned to the color of green gemstone. The fae blinked.

The moon spell had been lifted.

Then his eyes narrowed on her. Before Anova could open her mouth, he took several steps backward. "The blood crown thief."

"I didn't steal it," she said with clenched teeth. But she didn't dare move for the arrow that still remained in the air between them. "It's mine by rights."

"But is it right that it should be yours?" the fae asked. He closed the space between them. "Shouldn't one of its own rule over Fae?" His green eyes flashed over her form until they stopped on the crown.

Anova had no response. She didn't know what was right any longer.

She wanted to argue that she was going to destroy it. But was that better? Was that the answer?

You have a fae ruler, she wanted to say, but she didn't.

Before either of them could act, a light burst in the center of the fae's chest. His eyes rolled towards the back of his head, and he fell to the ground.

Where he was sprawled on the earth, Anova saw that the arrow made of magic had pierced his chest clean through from the other side. It dissolved seconds later.

Before her was the fae king, and his cloak of raven feathers rustled behind him in the breeze. He closed his palm to extinguish the magic he'd commanded to kill the wild fae on the ground.

His black-violet eyes stared through her. He snapped his fingers, and a nearly-invisible barrier coated the air around the two of them like a glaze.

"I'm going to need some answers, Anova. *Right now.*"

CHAPTER TWENTY-FOUR

What was she going to say to him?

What *could* she say to him?

Nothing was safe.

Before her was the fae who commanded the most power in their lands. The one who could set an army under the spell of a blood moon.

The one who she might …

She swallowed down the word. It was a pitiful, vulnerable thing. He looked ready to kill her. And the moon was high yet.

"I know," he said. His eyes were like a cat's in the night. "I know this fire was your doing, my darling. Tell me the truth."

"I … became aware of something in the archives," she said. For just a moment, his eyebrows flicked skywards.

He must have found out from Letharia that I snuck into the archives.

"Your anti-human weapon," she continued. Anova couldn't hear herself over her heart. "I couldn't allow it to continue existing here."

"There is no such thing." His expression fell into shadow. Controlled. "Trust that I would have been aware of it, had it existed." But as he looked upon her face, his eyes flashed with some quick fae emotion. It was gone before she could decipher it.

Before she could divert him from discovering more of their plan, he guessed, "The girl. That's who set the fire."

Calm your heart. Calm.

"It was my idea," she said.

Allow the calm to fill you.

"She'll be going back to where she came from," Hellmyr said. "I don't like the look of that one."

"No—I—" What could she say? The truth blurted out. "I need her."

Hellmyr had a strange look on his face.

"You what?"

Anova searched for the truth. What was the truth?

She's a witch. She's working with me to destroy your most sacred yet destructive artifact.

But what else was the truth?

He was before her in a blur. His hand had tilted her chin up towards him. His voice was flat. "Why? What is she doing here?"

Anova looked away. What was the truth?

His thumb brushed the bottom of her lip. "*Tell me.*"

"I ..." Her voice was hoarse. He moved her head so that she couldn't look away from him.

As she stared into his face, all other sensations fell from her like water from fish scales. The bitter smell of fire faded alongside the aching pains buried in her body. She couldn't remember why she was there.

Somewhere, a glimmer sparked in the air, and it reminded her of something. The memory fell away, too, and she was left with only what was important. *The voice.*

When he spoke, it was the most beautiful sound she'd ever heard.

"Anova," he murmured. "It would make me happier than I can describe if you told me a few things."

Anova nodded. She found she would do anything to keep that voice speaking, and she didn't want to talk over it.

His lashes brushed against his cheek as he looked down at her. "Tell me. Who is the girl?"

Her mouth moved without thought to check it. "She's a witch. The last one."

Something changed in his expression. She couldn't focus on more than one thing, however.

I wasn't supposed to say that.

But the voice made of honey and sweet promises was speaking again.

"Why is she here, Anova? What is she trying to do?"

She could feel her heart struggle in her chest. There was a reason the voice was asking this.

Her tongue was heavy, but it came out anyway. "To destroy the crown."

No!

He's using magic on you.

"Good girl," he murmured. His thumb moved across her lower lip. Her heartrate picked up. He stared at her, watching something in her face.

She wanted to obey the voice. She wanted to do its bidding more than she wanted anything else.

He's using magic on you.

Although its pull was still there, begging her to obey the voice at once, a new feeling surfaced within her. In her palm, her nails dug hard into her skin.

How dare he?

Her teeth bit into the edge of her tongue. *Does he think me so easily made a fool?*

But then, wouldn't she have done the same at the first opportunity?

Her heartrate slowed, though barely.

Wouldn't I have done it sooner to him?

She swallowed the bitterness on her tongue. *The liar and the manipulator.* They truly deserved each other.

"Why are you here?" His lids lowered as his expression changed. "You know what I ask."

She breathed in deeply. His honeyed voice had stopped talking, and she needed to do anything to have it speak again. Whatever paltry words she had to give in exchange, it would be worth it just to hear it again.

He's using magic on you.

"I ..." Her mouth dried. She felt dizzy.

Find the witch magic inside the crown. Find it, and use it. Break the glamour spell.

His voice was low as he spoke again. "I need to know, Anova. I need the truth. Why did you come back to me?"

Anova felt the moment she broke the truth spell.

The bastard that was the pain came back first. The choking smell of ash. The aches buried inside her body.

She was freed of truth-telling. Anova's thoughts circled her like a typhoon, pointing her to all the solutions and lies she could leverage. She would force him back where he'd been, tied like a ribbon around her finger. Or as much as he could, now that her fool mouth had said all that.

But you have to act as if you're still under the truth spell.

It would be no challenge for her, though. She could fake the doe-eyed damsel as well as she ever had. She was, even more than he, the faker.

She would be the better manipulator, too.

His voice broke the silence around them. He was frozen in the darkness, his expression indecipherable. His hand remained on the side of her face.

"Why are you afraid?" A pause that felt as long as a lifetime stretched between his words. "Anova. What happened to you?"

His question broke some small piece of her. It was so small that it was almost unnoticeable—like a piece of ice chipping from a frozen bough in midwinter.

But it was enough.

"Hellmyr." It was perhaps the first time she'd said his name to his face. She breathed in a gasp. "I have to destroy it. It's killing me."

She swallowed and said out loud the final piece. "I'm dying."

"No." His jaw flexed in an odd place. He pushed the hair from her eyes. "You're not."

He was suddenly angry—angrier than he had any right to be.

Anova bit down on the inside of her cheek. What did he care? He hadn't needed the crown tied to her life to claim his throne.

What did it matter to him if she died?

She couldn't look at him. He was making this hard. "You know the truth. You can hear my heart."

It was calm.

Too suddenly, his mouth was on hers, and the world was lost to her. This time, she let the abyss swallow her whole.

After all, there was relief in forgetting. Numbness. Nothingness. If only temporarily.

CHAPTER TWENTY-FIVE

The brush ran through her hair with more than a little resistance. Della made a noise behind her teeth as she took to detangling Anova's hair, a task that truly should have taken several people.

A series of knocks interrupted Della's fussing.

Maris narrowed her eyes at the door. "More fae healers, hm? What could another one do that the first twenty couldn't?"

But she went to Anova's door regardless.

She hadn't exaggerated, at least by much. When they'd arrived back at Eastwoe palace, a retinue of fae healers had awaited her. After mending her injuries, they'd examined every part of her from her toes to the top of her head, but so far, none of them had discovered anything promising.

Other than confirmation of what she had known already but didn't particularly want to hear: her relationship with the blood crown wasn't a normal one.

Anova processed these things with what felt like an alarmingly low amount of interest. She felt as if she were watching these things happen to someone else.

Her wedding to Hellmyr was tonight. As was the full moon.

Alys was imprisoned inside the palace's dungeons. Officially, it was because of her crime of arson.

Unofficially, it was for too many reasons to count.

It was dawn, which meant she had half a day to figure *something* out.

She wondered idly if she would be able to convince Hellmyr to support destroying the blood crown. She wondered if he would try to kill her for it now since she was dying anyway.

She wondered if she should care more. Either way, she would destroy it.

So long as someone else doesn't kill me first, she considered. Anova weighed her options.

She could run. Perhaps she should've from the start.

But there was no abandoning Alys, Della, and Maris. Anova considered what would happen to her friends and companions if she were to leave.

Della and Maris ... she would have to take them with her. Anova wasn't sure where she would hide them as they couldn't go back to the human lands now, but hopefully they'd find somewhere safe.

But there was no chance of the fae surrendering Alys now that they knew what she was.

Whether he admitted to it or not, Hellmyr had at least one prisoner to ensure she stayed in line and did as he wished. Though, she'd always known choice was an illusion with the fae.

You do what they want, or you pay the price.

She could accept her situation. Marry Hellmyr and take her bride price of death.

The fae would get what they want—a king with as much legitimacy as was possible in a blood crown-less world.

And she would get what she wanted. In a way.

If my death destroys the succession of the blood crown, that is.

Her morbid ruminations were interrupted by her visitor's voice. Anova's stomach twisted. It wasn't more fae healers.

"The presence of the fae king's bride is needed." Letharia's golden eyes stared from the doorway to her suite.

Maris crossed her arms. "What is it now?"

Gods bless her.

If anyone could face off with the mother of the fae king, it was Maris.

Letharia's mouth twitched upward for the barest of smirks before it settled into a sneer. She looked at Anova. "You would do well to remember to control your servants."

Anova pushed to her feet. "They're *friends*, not servants." She narrowed her eyes at the fae lady. "Although I'm sure such a concept is foreign to you."

Della's hovered at Anova's ear. "Careful, Nove."

Anova still seethed but came to her door. Della was right. Even so, she made sure to thank the two of them for their help before leaving with the fae lady.

As they walked, a dress made of sheer golden material swished the ground at Letharia's feet.

"Your request to see the prisoner has been granted," Letharia said at once.

How gracious.

Even so, Anova was surprised to hear it. It seemed the fae king had had a change in heart.

That doesn't mean he'll release Alys.

After a moment, she found her voice. "Just where is Hellmyr?"

"He has business elsewhere before tonight," Letharia said. "But he wished me to relay something to you in his absence."

She could feel the skin around her eyes wrinkle in suspicion. "What is it?"

"'It doesn't exist. It never did. I checked,'" she said.

"What are you talking about?" Anova said.

But she continued leading her forward without a word. She caught up to Letharia again and said, "What does that mean? I know he said more than that."

"That was the end of his message," said the fae. Her voice was flat. "I have nothing more to tell you about it."

"It doesn't exist. It never did. I checked."

Anova only had to think on it for a moment to understand what the message was talking about.

"There is no such thing. Trust that I would have been aware of it, had it existed."

He tried to find the anti-human artifact.

Anova shook her head. Of course, he couldn't find it. Alys was the one who destroyed it.

Or, rather, she hoped the witch had. She hadn't talked to her since the night of the blood hunt. The closer they got to the cells deep inside the palace, the more her stomach twisted.

She'd betrayed her. She'd done this to Alys.

Anova's head snapped up. "This isn't the way to the dungeons, fae."

They were standing at a window that faced the front of the palace. They were still not on the ground floor, however.

"Anova." Letharia leaned her hips against the ledge of the window. "Don't throw this world into chaos. You must marry him."

She stared back at the fae lady. Had she taken a blow to the head during the blood hunt? "I *am*. Tonight," she said through her teeth.

She had no other plan anymore. She couldn't run. And without Alys, there was no hope of destroying the fae artifact on her head.

Soon enough, she was going to die.

And it was possible the blood crown wouldn't die with her.

Her eyes narrowed on Anova. "Hellmyr told me about what's happening with the crown. With you."

The air left Anova's lungs. Of course he did. It would have been a feat to keep such a thing from the king's mother, but even so, she felt the bitter sting of something like betrayal.

Letharia held her gaze. "Go through with it. Hellmyr will protect you until the end. Otherwise, you throw Fae needlessly into turmoil."

"What are you talking about?" Anova's heart throbbed. She didn't wish to be speaking to Letharia about *this*. About her death.

"Give up the pretenses, Anova. We both know you wanted this artifact only to destroy it." She walked forward, closing the distance between them. "If you refuse him tonight and henceforth, you will take with you to your grave not only the blood crown, but also any semblance of peace and calm we have managed to forge here. He is king now, even without the crown, but the situation is more tenuous than we would prefer." She tilted her head. "You might not care, but there are those who wish to end the struggle for power in Fae."

We. If it were possible for her anymore, she would have laughed.

"Those like the ones in power," Anova corrected. "Once he has the *blessing* of the blood crown by marrying me and once I'm rotting in the ground, do you think he'll be a better ruler than his father, or do you just want a bigger puppet?"

She was saying things she perhaps ought not to while there were no witnesses, but Anova couldn't seem to help herself.

Instead of rising to her bait, the ends of Letharia's mouth rose viciously. "You don't even know, do you?"

"I know I've had enough your games," Anova said.

Letharia stepped to the side. It was then that Anova saw it. The window was a wide-set arch window that afforded an unobstructed view of Eastwoe and the autumnal forests spreading beyond the palace. The trees were dressed in colors of orange, yellow, and gold among sparse evergreens.

But that wasn't where her gaze stopped.

A figure was strapped by their wrists to the front of the palace, their feet barely touching the doors' archway below.

And they were *alive*.

"Your assassin. Our fae discovered evidence incriminating her during the blood hunt," Letharia said. "Doubtless, she would have succeeded in killing you if we hadn't have caught her."

Anova swallowed. Even from this distance and angle, she saw who it was. It was the fae assassin who had tried to kill Anova right before she'd found Hellmyr. The one who had been carrying one of Leander's knives.

The one she'd assumed had been sent by him.

Lyrin. And she was bleeding from the head.

"What is this?" Anova's nails dug into the ledge. Her stomach roiled. She whirled to face the fae lady again. "Is this supposed to convince me of your point? *Torture* and *blood-spectacle* were the province of the previous high king," she reminded her.

Fae needed another dictator like it needed to invade the human realm.

"He did this for you—as a warning to your enemies. All the creatures attending your wedding will see her, slowly dying at our threshold, and know what fate awaits them if they so dare." Letharia's eyes were slits. "Unless you wish him to seem weak to those who would seize his reign? To those who would murder his betrothed?"

Her chest heaved like she'd been running. Letharia had a point, and she hated it.

"There are questions I would ask her, too," Anova said finally.

Her dark eyebrows lifted over her eyes. "As in? I assure you, we have interrogated her well, Anova."

"As in who she works for," Anova fired back. "I've encountered Lyrin before. She has a master."

"She knows nothing further. We have already glamoured her and discovered this."

Maybe it was pathetic now that she faced her end, but she needed to know if Leander had sent her.

Her heart twisted in her chest.

"Do what you may to send a message, but I need her alive, if only a little longer. I have my own questions." Anova locked eyes with her.

The human master of the blood crown and the mother of the king. Which of them was supposed to have more power? More say?

Letharia was asking her to trust Hellmyr. Well, she needed a little of the same.

"As you wish," she said at last. The fae lady turned away from her. "She will stay where she is. But we will treat her before her wounds claim her."

When they left the window, Anova wondered if she'd fought to keep her enemy alive because she truly thought she could extract more information from her. If Anova thought that the answers mattered at all anymore.

Or if it was because she simply didn't have the stomach to watch someone else die a slow death.

CHAPTER TWENTY-SIX

Letharia left her when they arrived at the dungeons, though the fae lady's words still rang in her head.

"You might not care, but there are those who wish to end the struggle for power in Fae."

Anova stopped thinking when the smell of the dungeons hit her. She surrendered her weapons, though it was too much like parting with a limb.

A guard accompanied her on each side and before her as they delved into the dark hall lined with cells.

"Is this really necessary?" she asked.

None of them responded to her. Her teeth grinded into each other. Whose protection was this for?

Perhaps it's just so he can spy on you, she considered. *And to keep you from breaking her free.*

The thought sobered her. If he thought it possible, then there must have been hope.

It was then that she saw Alys. One of the guards opened the rusted metal door, and inside was little more than a cage.

All her limbs had been chained to the wall with irons, though they weren't so short that she hung from them. Her stomach clenched the more she saw.

Alys didn't move to look at them. She was curled within herself and pressed against the wall like a beetle discovered under a rock.

"Leave me, you creatures," she said in a low voice.

"It's me." Anova stepped forward. "I've been trying to see you."

The witch finally looked over at her. "Fine. But not with you three in here, too."

None of them made a move to leave. "They're not as dull as they look, I suppose," the witch murmured after a few moments of silence.

Her blood pounded. Alys didn't have to say it. They were being studied. Listened to.

"It doesn't exist. It never did. I checked."

Anova bit her tongue. She needed to speak on too many things.

What did it mean that Hellmyr hadn't found any trace of the artifact? Had she destroyed it?

How was she going to destroy the blood crown now that Alys was imprisoned?

How much time did they have left?

But she could say none of these things, so instead, she said what she needed to.

Her voice cracked in a strange way. "Alys, I'm sorry."

"It's done."

Alys gave a shrug of her shoulders. Dirt was already smudged into her skin, but she still held herself with the pride of being the last witch.

She wanted Alys to be angry at her. To rage at her and call her names. But she did none of that.

It was worse.

A heavy silence grew with each passing second. The abyss inside her grew with it. She couldn't stand it any longer.

"Say something," Anova said through her teeth at last. "Anything."

Alys leaned back against her cell wall and closed her eyes. "There's nothing to say."

"Alys," she said, her voice in a tight whisper, "what can I do?"

"I don't know."

Anova felt the eyes of the fae guards on her. *Damn them.* She came to her knees before Alys.

"I want to help you. I want to do something," she said.

She already knew the logical answer, of course. There was nothing to be done. Their time was up. Her heart ached in her chest with each beat that went by.

Alys didn't say anything. Anger, the pulse-pounding kind, filled Anova. Even if she had forfeited her future, that didn't mean that Alys could.

Or, if they were both doomed humans living their last days in Fae, that didn't mean there was nothing they couldn't take down with them.

"A witch doesn't give up." Adrenaline spiked her body. Suddenly, the fabric of Alys's clothes was bunched in her fists. "A witch does better than this."

Out of her periphery vision, Anova saw the fae move in blurs at the sudden attack. But she didn't care.

"Even if it's the last thing she does," Anova said through her teeth, "she does more than this."

She wasn't sure when she'd stopped talking about Alys and started talking about someone else.

All at once, strong arms found their way around Anova's as they yanked her backwards. The force left her on her back several paces from Alys.

The nearest guard shot a look at her. "It's time for you to go."

Anova lurched to her feet before the fae could touch her again. She discovered she was afraid to look at Alys.

When she finally did, Alys was back to looking at the walls of her cells. Back to ignoring all of them.

Just before she was ushered out of the cell, Anova saw that the witch's hands formed fists where they were pressed against her abdomen.

Anova's hands trembled as she removed layers of her clothing. She'd asked, as politely as she could've, for Maris and Della to leave her now.

Their comments would have been encouraging. Hopeful. But she knew they were only words crafted to take the bitter sting out of their own hearts.

Anova knew she should have appreciated that she still had friends and companions willing to sit with her. Perhaps even cry with her, if she'd asked them.

But she didn't want that, now.

Before they'd left, Della had run some bathwater for her. The smells of the soaps filled her nostrils. Notes of lavender, rosemary, and pine drifted through the air.

As she piled her clothes on the floor next to her, something fluttered to the ground beside them. Anova stopped and stared at it before touching it.

It was a scrap of paper folded several times over. Carefully, she flattened it out.

The words scrawled across it were written in an ink like blood. Anova realized belatedly that it probably *was* blood—Alys's.

She must have put it somewhere on me when I grabbed her, Anova realized.

She read it several times in a row before the words started to sink in. When she'd memorized all of it, Anova dropped the note into the steaming tub of water where it dissolved within seconds, macabre ink and all.

Anova turned the words over in the silence of her mind, examining them like a piece of food.

"Revenge me by destroying it yourself. Leave nothing to chance. If we both yet live after, find me.

There is much we could do."

Underneath those words had been a list of ingredients.

CHAPTER TWENTY-SEVEN

Anova opened the door to Alys's bedroom. Things of hers that weren't smashed to bits were scattered everywhere.

She pushed past the tattered remains of her books.

Please, let it be here. Please.

Most of the ritual spell's ingredients were things she could acquire on her own easily enough. But at least one of them would be near impossible to replace.

The blood of a fae who loves you. The blood of a fae you love.

Anova plucked a small sachet that had been left intact. When she opened it, she found only salt, but she pocketed it anyway. Already, she'd found one of the ingredients.

Shards of glass littered the floor. She danced between broken glass containers as she rifled through what was left of Alys's belongings.

It didn't look good.

Her herbs had been crushed—or likely thrown out of the window, she realized when she saw that they were scattered across the sill. Anova didn't give up.

Her hands found the cold surface of a glass vial. She swallowed the hope that rose in her chest, trying to keep it at bay. It didn't work, and a smile spread across her face.

No blood yet, but she had an intact vial.

Two ingredients down.

Anova recited the list in her head as she continued to look.

One glass vial.

Unspoiled water.

The blood of a fae you love.

The blood of a fae who loves you.

Your blood.

Salt.

Poison enough to kill a man.

Place these within the glass vial. Allow the light of the full moon to touch the glass as the last ingredient.

Activate with magic of any intent.

Anova stopped what she was doing and sat on the floor. Her palms pressed against her face.

It was gone. Or more likely, destroyed.

Hellmyr wouldn't be back until the moonrise, and she had no more of his blood.

So, that's it. I can't destroy it by tonight.

And this would be the last full moon she saw. Her hands started to tremble. She couldn't do it. The blood crown was going to kill her.

The blood of a fae you love.

The blood of a fae who loves you.

Anova came to her feet too quickly, and the world spun around her. She didn't have time for it and pushed herself out of Alys's room. She'd gotten all she could from the witch's belongings.

The realization made her blood run faster through her. Each part of the fae blood was listed on two lines because they were considered separate ingredients. Or, at least, they *could* be.

Anova shook her head. Alys could never be straightforward, could she?

As she entered her own bedroom, her heart throbbed in her chest. It wasn't easy to admit. She gritted her teeth.

The blood of a fae you love.

Anova pulled her sword out of its sheath. The last time she'd used it had been on their journey back to the Eastwoe palace. It had happened when she'd snuck out of her camp and found Leander. Though only by a small amount, she'd spilled his blood.

Her breath froze in her lungs. It was there.

The blood had dried and stuck to the edge of her blade. It was only a bit, but it would have to be enough. Her fingers trembled as she collected it and dropped it into the glass.

This was not the fae who loved her, however. Perhaps he never had.

Anova breathed. There was one place Hellmyr's blood might have been.

She flung open the doors to her wardrobe. On the floor of it were the clothes she'd worn on their trip to Westvalde and back. Since she'd gotten back and been subjected to the endless examinations by his healers, she hadn't let a single fae servant in or out. And Sera had been busy enough preparing her for tonight that her dirty clothes hadn't yet been washed or disposed of.

Soon enough, the fabric of the dress she'd worn that night was in her hands. The floor-length gown was beautiful, and it would be a crime to destroy it. But she found what she was looking for at once.

A dark red streak had dried into the outer gauzy layer of the skirts. When Hellmyr had carried her back to their camps, he'd been bleeding from some wound along his arm.

Anova took her small knife and cut the fabric until she had the blood-stained fragment in her fist.

The blood of a fae who loves you.

Did he love her? He'd gone against what any fae should have done—killed her for the crown. He'd supported her authority even when it had undermined his.

Anova stared at the fabric in her hands and remembered what had happened the night of the blood hunt.

The kiss they'd shared.

Anova blinked where she crouched on the floor of her wardrobe. She bit her cheek again to stem the moisture forming on her eyelids. The minutes were slipping by.

She rose and inserted the strip of his dried blood inside the vial. As she came to the window inside her bedroom, she looked over Fae. When her knife cut into her hand, she allowed a few tears to drip along her cheek from the pain.

With her finger, she collected both her blood drops and the drips along her cheek and secured them inside the nearly full glass.

She wiped her face and allowed her expression to turn into a blank mask.

Only one ingredient remained.

When she found Sera, there must have been some trace of emotion left on Anova's face—or perhaps it was the lack of any. The girl stared at her for a moment longer than she normally would've.

"Sera," she said. "I'll be leaving the palace for a while before tonight. Can you keep them from finding me?"

Sera's lips were tight. But after a moment, she nodded. Briefly, Anova wondered what she saw there. She wondered what she felt herself.

There was hope, though hope was unequivocally a bastard.

But maybe this time, she could try trusting it.

After all, she didn't have anything left that it could take from her.

She'd snuck inside the palace in the first place, so it wasn't a surprise to Anova that she could sneak out of it as easily.

Anova had tied a leather cord around the neck of the glass so she could keep the spell's ingredients on her at all times before the full moon rose. As she leapt the distance from the last tree branch to the ground below, it thudded against her chest inside her dress.

When she landed, she swallowed a groan of pain, though it wasn't her fall that had caused it. Her vision blurred, and primal screams roared in her ears. Her palms covered her ears, but that did little.

Sweat drenched her and glued her clothes to her body. She couldn't move.

Time passed. Anova lost track of how much.

After what felt like hours, she forced her legs against the ground and marched forward. She didn't dare check how far the sun had raced across the sky towards the horizon. She would either find what she needed in time or she wouldn't.

Anova passed among the trees draped in moss and the lanterns throwing their amber light on her path until she was deep within the woods of Eastwoe. She crouched and squatted among the vegetation for a sign of any number of the poisons that she knew.

Harmless clusters of bright orange flowers, trailing ivies, and bushes lush with safe, edible berries were all that she found. Anova pushed deeper underneath the canopy of the trees.

In her head, she recited the names of some that she'd been trained to recognize.

Wolfsbane.

Mountain Laurel.

Lily of the Valley.

Oleander.

Thorns scraped against her skin, and the pain at her temples was mounting. Against her better judgment, she looked to the skies past the boughs heavy with moss above her.

The sun was nearly touching the western horizon. Her heart lodged in her throat.

She'd gotten so far, but it hadn't been far enough.

Anova found a flat rock under the deep shadow of a hazel tree and pulled her legs against her. Her knees pressed against her forehead.

She wanted to right some of the wrongs in this world that she'd been forced to swallow.

But above all, she wanted to *live*.

Anova straightened. She would live. No matter what it took, she would make it work. No matter what.

Anova ran, her eyes scanning at a height from the ground much higher than before. She hadn't yet noticed any signs of poisonous plants yet, but that didn't mean there weren't any growing here.

I've been looking for the wrong ones.

In the Sorrelands where Leander's manor had been, the climate had been much warmer. Here, dampness invaded the land. As Anova ran, she started to hear the sound of a slow-moving creek.

Her heart thudded in her chest. She moved through the woods until she found it.

Water loving. Less heat tolerant.

Anova came to a spot along the river where the canopy of the trees relented, and evening sun poured down. Her breath froze.

Glossy, black berries clung to a tall shrub with soft green leaves. A few moments later, she found what she'd been looking for—purple flowers.

Belladonna.

For a moment, she considered gathering its berries to satisfy the spell's requirements.

Poison enough to kill a man.

She stopped. The fatal dose for an adult human would have been a dozen berries at least. There wasn't enough space in her spell bottle by far.

Anova breathed. After tearing off a strip of her dress at the hemline, she pressed it to her palm to use it as a makeshift glove. In one motion, she tore one of the plant's leaves from a stem and forced it through the vial's opening.

With the last ingredient, the glass was completely full. She replaced the stopper.

One leaf will have to be enough.

Anova replaced the necklace within the bodice of her dress when she heard a noise behind her. She'd already drawn her sword when they emerged from the woods all around her.

The fae guards were on all sides of her, and the sun was setting past the trees.

"His Majesty requests your presence." Something changed in the guard's face. Her voice lowered. "They await you, my lady."

Anova lowered her blade. She hadn't missed the word *they*. It was time.

Give them no chance to find it. Her heart thudded against the glass that contained the spell to destroy the blood crown.

Among the shadows of the dying day, she went with them.

CHAPTER TWENTY-EIGHT

After her guards handed her off to a team of fae attendants, they shoved Anova in the closest bathing chamber they could find within the palace. A team of them finished Della's handiwork from earlier and tamed the knots that had formed against her scalp and near the crown.

As they tried to undress her with their deft fingers, Anova snarled at the nearest of them.

"I'll do that myself," she said. Her heart thundered in her chest. *I can't let them see the vial.* Before their hands could rip her bodice apart for her, she said, "Let me. I have a recovering wound."

Fortunately, it was true enough.

Though the healing arts of the fae were impressive, an ache remained in her arm where she'd fractured the bone recently. As she went to work unbuttoning the back of the dress, she untied the leather knot holding the necklace together. When she shrugged out of the upper part of her dress and stepped out of it, she kicked the vial underneath the plume of skirts she left behind.

She didn't have the chance to blush at having so many eyes on her bare form. Anova was promptly scrubbed of the topmost layer of her skin in a steaming bath despite her protests.

At the same time, two fae went to work braiding her hair and interlacing live flowers within her strands. They worked expertly, barely touching the blood crown but for what was necessary. She felt as metal barrettes pushed against her scalp, but she kept quiet, her eyes on where she'd left the spell bottle.

They dried and dressed her even faster. Over her shoulders, layers of ivory fabric fell. The upper part of the dress had been sewn into the smallest lace patterns, culminating in a sleeveless bodice that closed at the neck.

Below a cinch at the waist, the snow-white fabric came to her feet except for a slit along one of her legs, starting at her right thigh.

Anova hadn't meant to look at herself, but she caught a glimpse of their handiwork in the surface of the lukewarm bathwater.

There was no other word for it. They'd transformed her into something out of a fae tale.

Anova almost lost her nerve then, but it was hard to resist a team of fae attendants when their sole purpose was to deliver her to the fae king on his wedding night.

Her cheeks heated at the thought.

Suddenly, she remembered the bottle under the heap that had been her dress. Anova dove for the pile, avoiding the grasp of her many attendants. Barely, she managed to slip the small glass inside the top of the dress where it nestled against her skin.

While they ushered her out of the bathing chambers, her fingers found the ends of the leather cord, and she tied them together once again. Hopefully, it would escape the fae king's notice long enough to for the curse-breaking ritual to work.

She felt that it was time.

The longer she walked, the more fae began to insulate her. Guards ringed them from all sides, the ones at the outer perimeter carrying lanterns on poles filled with bugs that had flashing thoraxes.

The moment they entered the ballroom, she felt his eyes on her. It was impossible not to feel it. For the moment, she resisted staring back and took in everything else first.

More fae than she could ever remember seeing lined the walls of the cavernous hall. Above their heads, the ceiling yawned open to a wide sky-window. The stars flecked the black sky, though she could feel the moon approaching its height. It would soon fill the hall with its madness.

Her heartbeat pounded against the glass hidden in her chest. She felt something stir inside her.

This vial contains real magic.

It was going to work. She just needed to time it. Perfectly.

Her blood pounded her veins as she stepped into the wide room. They were all looking at her.

It started with the guards who carried the poles fixed with light-bug lanterns at their ends. They bowed, and then her other guards and attendants bowed as one after. It was like a wave upon a beach as those before her pressed their heads against the floor. Anova held in a tight breath.

They'd parted from the middle of the room, the fae on each side like walls. On the other side of the room stood the fae king.

Hellmyr's eyes were cast in shadow, but even from this distance, she could see the fine clothes he'd donned. His clothes were as black as midnight, and across his back fell his cape of ravens' feathers. Mirroring the one that sat on her head, Hellmyr wore a crown of black feathers which was nearly lost in his hair.

His expression stole her breath. It was as if she were the moon, and he'd never seen her in his life.

She remembered his blood in the vial around her neck and forced one foot forward and then another.

As she moved, a smaller sect of her guards moved with her, angling themselves so that she was protected from the aim of archers and assassins. Anova focused on the dark sky above and the other side of the hall.

The minutes slipped by, and she was finally before him. Out of the corner of her eye, she saw movement. Maris was holding Della as she quivered. Along with the fae, they were pressed close to the ground in a bow.

Anova's heart squeezed. She would do this for them—and for the rest of her kind.

When she met Hellmyr's gaze, it felt as if her heart's rhythm had skipped a few beats. She swallowed. He may have been a manipulator and even a monster, but there was no looking away from such beauty.

After one last step to bring her close to him, he took her hand and pulled it to his mouth. She remembered the feeling of falling—the feeling of kissing him, and his mouth moved up her arm.

His lips rested just above her collarbone for one last kiss. But as he did so, he murmured so quietly that only she could hear the words.

"I have discovered a cure for you, my human bride."

It was then that she saw something peek from underneath his half-buttoned shirt. Pink, mottled skin gave way to a series of bandages wrapped around part of his torso. He'd been hurt.

Her heart stopped in her throat.

So, he believed her when she'd said it was killing her. What was more, he'd risked his own skin for her.

Her voice was nearly inaudible. "What is it?"

Ever so slightly, Hellmyr gave a shake of his head. "Too many eyes. It will have to wait."

Her throat felt like it was closing against her heart. Panic rose inside her like an overflowing well.

She couldn't do both. She couldn't trust Hellmyr and ensure the destruction of the blood crown.

It had to be one or the other, and she had to decide *now*.

They parted, and as he spoke, his voice rose the hairs on her arms. In his hand was a gleaming band of silver. "Will you take me as your husband by Fae's laws and the laws of your kind?"

Anova opened her mouth, but another voice rang out among the mass of fae.

CHAPTER TWENTY-NINE

Leander was saying her name, over and over. But by the time she found him in the crowd, Hellmyr's guards had, too.

Leander's chest heaved. His clothes had been torn, and the edge of a swordstaff hovered at his throat.

His eyes found hers. "Anova. Don't do this."

It felt as if time had sped up and slowed down all at once. Her head swam. He didn't feel real. She could do nothing but stare at him.

"Shut your mouth," snarled one of the guards holding him. "Or else we'll spill out your throat."

Anova could feel the blood lust rise in the room. The only thing the fae liked more than a spectacle under the moon was one involving blood. And there was enough moon-madness in the air this evening to demand its spilling.

"Don't," she said between her teeth. "Don't do it."

The guard looked from her to Hellmyr. She didn't dare look at him, but it only took Hellmyr a second to say evenly to the guard, "You heard her."

Leander said in a rush, "He hasn't told you the most important part of this ceremony. Fae marriages are made in magic and are thought to be one of the most binding contracts possible. No High King or Queen has married before in case it risked the blood crown's allegiance."

Anova held his gaze. "That's not possible. Only the spilling of blood can do that."

Leander stared only at her. "It hasn't been attempted before for the possibility that it *could*." The fae guard suddenly pressed the blade tighter against his throat, but he spoke against it anyway. "You could be considered of the same blood after a fae ceremony under such a bloated moon. More so than the child of a parent is of the same blood."

Anova jerked to look at Hellmyr.

"Possibly." His face seemed carefully blank.

Her heart kicked into a rhythm several beats faster than was comfortable. The first sliver of moonlight would pass into the hall in mere moments. She had to decide what to do now.

"You didn't tell me," Anova said under her breath.

Hellmyr brushed his hand against her cheek. "But my darling, there was even more you didn't tell me. Secrets even worse. Motives more wretched." His mouth hovered against her ear. "But I happen to like traitors and liars and manipulators. Together, we would be the worst of them all. You would live—and as my queen."

Anova held her breath. Leander's eyes were on them, and Hellmyr seemed to relish in the fact. In his hand was the silver band, and a spark of light travelled along its surface before it winked out of existence.

Bound by magic.

There would be no end to the blood crown. It would be allowed to continue existing—even if she died.

Anova pulled the leather cord out of her dress just as the smallest sliver of moonlight poured from the sky-window in the ceiling.

I will end it.

She held her breath.

I choose to sever the line of murdering kings and queens.

It all happened too quickly for her to realize.

A strange energy rose in the air, and a new kind of pain danced on her scalp like a moon-mad fae.

Leander shouted her name, but the sound was cut off in a noise like a gargle.

And next to her, Hellmyr fell to the ground.

Before his guards swarmed him, she saw him. Blood leaked from each corner of his mouth, and his eyes stared into the zenith of the sky above them. He was shaking.

The blood of a fae who loves you.

"Hellmyr," she gasped.

Anova tried to push past them to get to him, but something else was happening to her instead. The pain on her scalp grew to an unbearable degree. She slid to the ground, gripping the edges of the crown like it could hold her head together.

Through tears of pain, she saw the fae who still held a piece of her heart.

Leander had fallen, as well, but he wasn't moving. The crowd around him had started shouting and moving like a swelling ocean.

"No!" she shouted, but it was swallowed by the cacophony.

He's going to be trampled, she realized.

That was when she saw her. She moved like a ghost through the panicking fae, her hair pinned among an elaborate mask that she must have used to hide behind inside the crowd.

It was Lycasta. When she reached him, she held him tight to her chest.

The blood of a fae you love.

Lycasta looked past the heads of swarming fae at Anova. She didn't have to hear Lycasta to know what she was saying to her.

"It will kill him."

Would it be worth it—the end of the blood crown for the lives of two fae? Anova had already accepted the cost of her own life, so why should this have been any different?

The pain dancing on her scalp intensified then, and her vision went white at the edges. Her ears buzzed so she could hear no longer. She felt herself fall against the hard ground. The blood crown was resisting Alys's magic.

But it was losing.

Just as it had been made with the sacrifice of the original witch's life, to unmake it required a blood sacrifice.

A sacrifice not in hate but its opposite.

Anova tore the cord from her neck. The world moved around her as if she were floating on a sea. Bodies came and moved about her, but she couldn't lose track of the glass in her hand. The pain flickered her vision as it sapped more of her energy.

As soon as she could, Anova slammed the spell bottle against the ground. Mist rose up like a phantom where it had broken. The ingredients of the ritual dissolved like dust on the air. Anova slumped and nearly fell as she lost the feeling in her legs.

No matter what Leander thought of her now, she couldn't sacrifice his life to save hers. Not even to destroy the blood crown. And she couldn't sacrifice Hellmyr's either, she realized.

Coward, a part of her crooned. *Yellow-belly.*

She couldn't remain where she was. She needed to go.

Where she could go, Anova knew not. One by one, her choices had withered and crumbled to ruin. Her teeth dug into her tongue, and she pulled free her sword in the crowd of fae that had started to overtake them.

Alys had never told her that this was the price.

Would she have agreed to do it if she knew of it beforehand? Her head spun.

This is the last full moon before you die.

She needed to get out of here. She needed to escape now.

But to where? There's no other option for you now. You made sure of that.

The crown will kill you. You aren't going to destroy it—it will destroy you.

Anova's eyes stung, but she headed for the edges of the room anyway. She needed to think. She needed to plan. As she ran, she picked up a discarded cloak from the floor and shrugged herself into it. It helped disguise the stark white of her dress, some, but there was nothing to do for the crown atop her head.

She couldn't stay. She couldn't leave. She couldn't die. She couldn't live.

It happened in a blink. Fragments of the room's walls and columns burst apart, and a quick rush of heat surged across the area. The shrapnel soared from the burst point faster than anything she'd seen before.

The screams of the fae filled the hall, and all that wasn't bedlam reverted to it then.

Bodies pushed and pulled against her. Suddenly, she wasn't the bride-to-be of the fae king but another obstacle in the way of the crowd. Light surged among the night-filled hall where the fae called on their magic in their panic.

Anova ducked, her heart hammering in her chest. She needed to become invisible. She needed to find the wall.

Bodies, hands, and limbs pushed against her. She could hardly breathe.

In the sea of faces around her, Anova saw her. A wreath of fire danced at the edges where she'd blasted a hole through the wall.

Alys had taken one of the fae guards' swords. It, too, was alive with licking flames.

They had surrounded her, but she pitied the fae who tried to fight her.

Anova shoved through the tide of bodies to get to her. *Alys will know what to do. We'll leave this damned place together.*

If there was someone who could get her out of here alive, it was the witch. And if there was a way to end the crown of the blood curse without killing her, Alys would be the one to figure it out.

The closer she got, the more she heard her fight against Hellmyr's kings-guard.

"Give up, Witch!" The fae guards had circled her on all sides.

Alys gritted her teeth and parried an attack with her blade in one hand while her other conjured more flames in the palm of her hand.

"As if I wouldn't die before that," she snarled back.

"Alys," Anova called, but she didn't seem to hear her.

Her vision was swallowed by the wall of bodies around her again. Anova fought to squeeze through the moon-mad, blood-frenzied crowd.

With a final push, Anova shoved herself through the last of them before getting to the edge of Hellmyr's guards surrounding the destroyed wall. Anova smiled to herself. If there was someone who would rescue herself no matter what it took, it was Alys.

And she needed Alys on her side to do this.

The witch hadn't yet seen her. The flames on her sword flickered, illuminating her face in a strange light. One of the fae guards tried rushing her, but she dodged it and swiped him on the shoulder.

The fire took to the fae's skin faster than it should've.

Witch magic.

Alys's brown eyes narrowed on her foe. A breath dragged through her. "I should have killed more of you in that fire."

Anova froze where she'd been trying to get to her. She stared at her, and the witch finally noticed.

Hellmyr's words came to her then.

"It doesn't exist. It never did. I checked."

Hellmyr hadn't lied to her. There had been no anti-human artifact. She'd set fire to their training grounds for no other reason than to raze it to the ground.

And to kill some of them.

And she'd lied to her to do it.

In that moment, Alys saw that she understood.

She gave Anova a strange look—like she was pleading with Anova to agree with her. To understand that she'd done it for the greater good. For the good of humanity.

"You were in the High King's war notes," Anova told her.

"War notes. War," Alys had repeated dully.

To her, this is warfare, she realized.

Anova took a step back into the crowd. She lost sight of Alys in that short amount of time because she heard a furious voice ring out among the others. She dove back into anonymity among the limbs and bodies.

"Find her! Find her before—"

She heard no more. Before she could find her sword, something sharp slid into her skin along her hip.

Anova sank to her knees as blood spread across her white wedding dress.

CHAPTER THIRTY

She thought she stabbed her attacker back, but she wasn't sure. She couldn't even see their face. Anova lurched out of the way while she could still stand.

Her hand pressed tight against the wound. Dizziness washed over her.

I can't marry Hellmyr. I can't stay here.

But what other option was there before her? Warmth spread in her palm, and she pressed against it harder. It was only a matter of time before the moon-mad fae smelled fresh blood among them, and she would be caught.

There was only one choice she could make.

Leander … Please …

But it wasn't Leander who she found in the crowd of bodies. Anova's hand dug into Lycasta's shoulder when she sighted her.

"Get me out of here," Anova gasped, "and the crown is yours to destroy."

Lycasta jerked away from her. Her eyes flicked between Anova, the crown, and where Hellmyr must have been, clustered among his guards.

She made a noise behind her teeth but said, "Deal."

The fae lady twisted to look behind her. Leander was by her side instantly. Anova's heart lodged in her throat, but he seemed to look straight through her as if she were little more than an object. He settled his gaze on Lycasta.

Anova wanted to ask him if the ritual spell had had any lingering effects on him. She wanted to say anything, to tease out what hell this was between them if only to kill it, but there was no time.

"We'll leave with her. I need you to create a distraction." Before they were parted in the crowd, Lycasta stopped him and added, "Just please—make sure to come back."

"Of course," he murmured before slipping away again.

Her mouth was dry. She pressed harder against her wound and tried to breathe evenly. It was as if this Leander was a completely different one from the one who had stopped her from marrying Hellmyr.

And the one I plotted with to kill the High King.

Anova buried those memories. They were of little use to her now.

Lycasta smudged something over Anova's forehead before she could flinch away. "What did you do to me?" Anova snarled.

She could feel Lycasta rolling her eyes before she started to push towards the hall's exit. "I only altered your appearance and hid the crown. Keep up or you're getting left behind. Your witch's distraction won't last long."

Something settled low in Anova's stomach at the mention of Alys. The pain from the wound along her pelvis drowned out those thoughts, however. She was losing blood too quickly. It dripped down her leg and along the floor.

The moon-mad fae and his kingsguard were thinning now.

Before they reached the door, however, she passed by a reveling fae that grabbed her arm as she tried to slip past him.

The edges of his teeth poked past his lips as he spoke. "You smell of human blood." He sniffed, and then his eyes went to the dress she was wearing. Apparently, Anova's fae magic had done little for her outfit other than the crown.

"The blood crown," he snarled as he realized and pulled her to him.

Anova struggled against him, but the loss of blood made her too light-headed for her to grab her weapon in time. Metal flashed in the moonlight, and she knew without seeing it clearly that the fae had pulled out something to stab her with.

Her fingers went to claw out his eyes, but before she could get there, an arrow made of mist and whispers pierced the back of the fae's head. He slumped to the ground, bringing her with him.

Anova shoved her palms against the floor as she tried to slide the dying fae off her. But what she saw before her made her freeze.

In the center of the room stood Hellmyr. Above his palm hovered another arrow made of fae magic.

"The next fae to touch her dies," he promised. The cacophony in the room faded to dull murmurings.

Inside her mind, she swore. This was the end of the line.

But as she watched, a light burst behind Hellmyr. He turned, and Leander was behind him with a blade in one hand and fae magic in his other.

Anova wasted no time. Lycasta shoved the dead fae off her, and they started to sprint for the door. She knew she shouldn't have looked back, but she gave one last glance at the two fae who each held a fragment of her heart.

And she stopped. Leander had already been pinned to the ground by Hellmyr's guards. She couldn't see Hellmyr, but she was certain he was giving the command to kill him now.

"We have to do something," Anova said through her teeth when Lycasta turned to see the same. "We have to save him."

The fae lady only looked at her for a second before she seemed to decide something. Before Anova could get the question out of her mouth, Anova's back was suddenly pressed against the front of Lycasta's dress.

A knife had appeared out of nowhere, and Lycasta pressed it tight against her throat.

Lycasta's voice was loud. "Give him up or I kill her."

"Stop it," Hellmyr shouted at his guards holding Leander. When he saw Anova, something strange flickered across his face. His eyes travelled down to the red stain that had bloomed across her white dress.

Is that ... fear?

It was gone before she could verify it.

Even from this distance, she saw something pulse in the fae king's jaw. "Release him. Now," he told his guards.

Leander lurched forward holding one of his sleeves that had torn and started to bleed underneath.

Lycasta had already started edging them towards the doors. She cursed under her breath where only Anova could hear.

"The fae king is *not* an enemy we need."

Anova was silent. She needed this to work.

When Leander joined them in the threshold of the hall's doorway, they spoke no words between the three of them. In a blink, Lycasta had summoned a pool of moonlight with her other hand.

The air flickered around them, and then the doors slammed in on themselves, producing a click as they locked. Lycasta had locked the fae inside the hall.

"It won't hold them for long," Anova said, twisting to get out of Lycasta's restrictive grasp. "Especially since Alys already made them another exit."

As she spoke, Leander took the hilt of his sword and broke the nearest window. It was wide-set, big enough for any of them to get through. But it was too far from the ground to reassure her.

"We won't need long," Leander said as Lycasta came to the window and whistled.

Anova couldn't quite believe what she was seeing. She wouldn't have believed it at all if it hadn't been for Viridia and the other butterfly she'd watched transform into hoofed creatures.

Their orange and black wings fluttered on the air with ease. But they were much larger than any moths she'd ever seen.

Their eyes were black as pits, almost inquisitive as they beheld her. Before she could do anything, Lycasta took her by the wrist and dragged her to the closest one. Its insectile legs grabbed hold of her like a cage.

Was this the right option?

It's too late to go back, she reminded herself.

"Wait—she's hurt," Leander said.

Her heart shoved inside her throat. It was a fine time for him to start caring about what happened to her. But she swallowed that pitiful feeling as the moth released her.

"Quickly," Lycasta bade. "I can hear them down the hallways."

"Lay on your back," Leander murmured. "And don't move."

Anova tried not to think, but it was impossible. His hands worked quickly as he tore more of the dress to better reveal the stab wound. She sucked in a low gasp when he grazed it.

He seemed more careful of how he touched her after that. She felt the cool touch of fae magic on the wound. After, Leander took some of the torn wedding dress and tied them as bandages around her waist.

How she'd once dreamt of him touching her so closely. Anova looked away from his face.

And then her fool mouth said the words. "I guess none of what happened meant anything to you, is that it?"

But when she looked back to gauge his reaction, his face was unreadable. His eyes were tight.

"There is much you don't know yet," he said.

"Leander," Lycasta called.

They were coming. She heard their shouts.

The moth grabbed her once again, and Lycasta slid on the moth's back, just behind the joints of its wings. Beside them, Leander mounted the other moth.

The Eastwoe palace was gone from her sight in minutes.

CHAPTER THIRTY-ONE

When Anova woke, she was stiffer than usual. It was several seconds later when she realized that this was more than stiffness.

She'd been tied at her ankles and wrists.

Her breathing came too fast. It had finally happened. She was going to die. Some fae had finally caught her and intended to slaughter her to acquire the power of the blood crown.

Calm! Calm yourself! Note your surroundings and find out what's going on!

The fact that you aren't yet dead is a valuable clue.

But what it meant, she had no idea.

She was in a dark place. No, it wasn't that—it was simply nighttime. She was tied up on the earth, and the smell of smoke filled the air like a fire had started, but she didn't see its light.

It must be a small one, then.

Her breathing started to slow, though not by much. Her weapons were gone, of course. No captor would be daft enough to leave her with one.

Anova tried to crawl, but she was moving about as effectively as a worm in dirt. Her breath was ragged again, and she rested the side of her head against the earth.

What am I going to do?

She closed her eyes. She'd fought them off for so long. How had this happened?

The wedding. But I left …

She heard voices. Anova opened her eyes. There was still no sign of anyone or anything around her. She had to assume that the air around her had been protected from arrow strikes by the use of fae magic.

Their voices carried clearer when she held her breath.

"Where does that leave us, then?"

It was Leander. Sweat stuck her clothes to her skin. Her teeth grinded together.

She didn't care what was going on between her and Leander. She was going to murder any fae who thought they could tie her up like this.

And then, she heard Lycasta's voice, too.

"He wants to destroy the crown," she murmured. "But there isn't a way to do that without killing her."

Anova froze against the cold ground. Was it time? Adrenaline fueled her like food and steady drink. She would go down with a fight if she had to.

But is she right? Is there no other option now?

Anova bit down on her tongue. She could fall apart later.

But you traded the chance to be free of it—to live—for this fae bastard.

There had to be another way.

Hellmyr had another way, didn't he?

But he doesn't want to destroy the crown, she reminded herself. *He tried to transfer its power to himself.*

Another thought occurred to her then. She remembered Lycasta's words. Her brow creased.

Who are they talking about?

"We don't know that." It was Leander's voice again. His words made something in her stomach twist and crunch together.

He's not trying to kill me, then.

She squashed the hope within her. It was such a low standard.

"Regardless, he won't agree to the deal with the girl still alive," Lycasta said.

Anova stopped breathing. She needed to get out of here *now*. The edges of her fingertips could barely touch the rope they'd tied her with. But it would have to be enough to get her out.

Leander didn't respond for several moments. She wasn't sure if she wanted to hear what he had to say anymore.

"Is this the cost, Lycasta? Would you trade her life for this?"

There was something strange in Lycasta's voice. "With all we've been through, you wouldn't?"

"I don't know." Leander didn't speak for a moment. And then, he said, "We need to tell Cadmus. He's the one who wanted to go to the wedding and stop her. He'll wonder what happened to her there."

Anova stopped moving. She stared into nothingness.

Cadmus.

Her mind emptied at the name. She couldn't think.

She wished she could remain there like a grub under a leaf, undisturbed. There was too much meaning that came with that single word.

Cadmus.

The name was from a lifetime ago. It was Leander's real name—or rather, the name he'd had before his twin brother, Leander, had died in his place. It had been on a day that they'd been pretending to be the other.

That had been the day the fae known as Cadmus had died. He'd lived as his brother from then on to hide the fact that the High King had made a mistake and killed the wrong fae.

Or that was what *Leander* had told her.

She exhaled, and she felt as empty as a skeleton.

This—the fae who had rescued her with Lycasta—was Leander. The real one. The one who treasured books, knowledge, and ancient lore. Somehow, he was alive.

It explained why he seemed not to know her. It explained why he was comfortable working with Lycasta. Why he'd kissed her.

Her stomach dropped.

Where was the Leander she knew? Where was … Cadmus?

Anova thought back to what she'd heard during their conversation. They'd spoken as if he were alive and possibly even nearby.

"He's the one who wanted to go to the wedding and stop her. He'll wonder what happened to her there."

She swallowed. Trust was the fool's instrument. But it was as tempting as a breath on the bottom of a lake.

She had to find him. There were no others she could turn to, anyway. She couldn't remain with these fae. Lycasta needed her dead for a trade, and she wasn't about to stay and find out what it all meant. She'd heard enough.

Anova hadn't cut into her bindings at all, but she had to start moving. Her midriff ached as she crawled without limbs across the dirt. Somehow, she would untie herself.

As she crawled, she heard a sigh above her.

No.

With as much force as she could muster, she started moving faster. It did her no good.

A boot came down against the middle of her back. Anova twisted her neck to see the fae holding her down.

Lycasta frowned, the ringlets of her hair falling on either side of her face as she looked down at her. "He's not going to like this." Her lips pressed tight together as she considered something.

The fae added, "But Cadmus never liked me to begin with."

In the same second, Lycasta grabbed a fistful of her hair and pulled her head back. Her finger touched the middle of Anova's forehead.

Her magic was instant. She was out cold.

CHAPTER THIRTY-TWO

A persistent noise tugged Anova out of a deep, dreamless slumber. As soon as wakefulness was upon her, she wished for the numbness of sleep again.

Judging by the extreme stiffness that seemed permanently set into her joints and body, she'd been sleeping for far too long than was natural.

Anova opened her eyes as awful memories crashed into her.

She'd been captured and drugged.

Leander was alive, and Cadmus, the Leander she knew, was gone.

And she'd missed her one chance to destroy the crown without destroying herself.

Her breathing accelerated. It was going to hit her any moment now—the debilitating panic.

There'll be time later for that, she told herself, but it was hard to ignore a tidal wave. Anova focused on the small details near her first.

However, it was a struggle to understand what she was going on around her.

Although she was on a flat surface somewhere, she was clearly not on the ground. Anova stood and realized quickly that she was moving.

She was on a platform of sorts. At its edges was a glass dome.

Like a cloche, she realized. The realization did nothing to calm her nerves.

It was a cage, even if there were no bars or locks.

The platform was suspended in the air with a complex system of knotted ropes. The platform was swaying from side to side under a cathedral-like ceiling. As it moved, it paralleled another object in the air attached to the other end of the knotted ropes. It was a metal ball.

A counterweight.

Like a clock pendulum. Her stomach swam with the movement, though it was gentle. It wasn't the movement that had woken her but the sound of the metal whistling through the air past her glass cage.

Anova rested her back against the floor of the platform again. It helped to quell the feeling in her stomach that rose like bile. Her fingers ran over her body as she took stock of herself.

Like a stubborn old wound, the blood crown remained on her head. She supposed she should've taken that as a good sign that she hadn't yet died, but it didn't cheer her.

The wound along her hip had healed well. Her fingernail traced a pink scar that was the only evidence she'd been stabbed at her almost-wedding.

Her head sank back against the floor. There was too much to figure out and too much to do that was out of her reach now.

Alys had betrayed her trust. But then, so had Hellmyr. And Leander.

And Lycasta, though I was a fool to trust her in the first place.

Her hands bunched into fists at her side. She was done being the fool. Her breathing calmed.

What do you know of the situation?

As her mind went quiet, she started to hear raised voices from the other side of the glass cloche. She might have been suspended in the air, but there were people below her.

"This can't lead back to me." It was Lycasta's voice. Anova's teeth bit into her tongue so hard she tasted blood. "Swear it or the deal is off."

A laugh bounced off the many surfaces of the room. A fae whose voice she didn't recognize responded.

"Truly, Lycasta, what fool do you take me for? I'll swear under the moon if you so wish." His voice sounded careful and controlled. "Now, you have something to say about the details of our trade?"

"It has to be better than what you're offering," Lycasta said. "Something more."

Where is Leander?

"Something more than all my lands and all the contents of my treasury?" the fae male asked.

Lycasta made a sound with her tongue. "We could have that and more if we slew her ourselves. You know this." She paused. "My associates and I require something of more value than that."

Several seconds of silence passed in which Anova was sorely tempted to look over the edge of the platform she'd woken on to observe her captors more directly. But she stayed still.

The more she could learn about the situation before making her presence known, the better.

The male fae started talking again. "You and I both know there are no other associates, Lycasta. You came here alone with the crown."

She heard something like a hiss. Lycasta said, "As if I would do something like that. As if I would deliver to you the key to all of Fae with no safeguards. How daft do you think me, Artor?"

"You came to me because you panicked. Hellmyr has already sent his soldiers after you for her," Artor said. "And you don't want to become High Queen, or you would have made yourself that by now. No, you came here because you wanted the target off your back and a convenient trade in which you got the riches of a king without the mantle. You want clean hands and someone to kill the girl for you."

There was a pause before Artor added, "There will be no deal, Lycasta. I'm taking the crown."

"She's mine," Lycasta shrieked as Anova heard something break below her—or rather, many somethings.

Anova came to the edge where the glass cloche was and looked down. Artor stood in the center of his cavernous hall, his raised hand returning to his side. One wall of the room was crumbling into dust and mortar. Anova stared and tried to make sense of it. The crumbling wall wasn't opposite Artor but to his side. He wasn't even facing where it happened.

She saw the other fae then, a young one by the slightly rounder contours of his face and his smaller than usual stature.

"Excellent work. She might even be dead from that," Artor said, glancing at the ruined wall. "Now lower the human to the ground."

Anova's chest tightened. It had been a trick. While Artor had distracted Lycasta, acting as if he were going to attack her, his servant had come at her, unseen, and blasted her against the wall.

I can't underestimate this fae.

Anova flattened herself against the floor of the platform before it lurched downwards. His servant had loosened the counterweight, sending her much too quickly to the ground. In the silence of her thoughts, she plotted.

She was without weapons. They'd seen to that much. The most dangerous thing she could possess over this fae now was his underestimation of her.

I'll have to make it count, then.

She would feign sleep until they released her from her glass prison. When they stepped in to retrieve her, she would attack.

It wasn't one of her most sophisticated plans, but it would have to work long enough for her to acquire a weapon or her means of escape.

Though her eyes were shut, she considered just how she would do that.

Those moths. Lycasta doesn't go anywhere without them.

It was likely her only way out. Anova kept perfectly still as Artor's servant allowed the counterweight to finally rest at its zenith. The platform shuddered against the ground, and she dared not move or open her eyes.

There was a noise outside the glass, and Anova prepared her muscles for a fight. Artor was about to lift the glass from around her.

But the longer she waited for the moment, the more time seemed to stretch out before her. Anova dared not move the barest amount or fidget for risk of giving away the feign.

Her head grew heavy, and her body followed next. Her heart stuttered ahead at a new, disturbingly uneven rhythm like a wounded horse slogging through mud.

Anova forgot why she was laying there. It was better not to move, then, for risk of forgetting her reason for doing anything at all.

Her thoughts were slow to come to her.

What is going on?

A voice came from the other side of her glass cage.

"Hm. Most humans would be dead by now."

Anova opened her eyes. There was a thick gas collecting at the height of her cloche cage. It had fogged against the sides of the glass so that she could hardly see through the cage.

She knew she should've felt panic, but the feeling was as far away as the sun. It existed in theory, but it wasn't as if she could touch it.

He's poisoning me.

Anova stumbled to the glass. She needed to get out. Now.

Her fists pounded uselessly against the smooth surface. Tears started to streak down her face, but she bit down on the inside of her cheeks to stem them. She wouldn't give this sadistic fae the satisfaction of watching her weep while she died.

"Coward," she roared through her teeth. Anova leaned against the glass to keep herself upright. "Fight me."

On the other side, Artor was another breathtakingly beautiful fae. His brown hair curled at the edges of his face, framing his strong jawline. He smirked at her short words and her weakening state.

"The human queen of Fae. What an interesting creature." His hand pressed tight against the glass, and it clouded further. "It's a shame you had to die so soon."

CHAPTER THIRTY-THREE

Anova slumped against the ground as her breaths came shallower and shallower. There was little doubt now. She was going to die in this damned glass cage.

"I have too many plans for our worlds to allow your life to persist any longer," he said. "It's time the fae claimed what's rightfully ours."

For our worlds.

Anova had stopped moving to rest her head against the glass. The words ricocheted inside her empty mind, their meaning barely registering.

What's rightfully ours.

Hellmyr's voice whispered to her.

"Unless, of course, you wish to invade and start your reign over those lands, as well."

Once Artor seizes rule over Fae, he's going to come for the human lands. He's going to do what the previous High King failed to.

Anova's eyes opened. Her body moved as if it knew how to do this already—as if the energy within the crown had always been a part of her.

She stood in a fluid motion and placed her palms against the glass where Artor stood on the other side. For too many seconds, he watched with a bemused expression on his face.

"You will not get this," Anova said between her teeth. "You do not get to do this."

It was a matter of heartbeats before his amusement turned into frozen horror. Then, the light and heat consumed too much of everything for her to see his face anymore.

The world passed by her in a blur of motion and time, and she was suddenly on the ground. The pain searing along her nerves didn't subside for several minutes.

Once she could move, her hand went to her head. She winced from the pain. The crown still rested stubbornly there as if nothing had happened.

However, there was no sign of the glass cage around her, or Artor. Or even his young fae servant. She was alone on the floor of his hall.

Anova pushed herself off the ground before she could start finding bits of them. *A way out. I need an escape route.*

But there was no sign of Lycasta's moths. The pain behind her eyes built until it throbbed with each step she took.

What have I done?

With each time she tapped into the crown's magic, she dragged herself closer to death. Breaths huffed in and out of her.

There can't be much time left. I've used too much of it.

Anova addressed the painful truth.

She wasn't going to make it far in the fae wilderness like this. She might not even have days left to waste wandering about.

No, there was only one person who could help her now. And only one way to persuade her.

Anova kept one hand along the destruction that had been one of manor's walls. In her other, she held her palm before her.

Remember what it looked like.

She needed not to destroy the rest of the hall. She couldn't pass more hours or days knocked out by this cursed power on the floor of some dead fae's manor.

No, she needed access to it in a controlled manner. She needed a weapon.

It burst into existence with a crack like the sound of a man's back breaking. It hovered above her open palm, casting golden light like the sun on her skin. Its edge was keener than any metal blade's.

It was a loose replica of the knife she'd once carried with her in Irbess, though that one had never been this deadly. She knew without having to test it that the point would sink well past skin, sinews, and muscle with barely any effort.

The pain crackled in her skull, and she bit down on her lip. It became a currency for her. A taste of agony for borrowed power.

Even if it shortened her time and brought her closer to death. Right now, it was a necessary trade.

Anova straightened. In an odd way, the pain of the crown was her pet now: a clawed mountain cat that purred at the ends of her nerves.

She found the fae lady underneath a fallen column. It had caught on the crumbling wall, so while she was barely breathing, Lycasta was still alive under the pressure.

With visible effort, Lycasta opened her eyes at Anova's approach.

"Out of the two of you, I'm glad Artor was the one to die," Lycasta said in a series of gasps. Blood began to leak from the corner of her lips.

Lycasta smiled, and it was a ghastly sight as the blood spread. "After I die, at least Leander will be the one to wait this time," she added.

Anova's free hand pulled her by the front of her dress. "You will live. And you will tell me *everything* I want to know."

Dizziness flooded her, but Anova bit back the sensation. She'd never attempted anything with the blood crown's twisted magic other than destruction. In fact, she'd barely chosen to do that. Killing Strego and Artor and had been more instinct than anything else.

And it was a messy kind of magic. Consuming. Hungry.

Anova nearly lost her balance. Lycasta was staring at her. Perhaps she didn't have the strength to argue or resist what was coming.

Perhaps she wasn't as ready for death as she'd tried to seem.

With the hand that didn't hold the golden dagger, Anova pressed her palm against Lycasta's chest.

Mend her bones. Sew the puncture sites. Stem the tide of blood.

If only for a few more moments of life. If only for the answers I need.

It started with a gasp. Then, the fae lady was choking.

Anova removed her hand. This wasn't healing.

This was something else entirely.

Lycasta wasn't getting better, and she struggled to inhale even short gasps of air.

It's what she deserves, something inside Anova whispered. *This and worse.*

She should've felt satisfaction at seeing the fae who sold her die before her. Anova bit down on her tongue. She needed those answers.

It was the excuse she told herself when she shoved her hands on Lycasta again. The fae fought against her touch this time, but it was a losing battle.

Live. This time, you live for me. This time, you'll serve me.

Anova's vision flickered at the edges, but she pushed harder. Lycasta inhaled roughly, and with a few last bloody coughs, she was breathing normally again.

The fae lady wasn't doing well by any standard. But then again, Anova had only wanted to stop Death's date within the hour.

By pointing her fingers, Anova shoved the conjured knife at Lycasta. It stopped right before her throat.

Lycasta's voice was raspy. "What do you want?"

"You know what I want, Fae," Anova said. "I want you dead, but I need answers more."

"Fine," the fae managed to say.

"You were trying to sell me. Earlier, you wanted me to surrender so you and Cadmus could destroy the crown." She leaned close to Lycasta. "I want the truth. What do you really want here?"

"I don't care about the blood crown. I don't care about ruling Fae." The whites of her teeth showed as she lifted her lip. "But I wanted you gone with clean hands. Is that so hard to imagine?"

"I would be more careful with what you say," Anova murmured. She traced the blood trailing from the edge of Lycasta's face. She knew it would disgust her to have a human touch her so.

"It's the truth," Lycasta said, her eyes on Anova's hand. Her eyes flickered to her face. "And you know it. I just wanted … Leander. To myself."

Anova leaned closer to where Lycasta was on the ground. "Next. I thought Leander was dead. You know the brother I speak of. Not Cadmus. Leander."

Lycasta pressed her lips together. "That's not a question."

Anova shoved the point of the knife tighter against the fae's throat. "I don't like repeating myself," she said.

Lycasta swallowed as red beaded against her skin. "He was dead. *Is*. It's old magic that brought him back. Temporarily. It wouldn't have worked if not for Cadmus. And it wouldn't have worked for anyone else."

Anova tried to digest this information, but what she'd said only raised more questions.

Anova's voice was dry. "Why. How."

"Cadmus needed my services. I offered him a deal. He'd help me with the spell for bringing back Leander, and I'd help him find you."

His words came to Anova from when they'd met in the forest.

"I shouldn't have traded a thing to find you."

Anova's voice was tight. She felt when something rose in her throat. "Where is he? Where is Cadmus?"

What did he trade?

Lycasta was coughing. Anova jerked herself away from the fae lady. She hadn't realized she'd been pressing the knife into her throat.

She shot Anova a glare when her hand touching her throat came away red. Anova didn't care about that.

"Where is he, Lycasta?" she repeated.

Lycasta's eyes were like a cat's in the dark. "He's alive."

Anova stood. "You're going to take me to him, then."

CHAPTER THIRTY-FOUR

Anova's knees were pressed into the sides of the moth's oversized thorax, but it did little for her stomach. She needed to stop looking down so much.

The sun was hovering just above the horizon, as if it knew what horrors would be conjured in its absence by the fae below it.

In the moth's insectile arms was a barely-alive Lycasta. Their stint at Artor's manor had taken much more time than she'd hoped for. After she'd gotten information out of Lycasta, she'd stolen all that was useful and able to be carried on the back of a giant moth and left.

They'd been flying in silence for several hours, and Anova wasn't about to end the blissful nothingness between them.

Lycasta had told her what she'd needed to know. It helped make her feel better about leaving her alive, though she wasn't sure yet if she'd made the right decision.

She still couldn't believe that they'd raised the dead—though she'd witnessed firsthand a fae in the flesh who should've been dead. The thought made her stomach knot.

If that's possible, then ...

She stopped thinking on it. Lycasta had been certain to spell out what the magic had required.

Since Leander and Cadmus had been twins—*souls separated by the flesh* was her exact wording—they'd had a connection that allowed certain magic to pull him back from the realm of the dead.

Anova bit into her lip. There was no use speculating on it. Her mother was gone, and there was nothing anyone could do about that.

No magic fae spell could help that.

I still haven't even avenged you.

Lycasta's moth had started to lose altitude. They would land in a matter of minutes, now. Anova swallowed.

There was too much to think about, so she stared at the setting sun instead.

Inevitably, her thoughts went back to when Anova and Cadmus had talked in the forest. And when he'd crashed her wedding to Hellmyr to stop her.

Anova straightened. There was something wrong here.

Because that had been the Leander she knew. It had been Cadmus who had stopped her before she'd married herself to Hellmyr.

She was certain of it.

And yet, later that night, it had been Leander the scholar to mend her wounds. They'd left with him rather than Cadmus.

She recalled what Leander had said at the time.

"I guess none of what happened meant anything to you, is that it?"

"There is much you don't know yet," he said.

They were about to pass among the tops of the trees now. Her pulse pounded. Had they left Cadmus behind at the wedding?

Her eyes focused on the setting sun again. Something inside her brain clicked.

That's what he traded.

This time, she was going to strangle Lycasta.

Her hands gripped the moth's furred body. "We need to land. Now," she said.

If the moth had something to say about it, she couldn't hear it. As soon as she started to question if she should have said it, they started to fall like a stone through the air.

She held tight to the beast as they fell through branches and leaves. Lycasta's scream was cut off, and Anova's stomach twisted. The ends of branches scraped down her skin, and the three of them fell against the earth with a collective *thud*.

Anova was on top of her at once. Somehow, the fae looked even worse than she had before.

"Get off," she hissed at Anova, though she was too weak to fight much.

"That's what he traded, isn't it?" she said through her teeth. Her chest rose and fell too quickly. Anova's voice sounded strangled to her own ears. "Tell me the truth." Her hands pushed against her shoulders to hold her down. "He's using his brother's body. Every night."

At first, Lycasta stared, her bloodied lips tight. Then, she cracked a hair-raising smile. "You're losing time, human."

Anova bolted off the fae lady. As much as she hated her, she was right. She sprinted in the direction they'd been heading in the air.

It can't be much longer now.

Lycasta had explained in Artor's manor that Cadmus had hired her for her tracking abilities. According to her, she could find anyone in Fae with the use of her moths.

They were a species that had been trained with magic from the time they'd hatched.

Looking back, she was forced to believe her.

These thoughts fell away from her as Anova ran. The shadows grew as long as constricting fingers around her. She ran harder.

The scent of a fire laced through the trees. She broke through them to a clearing where smoke trailed into the sky.

At once, she saw him. And knew.

It was him.

His head jerked to look at her at once, his hand hovering over a sheathed blade before he recognized her. When he saw her, he moved faster than she could process.

His scent hit her before she realized he was before her. She drank it in.

"Cadmus," she gasped.

His dark eyes widened. "You know. Anova. You're alive." Each statement seemed a new realization for him. "That night, I thought you'd died—" His voice broke.

Her lips were on his mouth.

His hand was on the back of her neck, and he pulled her to him.

This time, she wasn't falling. She felt at home.

She knew she should have been disturbed by the thought, but she didn't care. She kissed him until she couldn't breathe, and then she kissed him more.

This was the fae who she had killed the High King for. The fae she would have died for.

Anova didn't notice when the sun set beyond the trees. But she noticed the shift in his weight and in the way he held her.

Before he could pull away from her, she slipped a knife free from her waist. She pulled away from his lips and looked at the face that was identical to the one she loved.

It wasn't him any longer. This was the original Leander.

She pressed the knife to his throat. As he tried to disarm her, Anova pulled the blade away and punched him along his jaw.

He staggered back several steps, his eyes dark in the shadows.

This is the other son of the previous High King's right hand. And judging by how he nearly disarmed me, he knows as much about weapons as his brother.

"You know." It was all he said.

Anova shuddered. It was exactly what Cadmus had said to her. And yet, the fae before her was a stranger.

Her voice was uneven. She hadn't quite caught up to the change. "She tried to sell me. Did you know she was going to do that?"

Her inclination towards hitting him again depended on the answer.

Leander took a step towards her. Instead of replying, he asked, "Where is she?"

She didn't mean to do it, but she glanced in the direction where she'd come from—and where she'd left Lycasta. He was gone.

CHAPTER THIRTY-FIVE

It was a meeting, as Leander called it.

It felt more like a hostage situation, though Anova couldn't figure out which of them was the captive and which the captors.

The three of them sat with their weapons before them. In Lycasta's case, her smaller moths had settled on the rocks around her, their wings fanning in the dim light cast by the fire.

Leander had healed Lycasta under the moonlight better than Anova had with her fumbling attempts in Artor's manor. Then again, she wasn't entirely sure she'd been trying to save Lycasta's life at the moment.

Even now, she itched to pull the weapons she'd stolen from Artor's manor into her hands.

Sweat slicked her clothes to her back. Were they accomplices? Enemies? Something else?

"The spell only worked because of who we were to each other," Leander said as he continued his explanation. His eyes lifted to the forest beyond them. "Magic like this must be accepted by the other party." He focused on her again. "Cadmus agreed to it."

"But how? How did it work at all?" She looked to Lycasta. "How did you know how to do it?"

The fae lady narrowed her eyes when she spoke. Anova held herself back from doing anything rash. "It's something I came across in the book I gave Cadmus."

Anova stared at her. "The book of fae tales?" Something else occurred to her. "You knew what we were using it for? That it had been written in code for the blood crown?"

Lycasta leaned back against the rock she'd propped herself on.

She must still be weakened from Artor's attack.

"I memorized it."

Anova's mouth popped open. She made sure to close it before Lycasta saw. It didn't matter. Lycasta's eyes were still closed when she spoke. "My father was the last caretaker of the Eastwoe archives," Lycasta said. "I memorized many of them."

Anova bit into her tongue. She didn't want to feel sorry for this fae. Or even impressed. But she couldn't help but pick up on one word.

Was.

She shook herself. The fae had always victimized themselves. What was new about that?

She was going to end that, though.

Anova breathed. She was running out of time by the second.

"But the spell only works at night, isn't that right?" Anova said. They were getting perilously close to the questions she dared not ask.

Is this permanent?

What's going to happen to him?

"Smart of you to see that. That's right," Leander said. He looked to the dark horizon. "And it will remain that way indefinitely unless the spell is completed or broken. Two of us in one body."

Anova's breath staled in her lungs.

Completed or broken?

She tried to appear calm, but her voice gave her away. "And what would complete or break it?"

Leander locked eyes with her. It was uncanny how alike they looked. "If each of us agreed, so it would be. The spell could be completed on the opposite of when it began—at daybreak instead of dusk." He leaned back again. "Or at least, that's my theory."

But she had a feeling his theory was correct.

"And ... what is it that you want?" she asked him.

Leander stared at the stars spread above him, tiny as specks of ocean spray. "I have decided. I was brought back to this realm for a reason." He looked at her. "There are things I excel at that Cadmus doesn't. I want to help you end it for good. The blood curse. There has to be a way to break it without more death."

Anova breathed. She wasn't sure what she expected, but it hadn't been this.

And then she remembered. She turned to glare at Lycasta. "And this one? She won't try to sell me to the highest bidding fae again?"

But when she looked at Lycasta—really looked at her—there was something strange in her face. She was allowing her moths to dance at the edge of her palm where the moonlight hit it.

Her voice was dispassionate when she spoke. As if it mattered not to her.

"What he wants, I want."

Something twisted in her chest.

She can see that it won't end how she wanted. Anova closed her eyes. *After he gets what he wants, she'll still be unhappy.*

Because he'll be forever gone then.

Anova swallowed those feelings. She didn't care for them. She'd gone long enough thinking that Cadmus had been trying to have her assassinated.

Lycasta got to her feet. Leander watched, ready to support her, but she remained steady.

She looked at Anova. "But your jilted lover is after us. He thinks we stole you."

Anova stood to face her. "Well then, you'd best tell me your plan to get rid of the crown so we can all be rid of each other as soon as possible."

When neither of them said anything to that, her mouth popped open. "Are you serious? What do you two have? Nothing at all? No ideas or leads?" Anova groaned and looked to the stars.

"We happened to be too busy getting you out of the lion's den first," Lycasta said from between her teeth.

Anova's head snapped to hers. "After which you tried to sell me for gold and land." Her blood throbbed in her veins, and before she was aware of it, her weapons were in her hands.

"I'm still considering it," Lycasta hissed, rising to her unspoken threat. "Exactly why are we helping the human again?"

"Why are you even here," Anova fired off. "Oh, that's right. Your fae boy. You'll do anything for *him*."

Leander was between them at once. "That's enough," he said in an almost growl. "Stand down."

He glanced down at her with a look that promised consequences if she didn't.

"Just make sure to control her," Anova said in a mutter, but she did as he said.

After they separated, Leander looked to Anova across the dying fire. "There is something we found between the two—three of us," he said, correcting himself. Anova bit down on her tongue at the exclusion. She needed to speak to Cadmus—soon.

Leander continued, "We might have a lead. It's from another fae tale."

"What is it?" She shifted where she sat against her rock. The fae tale about the blood crown's origin had been a code, and they almost hadn't figured out what it meant in time.

"The gist of it is that there could be an elixir that will cure all ills and purify any disease." He tilted his head. "And because the blood crown is a curse ..."

"You believe it will purify the curse," Anova said in a breathless whisper. She cleared her voice. "But where is it? What's the rest of the fable say?"

She couldn't let hope infiltrate her again. Not after the wedding.

But Leander was shaking his head. She went to him. "What is it?" she said between her teeth.

"You aren't going to like it," Leander said.

"Try me."

He looked at her like he was trying to understand why his brother wanted her around at all. The feeling was getting to be mutual—she wasn't sure what was so great about this Leander-lookalike.

Across from them, Lycasta said into the air, "Just tell her, Leander. She's not going to let it go if you don't. It's how she is."

Anova began to audibly grind her teeth, but Leander started speaking over the noise.

"Once, there was a girl and her mother who worked and lived together. They grew every type of herb and plant in their garden. They lived happily for many years until one day, the mother was stricken with a mysterious illness."

Leander continued, "The daughter fetched every remedy known to them and gave them to her mother. She tried alike witches' tonics and even fae magicks, but nothing improved her mother's condition. None of the herbs they grew improved her condition, either."

Anova was silent, listening for any detail that would provide them with the answer they needed.

He shifted. "The days passed, and she only grew weaker as the illness began to claim her life. The daughter counted down her mother's final days with a grim tally. After she had tried all remedies available to them, she cried during her mother's last days at her side."

Anova's stomach twisted. *It's just a fae tale,* she told herself, but she couldn't help the thoughts that begged to be acknowledged.

"Seeing her child weep so made her even more ill. When she called her daughter to her, she wiped the tears from her face and told her to cry for her no more. The daughter asked her why—after all, this was as difficult for herself as it was for her mother, even if she wasn't the one to suffer from the illness. Who would till the earth with her when she was gone? Who would rise with her to greet the sun in the hours of a new day? Who would enjoy the fruits of her labor with her after harvest?"

Leander's face was carefully blank. "The mother agreed with this. Her illness would last only a short while compared to the absence that would be inflicted on the daughter's life for the years to come.

"However, she told her that there was no reason for sadness. She had lived a good, long life with her daughter in the manner that she had wished. Her death may have been at hand, but there was nothing to mourn. The daughter knew that this would be the last time she saw her mother alive and stayed by her without crying until the girl fell into a deep slumber."

Leander looked at her. "In the morning, the daughter woke with a start. Her mother wasn't in her bed. Not finding any sign of her inside their cottage, she ran outside. She found her mother crouched among lilies, planting them along the edge of their modest home. She stood to embrace her daughter, alive and well again. She cried in her mother's arms, though this time with happiness at the many days they had together ahead of them."

He fell silent. Anova stared at the fae.

"That's all?" She narrowed her eyes. "You haven't forgotten something? Some innocuous detail?"

Lycasta said, "He's recited it nearly verbatim. That's all there is to it."

Anova turned to snap at Lycasta, but she stopped herself. She wanted to laugh. She'd allowed hope to latch onto her like a parasitic bug.

"We've checked every detail of the story just to be certain. Lilies. Tears." Leander pressed his lips together. "None of it has led to anything further."

Sometimes, fae tales are just fae tales. She wanted to say it, but the words got stuck in her throat.

No, she knew what she had to do now. It wasn't something she wanted to do. In fact, it was about the last thing in Fae she wanted to do.

Anova crossed her arms. "I have to go back to him."

At least Lycasta seemed cheered by the idea. Something in her face relaxed. She wanted her gone.

Leander turned to her. "What? We just got you out."

Anova looked away. His response reminded her too much of what Cadmus would have said.

I'll have to tell Cadmus, she remembered. But that was a problem for the day to come.

"Hellmyr told me he knows—" Anova bit her tongue. She'd almost said *he told me he knows what will keep me alive,* but she would have had to admit that she was dying if she were to say that.

And she knew she wouldn't be able to stomach Lycasta's reaction if she were to admit it. Her *joy*.

"He might know how to break the curse," Anova finished.

But that wasn't quite the truth. He'd only said that he knew what would prevent the crown from killing her. It was all she had now, though.

"He won't like it," Leander said.

They shared a look, and she knew that he meant Cadmus.

"He'll deal with it," she said. Her eyes left his face. "I'll tell him."

CHAPTER THIRTY-SIX

Anova wasn't tired. In fact, she was anything but. Living with the fae tended to make one nocturnal.

According to Lycasta, they'd been attacked most every night by Hellmyr's soldiers when they'd travelled. It was best that they moved during the day, then. And besides, as much as her stomach twisted at the thought, she needed to speak to Cadmus before they moved.

The fae had surrounded their campsite with barriers that she hoped would be enough to ward off both her assassins and Hell's guards.

Now, there was nothing to do but wait. But time was what she had least of.

The other two had curled up with each other on their roll of blankets. The weak flames from the fire barely touched their outline, but it was enough light for her to see that they weren't wasting their limited time together.

Any longer and Anova felt like she would vomit if she stayed there. She stood and announced generally, "I'll take first watch. If you're going to sleep, you should do it now. We leave at daybreak."

At which time I'll be able to stomach one of you at least, she thought but didn't say.

If the two fae who considered themselves the boss of her had anything to say about that, they kept it to themselves. She made a noise and turned her back to them.

Anova walked to where their magical barricades ended and gazed out into the forest around them. Leander had told her that they were fairly close to the Sorrelands. It was why the weather had been so temperate.

What was the real meaning of that fae tale?

Or was there one at all?

Anova allowed her mind to go blank as she stared out into the darkness. She found she did her best thinking without forcing it.

The moon passed overhead without incident. It stared down at her with its thinning face, reminding her of her mistakes.

How many more nights do I get?

The calculations would have been easy, but she wasn't ready for them. She'd passed too much time sleeping already.

Strangely enough, it was this thought she clung to as she drifted away from wakefulness. It wasn't her decision, but the body took what it needed regardless of deadlines.

She only realized she'd been dozing when she woke suddenly to voices raised just above a whisper.

Anova tensed. Before she pulled out a weapon, she realized it was Leander and Lycasta talking. The night hadn't yet passed, but it seemed they had stopped their incessant cuddling.

Lycasta's voice was unlike she'd ever heard it. Thin. Fragile. "So, you're giving up?"

Leander paused before answering. "None of what I said means that."

"But it is what you mean," Lycasta whispered. "After what I did—what we both did to bring you back."

"This is Cadmus's life." She imagined that he brushed the ringlets out of her face as he said it. "If I were supposed to have it, I would have lived that night instead of him."

Lycasta's voice was so quiet she barely heard what she said next. "But what if that's what he wanted, too?"

She heard one of them shift, presumably to glance at her, and Anova made sure to stay as still as possible to feign that she was still sleeping.

Leander's answer was equally quiet. "I don't think that's what he wants. I can't force him into completing the trade between our souls." He paused. "He cares for the girl too much for that."

Lycasta groaned. "Why are we trying to help her? It's not as if a human can live for much longer being such a target. She's like a piece of meat for hounds. Cadmus and Nerium should handle this themselves."

Anova hated how right she was.

He seemed to pause. Anova's blood boiled, but she stayed silent. "I believe in their cause. Maybe she'll surprise us," Leander said.

Before Lycasta could respond, Leander gave a sound like a snort and continued talking. "To think my brother fell for a human. He must have changed from the Cadmus I knew."

Anova was about to stop listening—as if she could force herself to stop—when Lycasta responded to what he'd said earlier.

"And what about your reason to live? There are those that care for you here, too." Lycasta's voice was little more than a breath. "I can't watch you give up."

Silence stretched through the campsite after that, and Anova could only guess what was happening then. She heard them no more after that.

Anova dozed, half-awake and half-asleep, until she shot awake at the realization that the new day was well started already.

Spears of golden light had spread across the belly of the sky above. The sun was properly clear of the horizon. She stood and turned. The two fae had fallen asleep holding each other. With a frown, she almost thought better of waking him.

He's not Leander anymore. He's Cadmus.

It was this thought alone that forced her feet towards them.

Anova crouched and reached for his shoulder. "Cadmus," she whispered to him.

His eyes opened at once, and his forehead creased when he saw her. He didn't seem to flinch from the fae lady in his arms, and his gaze shot to the horizon.

His name got stuck in her throat. This wasn't Cadmus. He untangled himself from Lycasta without waking her up.

Anova took a step forward when he took a step back from her and blinked.

"Leander?" Her voice was hoarse from disuse.

His gaze focused on her, and he came to her at once. After one head shake, he said, "It's me."

Cadmus. But she couldn't let herself be tricked.

Anova's knees nearly buckled, but she covered it up by taking a step back from him. "How do I know?"

His eyes smoldered with some dark thought. "Shall I recount every filthy insinuation you've used to distract me and cheat during our duels? Or perhaps every insulting name you've called me when I won in spite of your cheating?"

Anova's teeth gritted together. This was the fae bastard she knew. She narrowed her eyes at him. "Everything's fair in a fight to the death. Some fae once told me that."

His lashes brushed against his cheeks. "You're right, of course." He tucked a strand of her hair behind her ear.

She remembered the kiss they'd shared and nearly shuddered at his touch. *Control yourself!*

Anova swallowed. They needed to not waste this time they had, especially since they should've started moving by now.

She needed to tell him the plan while she could still speak to him.

"I've talked to your brother. We made a plan," she said. She watched his face carefully. "I'm going back to Hellmyr."

At once, his face twisted, and she saw the fae she met in the woods that day. "Are you so eager for a cage again?"

She couldn't look at him while she spoke anymore. She shook her head at the trees surrounding them. "There is no other plan, Cadmus," she bit out. "Surely, you know that." She swiveled to look his way. "You have no leads. And I do."

His expression was impassive, but his words were sharp. "And does this lead of yours involve attempting to marry him once more?"

"Of course not. I didn't know that it would risk giving rights to the blood crown away." She arched her neck to look at him. "You can't say without lying that you think I want that." She glanced away from him. "Not after what we did to try to destroy it."

Silence stretched between them for too long. Anova knew that he was thinking of the same memories. The death. The fear. The battleground on which they almost lost themselves a few weeks ago.

She'd been prepared to die if it meant destroying the blood crown—and if it spared him from the same fate.

"We can find it. The answer to destroying it." He snorted. "Believe it or not, he is better than me at something, even if it's only one thing." She caught sight of some rare fae emotion that flickered across his face. "I know with more time—"

He stopped. She wasn't sure why until he saw mirrored on his face the expression that must have been on hers.

Faster than she could blink, he was by her side.

"What is it?"

"There's not ..." She couldn't complete the sentence. She sucked in a gasp. She couldn't say those words anymore.

"There's not time," he said for her. His voice was strangely bereft of emotion.

They were only three words, but somehow, they were enough to undo her.

CHAPTER THIRTY-SEVEN

"The fable was right after all. It wasn't meant to be borne by a human." Anova didn't recognize her own voice.

"No. *No.*" Leander's chest moved up and down too quickly. "But you *lived*. It accepted you."

When she didn't respond, he forced her face to look at his. "Answer me, Anova. How do you know?"

Her voice was like fingernails scraping against rocks. She whispered, "It *hurts.*"

Silent tears fell along her cheeks as he pulled her to him. In his arms, she allowed that broken part of her to chip off entirely.

Against his chest, he told him everything. She told him about meeting the phantom of the fae princess. She told him about being hunted for the crown and accepting Hellmyr's protection in exchange for her hand in marriage. She told him about Alys's spell. And the blood she'd taken from him.

He was silent when he told her that—and what it meant.

Blood from a fae you love.

She found she couldn't speak after that. It was the closest she'd admitted to loving someone since her mother had passed.

But he wasn't saying anything. She couldn't stand the quiet. It had washed over them like a wave, and she was drowning in it.

"Forget it." She looked away from him, her teeth clenched against each other. "It was a fool thing to say. Even more foolish since I thought you'd sent an assassin after me. Which I still haven't been given an explanation for by either of the others, by the way."

"What assassin? What are you talking about?" His hold was iron.

She tried to pull away from him. This had all been a grave mistake. "As if you don't know. She was carrying one of your knives."

His jaw tightened. He lifted part of his shirt where his two blades were tucked at his waist, as plain as day.

Anova stared even after he'd allowed his shirt to fall and conceal them again. She didn't understand.

She'd broken the one that Lyrin had used to try to capture her.

Her voice was rough. "She had a knife like yours." Her gaze darted to his face. "Leander."

"These are each of ours. Our family only ever had the two," Cadmus said.

Anova shook her head. She'd assumed, just because the knife had looked similar, that it had been the same.

What a fool I am.

Cadmus seemed to understand her thinking now. She hated it. He said, "You really thought ..."

"Come on, it's not as if you didn't entertain it." She pushed harder against his arms and said, "Let me *go*."

"You thought I wanted you dead? Just because I wanted the blood crown destroyed?"

"Release me, fae," she said through her teeth. Her hands had gone to his wrists. If she applied enough pressure, he'd lose feeling and be forced to relent.

"Look at me." His hands found either side of her face.

"If I wanted more ridicule, I'd wake *her* up." She tried to jerk her head in the direction where Lycasta hopefully still slept, but she couldn't move.

His eyes were too mesmerizing to look away from, anyway.

"Listen to me," he said. "Before—until recently, the reason that I lived was to kill the monster who slaughtered them. Ending the line of High Queens and Kings was a mere bonus."

This version of him made her nervous, but she couldn't slip away from him now.

"And *after*—after we trained together, after I saw you every day," he said and paused. "After I started to understand you, it was nothing more than pure luck that I discovered the true price for destroying the crown before we enacted our original plan. That one of us had to die to do it."

"I don't understand," Anova said in a breath.

"Anova, I stopped living to kill him, and I started living because of *you*."

Her tongue felt too heavy to speak any longer. Such a thing was too much to accept.

"It made my decision to send you away—somewhere safer than Fae—all the easier. I would then be free to kill the High King myself and end the blood crown's reign with my own death," Cadmus said.

Anova's hands dug into his wrists. She didn't like these memories. *Safer than Fae my foot.* She'd been handed over to Hinterfell.

"A plan which we will no longer be considering," she said through her teeth. "You aren't sacrificing yourself for anything. And it's all a moot point now that I have it."

She narrowed her eyes at him. "Which brings us to another question—why stoop to working with her? It's clear she's only here for your brother."

"Anova," he said, and the way he said it made her want to shiver. "When I lost you after the High King died, I didn't know where you were. I didn't know who took you. I didn't know if you were alive." He breathed, and the air tickled her face. "I was afraid of finding you too late."

Her eyebrows pressed together. "That wasn't you? I woke up in a room." She struggled with the memories. She hadn't been well at the time.

And when she'd suspected she'd been captured, she'd escaped.

His mouth was tight. "We were attacked after the crown accepted you. Nerium and I couldn't find you anywhere." He gripped her tight. "Did they do anything to you?"

"No," she managed. "I got out before I even saw who it was."

"What about a name? A face?"

She shook her head. Not knowing their enemies didn't sit well with her, but the feeling was becoming familiar.

Anova realized something then. She held her breath. One fae was conspicuously absent. "Where is Nerium?"

But Cadmus was shaking his head. "For what I had to do to myself, I couldn't let him see that. He's been investigating leads for us. He'll back us up if we need it, though last time we spoke, he was in Farstar."

Anova looked to the horizon. They'd lost too much time already, but she didn't want to admit it. To her own surprise, she wanted nothing more than to remain here by their cold fire and talk like this.

But she didn't have forever.

He'd caught her looking. "How many days?" he asked her.

He didn't have to complete the thought. *How many days do you have left?*

It was something she asked herself too much.

"Maybe a week," she said in a tight voice.

"What?" He'd spoken much too loud. Anova tried to shush him, but she was fairly certain he'd woken Lycasta by now. He held her there, forcing her to look him in the eye. "Anova, what did you say?"

"I've lost track of a lot of days—"

"That's not enough time," he said for her. "Not enough for *anything*."

She felt like she couldn't get words out of her throat anymore. Fae always lived longer than humans.

Her lifespan should have been a blink to him. Always.

Young as he was for a fae, he should have been expecting that.

"What's a week to a handful of decades to you?" she said in an awful voice. "It was always going to be like this. This is what we humans are. Brief."

"Not like this." A vein in Cadmus's jaw flickered. "You deserve more." He held her face in his hands. "*We* do."

His use of *we* stopped her heart in her chest.

She couldn't speak anymore.

Cadmus held her against him in a silent embrace, and her face pressed into his collarbone.

For perhaps the first time since she'd been told she had a month left, Anova let herself lose track of her time. Like grains of sand in a timepiece, they fell without regard.

If she couldn't have this, then she would have nothing.

CHAPTER THIRTY-EIGHT

They came like an avalanche.

Anova extricated herself where Cadmus had been holding her on a soft woolen blanket. This paradise between them hadn't been meant to last forever, she knew, but it still stung.

Someone—or an army of someones—had found the three of them.

As the horses bearing the enemy tore up the earth surrounding their shelter, Anova prepared herself for a fight.

Lycasta was with them in a second, the supplies she'd gathered tossed on the ground when she saw them coming. She pulled out a small collection of knives between her fingers as her giant moth hovered above them.

They were magicless during the day like this, but at least their opponents were as well.

It was then that the arrows started whistling through the air around them.

Cadmus was a blur before her as he deflected their arrows. Lycasta settled into a battle stance she'd never seen from her. Anova pulled free her own blades, but fae mounted on horses met them at every angle.

In the back of her head, the buzzing started.

Not now, she bade the noise, but she'd never been able to calm the crown before.

The battle had smothered them before she'd had time to understand it. The fae closest to Anova leaped from their horses and came at her on her level.

A silver-haired one with sharp teeth beyond her lips grinned at the sight of Anova's blade. "The human-queen wants to play," she purred.

Anova ducked for the arrow she expected from her opponent, but it never came. Instead, fae arms came around her like a clamp.

Her stomach dropped. They were trying to take her. That could only mean one thing.

His voice soared over his squadron. "Surrender my queen to me, and I will consider sparing you of what I had in mind for you."

Hellmyr had found them.

Anova punched into the fae lady's gut who had nearly dragged her among his guards. She snarled at Anova as she slipped out of her grasp.

Hellmyr continued, "I will still kill you, of course, my dear friend Leander."

She heard his laugh over the sound of Cadmus slashing into the horse of his closest opponent. In front of her, Lycasta was barely holding the onslaught of his soldiers back.

Pain bolted through her, and she snapped back from the fae she'd been facing.

It wasn't that. It was the crown. Sweat stuck her hair to her head. Why was it happening *now*?

It wasn't as if she'd taken it off.

Lycasta threw a look behind her at them and said, "Give her to them. *Now.*"

"Not like this," Cadmus said between his teeth.

Anova was surprised to find she agreed with him even though returning to Hellmyr had been her plan. They hadn't even developed how they'd do it yet. They'd barely spoken.

It was then that she heard the sound of something metal piercing flesh. It was like the sound of clothing ripping.

Her heart was in her throat when she spared a look next to her to see him. Cadmus had taken an arrow to the shoulder, and red was already pooling under his clothes.

On her other side, Lycasta's screams joined the chorus in her head. Anova couldn't see what had happened.

Above the horses and the fae that had closed around them, she knew Hellmyr was watching.

She wasn't going to let them die for this. Not even Lycasta. It was time to end things.

But when she caught Cadmus's eye, the look he gave her was almost enough to make her stay.

There was no time to form a plan or even for a goodbye. But that didn't mean she was ready to leave him.

"We're going to live," she mouthed to Cadmus.

The skin around his eyes tightened for a moment, but she didn't get the chance to see his response. Pain, the kind that holds breath prisoner, flickered from the crown of her head to her feet.

She was on her hands and knees before she realized what had happened.

Somehow, Cadmus had kept the fae away from her when she'd collapsed. She came to her feet with a lurch.

Motion out of the corner of her eye stole her attention. It was the fae who had fired into Cadmus's shoulder. He was readying another bolt.

Anova didn't have time to decide. She shoved herself in front of Cadmus.

"That's enough!" she said. "Bring me the fae king."

She wasn't sure if they would obey her, but they parted, a wall of guards on either side, until he came forward.

He was as she remembered, far too pretty for one so wicked. His cloak of ravens' feathers cascaded down his shoulders and back until the end of it rested on his horse's romp. Hellmyr's eyebrows were near his hairline but his voice was lazy, as if she had interrupted him from some pleasure.

"You wished to speak to me?"

"I'm coming with you," she said, shooting a look at the fae guards around her who had accosted Cadmus and Lycasta, "but they leave from here alive."

The fae with the crossbow stood behind Cadmus, the edge of his next bolt pointed at the back of his head. Lycasta had been pinned to the ground by another one.

Before Hellmyr could respond, Anova felt as if a lightning bolt of pain had entered her through the base of her skull. Her hands pressed tight against her temples.

What do you want? You already have my life. What more could you take?

The ground rose up to meet her, but before it did, hands steadied her back on solid ground.

"Thanks—" Anova's teeth bit into her tongue. It was Hellmyr who had helped right her.

How did he get over here so fast?

She blinked. Cadmus's jaw ticked with visible anger. The edge of the bolt was pressed tight against his head.

"Where did you come from?" she managed to grind out.

"I wasn't simply going to let you fall," Hellmyr whispered against her ear. She could feel his eyes dart to Cadmus and Lycasta.

Before she could respond, he'd lifted her in his arms and started carrying her.

"I can walk," she said between clenched teeth.

"It's worth it for the look on their faces," he said, not even bothering to whisper anymore. The expression on his face slid off. He narrowed his eyes but kept his gaze straight as he carried her. He said under his breath, "Are you hurt? I told them not to hurt you."

"No," she said in a tight voice.

There was no need to explain. She was sure he knew what was going on.

She added, "There was no need for all of this, you know. I needed to find you."

He swallowed at her admission. He liked to hear it, she realized.

The last time I saw him, I left him at our wedding.

She looked away from the collection of faces staring at them. She couldn't believe she was feeling sorry for him. He was the king of Fae, after all. He took what he wanted when he wanted it.

He helped her mount his horse first before he got on behind her.

As his arms came on either side of her to hold the horse's reins, she tried not to think the thoughts she'd once thought about him.

He sighed and brushed his mouth near her ear. "Are you sure we can't kill them?"

"Yes," she said through her teeth. "Those are my conditions."

Just as suddenly as they'd appeared, they were leaving. His guards insulated them on all sides.

She hadn't meant to look back, but she couldn't stop herself.

They were already gone.

CHAPTER THIRTY-NINE

Anova matched the stride of the fae king as they stalked down the halls of Eastwoe palace. On the way back, she'd told him how many days she had left.

In reality, she had less.

Pain was still flickering through her skull, but she ignored it.

Hellmyr was already shedding his outerwear from the ride. He handed his feathered cape to an attendant as he said to none of them and all of them, "We'll be in my chambers. You are not to disturb me for any reason. Whatsoever."

She could feel the eyes of the fae on them. Perhaps her cheeks should have reddened at the thought of being alone with him in his rooms. She couldn't bring herself to care what they thought anymore, however.

The door shut behind them as his guards took their station outside his rooms. Her pulse raced fast enough to make her dizzy.

She said the only thing she could say. "At the wedding, you said you found a cure." She locked eyes with him. "Were you telling the truth?"

She wished she had his senses then. She wished she could hear his heartbeat hasten.

"Yes," he said.

She could have slid to the floor, but she balanced herself with the back of a chair. His eyes didn't miss it, but he didn't move.

"Hellmyr." It was strange to say his name again. She wasn't sure how she felt about that. Or him. She closed her eyes. "What is it?"

He didn't answer at first. After a moment, he said, "You can only live if you accept the blood crown. You must allow its magic to become a part of you."

She opened her eyes. That wasn't what she wanted at all.

"What?" The word was forced out of her gut. "No. I have to destroy it. I need to end it." Her teeth grinded together. "Why can't you see that? Its existence only hurts Fae and everything around it."

"Anova," he said, his eyes hard. "It will kill you. Whether you wish it or not, it will spill more blood to destroy it."

Anova pressed her palm to her forehead. This was the answer.

Live.

Or die for her cause.

But that's always been the question, hasn't it?

Anova's breath rushed out of her. She thought she'd been ready to die when she'd killed the last High King.

But that's because I was saving him, *too.*

She didn't like this voice. Who was she saving with her death this time? Another ugly realization hit her.

This time, if I die, he might, too.

Her stomach roiled. Cadmus had told her that he had chosen to live because of her. And if she died?

He'd take the deal with Leander and Lycasta.

"I can't," she said in a much smaller voice than she'd hoped to use. "It would never end. The assassinations." Her eyes darted to his. "They would eventually succeed."

Inside, she was a coward. This, she knew. Now that she'd had a damning sip of hope, she wanted to live. Badly.

"I know." His eyes darkened. "But it's not the only option, Anova."

"What are you talking about?"

His voice was careful. "I have a new offer for you." He turned from her to look through his glass doors to his balcony. "With no half-truths from either of us this time." He sounded as if his eyebrow was arched.

She crossed her arms. Last time she'd seen him, he'd conveniently not told her that the rights to the blood crown might transfer to him, too, if they married.

"Fine. What is it?"

"Joint rule over Fae. We spread the risk of the crown between the both of us. And the power." He turned around, and his face was straight. He wasn't joking. "We marry—but with no lies or manipulations this time. You will have my protection for the rest of your life." His voice went oddly hollow of emotion. "No matter who you choose to share your bed with."

"Hellmyr." She wasn't sure what else to say. She felt as if he'd taken a spear to her stomach, and she couldn't figure out why.

She took a step forward. And then another one. This was exactly how it was when she'd tried to seduce him.

He didn't care if she used him.

She took another step and forced the both of them against the wall, aware of how foolhardy she was being. He could have her head on a plate in a matter of seconds. He was the king of Fae.

"Why? Why are you offering me this?" she asked. "You should want to kill me instead."

Her blood ran with some irrational emotion, but it was too late to stop herself. She continued, "You could have all that and more in the blink of an eye instead of all this work to … to keep me alive and by your side."

Anova hated saying it but she hated being a burden even more. And she hated that he wanted her to use him like this.

He hadn't stopped her yet, so her mouth was still saying things. "But most of all, it doesn't make sense," she said. "Why. Why choose me? Why keep your human novelty around for all this effort?"

His dark eyes blazed as they glared down into hers.

"Novelty? Is that what you think?" His lashes brushed against his cheek. Was that anger?

Somehow, it made her madder.

"What else could I be to you?" she said.

He stepped even closer, and she could hardly breathe. "What is it going to take to convince you?"

Looking into his eyes was like gazing into a snake's. She couldn't look away. But she knew there was something more that she wasn't understanding. A missing piece of the puzzle.

Why did you go from taunting me as Cadmus's pet to this?

"The truth," she said. "I know there's more to it, Hellmyr. I want the truth."

He was silent so long that she wondered if he'd changed his mind—if he was contemplating how much more useful and easier to handle she'd be if she were dead.

A lot, she knew.

But a quick, startling smile spread across his face. "So, you want the truth. The ugly, monstrous truth." The smile fell from his face. "You're too clever for anyone else, to begin with."

"Clever enough to get what I want, perhaps," she said. She wouldn't be distracted from her answers.

"Very well." Hellmyr narrowed his eyes. "Some years ago, a fae lord brought the youngling he was raising past the barrier and into the land of your people. It was there that, as he collected the dues from the bargains he'd made with the foolish humans, the youngling was allowed to do as he wished. He cursed the humans there without regard to the rules that the rest of our kind adhere to. Old men became lampposts. Infants turned to stone. He was cruel. Malicious."

Anova stared into his face. She didn't have to guess who this youngling was, though she hoped she was wrong.

His teeth showed as he continued to talk, forming a bitter smile. "Not that the fae lord took any issue with this, seeing as they were humans. They would revert back to their natural state once the moon passed, but they didn't understand. They wanted something done about it." Hellmyr paused. "So, they consulted the only one of them who could hope to stand against a fae lord and his adopted son. A witch."

Anova couldn't breathe. "Alys," she gasped.

Hellmyr gave a short laugh that didn't sound like a laugh at all. "Not a young one. One wizened with years and fingers stained from poultices."

Anova's throat tightened. She didn't like this. "What happened?"

"The humans begged her to kill the fae lord's young, but she refused. A life hadn't been taken, she argued. It would be unfit. So, the next time the fae lord brought the youngling with him to collect on his bargains, the witch lured the fae child away and cursed him."

She could only stare at him.

He continued, "For this fae who so hated humans, he would be doomed to fall in love with one of her kind. A human. Only then would he find happiness in his cursed, half-filled existence."

By the end of his story, his voice had changed from one empty of emotion to one that sounded as if he were drowning.

"Hellmyr," she said in a breath. It was too much to understand.

He couldn't love her. Not like this. It was too much. Her heart felt as if it were being squeezed and drained of blood.

"I'm not done," he said simply. He was back to his strange, empty tone. "When the fae lord discovered what had happened to his claimed son, he took him back to Fae. At once, he sought an audience with the powerful High King.

"His son's life was ruined, he argued. He couldn't live a normal life cursed by a witch to love a human," Hellmyr said. "The High King considered the matter and agreed with him. Something must be done. There must be consequences. So, together with his kingsguard, they came to the human lands and killed the last witch."

Anova backed away from him several steps.

"No," she said.

Hellmyr wasn't saying anything.

"That was Alys's mother," Anova said. Her voice broke. "But that didn't solve anything, did it?"

"It didn't." Hellmyr's voice was low.

Her hands ran through her hair, running up against the cold metal of the crown. It was all too much.

"When I watched him bring you to Fae, I was angry. I didn't want anything to do with a human in case you were the one." His eyes flashed in the dark like a cat's. "And then, the more I saw you, the worse it got. The more I realized."

"And all this time." Her voice was almost silent.

He stepped closer to her. "I hated you for it, you know. I hated that you could hold this power over me. I hated that you reminded me of the foolish, proud fae who raised me and the witch he had killed because of me."

A long breath dragged through her. She remembered when she'd first met him in the boundary forests. The hate gleaming in his eyes at seeing her. "The feeling was mutual."

She swallowed. She hadn't even chosen to say *was* rather than *is*.

He was close enough to touch her now. He did so, brushing his thumb along her jaw until he pushed a strand of hair behind her ear.

"But you became more than the human come to remind me of my curse. Even if you were here to undo me, I started to want that, too," he said as his hand traced the back of her neck.

Her blood thundered through her. She couldn't accept this. Another fae had already stolen what remained of her heart.

His voice was dull and quiet. She almost didn't recognize it. "Anova. I need an answer."

Anova felt like she was being dragged down to the opaque depths of the ocean where it was quiet but suffocating and inevitable.

She envied the bottom.

In a single motion, she took a step back and left the room.

CHAPTER FORTY

A day passed in which she didn't speak to him.

In that time, however, he sent a messenger to her rooms. It was phrased as a request, but she knew it was meant to be taken as a summons.

To her relief, Della and Maris seemed to have been taken care of here and simultaneously left alone by the cruel fae. She supposed she had Hellmyr to thank for that.

Or maybe he knew that she wouldn't have forgiven him if something had happened to them in his palace.

Anova knew she should have been saying something to Sera by now, but she couldn't seem to parse through her thoughts enough to form any coherent answer. Her nails dug into the chair she gripped.

She'd woken up screaming again, but this time Sera hadn't checked on her. Perhaps she knew by now that the bolts on the windows were secure and that it was the blood crown's doing.

Hellmyr's words still ran through her brain.

"You can only live if you accept the blood crown. You must allow its magic to become a part of you."

And then, of course, there was his proposed bargain. She fought back the memory of him touching her skin.

He'd requested her presence at sundown in the palace's grand hall. She had little doubt that it had to do with what he'd told her about the *cure* for the blood curse.

"My lady?" Sera said. The skin around her eyes tightened. It must not have been the first time she'd asked that. Anova was aware she wasn't acting normal.

Anova blinked when her next step came to her. She knew what she needed now. She needed to talk to Cadmus.

What will he say? If my death is the only way to destroy it, what will he do?

All at once, she dreaded knowing. But she had to do something.

"I need to get a message out to someone before tonight. Please." She gripped Sera's shoulders. "Can you think of any way to do that?"

Sera's human eyes widened. "I don't—"

"Any way," Anova repeated. "If you can think of a way, even if it sounds ridiculous, *please* tell me."

Sera was silent when Anova released her. Anova suppressed a sigh. Short of asking Hellmyr for help, there was no other way, then.

And she couldn't let him know that she was trying to talk to Cadmus.

Breath dragged through her as she went to her window. She was on her own, then.

It was then that she heard a door close. Sera had left her, too.

What do I do?

She could leave. But where would she go? She had days. Maybe.

Anova sank to the floor and pulled her knees close to her. The motion triggered the pain hiding in her skull. She swallowed the cry of pain that rose up inside of her like an air bubble from the bottom of a lake.

There had been no answers here. Or, none that she could use.

Allow the blood crown to persist. Become a target for the rest of my life for power hungry fae.

Her heart skipped a beat.

Rule beside Hellmyr as his wife.

And then there was the other option.

Die and destroy the crown.

Her nails dug into her scalp as a new wave of pain washed over her. How was she supposed to accept the blood crown when all it wanted to do was to kill her?

The door to her room opened, but Anova found that she either couldn't or didn't want to move. It mattered not which it was.

If it was her assassin come to kill her, then her decision would be made at last.

But it was Sera who crouched beside her. Anova could only stare at what was in her fist.

"Where did you get this?" she whispered.

Sera stiffened, her lips tight together, and Anova thought better of the question. "Actually," Anova added, "never mind. I needn't know."

Anova took the vial without another word, and Sera left just as silently as she'd entered.

She stared at the vial, swishing the liquid within. There was no doubt. It was fae magic.

The intention behind the magic is set when it's summoned from the moon. Anova considered this. Wherever Sera had gotten this, some fae had likely intended to use it to communicate outside the palace with someone else.

She's stolen it from a guard, likely. Or even someone higher up.

Anova realized then. *It must be for her sick grandfather.* Her stomach swam. She hadn't even asked her about him recently.

This wasn't only about her. This was about fae and humans and who ruled this land. It was about wars and peace time and witches.

Anova put the vial on the floor. She was being selfish. Sera had risked much to be able to talk to her loved one.

But I have to talk to him. I have to know ... if it's best.

She couldn't bring herself to finish the thought.

No, she would use only the smallest amount of this fae magic. Then, she would return it to Sera's room and promptly forget that the girl possessed it.

Anova first pulled an empty wash basin before her but thought better of using it. With the vial tight inside her fingers, she froze in front of the floor-length mirror standing near her bed. She swallowed.

The last time she'd used stolen magic, it had resulted in unpredictable effects. There was no guarantee that this would work.

In fact, there was a strong possibility that this would backfire. Sera hadn't said what the fae magic would do—she'd only assumed it had been an answer to her pleas.

After she unstoppered the vial, her hand hovered over the surface of the glass. Anova allowed only a dribble of it to slide out of the bottle's mouth.

Where it touched the glass, it spread until it coated the entire surface in a cloudy white. She replaced the cork inside the vial and, with one extended hand, touched the mirror with the tip of her fingernail.

When it had no ill effects on her, she pressed the edge of her finger to it carefully.

The surface was much cooler than it ought to have been, but there was no change other than that.

Cadmus, please, I need to speak with you.

With a firm touch, she pushed against the surface, but it was a solid as it was before.

Anova closed her eyes. It wasn't going to work.

The pain flared again at the ends of her nerves, taunting her. It was as if it had watched and waited for her lowest point possible.

She slid along the side of the mirror until she came to the floor. Her teeth gritted together, but she couldn't hold back the gasp of pain that escaped her throat.

It washed over her like a wave and pulled her down with it. Sweat coated her back, and she focused on taking shallow breaths to keep breathing.

"What am I going to do, Cadmus?" she whispered against the glass. "Where are you?"

Anova jerked upright, her heart pounding at the sound of his voice. It had been too clear to be a hallucination, or had it?

"Anova?" Cadmus asked again.

She came to the mirror with the fogged surface, and her palms slammed against it. It was still solid, yes, but she could hear him as clearly as if he was on the other side of the glass.

The fae magic!

"I'm here," she whispered against it. "In Eastwoe palace. I'm using fae magic—I think." She swallowed. "I stole some."

It was easier than explaining the full truth, and who knew how long the magic would last?

"Are you okay?" There was an urgency to his voice that made her pulse race.

She knew what he was truly asking. *Are you alive? How much longer do you have? What's going on?*

"Are you alone?" she asked.

There was a pause.

"Alone enough—yes," he said after a moment. "I've been trying to get to you. The barriers on fae magic he's placed on the palace are difficult to break."

Thank you, Sera, Anova said in silence. She owed her more than that for passing her some of the stolen fae magic, she knew.

"What have you found out?" she said.

"Nerium came back," he said. Anova's heart soared. "He found no trace of the elixir."

She sank lower to the ground. Suddenly, she was glad he couldn't see her. But what had she expected?

"Anova?" His voice rose. "Are you there?"

She blinked. She realized she hadn't answered.

"I'm fine."

"You're not," he said. She narrowed her eyes. She thought she'd been careful in concealing her voice. "Did that bastard do something to you?"

"No, it's not that." Her voice closed around the words. She couldn't ask him what to do. Not anymore.

Anova was too afraid that he would choose the crown's destruction over her life.

But she needed to do something. She needed some other way out of this.

There's someone who doesn't want this. Someone who would do anything to destroy the crown.

She started again. "Cadmus. I need you to do something for me."

"What is it?"

Anova couldn't believe she was asking for *her* help, but she was at the end of her options. "Lycasta's moths are trained to track, aren't they?" She breathed, considering how to ask the questions she needed to. "How does that work?"

"They smell using their antennae. They're trained from birth with the help of magic to be much more sensitive to smell than other moths. Their size helps, too." Leander paused but only for a moment. "As long as they have something with the scent on it, they can usually find the person."

Something with the scent on it. She frowned. Anova had only the clothes on her back when she'd escaped her wedding.

And then it came to her.

"The sachet of salt I took from her room," she said. "I left it behind at our camp. That will have her smell on it." Anova realized she needed to explain herself further. "I need you to find the witch from the wedding. Her name's Alys. The salt was hers."

He was silent another beat before he said, "This is someone you trust, then?"

She wondered if she did. She decided to be honest.

"I don't think it matters anymore," Anova admitted. "There's no one else who can help us."

A noise from outside her bedroom stole her attention. There was someone else inside her suite.

"I have to go," she said in a tight voice, already pulling away from the mirror's cold surface.

"Wait," Cadmus said in a rush. "Did he have a cure or was it a lie?"

"It wouldn't destroy the blood crown," she said flatly, "so, no."

She didn't have time to stay and hear what he said next. There was a furious knocking against her door.

Sera said, "My lady, there's—"

Anova jumped to her feet, and the room swayed around her.

But instead of Sera, the fae king stood before her. His eyes narrowed on her as she backed into the mirror and tried to partially block it with her body with a casual motion. She hoped against hope that it wasn't still cloudy.

He took in her form. "What's going on?"

"Nothing," she lied.

I have to do better.

She stepped forward. Either the mirror was still enchanted by the fae magic Sera had stolen or it wasn't.

Her arms crossed before her chest. "Don't you usually have your guards do this part?" She cocked an eyebrow. "The dragging while I kick and scream?"

Somehow, his eyes were on her and not what was behind her. His thumb propped her chin up, and he held her gaze on his.

"Because I wanted to remind you," he murmured.

"Of what?" She glared at him. "Your power? Your position?"

"Of how much you want to do what I say." He smirked, revealing some of his too-sharp teeth. "I can tell by how your heart throws itself against your ribcage."

"Hellmyr," she growled under her breath. He wasn't being fair, outing her like that.

But it had worked. The fae king had turned away from her and the mirror. He hadn't even looked behind him to check that she was following.

Pompous ass.

Against her better judgment, she followed him out of her bedroom. Hellmyr took only a moment to examine how she'd showered her personal effects about her suite. It was less decoration and more disaster, and it unnerved her to see him look at the mess so closely.

"Looking for something?" she asked as she passed by him on the way to the door. The sooner they got this over with, the better.

He smiled his fae smile. "Just enjoying learning more about you."

He held the door open for her, and she walked through it with grinding teeth.

"If you're taking this as a *yes*, you should know I haven't decided on a response yet," she said as they walked through the palace's halls.

"You're wrong." He looked at her from the side of his eyes. "Or, at least partially. Your heart already has."

"That's not true," she said while adding, "and stop *cheating*. I'm just nervous about anything that involves this damned fae crown."

Next to her, he shrugged. "If you say so. Besides—"

He was suddenly in front of her, blocking her path with his body. Anova reached for the weapon at her waist and realized that it was gone.

"First, you will live." The darkness in his eyes smoldered as his lashes brushed against each other. "Then, I'll make you beg to marry me. And more."

Heat raced across her cheeks and ears. She hated how easy it seemed for him to rile her.

She pushed past him, her hand going reflexively to her waist before she remembered what had angered her in the first place.

She spun on him. "Did you take my sword and daggers?"

They were the first things she'd stolen in too long. For that reason alone, she missed them. The fact that they were her only defense here was fuel to the fire.

When had he lifted them? She pushed this concerning line of thinking aside to deal with it later.

Hellmyr lifted his shirt. Tucked inside the waist of his pants were her sheathed daggers. Inevitably, her eyes roamed to what they were shoved against: the bare skin of his lower stomach and the muscles underneath it.

"I can show you your sword too, but—"

"No, no. Don't," she managed to get out. "Just give me the daggers for now."

She held out her hand. She'd have to clean them, of course. Perhaps Sera would be able to find a good metal polish when she got back to her rooms.

Hellmyr let his shirt down again. "No."

"I'm not going to try to kill you," she promised. "So, give them back."

His arms crossed. "I'm afraid not. Not until we've tried this. You'll get them back at dawn."

Anova felt her eye twitch. Briefly, she considered fighting him for them.

Before she could convince herself of the merits of doing so, she pushed ahead of them again.

"Fine," she said. "We'll do it your way."

Best to get this over with, then.

She wasn't sure when she'd agreed to even do this. She certainly hadn't agreed to any of his other proposals.

Including his marriage proposal.

She breathed to calm herself. Hellmyr had caught up to her again and led them to the doors of the palace's great hall.

Anova wasn't sure what she expected inside—perhaps other than an empty hall—but she hadn't expected the figure standing in the moonlight before them.

CHAPTER FORTY-ONE

The fae lady raised her arms. Pale moonlight fell into her palms like water. It was the last Anova saw of her before white flames consumed Letharia.

Hellmyr pulled Anova back. She wasn't sure when she decided she would rush towards her, though it concerned her to see him so nonchalant while his mother burned before them.

"Just wait," he said next to her.

When Letharia emerged, the flames parted for her. She was utterly untouched.

As she passed, a flame caught on a single strand of her raven hair. It ignited immediately and sped towards the top of her head before the fae caught the errant flame and extinguished it with moon magic.

"You either control magic or it will control you," she said, stopping before Anova. "Including yours."

Mine? She had no magic.

"This is different—"

"It doesn't matter that ours is different from that which is contained in the crown," Letharia interrupted. "Witch magic. Fae magic. It doesn't matter."

Anova looked sidelong at Hellmyr. He hadn't mentioned involving his mother.

"In the archives," Letharia continued, "you wanted answers. You wanted to know about the crown." She tilted her head. "Or is this no longer the case?"

"I do," Anova said. "But that doesn't mean I want to use the crown."

"Hellmyr has told you the only way for you to live is to accept the crown. This means accepting its magic and allowing it to become a part of you," Letharia said. She stepped back a few steps. "We don't have time to waste. You'll either leave now, or we'll start already. If you still want that, you'll stand at the marked place on the floor."

"We'll see about that," Anova muttered, but she did as she asked.

Hellmyr went to the opposite side of the room, watching her with an inscrutable expression.

Suddenly, Letharia's white flames died. She stood in the ashes, allowing more moonlight to pool in her palm. "The moon gives us her gift. Our link to her is where our magic comes from." Letharia allowed it to pour on the ashes where green shoots began to form like a small army. "But the blood crown's magic comes from the earth." She shot a look at her. "As I'm sure you've noticed, it can be accessed any time."

"Like witch magic," Anova guessed.

"Correct." Letharia's golden eyes narrowed on her. "So you need to be able to control it. You need to find something to concentrate on to bring it out in a safe way."

Anova's fists tightened. "It can only destroy. I've tried."

Letharia's gaze was piercing. "You haven't tried hard enough, then."

She started forward some steps. Anova hadn't forgotten what had happened when she'd tried to heal Lycasta.

It hadn't been pretty.

"Is it not believable that something created from spite and hate could only harm?" Anova said. "I'm not using its powers."

Letharia and Hellmyr shared a look. At once, they both snapped their hands. The air around them shimmered into spheres.

"You're not going to get past our barriers," Hellmyr said with a flat expression. "Try it."

Anova breathed and thought of the angry buzzing at the back of her skull. She thought of the pain that gathered at the ends of her nerves. Her leashed mountain cat.

It didn't take her long to find it. It came readily to her like a dog called to a meal.

As soon as it was in her palms, it burst like one of Alys's explosives. She was drowned in white light as the screams came to a height.

She was on her back. Hellmyr helped her to her feet.

His hands remained on her for a moment longer than was necessary. He brushed the hair out of her eyes. "Are you okay?"

She stepped out of his arms. "I'm fine. But this isn't going to work, Hell."

"You're right." With his arms crossed against his chest, he leveled a look at her. "It's not if you keep thinking that."

Anova shook her head. "You don't understand. It's not some little thing you can move and manipulate. It's not like—"

"You're fighting it," Letharia interrupted. "You need to accept its presence."

She grinded her teeth together. Why did she have to put up with two of them now?

"This isn't working. I told you," she said.

Hellmyr met her glare with one of his own. Bathed in eerie moonlight, he looked the part of a powerful fae king.

"Would you prefer the alternative?" The skin around his eyes tightened. "Giving up?"

Seconds stretched between them. "Fine," Anova managed to say.

However, in truth, she wasn't so sure anymore.

They returned to where they'd been before and protected themselves with their magic. Anova didn't have to try hard to summon it again. As before, it lingered at the edges of her perception. Dark and hungry, waiting to be unleashed. She felt its need to consume.

It was evil. Hateful. There could be no other word for it. After all, this magic was an abomination created by a blood curse.

It wasn't supposed to exist.

But, then again, neither should I after becoming its keeper.

Anova breathed. It came to her at once, overwhelming and suffocating. Unearthly sounds filled her ears, and her vision danced around her.

Anova tried to pull it back in like a horse by its reigns, but it wasn't working.

Letharia was shouting something. It took her several seconds to understand any of it. "Allow it to become a part of you! You need to do this. *Now.*"

"I'm *trying.*"

The noises produced by the crown drowned out her voice. But she didn't need Letharia to know that it wasn't working.

The energy ballooned inside her like a dead, bloated fish on the surface of a lake.

Through the primal screams that seared her brain like a fish on a frying pan, she heard Hellmyr's voice.

"You have to accept it. It's the only way you can hope to live with it."

The crown's screams grew in volume. It didn't like being ignored.

"I can't. I can't hold onto it any longer." Anova said through her teeth, "It's going to destroy everything here if I don't let it go *now.*"

"Then destroy it," he shouted.

Through the haze that was her vision, she saw something that turned her stomach. Hellmyr had stepped forward so that he was steps before her. With a wave of his arm, the barrier on the air surrounding him dissolved.

"*Hellmyr,*" Letharia shrieked.

What is the damned fool doing?

Anova could barely keep herself upright. The pain demanded to be acknowledged. It wanted to be unleashed. It wanted to *hurt*.

Stop it stop it stop it.

He moved his head slightly as he spoke to Letharia. "It's my decision, Mother. I'll take responsibility for it."

His eyes cut back to hers. "For whatever she does."

STOP.

She tried to beat it back down—to smother it back into submission—but it started taking more of her in bits. First, it took her hearing. Then, the feeling along her extremities.

Her vision danced around her, taunting her. Hellmyr didn't move.

She couldn't contain it. She sipped air, but she was sure that she'd be standing for only seconds more.

Which will it be?

It was absurd. How could she accept something like a blood curse? It was everything she reviled.

Blood. Revenge. Oppressive power.

Fae power.

Anova saw him still. He stood before her, arms at his sides. Empty-handed.

"When I watched him bring you to Fae, I was angry. I didn't want anything to do with a human in case you were the one. And then, the more I saw you, the worse it got. The more I realized."

"I hated you for it, you know. I hated that you could hold this power over me."

I don't want it. I don't want any of this. Hellmyr's voice was mixed in with the cacophony.

"Even if you were here to undo me, I started to want that, too."

Undo me.

Anova didn't realize she'd been screaming until the sound cut off. Her chest heaved with breaths, but she still felt as if she couldn't get enough air inside her.

Her palms were against the ground. She didn't want to look up in case she'd done the worst.

But it wasn't like last time. A shiver ran across her spine.

It went silent—both the screams and the pain.

Finally, she looked up. To her surprise, the grand hall remained as it had been moments before. Her heart froze in her chest.

Hellmyr was rushing towards her. In one motion, he helped her off the floor. "Do you realize what you did?"

Anova opened her mouth and closed it again. She couldn't quite believe it. Her voice was scratchy, but she spoke anyway.

"I called it back," she said. "Controlled it."

Some distance away, Letharia was watching. Anova blinked. A slow smile crept along the fae lady's features.

She'd done it.

The crown was quieter than it had been since she'd woken up with it. Her body shuddered, and Hellmyr pulled her close.

Her voice was hoarse and barely audible. "I'm going to live. I *will* live."

The more she said it, the more she believed it. She stayed in his arms while the moon passed from the porthole above.

For the first time since she'd donned the crown, she cried.

CHAPTER FORTY-TWO

Once the sun rose, guards escorted Anova back to her rooms. For the first time in too long, she couldn't feel the pinpricks of pain hiding inside her body.

She knew they had more work to do, but she couldn't deny the signs of progress.

For once, the blood crown didn't feel like a splinter buried underneath her skin—a part of her and alien all at once.

Hellmyr had been right. Whether she liked it or not, this was the answer. All along, she'd been fighting the hybrid of magic that lived inside it and had suffered for it.

Anova sank into a plush chair inside her bedroom.

She could still destroy it if she wanted to. Now, it was her choice again. Even if she still didn't know what to do about the future of the blood crown, at least she had a future again.

Her lids sank as her blinks slowed. Although the pain from the blood crown was alleviated for now, last night had taken its toll on her. Exhaustion pulled her deeper into the chair's cushions.

A thought occurred to her.

I need to tell Cadmus about this. I need to speak with him through the mirror again.

But she didn't get up. Her body demanded sleep too much for that.

Once she woke again, she would first ask Sera if she had any stolen fae magic left. After that, she needed to practice with Hellmyr every waking moment from then on.

While they'd found a way to stop the blood crown from killing her, Letharia explained that she likely needed to work for several nights yet to fully accept the crown's magic inside her.

Was this the right decision?

Anova wished she knew.

A quiet yet persistent voice inside her whispered something else.

You've already decided what's right, anyway.

You've already decided to accept Hell's bargain.

It's the only way this can work while the blood crown exists.

Anova's eyelids parted. There had been a knock at her bedroom door. With muscle memory, she found the knife at her waist. She thanked her stars that she'd forced Hellmyr to surrender her weapons to her before she'd retired to her rooms.

But before she could stand, Sera's voice came from the other side of her door. "It's me, my lady. I've brewed you some hibiscus tea. May I come in?"

Anova breathed again as her body sank back into the cushions. "Yes, Sera. Of course."

When Sera opened the door to her bedroom, she carried inside a tray with two steaming cups. Anova breathed in the herbal scent and couldn't deny to herself that her timing was perfect.

She accepted the cup Sera handed to her and leaned back into the chair. She looked down into the red tea as she thought of her words.

Anova could feel Sera watching her. She cleared her throat.

"Thank you. Not for this but—" Anova bit down on her lip. She blamed the slip on Hellmyr's awful manners. "For the tea, too, I mean. But thank you for helping me. Earlier."

Sera wasn't saying anything. Anova's gaze shot up again.

"I'm sorry—"

Sera shook her head. "I'm not offended. Please, enjoy the tea before it cools."

Anova's eyebrows came together, but she did as Sera suggested. Anova cursed silently. She'd promised herself that she wouldn't pepper Sera with questions about the stolen fae magic she'd mysteriously possessed, but her curiosity was getting the better of her.

There was that and the fact that she needed it again. She swallowed as warmth spread down her throat.

Maybe if I can get her to tell me who she got it from, I can get some myself this time.

"Sera," she started, "I know I shouldn't ask you this. But I need to contact someone outside the palace again." Anova paused. "I need to use more fae magic, and frankly, I'm not sure where you got some. Well, *how,*" she corrected.

It was then that Anova realized what was bothering her so much. Sera was watching her. Not in a usual way, exactly, but in the way that one watches a dangerous animal from the other side of a cage.

Anova bit into her cheek. She shouldn't have asked. The fae magic must have had a high price.

She traded too much to get that, she guessed.

"Is there—" Anova's tongue refused to cooperate with her any longer. Her heart pounded, and she had to lean back into the chair's cushions.

Oddly, Sera seemed at ease at last.

A cold sweat broke out along her scalp. What was going on?

Anova rushed to stand but didn't get far. Her legs buckled underneath her, but before she could hit the floor, Sera caught her and lowered her back to her chair.

Her limbs were too heavy to move, but that didn't stop her from trying to grab the sheathed weapon at her waist. She didn't have the strength to speak, but inside, she screamed at her body to move.

Quicker than a blink, Sera pulled her dagger away from her.

It's her. It's her. It's her.

It was always her.

But she couldn't move.

"I was concerned when the poison didn't act at once. I've never seen anything like it in person," Sera explained as she looked upon her dagger with a slight frown. "The fae told me the first effects would be instant."

There was too much in what she'd said for Anova to concentrate on, though her mind was still as sharp as it had been moments earlier.

It was in the tea.

She saw Sera's cup, untouched and still on the platter she'd brought it in on. The signs had been there. When had she started to become so lax?

Her mind ran wild with a storm of thoughts.

"The crown ... isn't ... something to want," she gasped.

Sera's expression remained flat. "I don't want the crown. I'm not trying to kill you."

Anova's stomach sank. That was worse. She needed to figure out her motive and who she was working with.

There was no question that someone wanted her dead. Many fae did. But which one was it?

Sera got to work putting up her weapons and then clearing the tea from where Anova had been drinking it. She needed to do something, but she could barely move her mouth enough to speak.

Anova remembered their first conversation. She tried to get up, but her body wouldn't cooperate. Not even the magic inside the crown responded to her pleas.

"Three years of service here, and my grandfather's life is saved."

"Your grandfather," Anova managed. She stared at Sera.

That was the answer. This fae was threatening his life and had forced Sera to do this.

Sera placed the tray back on the table. Her shoulders shook, and at first Anova thought it was from sobbing. But she was *laughing*.

Sera jerked over to look at Anova. The amusement had drained from the girl's face. "I don't have one. That was a lie. I thought you'd be able to tell when I made it up."

Anova's tongue was getting heavier, so instead of trying to speak, she stared at her.

She went to Anova's window. Early sunlight streaked through it. "I did bargain with a fae, though." As she slid it open silently, she said, "She was right. You trusted me more than the others just because I was human. I couldn't believe my luck when you dismissed the other servants."

Anova stopped breathing. *She.*

There could be no other.

Through the open window came a red and orange moth as delicately as a petal blown inside. The insect landed on Anova's nose, its bead-black eyes staring down at her.

The urge to bite at it like an animal surged through her. *Lycasta.*

Her maidservant had emptied one of the teacups and held above it the vial of fae magic that Anova had used yesterday to communicate with Cadmus. The liquid poured inside, and the moth left her nose to perch on the edge of the teacup.

As Anova watched the moth sip the fae magic, she thought back to when Sera had given her some of the same substance.

Why did she do that? Why help me if she was only going to assist Lycasta in killing me?

She felt strangely calm as she thought it through. Perhaps it was because she could do nothing else.

Sera almost didn't help me that night. It wouldn't make sense for her to do so, after all. Whatever Lycasta promised her, it's certainly valuable.

The more she thought on it, the more she realized. Sera wasn't without compassion. In that moment, she'd felt for Anova when she'd begged her for help. And yet, she was fully cooperating with Lycasta today to ensure she killed Anova.

Fae aren't the only strange things living here, Anova considered with a shiver.

Anova breathed in a gust of air. She would need all her strength to speak. But now that she couldn't move and could do nothing else, she had to do it. She had to try to change her mind.

It was, quite likely, the only way out of this.

Anova pushed down the panic rising along her gullet. It would do her no good so succumb to it, no matter how tempting it was.

"Why?" The word rasped from her throat.

Sera stared back at her. Her lips were tight and her eyes wide. She looked like the young girl she'd defended that day against the fae servants bullying her. Anova knew she understood what she'd meant.

But another voice responded.

"Oh, she's still able to speak?" It was Lycasta. Anova looked around as well as she could, but she didn't see the fae lady anywhere.

The moth landed on her nose again, and she realized with an awful feeling that the fae magic was allowing her to speak, hear, and see as the insect before her.

Lycasta added, "A few more hours will take care of that." The shapes that looked like eyes on the moth's wings stared down at her, too.

"Try killing me," Anova said through her teeth. It took her entire concentration to glare at the moth on her face.

She heard Lycasta's sharp laugh in her ear. She would have traded anything to be able to swat away the moth at that moment.

Two sets of eyes stared her down as Lycasta said, "I'm not trying to kill you, human. No, that would run counter to the entire plan."

Anova's heart beat faster at her admission. She hadn't forgotten when Lycasta had tried selling her to the highest bidding fae for the honor of killing an unconscious human girl. It hadn't ended well for the fae lady, and she would remind her of it.

She would rip her apart when she could move again. Anova would ensure Lycasta never forgot crossing her. She swam in the idea of her revenge, drawing it out. It helped sate the panic, if only for a few more moments.

"Bad idea," Anova managed to growl.

Lycasta sounded like she was remembering the same thing. "It's quite a good one, actually." Her voice sobered. "And the only way any of this will work for us."

Us. She means herself and Leander.

Before she could say anything to that, Lycasta said, "No, I'm not trying to kill you. I don't want the blood crown. In fact, it matters not to me what comes of it—so long as your death isn't traceable to me."

Anova couldn't breathe. The moth moved along her face until it stopped at her ear.

Lycasta's voice was low. "They will find you unresponsive. The poison Sera administered was a very low dosage of belladonna. It would be enough to kill a human child, but for a human adult, it's just enough to slow your heartbeat that most would consider you dead."

No. No.

It couldn't work. One of them would hear her heart eventually—would realize what was happening.

It doesn't have to work for very long, she realized.

Anova felt something wet one of her cheeks. Belatedly, she realized it was a tear.

"Cadmus," she whispered.

They both knew what would happen if she was declared dead. Anova wanted to be angry at him—that the possibility of her death could do this to Cadmus—but all she felt was a hollowness in her chest.

Lycasta's voice was tight. "If you are declared dead, Cadmus will agree to complete the spell. He'll save Leander from death in exchange for his own life." She almost sounded remorseful.

A fog washed over her, though she fought it. If nothing else, she had to cling to her awareness. It was all she had left.

The moth climbed higher so it clung to the center of her forehead. She could feel its soft wings against her skin.

"Poor mortal girl. Sleep," Lycasta bade. "May you slumber through this final part of your existence."

CHAPTER FORTY-THREE

Anova woke up.

She wasn't sure whether or not that was a good thing.

While she couldn't move or even open her eyes, Anova heard raised voices around her. She remembered Lycasta's last words to her. The fae lady had intended for her to sleep through this, but she'd woken up. Aware, but unable to move or speak.

Worse. This is worse, she decided.

With a jolt, she realized Hellmyr was the one yelling.

"If you value your life, you'll start speaking, healer," Hellmyr growled. "What are you talking about? She's not dead."

"Her heart has failed," the fae tasked with healing her responded. "You can hear n—"

She heard a sound like a gurgle and realized Hellmyr must have done that to the other fae.

"I'll be the one deciding that, so I think it's time you did your job," Hellmyr said in a deadly quiet voice.

A sheen of cold sweat had dried to her face. *I'm alive. Please, Hellmyr.*

But it was as the healer said. With every second that passed, she felt a new wash of dizziness assault her. It was a wonder she clung to awareness.

The depths of her slumber beckoned to her. How easy it would be—just like falling asleep. It could be as Lycasta had suggested. Painless. Easy.

No. I need to live.

I want to live.

Anova had to signal to him that she yet lived. But she couldn't even force herself to breathe. Every so often, a trickle of air slipped through her nose and into her throat.

The fae healer was trying something else. She could feel his warm hands on her skin. She realized then that the healer's skin wasn't warm but that she was much too cold. She tried to find the magic that lived inside the crown, but it was silent of both power and pain.

None of the healer's efforts helped.

She drifted, lost in her fog again.

"Hellmyr." Letharia's voice pierced the haze that had descended on her brain. She was unsure if hours or days had passed.

Hellmyr didn't respond.

"Hellmyr, it's been long enough. They'll start to wonder when they haven't seen her in many more days. Some have already started asking." Letharia was silent for many minutes until she added, "The rumors have spread."

His voice was strained. "I'm not giving up." Something clattered around in the room they were in.

I'm alive, Anova chanted in her mind. *Don't you realize? The blood crown is still here!*

When he spoke again, his voice was different. It was quiet, though it had an edge to it. "Help me understand. It was working. She was starting to change."

Anova's heartbeat felt more than glacially slow. It felt like it was stopped for good.

Change?

Another too warm hand touched her. The lids of one of her eyes were pried apart, and she glimpsed the ceiling of the room she was in. The ceiling was too ornate not to be somewhere inside Eastwoe palace. In her periphery was Letharia staring down at her.

She tried to move her gaze to look anywhere—to at least suggest that she was alive—but it felt like trying to push an island through water.

"It's clear before you. We were wrong," she said simply. "Its magic was ultimately incompatible with her." Letharia frowned as she looked down on her. "Otherwise, her murderer would have gained the crown by now. It would have claimed them, fae or human." She paused before adding in a barely audible voice, "That's what did this, Hellmyr."

Letharia's eyes shut as if she were in pain. Anova realized why a moment later when a wordless yell reverberated throughout the space. It quieted as the seconds passed like a noise travelling through a tunnel. Hellmyr was gone from the room.

The fae lady carefully closed Anova's lids, and she removed her hand from her face.

All was silence, and the coldness came for her once more.

No. No. I have to stay awake.

As Anova struggled to cling to consciousness, she understood what Letharia had meant.

"That's what did this, Hellmyr."

They think the crown killed me at last.

But there was more to it than that. Their words echoed in her head until she gleaned more meaning from them.

They think their efforts to save me killed me.

The cold hovered around her, pulling at her extremities like a shadow monster. Its fingers slipped everywhere that she couldn't cover.

Like a pall, it threatened to pull her back into a dead slumber. Her thoughts were starting splinter once more. It was growing harder to remember the conversation she'd overhead moments ago.

She needed more rest.

But what was waiting on the other side? Would it truly be more dreamless sleep?

Or had Death come to collect like the spurned lover given hope?

I want to live.

I want to live.

CHAPTER FORTY-FOUR

The silence was broken not by a sound, but by a feeling. Anova didn't know what it was until it started to consume her.

It was more than the absence of cold. It was fire.

It was all around her.

Smoke filled her lungs, stifling her slow, laborious breaths. But she still couldn't move. To go from pitiless cold to such heat was a nightmare that Anova hadn't known existed.

She wanted to writhe. She wanted to scream. But there was nothing.

Past the jackal-like laugh of the fire all around her, she started to hear noise. Distantly, a haunting melody came to life. Music from stringed instruments filled the air around another sound.

It was a voice she knew too well.

Hellmyr.

Memories struggled to reform themselves in her brain, but they remained buried, heavy like bodies in a lake.

His voice was loud, even compared to the roar of the fire around her. "Get him," Hellmyr snarled. "Someone. Get. Him. *Now.*

What's going on?

But her heart wouldn't budge from the stutter that had awoken her. Despite the heat, the blood in her veins had slowed and cooled too much.

Belladonna, she remembered. She'd been poisoned. Now who had told her that?

If I don't remember, it's not important.

What was important was that she was going back to sleep. She was finally going to rest. Nevertheless, a whisper came to her in the silence.

What if it's not sleep? What if this is Death?

If she could've, Anova would have frowned. So, what if it was? Hadn't she contemplated this moment over and over again within the past few weeks? Wasn't she sufficiently ready for it now?

But the whisper wouldn't stop.

Remember. Remember what you said.

A gasp of smoky air filled her.

She wanted to live. She was going to *live.* No matter what.

Understanding flooded her anew. Anova realized what was going on, even if she couldn't open her eyes. Repulsive pain seared through her, starting at the tips of her feet.

They were burning her.

This was her funeral pyre.

Anova tried to scream, but nothing came out. She couldn't unlock her jaw to let it loose. Hellmyr's shouting was almost louder than the fire now.

I'm alive! Please, someone notice. I'm not dead yet!

The sudden realization that they were burning her alive assaulted her. Anova would die here, and whichever random fae had lit the fire would acquire the new blood crown. And this cycle would begin again.

And Lycasta—

The memory sparked inside her. She'd been the one to orchestrate this, and she'd used Sera to poison her. Her heart felt as if it were shriveling. She'd trusted Sera, but that had been her own fault.

Infernal heat began to wash over her, starting at her extremities. Flickers of lit ash fell on her, lighting pieces of her clothes aflame. She had moments now.

She was going to live. She *had* to.

Even if she had to fight and claw her way there—just as she'd always had to. She felt her teeth grit inside her skull. She was going to move if it was the last thing she did.

It may very well be.

Anova fought against her heavy limbs, taking them to war. But nothing else budged. Her breath was slow to move through her.

Just a budge. Anything.

When that didn't work, she turned to the crown. Curiously, they hadn't taken it from her. Or they hadn't been able to pull it off her head, more likely. Anova reached for the raw power inside it.

It didn't answer.

Panic clawed up her throat.

Suddenly, she felt something brush against her face that wasn't flame. Her heart felt properly stopped.

"My love. My stubborn Anova." It was Cadmus. His words were much too soft. "It's okay. I'm here now."

She tried to look at him, but it didn't matter. Cadmus had realized she wasn't dead. Her heart soared in her chest, and she couldn't tell if the feeling was like flying or falling. He'd heard her faint heartbeat. She was going to live.

The heat was consuming, flying across her clothes until it pressed uncomfortably to her skin. The agony raced along her body, searing her. They needed to move. *Now.*

Instead of that, however, Cadmus held tight to her. Something was soaking through her clothes that was thicker than sweat and warmer than it, too.

Blood.

No. This wasn't what was supposed to happen.

NO.

Anova screamed inside her head, screaming at the reality before her and willing it to change itself. Precious seconds slipped by like sand under the sea. Her eyes flew open at last, but it was too late.

Cadmus was slumped against her chest. He wasn't moving.

His blood had pooled across her, extinguishing the smallest of the sparks that had landed on her. It was thick on the air, the strange taste of fae blood and the heavy pall of smoke.

His head of raven hair blocked most of her vision, but she could see the darkening sky above. The last tendrils of evening light were receding. Anova sucked in another gasp when she saw the volume of blood that was coming out of him.

He'd carved himself open where his heart was.

He ... The bargain—

No. No. She couldn't think on that.

She had to act quickly if she were going to save him. Anova willed her stone joints and muscles to move. All she needed was to move a finger or a toe. Then the rest of her would follow.

The fire danced across them like a demon, flicking and darting out more and more like it was testing the limits of her pain. But she wasn't sure if she had a limit.

Cadmus. Cadmus. Please. Stay with me.

But the words wouldn't come free of her heavy tongue. She could still do nothing other than watch as his lifeblood left him. Her eyes bounced in every direction as the fire consumed more.

Pain raced through her, and the crown felt as if it would melt her head.

It was then that the last of the day must have passed from the horizon. A light sparked in the air above them.

But in the seconds before its flash, she saw something else on the air. It was a single moth, its wings dappled black and white over orange. It had been watching them.

Lycasta.

A plume of choking smoke rose up before her, and Anova saw her. On the back of one of her monstrous moths, Lycasta flew.

A primal anger rose up out of Anova so fast that it made her dizzy. Her heart began to thunder blood through her like a horse's gallop.

The magic on the air formed into something like a spear, and it pierced Cadmus's back. Anova couldn't think.

Before she could understand how it was possible, she hauled herself upright with a lurch. Now that her heart worked again, the pain was unbearable. She swallowed a scream as clothes melted against her body.

I just need to bear it a little longer.

Anova tried to jostle Cadmus, but he didn't respond.

"Cadmus," she whispered. "Please. You can't do this. You can't." She couldn't get out the words.

Even though she could move, she couldn't even crawl out of the flames. She didn't have the strength to move him, she found. She took in a series of shallow breaths. She needed to get them both out of here. Then she could figure out how to help him after that.

But something other than blood was spilling out of him now. A bright light was leaking from the wound at his back.

She was distantly aware of other fae shouting. She couldn't see past the flames and smoke. But they must have seen her by now.

Anova didn't hesitate. Her limbs were weak, but she forced her hand over the spot where the spear of magic was embedded inside him.

If you answer to anyone, you answer to me, she snarled at the crown.

But it wasn't working. Anova bit down a scream of pain as she smothered the flame licking along her dress. Her entire body was a pool of sweat.

Her head swam, but she pushed herself harder. Her hand formed a fist.

Pull it out, she bade the wild magic within her. She wasn't aware of when she'd started to cry. *Fix. This.*

The light grew brighter until it blinked out of existence suddenly, and the spear was gone with it. Anova slithered from under Cadmus. With shaking hands, she tried to heave him away by his shoulders. The fire had reached him.

Her lungs fought against the pall of smoke around her. She was on a wide platform somewhere. With a weak kick, she scattered much of her bed of branches at the flames. Even though they fed the pyre surrounding them, it was better to surrender the tinder before she caught fire in earnest.

For a brief moment, the smoke cleared as a light burst above them. Arrows flew into the air, but they all missed the fae lady. Lycasta's moth lifted ever higher, but not before Anova saw someone else on the insect's back.

She blinked before understanding what it was that she saw. It was Leander. Alive. Coughing up a lung, but alive.

Lycasta won. She got what she wanted.

He thought I was dead, and he allowed them to switch his life for his brother's.

Anova went numb. The spell to switch their souls had been completed. And the fae she loved was dead.

He's not. He can't be.

A part of Anova's brain had processed what had happened, but her body hadn't. She continued to try to heave Cadmus out of the funeral pyre.

She didn't realize until she was on the ground that the smoke had filled her lungs entirely. She wasn't breathing air anymore.

"Cad—" His name turned into a gasp, and she swallowed ash.

There was no denying it any longer. She was suffocating.

Screams and shouts filled the air as thickly as the smoke had, and she wondered if this was the blood crown's last gasp of life, too.

At least you're going to die with me, she considered with a spiteful heart as she thought of the crown. *With us,* she amended after a moment.

Her thoughts were cut short as more ash filled her mouth. She felt as if she were a fish gasping for air on a ship's deck, one eye hopelessly to the sky.

Dead already.

Anova curled closer to Cadmus. There was no moving him. Sweat clung to her back, and she had no energy left to smother the flames that snuck at their elbows and feet.

She closed her eyes and faced him.

I love you, she told him silently.

Anova felt a tear fall along her cheek. If only the poison had worn off just moments earlier.

No, she realized. The problem hadn't been the poison.

It had been *her*.

It wasn't only that she'd trusted the wrong people. She had. But she also hadn't trusted the right one.

The one that had truly cared about her. The one that wanted her to live—even if it meant letting go of his dream and the only thing that had motivated him to action after his family's deaths.

Remembering what she'd last said to him hurt more than the agony inside her body. Maybe it was the knowledge that the pains living inside her would only last a few moments longer that relieved their sting.

"Did he have a cure or was it a lie?"

"It wouldn't destroy the blood crown," she'd said flatly, "so, no."

Her last words to him had been a lie. Anova had been unsure of his allegiance—unsure whether or not he would have preferred her dead and the crown destroyed versus her alive. Alive, and she would have been using the crown's cursed magic. Allowing it to thrive inside her.

If I had only told him about Hellmyr's solution and about the progress I was making with the blood crown, he wouldn't have believed my death so easily.

Anova, you fool.

She tucked herself closer to him. She couldn't have lifted herself off the ground if she tried, but she could do this.

There was no more air to breathe, and her lungs cried out. But she pushed that feeling down, as far down as she could.

I'm sorry.

Hands were on her. They'd found her. When they touched the burns, she screamed.

She was alive.

Even if she didn't understand why life had chosen her instead of the one lying next to her.

CHAPTER FORTY-FIVE

When Anova woke again, she noticed the difference at once. She was more than hot.

Everything was hot.

She was in a room she didn't recognize, blessedly alone. A curtain was drawn across a single window, and a low table was pushed close to her bed. A glass of water sat on top of it.

Her blood raged through her, but she needed to prove to herself that she wasn't still drugged with belladonna poison.

Anova lurched up, dragging the blanket off her. But when she shifted against the covers barely touching her, a wail escaped from behind her clenched teeth.

It all hurt. And this time, it wasn't the blood crown's doing.

A breath of cold air settled inside her. As far as she could see, her limbs were wrapped tight in gauze. A gasp rose to her lips, but she suppressed the urge to make more noise.

She couldn't afford to forget that there were enemies here.

They had outmaneuvered her once. It didn't matter if Sera was still here or not. If Lycasta was smart, she'd have had the girl killed.

It's what I would have done.

These thoughts helped to distract her from what Anova saw under her bandages. She'd started to peel them from her skin, and they came away heavy with some fae-made ointment.

Her fingers shook, but she couldn't stop herself.

Blisters dressed her legs where she was least injured. They ranged in size from freckles to ones the size of her thumb pad. She couldn't help but think that they looked like little suns.

Anova sucked in something between a laugh and a muffled cry.

Of course, there was worse.

All along her arms was a bright, concerning red area—and a layer of skin that shouldn't have normally been visible. Her burns were in various stages of healing, ointment still plastered to spots, but too much of it looked like this.

Fresh as when she'd been burned on her funeral pyre. And yet, the aches in her body told her that she'd spent days in this bed.

Anova swallowed. She didn't have to hear it from a healer to know that even fae magic had its limits.

With that thought came another.

She sank against the bed. Anova bit down on her lip to stifle a cry of pain from the movement.

He's gone.

Suddenly, Anova couldn't feel the way that air brushed against her wounds too harshly when they were uncovered. She couldn't feel them at all.

She stared straight ahead at the window, not quite seeing it anymore.

Cadmus.

She'd been a damned fool all this time, but he'd been worse. Her hands fisted some of the blanket next to her. She wanted to be angry at him. She wanted the anger to feed her like feast could've.

He'd taken the weapon to his own flesh. Anova was shaking, but she didn't care.

He'd done it himself. And for what? That lying she-fae? What a stupid, backwards-ass reason.

But the answer sat deep inside her. It was quieter than the anger, so it took her longer to hear it.

He'd thought that the blood crown had destroyed both of us.

That I was gone. And it was to be buried with me, no longer able to crown another High King or Queen.

It was what he wanted all along ... and not at all what he wanted, if his words are to believed.

After that, he had the chance to make someone else happy. To save his brother's life. To make his own mean something. I suppose he took his chance.

Anova's hand ached from clenching it. Slowly, she opened her fists.

Even if he'd been a fool, she'd been a worse one.

A ragged breath filled her, and she smudged away the tears on her cheek. She'd heard footsteps in the hallway leading from the room.

The decision was quick, easy even. Anova's hand wrapped around the glass of water in nearly the same instant that she slammed the side of it against her bedside table.

Tiny shards rained to the floor like snow powder and were washed away by the water. The bigger pieces clattered to the floor, too, except for the shard she still held in her shaking grip.

To the fae, she said, "Don't come closer. Or else."

His eyes went to the broken glass and back to her unbandaged limbs. "What are you doing?"

She recognized him from his voice. This fae was Hellmyr's healer. Or one of them, anyway.

He took a step toward her. "You're in no state for this."

"No," she snarled. "Don't come any closer. Not until someone brings me your High King."

She could see the debate on his face. Even if she possessed the blood crown, she was only a human, and a weakened one, at that.

Anova realized with a jolt that likely no one other than Letharia and Hellmyr knew that she'd been able to access the powers of the blood crown.

Blood surged along the surface of her wounds. She was pretty sure some of them were oozing.

She didn't know how deep Lycasta's network went here. Anova remembered that a servant other than Sera had arranged her and Hellmyr's wedding date.

She wet her lips. She was going about this the wrong way. She needed to convince them she was as she appeared to be—a human clinging to tenuous life. One they'd nearly killed accidentally.

At once, Anova dropped the glass shard to cringe back as what she hoped looked to be a fresh wave of pain took her. This farce was easy because it was the truth.

The best kind of pretending.

A low wail escaped her tight lips. She allowed the pain to roll through her, and, unchecked now, it took what it wanted. The gasps were real by the time the fae healer was by her side.

His eyes were narrowed on her but his voice told her that he'd expected this weakness.

"No moving anymore," he said. "It's not necessary for you right now. Someone will be here at all times going forward."

The fae's hands were fast and his touch light as he applied new bandages to her limbs.

Through a mouth she barely opened, she said, "Alright."

But her cries had brought more of them in. She caught a glimpse of Hellmyr's guards at the edge of the room.

Without taking his eyes off her, the fae healer said to them, "It's fine. But bring the king."

Anova couldn't allow the emotions to cross her face. It wouldn't have made sense with the part she was playing. But she felt equal parts pleasure and surprise at the ploy's success. It had worked.

She breathed through her nose. *Focus,* she bade herself.

Plot your next move.

She swallowed the panic rising in her throat. There was always a next move. First, she needed to get somewhere safe.

But she couldn't let up the act in front of these fae yet. Not until she understood more of the situation.

He was inside her room before she had time to come up with more of a plan. His grackle eyes were ringed with dark circles. She'd rarely seen any of the fae look tired, and the sight made her pause.

They stared at each other, he only taking his eyes off her to watch the healer finish wrapping her limbs in new bandaging.

As soon as he was done, Hellmyr announced to the room around them, "Out."

His face was unreadable. When they were alone, he asked, "How are you?"

Anova couldn't even pretend to laugh at the question like she probably would have under other circumstances. She was as far from fine as one could be.

So, she decided to ignore the question. There was too much ground to cover. Too much to do, and she'd hardly been awake for half an hour.

His name came to her lips, unbidden.

Cadmus.

She nearly lost her nerve, then, but she had things to do before she broke down entirely.

Soon, she promised her frayed nerves. Soon, she would allow herself to become lost to the sorrow and anger threatening to swallow her.

The question rushed from her lips. "Do you know about the belladonna?"

His jaw tightened. "I found out afterward."

He didn't have to elaborate. She knew what he meant. He'd only discovered that after they'd tried to burn her in her pyre. The reminder of those moments made her eyes water in pain, but she bit down on her tongue to stem her reaction.

"It was Sera, my maidservant—" Anova started.

"Gone," Hellmyr said, pacing around to the side of her bed. "I suspect either the she-fae arranged for her departure in the confusion or she killed the girl herself."

Anova's back thudded against the bed's carved headboard, though everything hurt to touch her skin.

Had she wanted the girl dead? She wasn't sure.

Anova's hands tightened to fists. She had facilitated Cadmus's sacrifice. So, yes, maybe she did.

Either way, she wanted to find out. And there was still the matter of Lycasta.

Anova jolted up, though the movement made an involuntary gasp come to her lips. "I need to find them," she told him. "Sera. Lycasta." She swallowed. "Leander."

At his name, she saw something flicker in Hellmyr's eyes. She remembered that he and Cadmus had once been friends.

"I'll send my most trusted to hunt them," Hellmyr said. His eyes moved away from her, and his jaw clenched. "Though, if they have any sense, they're well away from my reach by now."

Anova realized then what it was that she saw in Hellmyr's strange expression. It was fury. Fury and ... something else she'd never seen in him.

"I need to go, too," she told him. "I'll know how to find them."

"Anova. You're not doing that." Hellmyr's eyes were hard on her. "You're not going anywhere. Not like this."

Maybe he was right.

She felt his eyes on her limbs. The bandages. How pitiful she must've seemed to him.

And maybe he was *wrong*.

Her teeth gritted as the pain washed over her anew. She wasn't just going to sit here while those responsible for leading Cadmus to his suicide fled for the most remote part of the world.

But even when we find them, what then?

Revenge, a voice inside her cooed.

Hellmyr must have seen something in her face because his next words were dulled of emotion. "I know about the spell. And Anova," he said, pausing as if to study her reaction. She wasn't sure what he saw, but he continued. "He's gone."

Anova tried to keep her breathing even when he said the words. He was silent as he watched her. She tried to tell herself that she'd known this already, but it was difficult to tutor her body into agreeing.

Cadmus was dead.

And when Lycasta died, Cadmus would *still* be dead.

Everything hurt to move, so instead of crawling into a ball on one side like she wished to do, she closed her eyes. Blood or pus or something oozed from one of her burn wounds, but she didn't care.

She'd lived. She'd survived the belladonna and the blood crown. But for what, exactly?

There was Hellmyr's offer from before. The blood crown would persist, but then, so would she.

It would be more than that. What he wants is a wife. Someone to rule beside.

Is that what she wanted? Maybe she could ensure no one abused the power of the crown by controlling it herself.

The thought jolted something inside her. *The blood crown's magic can be more powerful than a regular fae's moon-given magic. It works differently.*

Maybe something can be done. Maybe the spell can be reversed.

Leander's words returned to her.

"The spell only worked because of who we were to each other. Magic like this must be accepted by the other party."

Anova knew who she needed then. Her blood pounded in her ears. Even if she couldn't do much like this, there was someone who could. Someone she'd sent Cadmus to find before Sera had poisoned her.

She chose her next words carefully. "When you were burning me, they got past your guards." It was a guess, but she'd pieced together the story by now.

At her words, Hellmyr stiffened. *Guilt,* some part of her realized. *He feels guilty.*

Good. Maybe I can leverage it. I need some information out of him.

"All three of them," Anova said significantly. It was another guess, but it had worked for her so far.

His face was smooth of emotion, but she saw the truth in his eyes. "I'm not releasing her, if that's what you're asking," he said.

Her stomach clenched. At once, she understood. *So, Cadmus did find Alys. She'd been with them when they'd interrupted my funeral.*

And he captured her.

"I need her," Anova said.

"I'm not going to do that. She's too dangerous." Hellmyr's eyes flashed. "When they got here, she tried to destroy the entire palace. I found the evidence on her." He shifted. "The witch has demonstrated over and over that she is a danger."

"Then release her to me under supervision," Anova said between her teeth.

When Hellmyr didn't say anything to that, a gust of breath left her. He didn't trust her.

Well, it was about time.

"Then what are you going to do?" She shot up, slinging her legs over the side of the bed despite the pain it brought. "Keep her here until she dies in your dungeons?"

Hellmyr stared back. "The thought has crossed my mind."

She wondered if they were still talking about Alys or not. Heat rushed across her skin, and she cocked her head at him in a challenge.

"You seem to be in the habit of keeping prisoners," she said with bared teeth.

Hellmyr crossed the distance between them in a blink. With a finger lightly pressed under her chin, he lifted her gaze. "If it makes you hate me." His lids lowered as he looked at her. "Then hate me."

Anova's heart galloped into a new, frenzied pace that she wasn't sure was due to her anger or something worse. She focused on the hate, ignoring what else may have lingered within her.

But before Hellmyr left, it left her body for a fleeting moment. She knew what was behind his vehemence and possessiveness, even if she did hate him for it.

"You didn't kill me, Hellmyr," she said. "Not by the crown. Or the fire. I'm alive."

She wanted to say *I'm fine,* but that would have been a blatant lie.

He stopped, not turning to address her, and said only, "I could've." The voice sounded entirely unlike his own.

After a pause in which she said nothing to that, he left.

CHAPTER FORTY-SIX

In the first two days, Anova had memorized her guards' schedules entirely. In that time, she'd successfully convinced her fae healer that to move was pure agony for her.

The downside was that she had to keep the charade in place and resist even the smallest stretches. Her legs grew sore from inactivity, and her arms ached.

Just a bit longer, she promised her body.

During the day when they left her mostly alone, her most ugly sobs escaped from her lips. In those moments, her guards would look away.

Not yet, she bade herself during those moments. *Later,* she promised.

Later, there'll be the chance for breaking down entirely.

For now, she had a date with revenge. And she was going to get some answers from a witch who owed her big.

The shard of glass from the cup she'd broken rested underneath her pillow. When the healer and her guards weren't looking, she ran her thumb along it to test its edge. When she slept at night, her nails honed its edge into something like a weapon.

By the fourth day, it was time.

Daylight wasn't when she normally liked to do something like this, but it was when she'd be least watched in this place and her captors would be generally without their magic. She rubbed the tiredness from her eyes. Anova wasn't sure when she'd adjusted so well to the fae way of life—sleeping during the day and waking at night.

For a moment, she remembered how Juras had charmed a jail guard to break her out of imprisonment in Irbess. Her heart thundered in her chest.

I'll come find you. Soon.

Anova frowned for a moment. She was making promises she couldn't keep again.

Abruptly, she rolled to her side, clutching her knees to her chest. Pretending wasn't hard when a real screech of agony rose to her lips from the sudden movement.

"The healer," she said between gasps. "I need the healer."

Out of the corner of her vision, she could see her two guards glance at each other. Hellmyr had ordered them to never leave her alone, but he'd also ordered them to never be alone with her.

Undoubtedly, it was because of the blood crown and the target it pinned her with. Anova waited with held breath to hear if this would be easy after all—if they would both leave her instead of risking that one would get his hands on the crown.

"Send Garrick here on your way to the healer," said one of them at last. "I'll stay."

"I'll be sure to do that," responded the other one.

A warning.

If I can't pry it off the head of this nearly-dead human, then neither can you.

And as easily as that, she was down one fae guard. She knew she probably should have feared being alone with one of them, but she didn't. There wasn't much time, especially if another guard or the healer was coming.

Especially if she planned to free more than herself this day.

The shard under her pillow sliced into her palm with ease, wetting her cotton covers. Ignoring the pain, she formed a fist as she brought the hand against her side to make it seem as if the blood was from elsewhere.

"No. One of my wounds opened," she gasped. Her eyes went to her sole guard. "Please," she whispered. "Help me."

Red seeped from the wound, winding down her arm among the pattern of burns she wore. She swallowed. It was more blood than she'd expected to draw.

The guard came to her side as she'd asked, but she saw at once this was a mistake.

As his sharp eyes took her in and his mouth smirked, recognition shot through her like a potent drug.

She never forgot the face of someone who tried to kill her.

Anova rolled off the bed before he could get a proper hold on her. The fae snarled and finally pulled free the weapon strapped to his belt as he came after her.

Breath rushed out of her as she clutched the piece of bloodied glass in her palm. Dizziness assaulted her. She hadn't moved so much in several days.

His blade missed her by a few hairs. Anova's breaths came heavier and heavier with each of his lunges. She was out of practice.

"You faked your death," she realized. This was one of the fae who had attacked her in Irbess—one who she'd thought they'd discovered dead beside his co-conspirator, one of Hellmyr's other kingsguard.

We only saw the face of the female, she considered. *The other body was too mangled to identify. We'd assumed it was him.*

"Once I was declared dead, I didn't have to answer to the moth tamer who had wanted us to kill you," the fae guard said above her. He held his swordstaff low in a threat as he said it. "After that, it was an easy matter to integrate into his forces again. He was desperate for more fighters after the fire in Westvalde."

His weapon came in a wide arc for her. Anova forced her body to cooperate, though tears sprang to her eyes. Her body needed a reprieve and sooner or later, she knew it would get it.

Her tongue was heavy in her mouth, but she spoke anyway. "You were waiting for this," she accused him.

He showed his teeth and paused for only a moment. "I was waiting to smother you in your sleep, actually." The smile faded from his face. "But I knew better than to expect an easy death out of the human who slew the High King." He crouched to aim better for her. "No, Human, I've been preparing for this moment in all my nights since then."

"I'll be happy to save you the trouble by killing you first," she said through her teeth.

Neither of them had time left for this, and she felt they both knew it. From where she'd been driven to the ground, Anova hooked her leg on his as he aimed for her abdomen. He faltered, and her adrenaline coursed through her. This was her opening.

Even if she'd been trained for the last few weeks in Fae by the son of a respected fae general, she'd thrown her first punch on the streets of Irbess. Anova's fist was fast and fleeting like an insect's bite.

The glass cut further into her palm where she'd held it, but it had cut into his skin more. Red splattered from the cut along the arm that held his weapon. She didn't have time to celebrate, though she couldn't help but smile.

It didn't stop him.

Rather than reacting to the pain by clapping a hand to the injury like most would've, the guard's severe eyes flashed. Anova tried to scramble back and come to her feet, but the reach of his weapon stopped her. The blade hung above her head. His eyes glossed over the black twisted piece of metal on her head.

"You don't deserve this power. Or the honor," he said. "No, our folk need a fae ruler. And not a puppet king."

Anova sucked in a breath of air. With a push, she rolled out of the way, but not before his blade grazed the peeling skin along her arm.

She swallowed a scream.

"No one deserves it," she said through clenched teeth. "Power like this always corrupts."

"Corruption? Is that what you think is important in Fae?" The fae gave a short, strange laugh. "Your human morals are of little consequence here."

Everything was on fire. Her vision started to run. Her body was failing her at last.

Anova waited for the strike she knew was coming. For the pain that would eclipse all others.

Instead, the edge of his blade hovered at her throat where her pulse pounded against it. Anova couldn't move without opening her throat. There was nothing to do besides meet the gaze of the fae who was going to kill her.

"Leaderless and directionless. Did you honestly think Fae would be better this way?" he asked. He laughed again. "No, of course that's not it. You don't care about that at all." He narrowed his eyes as he refined his guess. "You killed the High King because you despise fae like him. Not for *corruption* or any of your noble excuses."

Anova's mouth hung open. Of course, she hadn't only killed the High King because she'd hated him. But she couldn't seem to make the words come out of her mouth to say it.

Before she could respond, the fae guard shoved the blade forward at her throat.

It hadn't been Anova's choice.

Ever since she'd woken from the belladonna poisoning, the crown hadn't felt the same. It didn't clamor as it had before.

She'd taken it as a sign that it had settled. But maybe something inside it had broken—even more than it already was.

It happened in a blink.

Just how the crown's attacks had been before, the light was sudden and piercing. Heat washed off her in a wave, and she felt she would peel her skin off herself if she continued to feel this warm for a moment longer.

The crown will kill him, she realized in those seconds.

An image flashed before her face. It was Cadmus as she'd remembered him—alive, too conniving for his own good, and an expert at chipping down the walls she'd carefully crafted in her life.

"You hate us. You hate me. It's clear in the way you speak and act."

No. That's not how it ended, she reminded herself. It had ended with the both of them in each other's arms. She hadn't hated him. Ever.

And then the other fae's voice came to her.

"You killed the High King because you despise fae like him. Not for corruption or any of your noble excuses."

Before the crown's brutal magic charred the body of the fae guard who had attacked her, she called it back to herself. Anova shuddered from the force of it. It was like breaking the surface of water while a chain tried to drag her to the bottom of the sea.

When the blinding light faded, they were both on the floor. Anova pushed herself up. The residual energy from the crown's magic flooded her limbs, and she felt almost drunk with it.

Across from her, the fae guard was on his side facing her. Quicker than a blink, his weapon was in her fists.

Useful thing, she considered, hefting its weight. She had no time at all left, so she sprinted to the door, ignoring the way her skin felt like it was on fire.

Until the moment before she left the room behind, she hadn't been going to check. But she had to know. Anova threw one last glance at the fae on the floor.

He hadn't moved from the spot. Even though she had no time for this, she stopped there and held her breath.

Ever so gradually, his chest rose and fell. She hadn't killed him.

Anova wasn't sure if that was a good thing or not.

CHAPTER FORTY-SEVEN

Anova may not have been able to shift into invisibility like perhaps the fae could or melt into the shadows, but she hadn't needed magic to make herself unseen before.

When she heard them approach in the palace's halls, she shoved herself behind staircases and pedestals. But the fae who ran to her rooms weren't looking for a sneak thief. Or even a dethroned queen.

They were looking for the burnt, disfigured human girl who they'd nearly killed by mistaking her as dead. To them, she might as well have been dead already.

"No moving anymore. It's not necessary for you right now. Someone will be here at all times going forward."

As she emerged from her hiding place in the palace's halls, Anova considered how her assassin had been the first person to treat her like a threat after her belladonna poisoning. She would have laughed if she'd been able to anymore.

Maybe that's why I wanted him alive.

Anova pushed herself harder. Her breaths were shallow. The pain flared in her body again, though by now, she was well used to such things.

She had no time left, but she had to get them out. Anova found their shared quarters with ease. Her body heaved with pain, and she leaned against their door.

"Della. Maris." Anova dared not raise her voice any louder. After a moment, she gave a soft knock and hoped her luck would hold for the thousandth time.

When the door opened, Della only took a moment before enveloping her in the tightest hug she'd ever received. Anova squirmed from the pain of touch.

"Della, please—" she gasped, and the woman released her hold on her some.

Della launched into an explanation faster than Anova could take a breath. "He said we weren't allowed to visit you. He said that you needed to rest first."

Of course he did.

Anova held her mother's friend close. "I'm leaving the palace. For good this time. But they'll drag me back once he finds me, so it has to be right now." She swallowed. "Are you coming? Is Maris there?"

Della took only a moment to consider it and nod. Without taking her eyes off Anova, she called, "Maris? You hear all that?"

But Maris was already coming through the door. "I've had our essentials packed since the wedding." She stopped and looked Anova in the eye. "This is about him, isn't it? The one who loved you?"

Something lodged in Anova's throat at the way she'd said it. But a noise down the hall interrupted her answer.

"We should go," Maris said for her, and they ran.

On the way down, Anova explained her half-formed plan to them in fits of whispers. They remained quiet, their breaths almost silent *huffs*.

It sounded nonsensical to her own ears. But Anova had to believe in *something*.

Because, if she didn't, there would be nothing else for her to believe in. Her heart tremored inside her for the possibility. They waited on the corner of a hallway for a group of his guards to pass.

As they rounded the corner, Anova froze. The others had heard it, too.

The sound of two fae guards speaking filled the hall. They were close, and the guards they'd narrowly avoided were too near in the other direction to turn around.

They were stuck.

The magic of the crown prickled across her skin. She looked to her companions, but she couldn't risk hurting either of them.

I have to fight my way out for us.

Anova swallowed. "I'll do it. Stand behind me."

But the other two didn't move. They stopped like they'd been talking. Before she could ask, Maris's hand found her shoulder.

"We'll head them off. There's a split in the hallway. Once we distract them, go."

Anova's mouth hung open. "I can't leave you to them—It's too dangerous."

"Come on, Nove. You can't hog them all for yourself." Della's mouth turned up in a mischievous grin. "You're not the only one who can charm a fae boy."

The guards' voices were almost louder than their own, now. In her ribcage, Anova's heart thundered. She looked at the two women who had become not quite like her own mother to her but something similar.

There was no time for a goodbye, but Anova squeezed their hands as tears dotted her eyelids.

"I'll come back for you," she promised. "I swear it."

Anova flattened herself against an alcove as Della and Maris stopped the oncoming fae guards. She dared not take a breath until she heard their eventual steps away from her.

Anova wasn't sure what she'd done to deserve those two. She took Maris's orders and sprinted the rest of the way.

She knew where the dungeons were from the last time Alys had been imprisoned there.

When she reached the entry room into the palace's dungeons, Anova froze. There were no less than three guards in the space, but she didn't have the time to deliberate or fight.

This time, she had to deal with them.

At once, they surged forward to stop her. Now the energy buzzing inside her was easy to find. It willingly came to her fingertips, her leashed mountain cat.

Not to kill them. To stop them.

Anova had no idea if the magic inside the crown cared about what she wanted.

What am I thinking? It's not as if it's sentient.

She gritted her teeth, trying to focus and call the blast back to her before it grew too much in power. The buzzing all around her quieted, and the light cleared from her vision.

Slicked in sweat, Anova rose from where she'd been crouching near the ground. The dungeon guards were littered on the floor. After she found a ring of keys on one of them, she didn't pause to check if they yet lived.

Distantly, she thought she heard the reverberations of boots or shouts in the palace above her head.

They'll have discovered what's happened by now.

And Hellmyr was no idiot.

As Anova passed the empty cells, her eyes scanning them for any sign of the witch, she saw a different familiar face.

She didn't have time for this.

But there was something to the fae lady's face that made her stop. It was strange to see a fae so bruised and disheveled, even if it gave Anova a sick sort of satisfaction to see one of her enemies so beaten.

Anova found the key to Lyrin's cell and stepped inside before she could stop herself. This could be the last time she got her answers.

Even if it was too late.

"Lycasta was your master," Anova said. It was an assumption, but it was the only one that made sense now.

At her approach, Lyrin's head shot up. Her hands had been bound at her back and an iron chain kept her near the wall.

It was Anova who had kept Hellmyr from allowing her to die on what was supposed to have been their wedding night, on display for all of Fae to see. But that didn't mean they were on the same side.

Lyrin almost killing her had seen to that.

"I never saw her face. She could always find me. Messages were left for me on birdwing." Lyrin tried to shrug, but it was more a shudder.

"And the knife?" Anova asked. "I know it was made in imitation of another."

It was much too similar to be a coincidence.

"You saw it yourself when you broke it," Lyrin said. "I know not why she chose that one for me to use against you, though it broke easily enough. Unlike the other fae here, I know my blade craftmanship. All I can say is that it was hastily made."

Anova stepped forward a few paces. From the start, it was Lycasta who had wanted to drive her and Cadmus apart so she could have Leander.

That, she understood. But she still didn't understand the fae before her.

"Why." The word came out of Anova's mouth less a question and more a statement.

"Despite training for it most of my life, *someone else* had the pleasure of killing the old High King." Despite her state, Lyrin reluctantly lifted her chin to Anova like she was lifting a glass of wine to her.

Anova hadn't responded, but her almost-assassin kept speaking. "My mother was one of the king's consorts. She wasn't one of his favorites like the king's mother, Letharia." She rolled the fae lady's name around in her mouth. "I wanted to kill him for hurting her."

What Lyrin had told her felt much too familiar.

"You're … one of his heirs?" It was all Anova could say.

But she didn't remind Anova of Hellmyr. Lyrin reminded her of herself.

Lyrin laughed. "Not quite. The old bag wouldn't have let me walk around with my head so freely if that were so."

"But he didn't," Anova said. "Not at the fête."

Her fake mirth disappeared. Lyrin was silent.

And I saved you from him, Anova said in her mind but not out loud. *And then you tried to kill me.*

Instead, she said, "Where is she now? Your mother?"

Lyrin was silent in answer for that, too.

She should have been gone from the palace by now. They were searching for her as she stood there like a fool.

And perhaps she was still acting like a fool, but she removed the key to Lyrin's cell from the others.

She held it in her palm. The cold bit into her warm skin.

"I never want to see your face again," Anova told her.

And she dropped the key at Lyrin's feet.

She was gone before she could change her mind.

If nothing else, she hoped Lyrin proved to be a distraction for the guards after her.

But that's not why you freed her, is it?

Anova ignored this voice. She ran past all the other cells until she came to the one that had housed the witch the last time she'd been Hellmyr's captive. Her heart jerked in her chest at what she saw.

This time, Hellmyr had made sure that Alys couldn't have broken out of her cell. Circling the witch's wrists and ankles were metal chains that were welded to her cell's walls. A bigger shackle hung around her neck, keeping her close to the edge of the dank room.

The witch had been bound much more securely than her own assassin had been.

The witch's gaze jerked up at the sound. Alys's dark hair was a mess, and her clothes, clearly well-made and well-kept at one point, were smudged with dirt. Her eyes were like a cat's as they looked at her in the darkness. Silent and unblinking.

The witch took in the burns across her body and the red seeping from her wounds from the fight with the fae guard. She didn't look surprised to see her alive, but maybe she hid it well.

Through the barred window, she heard her speak. "What is it you want, Anova the burnt girl?"

Anova stepped forward, one hand on the metal door, as she looked back. The sounds of the guards' footsteps were unmistakable now. They were coming.

"A lot. And you're going to help me get it."

Her tongue ran over her teeth. None of the keys on the ring were working.

Dread curdled in her stomach.

Hellmyr himself carries the key.

She had the fae guard's weapon, and she could use it to pick the cell's lock. It was her only hope, now. Sweat poured down her spine as her hand grazed the handle of the blade. She'd done this many times before.

Their shouts bounced across the wide walls of the dungeon's bowels. They'd found her. Her fingers were sticky with sweat as she fumbled with the lock.

There's no time for this.

Something lodged in her throat. The first of his soldiers were visible as they ran towards her, the dim light of the dungeons catching on their drawn weapons.

Anova shoved her palm against the grimy door as she ordered Alys, "Get to the far corner."

What if I hurt her? What if I can't control it?

Will it have been worth it then?

But she felt as if she were watching someone else do these things. The light gathered in her vision until it drowned all other images away.

Anova closed her eyes as the heat spread through her. She focused on the feeling of the magic coming back to her like a whip.

You'll come back to me or not at all.

She pushed the energy out of her body in the same breath that she demanded it back, back inside her body where it had inflicted its pain on her for so long.

If this agony is mine, then let it be mine in its entirety.

Anova was shuddering when the consuming light and heat faded. Smoke trailed from the stone around her. The blast had reduced much of the cell's walls closest to her to rubble. Alys was standing in the far corner of it, the far ends of her chain tethers gone with the stone wall.

The shackles still remained around her limbs and neck, but there was no helping that now. They had to move.

Alys's lips were thin as she took in the damage around them.

Her eyes stopped on Anova where the crown rested. "What have you become?"

Anova swallowed. She wasn't sure what they were to each other anymore. Allies. Enemies. Friends.

Conspirators.

She settled on the last. It was perhaps the least complicated, even though whatever had happened between them wasn't what she'd call easy or simple.

"I became what I needed to be." Her eyes went to the destruction that was the hall beyond her cell. "Come on. We're going before they catch up."

There was a pressure along her arm before she realized the witch was holding her there. "And then what? What do you want with me?"

Something tightened in Anova's throat. They didn't trust each other anymore. It was beside the fact that they would both get caught and captured if they lingered here.

She settled on the truth, or at least a portion of it. "I need your help."

"It's over, Anova." Alys stood there, her chains rattling as she crossed her arms.

Anova wanted to shake her. It wasn't even nearly over. Why were they still standing here? Hellmyr wanted them both imprisoned in his palace, even if her recovery bed wasn't near to the conditions of Alys's cell.

"We need to go." Anova said, pulling the witch forward in one motion. There was a clear path through the rubble they could take out of the dungeons, though they'd have to climb through the debris some.

"He's gone." Alys's words were barely audible over the shouts from Hellmyr's guards. They'd found them.

"Of course, I know that," Anova said in a voice that struggled to get out of her throat. But the witch had heard.

"Surrender your weapons!" Their voices bounced off what was left of the stones. Another of them sent out the order for the fae king. Once Hellmyr knew where she was, there would be no stopping him.

At the same time, Alys turned and asked her, "Am I coming with you by force?"

Anova understood the question even if she hated it.

Are you trying to force me to do this?

Since neither of them had responded to the guards' orders for their surrender, the fae had decided to charge. After all, they were only two human girls.

The fae closest to Alys fell to his knees, clutching at his throat after Alys had flicked into his face what had appeared to be a clutch of black dust in her fist.

It was enough to make the rest of the guards falter, if only for a second.

Anova didn't dare waste her moment here. It was perhaps her last chance at convincing Alys to work with her.

Her last chance at … Anova couldn't think the words.

She betrayed you. She lied to you.

Anova's heart kicked up again. But she had also betrayed Alys's trust, even if indirectly. She had trusted Hellmyr, and he had magicked the truth out of her to discover what Alys was.

And there was one person left in this world who could begin to help her with the only thing left she wanted.

"A trade," Anova blurted suddenly. Her palms itched. The blood crown knew when she was thinking about it. "Something I want for something you want."

"You know what it is I need." Alys's eyes cut to her. "Even if what you want is impossible."

"Get the witch first," came the next order from one of the guards. "The king has ordered her never to walk free."

Anova's pulse flicked through her veins harder. He'd never consulted with her about that particular order. In fact, he hadn't shown much interest in having Anova as a ruler by his side. More as a prisoner.

Her nod of assent was quick and subtle. She doubted even the fae would have caught it. But Alys had. Alys grabbed her by the hand and jerked her backward into the stone rubble in the same moment that the witch's fist opened again.

This time, a cloud of black smoke came from it and swallowed her sight whole.

CHAPTER FORTY-EIGHT

"Are you going to tell me what that was? Or was it more unexplainable witch magic?"

Despite their circumstances—despite the pain working into every part of her body and the fae who were after them—Anova couldn't help but smile. Though she wasn't sure they were even on the same side anymore, Alys had always been something of a kin soul to her.

She reminded Anova of a more serious Juras, and her heart hurt at the comparison.

I have to believe he's safe. As long as he's far away from this.

It would drive her insane to think otherwise.

These thoughts left her when Alys actually snorted. She couldn't see the witch's face from where she was in front of her on the horse they rode together, but she didn't have to.

"Nothing magical about it," Alys said. "Black mold. I scraped it from the walls of my cell until I had quite a collection of spores. Well, I turned it into a more inhalable smoke at the end. But otherwise, it was plain mold."

Anova's brow creased. "Dramatic," she murmured, remembering the fae's reaction to having mold blown in his face. She sniggered.

Alys was quiet for a few breaths before she added, "I'm sure you've noticed. Just think on it for a moment."

It took her only seconds to realize. Her mouth formed a straight line. "They haven't been exposed to it here."

None of them had lived in poverty. None of them had to resort to eating old, molded bread when moonlight graced them with gifts beyond imagination. All a hungry fae had to do was snap his fingers if he wished all the fish of a lake would come to the surface.

Or perhaps some of them had handled molded food before. Food stores spoil. Even moon magic couldn't stop nature's processes. Probably.

But they hadn't lived like humans. Anova wasn't sure if there was anyone in the city of Irbess who hadn't handled mold—and even eaten it at points.

Anova allowed the silence to build between them. There was much to say between the two of them, but there were things she wasn't ready to say out loud yet.

The forests of Eastwoe flew past them, low branches heavy with moss grazing the tops of their heads as their stolen horse flew through the brush. This steed was one of Hellmyr's best, and she'd claimed him because she knew he had better endurance than the horses his guards would be chasing them on.

They'd been riding for days, but there was still no sign of the forest she was looking for. Her heart sped in her chest at the possibility of not finding it.

Alys had known what she'd wanted. She was sure it had been written on her face from the moment she'd stepped into the witch's cell.

She wanted to save Cadmus.

She had once talked to a long-dead fae princess in a forest where not even her shadow had followed her. If she needed to get to the dead, the Lost Forest was her only lead to him.

Anova had told Alys everything she knew. In return, Alys had listened and made no promises.

But a strange look on her face had told Anova all she'd needed to know. There might have been a way. She didn't pester the witch for answers.

Though we need to establish some things first, she considered.

The farther they traveled through the lands of Fae, the less evidence they saw of its inhabitants. It was as if the world had gone quiet in shame and disbelief at what had happened at Eastwoe Palace.

Anova glanced down. Their shadows had combined to form a flickering black mass that roved over the ground beside them, racing them.

Where is it?

Anova spoke. "We need to discuss the terms of this bargain."

All she saw of Alys was her tightly woven hair in front of her. "We'll see to that once we find your mythical forest."

Even though they were so close to one another—a necessity because they shared a horse and were being tracked by the king of fae across his lands—Anova couldn't decipher her mood.

"We can't *not* speak on it, Alys. I need something else to go on other than blind trust." The words came out like a flood past a dam.

The stiffness came then. "I did what I had to."

"What you had to? Alys, you could have told me." She was surprised by the hurt that had slipped into her vocal cords.

Anova yearned to see the witch's face, but she held it straight ahead.

Her companion was quiet for so long that she thought all hope for conversation had been lost.

Many minutes later, Alys broke her silence.

"The night they came to kill my mother, the fae claimed they would allow her to live—if only she told them where the rest of our kind was. They argued that there were obvious signs that she was teaching an apprentice to take her place, though she never relented and told them where I was."

Anova swallowed. The memories of her own mother's death pulled at her and demanded to be acknowledged. Her heartbeat raged in her chest.

Maybe there's someone else I can save. For a moment, Anova felt like a scared child again.

Without a home where she belonged or the people that should have populated it.

Anova's voice was rough when she spoke. "She hid you from them."

Alys looked straight ahead of them. "It was a spell of my mother's creation, and one of her finest works. I was in the hearth when they raided our house. The smell of soot disguised my scent from them, and her spell hid me from sight so long as I didn't move." She paused before adding, "I was in there for two days before I moved. I never forgot what they said before leaving."

Anova thought she knew, but she said the words anyway. "What was it?"

"With a witch alive, Fae itself would never be safe."

Anova's mouth parted. She knew about the previous high king's obsession with witches, but to claim that their entire land could be threatened by one human with magic seemed a degree farther into madness.

She thought then about how severely Alys had reacted when she'd told her that Alys had been mentioned in the High King's war notes.

She'd been convinced a war was coming.

"That High King is gone," she reminded Alys.

The witch in front of her looked to the side for a moment so she could see her face. Her eyebrows raised delicately above her dark eyes. "So, the current king of fae would never invade our lands? Never wish to subdue our people?"

Anova stared ahead and tried to answer. She couldn't. For many more heartbeats, the only sound was the rustle of vegetation around them as they ripped through limbs and leaves and the gallop of their horse.

Eventually, Anova found her voice.

"I trusted him ... with secrets that weren't mine," she admitted. "Even if I hadn't chosen to reveal who you were." Anova swallowed. She was trying to say something here, but she wasn't getting anywhere.

Perhaps unfortunately, Alys didn't interrupt.

A shuddering breath flowed through her. It didn't have to be this hard.

"I was the reason you were captured by them—both times. And you trusted me." Anova schooled her burnt body into compliance. She'd been shaking. "I'm sorry, Alys."

Alys's response was as low as a whisper, but she heard it. "I am, too."

Anova digested the witch's words in silence. Aches burrowed into her joints as she thought. Her body begged to be allowed to stop moving, but she ignored it. Had they been on foot, she wouldn't have made it a quarter of this distance before collapsing. Alys's quickly-made ointment had soothed the worst of her burns, though she had already begun to suspect at least some of the damage was permanent.

Alys spoke first, her tone careful. "And you'd go through all this for one of them? For a dead fae boy?"

Anova cringed at her words, though she knew they were true. "He's done something like it for me too many times."

In the horror and chaos that had come after she'd killed the High King, she'd been lost and on the run by herself with all of Fae after her. It was then that he'd made the damning trade with Lycasta just to find her.

The same trade that had resulted in his death.

You fool of a fae.

"This is all conjecture," Alys murmured.

"You wouldn't be out here with me if you didn't think it was possible," Anova countered. She had to hold onto the belief. Because, without it, there was nothing left for her but a cold, empty world—along with the black crown wrapped around her head.

"If this place exists ... then I'll do what I can." Alys's eyes narrowed on the path ahead of them. "There are tales that Death favors deals like the fae do."

Anova licked her lips. She knew where this was heading, but she had to be sure. "And to trade for his life ..."

It was the first they'd spoken out loud of what they were attempting, though there could be nothing else that Alys wanted greater than the crown's destruction.

Anova quoted the witch's words back to her. "What was once made can be unmade." They were the same words she'd spoken to her the first time they'd met.

"That's right. If this place exists," Alys said, her breath hitching, "I'll get you in on the condition that you leave the blood crown with the dead. I've been thinking on it, and it might be the only other way to destroy such an artifact—other than the unmaking spell I created."

The witch looked at her, her brown eyes catching on the light that filtered below the trees. Her teeth gleamed as she smiled. "Unless you wish to sacrifice a life for your fae boy's life?"

"Somehow, I don't doubt that you have a list," Anova said with raised eyebrows. "And that you'd refuse to do that when destroying the crown is an option."

Alys smiled. "Are you so sure—"

Anova had seen it, too.

There had been a flicker of something on the path before them—almost like a blink in the air.

A moment later, their horse whinnied and came to a sudden, forceful stop. The misplaced energy traveled from his body to theirs, and Anova was suddenly airborne. Her flight lasted only seconds in which she barely remembered to tuck her head close to her body.

A low groan left her lips. She dared not move for the pain spreading steadily throughout her. It took her too long to realize the pain was mostly not new, and that the injuries from her burns were flaring up from hitting and scraping against the ground.

She uncoiled from her balled-up position to see Alys slumped against the base of a juniper tree a few paces from her. Nowhere in sight was their stolen horse.

Her heart threw itself into her throat, and she came to her feet too fast. Her vision swam, but she ignored it.

"Alys," she said in a strained whisper. "Alys, please."

Anova's hands found the witch's pulse, and it was a steady, stubborn thing. That was a start, at least. Her fingers probed Alys's head in search of any head injuries, but they came away clean of blood.

"Alys," she repeated, holding her by the shoulder, though she remained unresponsive. Her voice pitched higher as she called her name again.

Unseen injuries could be worse than the visible ones. Much worse.

"Don't worry about the witch. She'll be fine."

At once, muscle memory took control of Anova. They'd been ambushed, and her body had known sooner than her mind could've caught up.

Her claimed weapon was in her hands at once. Its blade gleamed in the filtered light, and she was back on her feet faster than should have been possible for her.

But the figure on the path before them wasn't one she'd ever expected to see again. Her mouth parted in a silent gasp.

It was the goblin, Rietvar.

CHAPTER FORTY-NINE

He was as she'd remembered him the first time they'd met. His silver hair framed an expression that was one a host might've worn when he found his houseguests already drunk upon their late arrival.

"What—" The word stopped somewhere in her throat. Her eyes went to her feet.

Her shadow was nowhere to be found. They'd made it inside the Lost Forest.

It was at that moment that Anova remembered she owed the goblin in front of her. And then she looked from her companion to him as his words untangled in her brain.

"What are you doing here?" she asked him.

Rietvar's laugh bounced off the trunks of the trees around them.

"You come to my home and ask me why I'm here. Humans." He shook his head. His eyes moved to what she still held in her hands. "You can lower your weapon now."

She showed her teeth in an approximate smile. "I don't think I will until I have some questions answered. How do you know Alys is fine?" Her eyes went to her again. "Did you hurt her?" The question she didn't dare ask bobbed in her throat.

Can you help me find Cadmus here?

"So serious." Rietvar's eyebrows went up. "And so many questions." He looked at the witch that Anova was guarding with her body. "She isn't unconscious because she hit her head. I just put her to sleep for the moment."

Anova's eyes swung back to the goblin. Alarms were ringing in her head. "I need more than that, Rietvar. Why."

And *how*, she added in her head. But she was done being surprised by the fae's abilities at this point. She knew not enough about faekind in general, and much less about goblins.

He actually rolled his eyes. "Alright. Enough of this. He wished to talk to you alone, if you insist on knowing why I did that."

Unbidden, a breath came loose from Anova's tight throat. "He?"

Rietvar held her stare. "Not the fae you're thinking of, your lover-fae, but the one who deals in spent lives. The one who makes deals."

Anova froze. She remembered Alys's words.

"There are tales that Death favors deals like the fae do."

"He'll speak to me, then." Her throat was too tight for her voice to carry, but the goblin seemed to have heard her.

"He agreed to your wish to speak is all." Rietvar cocked his head at her. "Why else do you think you were allowed to enter this place?"

Allowed. That's why we couldn't find it earlier. It requires permission to find it at all.

Her gaze fell on Alys again. She couldn't leave her unattended here.

It was only her second time in this strange place, but who knew what other creatures lurked under the tree branches?

To Rietvar, she said, "I don't suppose you can make our horse come back, can you?"

Rietvar appeared to consider it for a moment before he said, "Possibly. But I don't feel like it."

Anova narrowed her eyes on the goblin. He was beginning to be a little pain.

"It's not far," he added. He pointed at her forehead. "Though I suppose you could use that to help you carry her."

She ignored the goblin's suggestion to use the crown's magic and crouched beside Alys. She wanted the witch near her for what was going to happen next, though she wished she would wake up.

Anova exhaled and gathered the witch in her arms, her legs straining as she pushed against the ground. Her body's wounds pounded with blood flow in protest.

She couldn't do it. Cadmus had made it look so easy, too.

She stopped breathing. She couldn't think of him—at least, if she wanted to hold it together in front of the goblin.

Anova bit into her tongue. She would have to leave Alys here, alone, while she went with Rietvar. Even if it wasn't far, she felt like it was another betrayal. She left Alys propped against the base of the tree after reassuring herself that there was no hint of any wound or impact trauma on her. She spared one sidelong look at Rietvar.

Friend. Enemy. Co-conspirator. The distinctions in her brain blurred. *She'd better be fine.*

"Lead me to him," Anova said, standing again.

Anova recognized this place at once. It was the fae princess's lake.

She'd been wrong, Anova realized. There had been a way to live as a human with the blood crown. She was trying to untangle what this all meant when Rietvar spoke.

"It's time," he said simply. He was standing several paces away from the lake.

"Then where is he? You haven't said how this is going to work." Anova said. She couldn't stop checking every corner of the clearing. She couldn't allow herself to relax when so many wanted her dead or captured.

Rietvar's eyes were on the lake. "He is most eager to meet with you. But you must pass through to the other side first."

She could feel a vein in her hand twitch. "Other side." She didn't like the sound of it. "This is a trick." She smiled a fake-sweet smile as she accused him.

Rietvar smiled a fake one back. "If it were, it would be a trick to eat you. And I would've by now, human."

The hairs on the back of her neck stood up. It wasn't that she'd forgotten his strange beast-form ... she just hadn't wanted to address that fact.

Anova looked back at the lake. Clearly, this was the key to get to the other side.

"Orrr," he trilled, "you could go back. You have a choice. You always have choices."

A dry swallow sucked the last of the moisture from her mouth. He was right.

She could turn back now. Drag Alys out of range of this place so it no longer had a hold on either of them, and they'd be free. Probably.

She didn't have to go to where the dead rested to make a deal with Death.

What if I never come back? Rietvar might not be tricking me, but the entity on the other side of this lake might be.

Anova closed her eyes and felt warmth on her face as she angled it. The sun was high, but she knew it was false. The sun never moved here.

For the first time since it had happened, Anova let herself remember him and what had happened. After all, this was the end, right? She was going to face Death for his soul, and if Death didn't like the idea of her stealing one of his?

Then what?

Anova breathed out. *Don't think about that.*

It was a relief that she could confront it at last. Cadmus's death and the fact that she'd loved him. It was all wrapped up together, now.

She wondered when it had happened and why. How did a heart do this to itself when it would be magnitudes safer not to?

What a fool heart.

She breathed in. She couldn't stay here forever between life and death.

Cadmus gave himself up for everyone that he loved. He tried to save me by ending the crown with his life first. Then, he chose to give his brother his own life.

She remembered that Cadmus had thought he'd never been the one meant to live after the massacre of his family. He thought that their places should have been switched from the start.

But he was wrong. He'd deserved to live then, and he deserved to live now.

And only she had something valuable enough to trade for his life.

Maybe.

She stepped forward.

"I'm ready."

CHAPTER FIFTY

"Step into the lake," Rietvar commanded.

Anova stepped forward as the water lapped at her ankles. She might have balked if she hadn't been an excellent swimmer. Growing up next to docks and shipyards tended to have that effect on a street rat.

However, Anova wasn't ready for the lake to pull her into it.

Water gushed into her lungs at once, and she fought against the force that had pulled her under.

And yet, suddenly, it wasn't *under* at all. Anova was being pulled up out of something.

She broke the water with an inhale that burned. Anova pushed herself back to the edge of the lake, and she slogged out of it with coughing fits that wracked her lungs.

"I'm going to choke him," she muttered between breaths.

"I'd like to see it," a voice said.

Anova's gaze shot up. She was in the clearing that she'd been in with Rietvar before, but ...

Something was wrong. Instead of midday sun streaming above, there was only an inky black sky. Not even stars dotted the heavens.

This was not where she'd been before. That was when she saw him.

He was a full head taller than her with eyes as black and dull as coals. His hair was pure silver and cut to his chin. It was strange—he looked nearly human for the lack of points to his ears.

His fake smile returned, and he padded from where he stood on the surface of the lake to the land.

"Welcome, Anova, to the afterlife."

Anova couldn't breathe. Rietvar was no mere goblin.

He's ...

The knowledge was enough to cause her knees to buckle, but she stopped herself before she fell down.

He's just the trickster goblin I met earlier, she tried to convince herself.

"You ..." It turned out, she couldn't finish that thought.

Even so, he correctly guessed her thoughts. Or he somehow knew, she considered with a shudder.

"I have many forms." Rietvar cocked his head. "Just as I am called many names. Death. Purveyor of souls. Bastard." He narrowed his eyes and smiled again. It was unnerving now.

Something between a laugh and an exasperated gasp escaped her. "You arranged the entire thing." She cut short her thought.

Anova remembered the first time she'd met him. "Did you lure me to the Lost Forest to meet the fae princess?"

Rietvar considered her from an angle, his chin pointing to the side. "Is this why you sought me out? To answer your troubling thoughts such as these and soothe them like some sort of balm?"

"You already know why I'm here," Anova said, though the words came out softer than she'd wanted them to.

She swallowed and stepped forward inside the space that wasn't the space she'd known moments before. In a louder voice, she said, "I'm here to make a deal with you." She breathed. If she wasn't going to say the impossible, now was the time. "I need to bring back one of the deceased. Back into the living realm."

The face before her shifted, though his smile never faltered. Staring at her was the face of a beast, his long tusk-like teeth parting his lips in his wide grin. There was no light here, but somehow, his silver fur shimmered.

But his eyes never changed, she noticed.

"And what is it that you offer in exchange for such a thing?"

Anova focused on keeping her voice steady. She felt the weight of the crown on her head, so she knew it had come with her into the afterlife.

If she had to be careful with how she phrased her bargains with the fae, Anova had to be absolutely exacting with how she bargained with Rietvar. If she said the wrong thing or used phrases that meant something else ...

Best not to find out.

After several moments in thought, she said, "In payment for Cadmus's return to a hale life, I will give up the fae artifact known as the blood crown."

His grin widened.

"I don't want that."

Her chest was tight. She'd gotten this far and sacrificed so much to get here. She'd slipped into a space not in the living world.

It took most of her willpower not to demand an explanation. It should have been enough. Fae killed each other for the object—it should have been enough of a trade for one fae soul.

But there was something else, something worse concealed under this thought. Rietvar didn't owe her anything. He didn't have to take this cursed crown from her head. Why should he?

No, the worse thought was that she'd come here without anything else to offer.

"What do you want?" She clenched her teeth. "Why don't you just tell me, then."

She stalked to the edge of the water where he waited. As quick as the wings of a bee, her hand went to her waist. She found nothing there. Her weapon hadn't followed her to this place, she discovered too late.

He hadn't missed the gesture and what it had meant, it seemed. All pretense of levity slid from his face.

"What I want is what any bargainer wants. A fair trade. And a deal valuable to him."

Rietvar started to walk around her in a slow circle, his eyes never leaving her.

"How is that not fair?" Anova twisted to keep him in her sights. "It's one-of-a-kind. Powerful. Created from a blood sacrifice. If that isn't sufficient, then tell me what you want."

Rietvar licked his lips. "What would my use for such a thing be? I already have all the power I need." As he spoke, his teeth clicked against each other. His canines looked too large for his already large head. "I have blood sacrifices made to me daily."

Anova didn't dare breathe. She wasn't sure what the answer was.

"Just tell me." She took a step towards him.

The beast known as Rietvar stopped his pacing. His eyes pinned her to the spot.

He grinned, and she knew it was as much an illusion as anything else here. "You already know, Anova."

Before she could speak, his voice filled the air and became heavy and droning. The sound plugged her ears so that she couldn't hear her own heartbeat.

"You have survived the trial of the blood crown. You came here and knew to seek me out. You've turned out to be more than the scared human who broke into my domain the first time. Because I am gracious, I will allow you to see the one you want.

"Pay my toll, and I promise to restore his lifeblood. Or refuse and come back alone. Make your choice."

The beast Rietvar darted forward faster than she could process. His jaw opened to a black pit inside where his throat should have been.

She didn't even have the time to draw breath before it happened.

CHAPTER FIFTY-ONE

Anova was on the ground somewhere. Instead of reaching for a weapon when Rietvar charged, she had reached for the slumbering power in the crown.

But she hadn't been able to find it in time. She brought one hand to her throbbing burns along her other arm as she slowly sat up.

It didn't make sense, so her brain rejected the vision. But the longer she sat there in silence, the more she was forced to admit that she recognized the place, even if nothing else about the situation was familiar.

Mirrors lined one wall. She stared at herself, as she looked as she always did with the cursed crown bound to her. Like she needed more than a little sleep. But now, there were her burns.

Anova cringed from the vision. She hadn't properly looked at herself since almost burning alive in her funeral pyre. And she didn't want to now.

Even so, she'd caught a glimpse. Bandages still covered much of her skin—curiously dry despite her dip in Rietvar's lake—but some had unraveled by now. Mottled red skin that looked like a map spread from under her sleeves.

Anova fixed what had come undone under her sleeves as she quickly took stock of her surroundings. A bed was at one end of the room, but she didn't dare look. She knew she had to work up the courage for that.

It was Cadmus's room.

Somehow, Rietvar had transported her here—or he'd really eaten her this time and this was what the afterlife was like.

She halted her raging thoughts before they overtook her. She had to breathe more evenly if she were going to stand.

After a moment, she came to her feet and started to walk towards the bed.

"You already know, Anova."

His words murmured in the back of her skull. She tried to shut out the sound, but she couldn't.

When Anova saw his face, she stopped suppressing the urge any longer. She ran to him.

His eyes were shut, and his lips were perfectly still. For one of the few times she'd looked upon his face, he wasn't wearing a hint of his usual mask of distrust and bitter sarcasm.

Cadmus was laying in his bed, his hands placed on his stomach like he'd fallen asleep outside under a warm sun.

Or like he's dead, another voice in her chimed, but she hated the voice for saying so.

Anova came to the side of his bed. Slowly, as if he were asleep and she could wake him, she leaned over him as she looked upon him.

"Why did you do that?" she whispered through a constrained throat. "You idiot."

When he didn't wake up and return her insult, something ugly reared inside her. A pitiful sob rose to her lips, though she swallowed it back down.

She hated Rietvar. She hated the world at large these days, but she hated the goblin-turned-death-bargainer most of all.

He'd brought her here just to torture her. To entice her into seeing what could have been.

You already know.

She did. Because the only equal or fair trade which brought back to life a dead soul required another to die.

It was simple, cold logic. To give Cadmus his life back, she would have to die in exchange.

They would have no happy ending together.

"Cadmus, I'm sorry," she whispered. Her lids filled with moisture, and she brought her lips to his in a silent farewell.

Her heart shoved into her throat at the feeling of his lips against hers. How she'd once craved this. How she'd imagined it and relived it in her head when it had happened for the first time.

It was then that his lips crushed against hers, and a strong hand found the back of her neck to pull her closer.

Her eyes snapped open in shock. Cadmus was kissing her back. Adrenaline and desire flooded her veins. It was like drowning in a river that wasn't quite going fast enough for her tastes.

They pulled apart for a gasp, and his lips were already red from their kissing. He got out the question first. "How are you here?"

What do I say? What does he know? Her pulse pounded faster. This was going to be much harder now that he was awake. She couldn't admit what she was doing here.

He'd try to stop her.

So, instead of saying that, she shook her head.

Cadmus's eyes narrowed on her. "Another one of these dreams, then," he said in what was not quite a question but not a statement either.

Another? She didn't have time to blush.

"Yes." The word squeaked out of her throat. This was what she needed to distract him.

She needed some way to leave here and tell Rietvar she was going to accept his one-sided bargain.

Somehow, she felt as if she'd known this from the start. That everything would come back to her saving his life one last time.

His mouth widened to show his teeth. She didn't have the chance to get another word in before he pulled her underneath him. At once, Anova was assaulted by his smell. She drank it in.

She wondered how it worked here. *Maybe this is his afterlife. His manor.* Her eyebrows came together. *He must not be aware …*

But if this is how it is, then maybe it's not so bad here. She wondered where she would wake up.

Her thoughts scattered from her brain. His mouth hovered barely over her skin, moving from the edge of her jaw to her neck. She chastised herself. Cadmus was enjoying himself, and she would, too.

No matter how this ended, it would be the last time either of them saw the other.

"Cadmus," she whispered as she tried to cover up her shiver. "You are suspiciously good at kissing." She pretended to glare up at him. "I never asked. Who taught you?"

She got what she wanted out of him. His thick lashes brushed against each other as he looked down at her with a look of fake incredulity.

"Is it so unbelievable that I'm not naturally talented in this?" His eyebrow arched as he traced her collarbone. And then traced a line that led elsewhere along her chest.

"Yes," she said through her teeth, though it was a terrible lie.

Cadmus's grin dissolved from his face as he watched her. "Is something wrong?"

No. Not right now.

Her heart threw itself against her ribcage in protest. *Yes. Everything.*

But she saw it in his face. Once she traded her life for his and he woke up somewhere in Fae, alone, his life would be as cursed as hers had been.

He would never forgive her. She could see that, too.

I never forgave you for what you did, either. But the words stayed in her throat.

This was the real prison. No matter her choice, they couldn't make it out of this room together. Not both alive.

"Cadmus," she said. No matter what, she didn't want to break the spell. She wasn't sure what was safe to talk about and what would make him aware of what was coming or that he was dead.

But she thought this memory might have been safe.

He'd waited for her. She continued, "There's something I've wanted to know." She couldn't say the rest of it.

He whispered against her skin. "Tell me."

"Why me?" The words slipped out of her. "Why ... the trash of the streets?"

His breath rushed out of him. When he spoke, he sounded furious.

He moved her head so she was forced to meet his gaze. "You are many things. But trash is as far from them as is physically possible. You are deadly smart. To a fault, almost. You are resourceful. You are far too dangerous with a weapon. Actually, one of the things I love most about you is you can best me even without a weapon. I like that you are better than me at many things that I never would have thought I'd like being better at."

Cadmus closed his eyes as if to refocus himself. "But most of all, you never give up. You survive."

They stayed liked that for a few seconds, his eyes still closed, until he added, "I think *persist* is the right word because it implies you fight rather than merely endure. But you have never been trash." He opened his eyes. "However, I have always been an asshole. Sometimes, an oblivious and stupid asshole."

She smiled at him and didn't correct him.

At her expression, his eyebrows came down in a mock expression of anger. "You dare not contradict the last remaining member of the Wolfsbane house?" His mouth went back to her neck where he peppered the skin there in tickling kisses.

"Cadmus," she said, the breath rushing out of her in protest between forced giggles.

He doesn't remember his death, she realized.

As he tickled her in his bed, she pulled his wayward mouth back to hers. To her pleasure, he gave in easily.

When she pulled back for a breath, he asked against her ear, "Will you be in my dream tomorrow?"

Her heart felt like he'd squeezed it. Somehow, this question felt more vulnerable than hers had been.

You already know. It was true. She knew what she had to do now.

Anova rolled Cadmus to his back and placed her head on his chest. It gave her an excuse not to meet his eyes that wouldn't have been suspicious.

"Yes," she said in a voice that almost didn't carry. "Yes, I will. I promise."

Time stretched out until she couldn't put it off any longer. Cadmus had gone still again like he'd been when she'd found him.

She was certain he was sleeping again.

Anova slipped off the bed with as much care as possible. Her eyes went to the door to his room, the only way out. She knew it would take her back to Rietvar or wherever was next.

It had given her the time she'd needed to think. Maybe there was a way out of this. A way for the dream to come true. She wanted this more than anything. Her eyes closed as she thought.

We'd almost had it. There must be a way out for us both.

She barely felt the crown on her head anymore, though it had become a permanent piece of her in so short a time.

In the quiet of this room that wasn't a place and was all at once, Anova remembered the words of her enemy.

Maybe there's a way.

She wished the moment of peace could have lasted forever.

Anova opened the door.

CHAPTER FIFTY-TWO

"And you've made your decision?"

Rietvar was back in his human-like form. His neck cracked as he looked at her from an angle like he was still a beast.

After Anova had opened the door to Cadmus's room, she'd taken one step into the hall beyond it. When she'd blinked, she'd found herself standing on the shore of Rietvar's lake again.

The strange, starless night looked upon the two of them.

She stared back at the shapeshifting bargainer. "You know I have," she said. "And you know what it is I'm giving you." Her heart thundered in her chest. She wasn't sure at all that this would work.

"I need you to say it, Anova," Rietvar said, his eyes greedy and burning like a furnace.

Anova swallowed. There was no way around it. There was no way to trick a trickster. "In exchange for his, you'll have my mortal life," she said.

Rietvar smiled. "There's a good bargain. Yes, human. I'll accept that deal."

Anova blinked again. On the ground at Rietvar's feet was a motionless body. Her heart jumped into her throat.

She rushed forward, her hands already around him as she started calling his name.

"Cadmus. Cadmus, please." But this time, he was still.

Anova held tight to him even as she forced her gaze away. She could barely stand to look at him when he was like this.

"You said—" The rest of her words got lost somewhere in her throat. Rietvar was gone from the lakeside.

It was just her and Cadmus.

And something was happening to him. He'd been … not warm when she'd held him, but not cold, either.

By the second, he was growing colder. Anova jerked her gaze back to him despite the pain it ripped through her center. His face was growing more pallid, and she watched as the skin thinned around his face. Seconds more passed, and there was no other word for it. He was gaunt.

"Cadmus. Cadmus," she said through her teeth. It hadn't worked. There had never been any hope for a deal. It had all been a cruel joke.

Nevermind what she'd thought she'd figured out. She'd been wrong. She'd been ill-prepared.

She'd been stupid.

And the fae had played her again.

Anova hadn't realized when she'd started shaking, but she couldn't control the tremors by now. Cadmus was dying all over again in her arms, and this time, it was entirely her fault.

The back of her hand wiped the tears into her skin. She needed to do something. Now.

She couldn't watch him die in her arms again.

Not. Again.

In the back of her mind, the power of the crown lurked. Anova grabbed for it like she was grabbing for the light of the sun in bleak darkness.

Come to your master, she bade, and the feeling of the crown's power filled her like stinking ale.

Save him.

She forced the heat off her and towards him, and it travelled along her nerve endings until it jumped from her hands like a spreading brushfire.

She bit into her tongue. The crown's magic funneled from her center until she became dizzy.

Save his life.

But something was wrong. The heat burned at her hands, biting along her skin like it resented the command.

Her leashed wildcat roared in her ears, and an image of the dead High King filled her mind. She remembered that the last time she'd seen him use the crown, he'd used it to execute Iona. The realization struck her like a blow to the stomach.

It can only destroy.

Anova was barely breathing. The light had almost consumed her vision, and the heat was burning her all over again.

It was going to destroy him for good.

"No," she grinded out from between her teeth.

Remember how you called it back before. Remember training with Hellmyr and Letharia.

Sweat slicked her back, and the power in her hands had reached a breaking point. She couldn't contain it any longer. The thought of them was almost enough to foil her concentration, but before her focus snapped in half like a branch, the crown's cursed magic flowed back into her body.

Anova's back hit the ground with a smack. The sky above her was still an empty black. They hadn't gone anywhere.

She darted up again, and her heart dropped somewhere past her stomach.

Cadmus was on the ground as he'd been before she'd attempted using the crown. But he was so much worse.

The skin of his face was sunken in, and his eyes were like dark pits. His lips were white.

She'd failed. There was nothing left. They were both going to die here.

And something told her the afterlife wasn't at all like the illusion that Rietvar had conjured up to drive her to accept this bargain. And then he'd left without another word to watch her delve into insanity.

It was then that she noticed. The shoreline of the lake had receded since she'd returned to the area. She could still see Rietvar's footsteps from where he'd been a beast, and they were much farther from the edge of the lake than they'd been before.

It's growing smaller.

Anova came to her feet as a deadly quiet overtook her. The storm raging inside her was still there, but there was something new smothering it all. The path ahead of her cleared.

It was time to pay her half of the bargain.

This time, she found it easy to heft Cadmus in her arms. She pushed away the concerns that gathered at this thought as well as the pain in her limbs.

When she hit the water, she felt an object tucked at her waist. It was her weapon that she'd thought had been left on the other side of the lake.

She didn't stop, and the water surged over their heads as she dove into the lake with Cadmus.

The lake water filled her lungs at once, but she couldn't return to the surface for air without giving up. The surface of the lake above her had narrowed to the size of a tide pool.

The only way forward was down, but as the water at the bottom resisted them more and more, she knew it was time to pay her due.

It was time to sacrifice her life so he could pass through to the living realm.

The thought that had been a whisper in the back of her skull grew louder.

Maybe I can trick the trickster. Maybe I can live, too.

Her world blurred as the darkness closed around them. Cadmus was much too light in her arms.

But she couldn't quiet the whisper.

There was a way. There had to be.

Anova's hand shook where the dagger was poised above her heart. Her other arm ached from keeping Cadmus by her side. He wasn't moving. She had to finish it to get him to the other side.

Soon, there would be no life to give up.

In the greedy darkness of the lake's abyss, her body grew as cold as Cadmus's. Her veins were like ice.

I'm drowning.

It was this infiltrating numbness and cold that reminded Anova of the belladonna's grip on her sluggish heart. During the blur of the poison's spell, she'd felt as if she'd already died and had been trapped inside her cooling corpse.

There were voices, she remembered. *Hellmyr…*

As darkness glimmered at the edges of her vision, she realized they were both fading. Her arm relaxed her grip on Cadmus, and he floated from her. The blade in her hand nearly slipped from her fingers.

There's a way. There's a way.

Hellmyr's words filled her emptied head.

"Help me understand. It was working. She was starting to change."
Change.

Anova reached for the slumbering power of the crown at the same time that she steadied the dagger in her fist.

I'll accept you. All of you, she spoke into the silence.

Anova plunged the knife into her heart, tearing open her flesh.

At the same moment, Cadmus opened his eyes where he faced her in the water.

CHAPTER FIFTY-THREE

Too much happened at once. The burning in her lungs combined with the searing pain from the wound, but she didn't stop. Cadmus focused on her face. Then her bleeding chest.

"Anova. NO," he mouthed.

He reached for her, but the lake had already taken hold of him. A rush of water pummeled his chest, dragging him down—or rather to the other side.

Her energy seeped from her, and red twisted around her like snakes in the water. She was dying. Blood gurgled to her lips.

Her body was finally failing her.

"No!" This time, she heard Cadmus's scream through the dark waters.

His arms fought the currents, but it couldn't be stopped. It had already accepted him. He was going to *live.*

Tears blurred her vision as her body refused to move any longer. Her plan wasn't working. The darkness clouding around her had almost stolen the sight of Cadmus from her.

Despite the futility of it, he was fighting the force bent on keeping the bargain she'd made. They locked eyes, and Anova saw it then.

Somehow, he loved her. Her weak heart sputtered and thrashed.

He loved her so much that this was going to destroy him.

It has to work.

Even if she had to give up her humanity for it. She was going to survive. Persist.

Screams pierced the dullness beating against her ears. It wasn't long until the screams started to form words.

"No. No. No! Please—"

But this wasn't Cadmus. Anova fought to clear her vision. These were the screams that had haunted her nightmares since she was twelve years old.

If only she could find her mother here—

She would give up anything to give her the life she was robbed.

But as the screams repeated, and her hands found only dark water, Anova stopped.

She's not here. It's an illusion.

Anova shut her eyes. *If that's so, then why does it hurt so much?*

I'm sorry, Mother. I'm sorry I couldn't stop the fae from killing you.

"Then why are you allowing it to make you one of them?"

Her eyes opened as pain lit her nerves on fire. Where it wrapped around her head, the blood crown felt like it was constricting her flesh, biting into it with each second.

Cadmus was almost too far away to see, and she realized she was on the bottom of the lake while he was at its surface.

He'll be saved. He'll live.

Her heart soared as if it could catch up with him.

I don't have time to save myself anymore.

"Mmf—" Anova tried to shout, but water filled her mouth instead of air.

That voice wasn't her mother. *She would want me to live,* she argued in the cacophony of her head.

She would want—

"Better dead than a monster. Better to be rotten than something you hate."

No.

This was her mother's voice, but Anova knew she wouldn't want her daughter dead. *Even if I have to do the unthinkable, she would want me to live.*

Anova's fingers curled around the black metal. It was too tight against her skin and would soon break past it.

Stop using her voice! That's not her, she screamed at the voice.

"Are you sure, Anova?"

And she was there, floating above her. Her clothes and hair were lifted and dragged along by the waters that kept Anova at the bottom.

She was exactly as she'd remembered her. Her honey-brown hair cascaded around her heart-shaped face with delicate cheekbones and arched eyebrows.

"Come with me, Darling." Her mother extended her hand to her. She might have been pale, but she didn't look like Cadmus had when she'd dragged him into the lake—gaunt and plucked of life.

Anova's eyes filled with tears. Her body was so cold already. She couldn't really take more of it. And how bad could death be if she was with her?

Before their hands met, Anova looked down. In her mother's extended hand was the blade she'd lost in the depths of the dark lake. She looked back to her face.

"It won't hurt for long," her mother promised.

Anova nodded. Her belly constricted around swallowed water, and her throat tightened around the words she couldn't say. She accepted her weapon and took it in her fist.

With her wounds and the water in her lungs, she should have been dead already, but the crown had kept a part of her alive. It was the same part that Hellmyr had manipulated her into forming.

The part of her life that was intertwined with fae magic.

As the tip of the blade touched the bleeding wound on her chest, she faced her mother.

I don't hate him.

Anova stuck the weapon deeper this time, pushing past sinew and muscle.

At the same time, a new energy surged through her, replacing the lifeblood she'd lost to the abyssal darkness around her. Anova followed the feeling.

And opened the block between her and it. The block keeping her safe from what was on the other side.

Take this body. All of it!

Above her, her mother dove for her with extended hands. In a blink, her face changed. She was no longer her mother but a stranger with a furious expression in her dark eyes and layers of necklaces around her throat.

She'd never seen her before. But she knew who this was.

Witch, she mouthed to her as she moved out of her grip. A name bubbled to the top of her brain.

Gwenore.

"I couldn't save him from becoming one of them ... so I let it happen." Gwenore's lips pulled down when her lunge didn't touch Anova. "I saw his death and allowed it. But I couldn't let them get away after killing my boy. So, I cursed them with power." She smiled. "And suspicion. Paranoia. Death."

This was the witch who had created the blood crown with her revenge spell. Anova's heart was too slow. She'd lost too much blood.

I can't fight her, she realized as her body tremored in pain.

Gwenore's eyes narrowed on Anova. "But my creation was never meant for this."

The witch lunged for her throat before she stopped speaking. But before she could touch her, Anova allowed the crown's magic to blaze through her veins like fire.

Her own screams filled her head as Anova dug the knife deeper into her heart, and black eclipsed her vision.

When the last of her life left her body in the deepest part of the black lake, an overwhelming quiet smothered her. But not before she heard the voice of someone else entirely.

It was that of a goblin she'd met in the wood surrounding a lake.

"You will pay me what I'm owed. One way or another."

CHAPTER FIFTY-FOUR

"You woke her up. I told you that you were clattering them."

Anova opened her eyes. She knew that voice.

"Maris," she breathed. She shot up. Her surroundings were familiar, too, although they didn't make sense.

She was in her bedroom in Wolfsbane manor. Soft morning light streamed through her window. Her bed was plush and warm.

Maris and Della were at her side, and the latter started speaking at once.

"Anova," she gasped. A sheepish look crossed Della's face as she talked to her headboard rather than her. "I may have been a little too loud on purpose." She bit her lip. "To see you awake at last."

But her mother's friend's face had been so full of pure joy that Anova found herself grinning so wide it hurt.

"Please. Don't be sorry. I'm relieved you're safe. And I'm glad to be ..." Anova's eyebrows came together. Was she alive? Awake?

"Here," she finished awkwardly. Though the other two didn't seem to notice. She swallowed a bulge in her throat.

There were too many questions for her to get out. But it was the first that could be the most painful. Her memories inside the lake played at the edges of her mind, taunting her. Which had happened and which had been a nightmare? "Della. Maris. There's something I need to know …"

Ever the open book, Della's face went white. Anova's hands clamped around her upper arms. She said in gasps, "He's—he can't be—"

At the same time, Della sputtered out, "He said he wanted to be here when you saw. To explain it."

Anova slumped against her headboard. She blinked.

He's alive. Cadmus is … alive.

At the same time, her hands wandered to her head where she found the blood crown still planted there.

It wasn't all she found.

Anova darted to her feet.

"Where's a mirror? I need one."

"He said—" Della started again.

"Anova," Maris said at the same time. But Anova easily slipped out of her range of grasp before she could stop her.

The mirror was where it had been when she'd lived here. A cloth had been thrown over it.

Like that was going to stop her.

The fabric was lying in a heap on the floor before either of the other two could get to her. Anova stood there, watching herself touch her ears that came to sudden tips. Watching the Anova in the mirror examine how her eyes shifted in the light.

She kept looking until she found the angle where she could see her mother's eyes in her own. But maybe she was seeing what she wanted to. Anova slid to the floor and joined the fabric piled there.

"Anova," Della gasped, crouching beside her. "I'm so sorry. Cadmus went out to patrol the land here. But he said he wanted to be here when—to tell you before you saw. To explain it all."

Anova shook her head. They didn't understand.

Maris joined her on Anova's other side. Her soft hands found her face and pushed hair behind one of her fae ears. "You're in shock," she said quietly.

"I'm alive. And so is he. Who cares if I am?" Anova threw her head back and started to laugh at it all.

Her body shook with convulsions. Her throat felt raw, but she didn't think she wanted to stop laughing.

It was supposed to have been impossible.

She could feel the other women's eyes on hers and the concern radiating from them. For their sakes, Anova allowed her laughs to come to a stop.

Her voice was rough when she spoke again. "Sorry. I just—" Anova swallowed. "So, my plan worked? He's alive? I'm alive? All of us ..."

Maris nodded, once. She seemed to choose her words carefully. "Whatever you did in that lake ... He's alive again. What Della said was right. He left a few hours ago to ensure this area was secure."

Anova squeezed one of each of their hands. "And you two ... You're really okay?"

"Yes. Nerry got us out of the palace." Della grinned. "And then he found your fae boy and you."

"Nerry?" Anova wondered out loud.

"I had anticipated it to be harder to steal two prisoners from the fae king himself," a voice said behind her.

Anova twisted to see Nerium in the doorway of her room. A wry expression was beginning to form at the edge of his mouth and his eyes.

He continued as he walked forward, "He was a fool to underestimate these two."

Maris and Della helped Anova to her feet. Della's grin was wide as she said, "You're going to have to show us some of those tricks again."

Anova couldn't believe it. If she hadn't, moments ago, seen something just as impossible in the mirror, she wouldn't have believed it.

Nerium was blushing.

As Della and Maris helped her dress for breakfast, Anova avoided looking in the mirror. She felt that the other two saw and understood.

I'm alive, she repeated to herself. *That's what matters more.*

But there were other things that mattered, too.

Like not recognizing the girl in the mirror. Or rather, the fae in the mirror.

But as they helped steady her while she slipped out of her shirt and pants, Anova couldn't help but see the body below her.

She sagged at the sight, and breath rushed out of her.

"Anova, it's okay," Maris urged. Her voice rose uncharacteristically. "You're going to be okay."

Anova gave another shake of her head. "No, it's not that." She leaned against one of her bed posts. A tear ran along her cheek.

Della tried to touch her but retracted her hands at the last second. Probably because of the burn scars along her body.

"I'm sorry, Anova," she said again. "I know it's—"

Anova met her eyes. "I'm glad. It's me." A strange note had entered her voice at the last two words. "I'm glad they stayed on me."

Della nodded. And she hoped she understood.

It was maybe the last part of her that she had left to prove who she'd been. Even if the scars were a symbol of when she'd nearly been burned alive on her funeral pyre.

A symbol of humanity, then.

The fae were beautiful and flawless and ageless. But then, maybe she was something else. Not human. Not quite fae.

When Anova descended the stairs of the manor in a soft, shimmering dress that was either blue or gray depending on the lighting, someone was waiting for her.

Cadmus ran to her and spun her in a circle across the parquet tile floor.

In her ear, he whispered, "You must know by now that I'm going to have to prove my natural skill to you. My pride won't allow me to accept the insult gracefully."

Anova looked at him quizzically until she remembered.

It was our conversation while he was in the afterlife. He remembered.

And then she remembered the kiss they'd shared.

She pulled his mouth to hers to give him the chance to prove it.

CHAPTER FIFTY-FIVE

In a dark wood, a witch rode on horseback. Strapped to the horse and her were bags of salt and all the food she'd managed to find on her own.

Which wasn't much to begin with.

She itched to look around her, but more important than keeping an eye out for *them* was keeping the horse on a path not directly intersecting a tree trunk.

She knew it was the wrong decision when she felt it in the back of her skull where her magic slept. *Something* was coming for her.

A dry swallow scratched her throat.

Damn all of you.

There was no time for spells or curses. Even if she had the proper materials or time for such a thing.

She whispered calm words to the horse, though she wasn't sure if it did him any good. She gritted her teeth as she considered it. They might kill him for sport when they didn't find her.

The witch cut open one of the bags of salt so that the horse was covered in it. It would buy him a little time from their horrors.

She leaped from his back the instant before a low branch struck her in the face. As she climbed to the top of the juniper tree, she watched the last stores of her food and spell materials ride off without her. Bright flares of fae magic lit the woods below her as the fae king's soldiers looked for her.

Alys looked to the pale moon hanging in the night sky above her as she considered her next steps.

She never forgot a promise or betrayal.

Acknowledgements

First, thank you to all my fabulous readers for making what I do possible. Without you, there are no more stories. I hope you're loving this new series so far. Our plucky con-woman heroine has a special place in my heart. I can't wait to show you what else I have in store for her and the others.

Thank you, Beba Andric. You've been with me through so many pages of adventures. Here's to many more, my friend.

I am also incredibly grateful to Amy Eversley for all her valuable feedback.

A warm hug each to Myriah Webb, Leah Macias, and Jennifer Aceves for listening to my rants, woes, and victories.

And thank you most of all to Roman Smith, without whom I would be a big(ger) mess. Thank you for your unending support. I love you more than I can say.

About the Author

From the time she "borrowed" a floppy disk from her school's computer lab at the age of 12 to type her first story, Joy Lewis has been dreaming up tales of adventure and danger for most of her life. In 2017, she graduated with highest distinction from Middle Tennessee State University with a B.A. in English. She lives in Tennessee where she can be found in her garden when not writing.

Sign up for her newsletter for a free book at www.joylewisauthor.com.